MW00610679

SKYSKAPE

DAVID MRUZ

FpS

Greenville, S.C.

SKYSKAPE

First Edition

ISBN: 978-1-952248-94-8 (print)

Printed in the United States of America.

FpS

www.fiction-addiction.com

To Grandpa Rowley,
who loved nature and served for our freedom.
May you tie new knots.

Acknowledgments

I started writing Skyskape in January of 2020, and I believe the story would not be the same had it been written in any other year. When I was able to finish the first draft a full 30 days after I started, I knew the story I was telling was worth pursuing.

As the quarantine began, I knew I had no time to delay, because the message of Skyskape was too important to wait for better days. Skyskape is a story of the unexpected hardships people endure in times of crisis, but also the unalienable truth that no undertaking is achieved alone. As Duun saw his life's journey held together by the connections he had with people and places in uncertain times, so too did I write Skyskape with the help of many others.

First, I need to thank the test readers who listened to me as I read the story several times over the past year as well as those who read it themselves. I thank my parents Sue and David Mruz for sitting around the kitchen table with me listening to my story and offering input where it was needed. I thank Cameron Cook for being the first other person to read Skyskape in its entirety, and who motivated me to get this story published. I thank Todd Brown for reading my first chapter and offering his input to the story. Marcus Vance helped give me pointers on the basics of WWII era aviation to incorporate into the worldbuilding of Tarrkaven. I thank the Presbyterian College English Department for their part in shaping my skills, and I thank Robert Stutts especially for reading through the first four chapters and encouraging me to continue telling the story. I'd also like to thank Dr. Patrick Cosby for this acknowledgments section as he opened my eyes to the treasure trove of acknowledgments in books.

Though I spent most of my time writing later drafts in my home library or at my dining room table during the quarantine, I'd like to thank the local Starbucks and Greenville County Library for offering me places to write my novel. I thank my brother Will and my sister Katie for working together on the cover art. I'd like to thank David Romba for the author portrait. I also could not have published this story without the assistance of my editor Vally Sharpe as well as Jill Hendrix of the Fiction Addiction bookstore. Most of all, I would like to thank my readers for taking a chance with my debut novel.

Larry

SKYSCAPE

Chapter 1

In the final week before the final exam of the final year, Avo Howl didn't anticipate he would need to use his education to survive the night. His secret, built over four years, had been discovered in an instant, and he knew his old life had ended. He'd been careless, and now he'd have to start a new life or die trying.

He didn't know what had given him away. Perhaps it was a stare that lingered too long or a stray gesture picked up by the predatory eyes of the envious or spiteful. In any case, the prefects knew where to find Avo that evening just before the curfew, and in that instant, he needed to become a shadow—a task at which he seldom succeeded. Perhaps, he thought, the creation of chaos would allow him an exit. Even the brightest lantern disappears in an inferno.

To stave off the frozen air would involve finding a shirt and coat, perhaps even a scarf—if one could be located. His emerald green complexion made him stand out against the brown grass and yellowing leaves.

Avo dropped down from a second-story window of the dorm tower as the prefects fought to break down the door. The frozen night of an autumn's end proved harsher than any he'd ever known—the whole of nature seemed to turn its back on him.

It didn't matter; he would endure the world's rejection. Attending this academy had already threatened his family's values, and now those values made him a target of a hidden enemy within the kingdom. He would weather the cold because it would be too cruel to let his enemies steal his fierce spirit.

The speed of his departure had left him under-equipped and he underestimated how soon he would be surrounded. The skies would only be colder and yet somehow more welcoming.

His mind raced as he fled around the perimeter of the citadel toward the airfield along the rocky cliffs below. Over the sound of crashing waves along the cliffs, Avo heard hounds baying behind him —their handlers hovering behind. He understood the ways of nature and knew the dogs could handily outrun him, even if the handlers dared not brave the stony cliffside. He would rely upon his gift of guile to avoid the beasts.

"Ivy are you there?" he spoke into the air. "It's me, Avo. We haven't spoken in a minute. Can you cover for me? I don't want to be a chew toy tonight."

As he leaned against the stone wall, sudden sprigs of ivy descended to encapsulate him and the surrounding turrets in swarms of leaves and vines, releasing a pungent aroma foul and unpalatable but only to canine senses. The dogs drew near but upon catching wind of the stench, they doubled back and went another way. Once confident they were gone, Avo poked his head from the thicket and continued toward the airfield. As he departed, the ivy already began to wilt in the icy air.

Avo always felt free in the sky, unfettered by the law of the land. Getting into the sky was the hard part, but once there, not one of the shadows of the kingdom could stop him. Avo was matchless in an airplane. He would own the skies from the cockpit of a Liberty.

He didn't know where he would go when he was airborne. Buldwikk was off the table from the start. A nation of sorcerers that had stomped out the life from all the nations they conquered seemed a poor choice. Visolia would want his plane more than his piloting—the nation of factories and foundries wanted any edge over Tarrkaven in aviation. However, Avo knew everything in Visolia was expendable, and its excess flew in direct defiance to the Kovenant's teachings. No matter where he chose to go, he would need to evade anyone who pursued him first, but he felt confident he could manage that.

Thankfully, Avo's key to the hangar kept his plan in motion so he could determine where to spend his exile later. As he rose from the cliffside with the key in his pocket, he slipped through a gap in the fence to sneak toward the hangar. At the locker in the hangar, he donned the sweater he saved for the frigid skies of winter. The detailed patterns of wool spun by his mother might draw unwanted scrutiny, but he was bound to raise more questions venturing about without a shirt in public spaces.

He heard the klaxons scream outside and threw his aviator jacket over his shoulders. No time for a helmet, but he managed to secure the goggles over his eyes before boarding the Liberty.

He had flown almost a hundred training exercises and had passed several exams in this fighter. He'd earned a place in this plane instead of the sluggish bombers that groaned through the clouds, usually reserved for students of his house.

The Liberty was fueled and ready for the exam that had been in store in the morning. He climbed into the cockpit and put the propeller in motion. Two rockets were mounted under the wings, not enough to engage in any prolonged combat, but just enough to get him into the air. He heard the noise of machine-gun fire, but the six-wing-mounted cannons could clear the field in the short term. Hidden enemies from the academy fired pistols that bounced off the fuselage of the plane. The time for caution ceased; the time for action was upon him.

Avo fired the first rocket into the hangar door. Blown from its hinges, it created a hole that would be a tight fit for the wings of the plane, but Avo knew the span of his wings as though they stemmed from his own body. He pushed the plane forward and through the doorway out onto the airstrip. Searchlights trained on his plane as an anti-air gun rolled into position. Academy security turned the cannon in the direction of the plane.

As soon as the plane cleared the hangar, he shot the second rocket. Avo hadn't expected to need to expend the second rocket so soon, but his every action rose from desperation. He hoped to avoid further bloodshed as the scent of a flare expended indoors filled his nostrils with guilt and shame. Using the wire guide, he hooked the rocket around and aimed for the gun battery. The wire connecting the rocket to the plane commanded it to turn it toward Avo's aggressors. Recognizing the accuracy of the rogue pilot, the guards fled before their cannon erupted in the explosion.

Avo needed to move before more arrived. He pushed the throttle against the console and pulled back the stick with practiced precision. Trucks moved into position to try and cut him off, but he clipped the canvas of the vehicles with the landing gear—just enough to tear the cloth free. He turned the plane away from their small arms fire as he swung back toward the academy citadel. The thunder of his pace would awake the stodgy old headmaster who had sent him to his doom.

There would be other planes in the air soon to chase him, but the sky was wide and empty and perfect, and he would be long gone among the clouds before they could catch a vapor of his trail.

Thoughts raced through Avo's mind. *So long Skyskape, so long family and fealty, so long security and hospitality. Farewell to the law and may the Kovenant forgive the breaches to the tenets I made to survive those four years.* Avo made mistakes, but his convictions would not be among them. If any fault was to be found, it had been in the people in whom he had placed his trust.

Avo flew on, knowing that when he landed the plane, he would make use of his talents to bide his time and strike back against Baron Blau. Until then, he needed haven, sleep, and solitude.

Chapter 2

In a remote edge of the Kingdom of Tarrkaven, a canyon where the Tarrbly river runs just south of its source surrounds the grounds of a great hero of the War of Kalamity. Baron Orson Blau reigned as an example to all nobility and an asset to the royal family. A magnificent specimen of the human race, he made conversation with such an ease of expression that, in each beat and bar of speech, there was a focused charisma that inspired and informed everyone around him.

With steely hairs cut close to his head and easy blue eyes, the Baron proved popular with the dreamers and darlings of the kingdom. Because he was forty-two years old and still unwed, it was pertinent to ask what his plans were for the future of his domain. Unless, of course, he expected immortality to be granted to him.

Still, his answer about his plans was always the same, that there were wrongs in the world that still needed to be corrected. In the Baron's charisma lay seeds of dissatisfaction with the factious and corrupt crowds of lesser nobles and peers making secret deals with the merchants and industry makers of the cities and lands abroad. Baron Blau existed as a vanguard of the values and expectations of a gentleman from the legendary history of Tarrkaven. So storied were his exploits that he seemed to make the legends jump from the page.

Among the first flying men in the War of Kalamity, Blau set the bar for every pilot to follow in his wake. A lofty goal for so lofty a profession, but even for all his deeds of great standing, there existed the simple kindnesses he prided himself in—kindnesses few others would willingly stoop to perform.

In the final years of the War of Kalamity, Buldwikk dealt a devastating blow to Tarrkaven's western neighbor of Ulkirn, rendering the land uninhabitable and the people broken and scattered. Where once existed a land teeming with great bounties of life now only remains desolation and graves. Refugees scattered to the other nations following Buldwikk's domination and would've known the terror of sorcerous powers had it not been for the stand Tarrkaven took with technological supremacy. Taking to the skies in flying machines, Tarrkaven and its allies halted the conquest of Buldwikk and a new name in justice ruled over the continent. Baron Blau, among the most intrepid spirits of this new Tarrkavian military, brought it upon himself to welcome the refugees of Ulkirn to his lands.

Among the great forests and fields of Ulkirn, a faithful sect—small even in their home nation—followed the path of the Knot Kovenant. Unlike the Ministry of the Four that was prevalent across the continent, the Knot Kovenant did not proselytize or seek to convert others to their tenets. Instead, they passed them from generation to generation. They were a people with a responsibility to the natural world. From this faith in the lands of Baron Blau came a boy by the name of Duun Howl.

To mistake Duun as a girl would not be an uncommon mistake. At the age of fourteen, Duun had deep red hair grown down to his shoulders, accented at the temples by natural plumes of white like a fox playing at humanity. With exuberant amber eyes and a profound sense of curiosity, Duun poked about in all corners of the Baron's land. When he finished tending the animals for the day, Duun rested in the woods or along the canyon sides, watching the fish travel downstream or the birds land at their roosts along the rocky crags. He would watch the goats scale up the stones to lick the salt deposits behind the cascades of the Tarrbly River. He would watch how deer walked with long measured strides, and he'd smile when the foxes of the forests canter about on little gloved paws like capering thieves from an old fairy tale.

In the late hours of such a day, when all labors were put away, the fox-haired boy Duun heard a low hum of propellers descending upon the canyon. He paused and tilted an ear to the sky. His knowledge of aircraft was limited to what he encountered in the skies of the canyon and what

Avo had told him, but his enthusiasm for flight rivaled that of his passion for nature.

Judging from the low hum of the plane's engine, Duun guessed it was a two-propeller design. The direction from which the gentle thunder originated appeared to move away from the direction of Blau's manor. It could've been leaving the estate, he thought, but Duun would've remembered hearing it arrive beforehand—and he had not. He deduced the plane was preparing to land along the river and the only plane that could land in the canyon was the one that brought Avo home from the academy. He ran back toward town to greet his brother. It seemed strange that he would be back so soon, but it was a welcome surprise, nonetheless.

Having traversed this span of woods that lined the canyon walls countless times, Duun knew the hidden paths of tree branches that would quickly lead him back without his setting a foot on the ground. Under most circumstances, such a journey would be fast and safe, but as Duun swung down from a dogwood branch, a great mass of paper and wax shook loose and crashed to the ground below. Duun's grip loosened but then immediately tightened as the first of the bees swarmed from the hive. His palms sweat as he suspended himself as still as possible as the storm of insects drew nearer. His nose began to itch, and he felt his fingers begin to give when a series of blossoms sprouted from the nearby apple tree. The bees slowed their frantic torrent and then gently gathered among the petals. From around the tree stepped a woman with bright green skin and wavy verdant hair to match. Her hand rested gently upon the surface of the bark. She looked up at Duun with disappointment.

"Care to explain what happened to these slumbering bees?"

"Well, to be fair, I don't recall there being a beehive on this branch last month."

"Come on down, quietly. I've calmed them for now, but they'll get riled up if you disturb them again."

"All right, Leleen," Duun said. It was hard to argue with a sister who spoke the language of the forest.

Among the most sacred and guarded rituals of the Knot Kovenant was the turning of eldest children to forestfolk. At the expense of having children of their own, the forestfolk kept and held sway over the plants and, to a lesser extent, the animals of nature's domain. To the Knot Kovenant, it was a sacred responsibility; to anyone else, the power aroused suspicion and fear. Duun loved his sister but found it frustrating how she seemed to appear from behind every tree—when he slipped up. She was never around when he had anything interesting to share.

Leleen took Duun's hand and helped him down to the earth's surface. "What's got you in a hurry?"

Duun pointed upward. "That plane is coming back from the academy. I think Avo is on it."

"Are you sure? He shouldn't be back for another week or two."

"Why else would an amphibious plane be arriving at this time of year?"

"Yeah, I get that you two are into all the flying machines, but I don't really think about that sort of thing. I keep my feet planted on the ground." Leleen smirked, mostly to herself.

Duun pinched the bridge of his nose and groaned. "Leelee, please leave the bad jokes to Avo. He at least makes them charming," he said.

"My jokes aren't bad," she replied.

Duun decided not to suggest otherwise. "Well, since you're here, wanna go down to town to see Avo?"

"I would, Duun. However, forcing blossoms on this tree this time of year will cut years from its life and decrease its yield in the coming season. I'm going to see if I can restore some of its vitality from the surrounding flora. Don't worry. It's not like I won't see Avo. I doubt he's going to hop on the plane so soon after arriving. If you see him, tell him I'll be right there. I'm sure he'll understand."

Duun nodded.

"Also, next time, be careful to look where you leap. I may not be around to save you from a future as a pin cushion."

"Yes, Leleen," Duun said, with less enthusiasm.

Outsiders viewed forestfolk as something "other" at best or inhuman at worst. Duun figured Leleen was like any other older sister, but he couldn't say for certain as he was the youngest of three and had only an older brother. In any case, he was thankful he had been spared from the bee stings. Nothing would be more embarrassing than greeting his brother as a swollen lump of agony.

Upon clearing the forest and catching sight of the plane swooping in for another pass over the river, Duun broke into a sprint into town. Upon reaching the street, he slowed his pace. While Duun moved with haste within nature, he took a more cautious stride in the more settled portions of the Baron's lands. From time to time shards of glass were left along the road from milk bottles set unsecurely upon doorsteps or from the careless hands of a delivery man. He had considered making shoes for these occasions but hadn't happened upon a suitable animal's skin to fashion for this purpose.

Upon reaching the waterfront, he saw the crew of the aircraft mooring the plane to the dock. Its pontoons rested upon the water's surface. A crowd had already gathered to determine why the plane had arrived. Murmurs and hubbub guessed at what would come from the plane. This portion of the crowd was among the generations that had grown up in Tarrkaven under Baron Blau for their whole lives. The older folks wore suits and dresses of decades-old fashions that had been good enough in the previous century. Women in wide-brimmed hats and bonnets strained in curious observation. The younger folk wore cotton shirts and blouses. Men wore denim pants while the ladies wore skirts and bicycle shorts. The people of this country had cosmopolitan ways and always found ways to stand out. They had the money to explore such forms of expression.

This was not the group Duun usually watched from. He was generally not welcome, especially among the older folks. Instead, he would watch the plane from the less advantageous side of the river with the rest of his fellow refugees. It had been twelve years since he had left the land of his birth, and yet, despite living most of his life in Baron Blau's territory, he still felt like a stranger among the locals.

Today, the crowd he stood among dressed more in custom with his own fashion, nomads with—clothes made of flax, cotton, and wool. Some of the older folks and laborers wore shoes, but many among Duun's company were barefoot as he was.

A few forestfolk were present—easily identified by their brilliant green skin. Two-toned hair grew long from the scalps of others among the crowd.

Several men even had great colorful beards. There were some among the refugees who dressed as ones assimilated into the culture of the locals, but they had no real place to stand between the two groups. Although the Knot Kovenant didn't recognize these modern people of Ulkirn as being the same in purpose and practice as their most faithful, they did share the national heritage, so they welcomed them as fellow displaced citizens.

Duun wormed through the crowd through each gap and opening that presented itself until he made his way to the front of the group. He hoped with great eagerness to see his brother, but to his surprise, instead he saw a small squad of soldiers step from the plane to the wharf. Each wore a deep maroon uniform, carried a bayonet-bearing rifle, and bore stern looks as they glared in the direction of the refugees. As they marched down the dock, they turned toward the crowd Duun had embedded himself within. Those who were not of Ulkirn fled indoors to continue watching from windows and doorways to see what would unfold.

The soldiers formed a line facing the crowd, and their commander stepped forward with a rolled-up piece of paper. Watching the people with caution, the officer untied the knot around the paper to reveal a wanted poster—bearing a face Duun knew only too well.

The commander scanned the crowd. "Who among you is harboring the fugitive known as Avo Howl?"

Chapter 3

A silence descended upon the crowd. Everyone among the refugees recognized the face depicted on the poster. Avo was a divisive figure in the community of the Knot Kovenant—he was one of the children who had escaped the War of Kalamity to thrive in this new land, but he was known also as one to use the technology of this kingdom while interpreting the tenets of the Kovenant liberally. Leleen's younger twin brother, he'd worked hard to support his family after the loss of his father in the final days of the war, tending to the herds and assisting in the home of Baron Blau, even as a green-skinned forestfolk. Some felt his actions had endangered the Kovenant, while others saw him as the latest culmination of their faith in foreign soil. In the passing of the silence, an older woman among the crowd finally spoke. "Avo hasn't come home all year. There must be some mistake."

"There is no mistake, witch. This heretic has made himself an enemy of the Kingdom of Tarrkaven. Our best investigators have deduced he would have few contacts or hideaways outside of this community, and if you are unwilling to cooperate, then we will be forced to search your homes and arrest you as suspected collaborators."

The crowd grew restless at the mention of being held in custody. What's more, they had no knowledge of what might have happened to Avo to cause him to break the law. While some in the kingdom held contempt for the Knot Kovenant, it had protected the country from criminals and the ever-growing threat of Buldwikk. Surely if the refugees assisted the soldiers, they would even learn to trust the refugees they'd allowed into their borders.

However, Avo could've done something wrong. Duun found himself hidden once again by the crowd. If the law was pursuing Avo, danger could befall Duun's only brother—both of whom were important members of the family and the greater community. The extreme rarity of a household having two forestfolk had granted the Howl family a special place. Paralyzed by indecision, another of the Knot Kovenant spoke.

"What is Avo's crime? Help us understand, and we will play our part."

"This lime whelp abused the hospitality of the Skyskape Royal Flight Akademy by making contact with enemies of Tarrkaven, assaulting a teacher, and stealing a military aircraft. Have any among you seen such an aircraft?"

A soldier standing by the officer procured an image of the fighter in question. Duun recognized it as a MP-30 Liberty, a multipurpose aircraft that Avo had told him about when he came home from Skyskape. It was a black and white print, but there was no mistaking the shape of the wings.

Duun paid careful attention whenever a plane entered the canyon, but due to the lack of potential landing zones and the Baron's own private airstrip, he thought it unlikely that any such plane had arrived unnoticed—carrying Avo or anyone else. He inched toward the officer, but still felt, deep within his throat, a catching tightness that kept him from speaking. He hadn't gotten far before the officer noticed him and stepped forward.

"Boy, what can you tell me about this fugitive?"

"I..." Duun began. He wanted to say he didn't think any plane had arrived in the canyon, but the words wouldn't come out.

"Young Duun is the brother of Avo," said one of the Ulkirn citizens, not of the Kovenant. Perhaps he had intended to be helpful by answering so that Duun would not have to strain himself to blunder through the interrogation, but his choice did not have the intended effect.

The officer raised his eyebrows. "We will take this boy in for questioning then. He will tell us what he knows about the fugitive, and if we can corroborate his story, he will be released. Men, do what you must," the officer said, and to the soldiers with guns. Duun froze in place. He thought to run, but in the split second in which the soldiers closed the gap to him, he realized cooperating might allow him the chance to discover what had really happened to Avo. He remained steadfast and stepped forward even as others of the Kovenant tried to protect him.

"He has no part in this," protested a woman of the forestfolk. Older than LeLeen, there were opened flower blossoms nestled in her hair.

The commander pointed an accusing finger in her face. "Out of my way, lime."

Among the Knot Kovenant, forestfolk often had it the worst. The Kovenant's views were contentious at best and blasphemous at worst in the face of the faith that had presided in Tarrkaven for thousands of years. However, forestfolk had the added curse of looking different and having means beyond normal human capabilities and hidden knowledge. This made them an even bigger target—especially in the shadow of Buldwikk's sorcery. Due to their bright green skin and hair, many Tarrkavians scornfully referred to forestfolk as limes. Use of the expression caused unrest to mount among the crowd.

Duun tried to push forward as best as he could to settle the matter sooner than later. But he didn't move so fast as to seem aggressive to the soldiers. Everyone around him continued to collapse around him, making his efforts a greater struggle. If something didn't change soon, the encounter could turn violent.

The tenets of the Knot Kovenant carefully outlined conduct relating to violence and when it did or did not warrant action. In this situation, where a wrong move could spell the deaths of many of the Kovenant, the tenets would offer leniency to harm the soldiers if they threatened a greater abundance of life. The crowd proved much larger than the soldiers, and as the saber-rattling increased, violence might break forth.

"I will help however I can if it will help us find my brother," Duun said.

This caused a hush to descend over the crowd. The forestfolk woman turned to regard Duun and backed away to the side to avoid opposing their kin of the Kovenant. However, the soldiers, less than eager to talk, had already procured handcuffs for Duun. As the irons were put on his wrists, he feared for what would become of his mother and sister.

Hope seemed lost until a luxurious motorcar drove up along the riverside down from the baron's magnificent manor. The engine purred in place. From the door emerged the hero of heroes: Baron Blau in the flesh.

To understand the baron's gravity, one may imagine a quite different sort of man than the one who performed the great heroics of his day. He stood just below six feet tall but as soon as he rose from the vehicle and approached the soldiers, the shape of his greatcoat swayed within the air, evoking the image of a shapeless sea creature. The baron's wardrobe never appeared gaudy, and one who did not know his legend (if such a soul existed) might mistake him as an ordinary business executive. The car he drove in, however, spoke to the merits of his taste for performance engineering.

Duun could feel the growling of the engine through the stones under his feet. With hair of white gold and sky-blue eyes, Blau's countenance flashed over the soldiers and the crowd like a signal light guiding ships in stormy waters. When words rose from his lips, they rang true with the voice of a man well educated, a man who had spent many years touring the cities of the world.

"Good soldier," he said, "would you care to explain why you are harassing my people? I was told the plane was landing for routine arrivals and departures."

"Baron Blau," the commander said as he took two small steps backward and stood at attention with the soldiers around him. He dared not say another word until the baron commanded it.

"These are all good men, women, and children enjoying their afternoons, just as you are good soldiers likely following orders. However, I see six soldiers making waves in the reflecting pond. I would ask why."

"Well, you see, Baron, we've been ordered to search for a fugitive from the Skyskape Akademy who stole a military vehicle. This fugitive, Avo Howl, damaged property and caused quite a fuss."

The baron smirked. "Avo stole a plane? He's a willful boy to be sure, but he wouldn't start trouble unless provoked. This story of yours seems to be missing a few pieces. Why would a model student just weeks from graduating feel so threatened as to steal a plane and damage school property?"

"Well, your baronhood—"

"Baron's fine…or Your Lordship," Blau said.

"Baron, we believe Avo has made alliances with subversive elements from neighboring countries. Perhaps they are planning a rebellion with the Knot Kovenant in your very community. This...child…here is kin to the fugitive and we sought to question him."

Duun didn't much care for the suspicious pause in the commander's voice before being identified as simply the child.

"Perhaps if you understood the Knot Kovenant, you would know that their sacred tenets forbid widespread violence. They don't even work in slaughterhouses and tanneries because of it." The baron turned to Duun. "Did you say you would help these men?"

"I did," Duun answered.

"Then let the boy help you."

"We were going to take him somewhere safer for questioning," the commander said.

Baron Blau looked around then looked back. "Safe from what? Trout? Herons? Sheep?"

"Hidden insurgents, Baron," the commander said. His lips tightened as he felt he was being mocked by the noble.

Blau frowned at the soldiers. "I don't know of many rebels in towns where people are happy, employed, and fed. Have you answered my questions truthfully while we've been out here?"

"Of course, Baron," the commander said.

"Then I'd say right here and right now we are safe for questioning. Duun, your brother says you have a particular interest in planes. Have you seen or heard any other planes arriving in the town?"

"No, your Lordship,"

"Why do you think so?"

"The only airstrip is on your estate."

"That is correct, and I think I would know if there was a plane I didn't recognize on my doorstep. Perhaps the plane lands on water, but I see only your plane upon the river. I think we can safely conclude Avo did not come here, and these people are good innocent folk with no knowledge of this apparent crime."

"Yes, good baron," the commander said.

"Now go back to the academy and tell them that as sure as there are four gods in heaven, there is one baron of this domain and if anything moves out of place, I'll be the one to judge it. I won't have anyone treading upon my lands or affairs unless I desire it. Understand?"

"Yes, yes, of course, Baron Blau." The commander dropped his head downward to avoid his luminous gaze.

The baron walked up to two of the soldiers and placed his hands upon their shoulders. "Excellent. Now that the matter is settled, I would ask you to come to my house for some warmer hospitality. What do you say to wassail, gingerbread, and a warm hearth?"

"We'd like that very much, your Lordship, but we don't mean to intrude any further."

The baron shook his head. "Oh, nonsense," he said. "There's nothing like the miracle of aviation, but it's not the most comfortable of circumstances. You've traveled far, and I'd say we've settled our business rather quickly. It would be a disservice to send you away so empty-handed."

The commander's visage brightened. "Then we would be honored."

"Excellent." Blau walked around the commander and stood in front of the soldiers. He waved his hand to the car and the chauffeur stepped out from the passenger side and took the driver's seat. "Parker will bring the limousine. I fear the horse I rode in on may be a bit crowded for all of us."

Blau then turned his attention to the people of the town. "As for all my dear beloved subjects, I ask that you harbor no ill will. As you are subjects of the crown, so are these soldiers. And just as they will not take up your time any further, I'd ask that you welcome them as our guests as I have welcomed you. I do not wish to keep you from your evenings any longer."

The people answered with affirmations and dispersed, in most cases, to head home. While the matter had been resolved, none were too comfortable or too trusting to risk further interaction with the soldiers.

Duun watched as the baron conversed with the soldiers. They laughed and delighted at what were obviously the baron's tales and jests. Then he noticed an odd shape on the commander's sleeve. On one of the buttons there was an image—a white oval with two purple dots like eyes staring back. He didn't recognize this image but didn't try to get closer. He did not want to draw further attention to himself from the people who had nearly swept him away.

The limo came down shortly after, and the soldiers entered the vehicle one by one. As the commander at last went to the side of the car, the baron went to the driver's side door and the chauffeur swapped places with him. The chauffeur shook the commander's hand with the familiarity of friends and then closed the car door. Baron Blau took his seat at the wheel and drove away toward the mansion.

On the walk home, questions raced through Duun's mind. Had Avo been different when he last saw him?

Chapter 4

Duun walked through the pastures on his way back to the family cottage. The light of the hearth shone through gaps in the shutters and smoke rose through the chimney into the night sky. As he approached the door, he saw Leleen standing there. She held up her hand to stop him.

Duun froze in his tracks and looked at his sister, who pointed down toward the grass. Just shy of his next step was a large pile of sheep poop. He stepped around the landmine and onto the stones of the doorstep.

"Didn't we just talk about watching your step?"

"Sorry…it's just…it wasn't Avo on the plane."

Leleen stood up straighter. "Is everything all right?"

"I don't know," Duun said, "Avo's gone."

Leleen paused. "*How* is Avo gone?"

"They said he's stolen an airplane and is a criminal," Duun said. The words sounded foreign, incorrect as they left his mouth, a lie burning him deep inside as though they carried a venom that would poison Avo's name.

Leleen frowned. "Why did they say he's stolen a plane?"

"I don't know. It sounds like they think Avo's part of some underground movement to attack the kingdom. The soldiers nearly took me when they found out I'm related to him."

"Are you okay?"

Duun nodded. "Yes. But what if Avo did what they said? Do you think there's a rebellion against the crown? Why would Avo want any part in that?"

Leleen silenced Duun by pulling him into a hug. Her younger brother was closer to Avo than she was. It hadn't been unusual for the twins to lock horns, but Duun loved his older brother and sister in equal measure. They had made up for his not having many friends, other than those that tended to walk on all fours.

Leleen imagined the idea of losing Avo felt like losing a right arm to Duun. When he calmed down, she smiled at him and gestured to the door. "Come inside, I'll make you some tea."

The cottage was small and sparsely furnished. There were only two rooms—one for gathering and one for resting. In the gathering room was a table low to the floor and a hearth with a kettle cooking over the flames.

Their mother sat at the table. From her side, a mighty cloud of wool stirred and trotted up to Leleen. It nibbled at her hand and followed her around the table. "Hello Bigby," she said.

"Mom," said Duun, "why is Bigby in the house right now? We've got a fire. We don't need a sheep in here."

"Bigby is a valued member of our family, and he pulls his weight same as all of us."

"So do Tippy, Toppy, Floppy, and Thunderburgh," Duun replied.

Leleen rolled her eyes. Avo had named the sheep—she knew her twin had done it as a sadistic pleasure, forcing others to say their names aloud.

"Well, tonight is Bigby's turn in the house," said their mother.

Leleen turned to Duun. "Can you hold onto Bigby while I make some tea? It would be bad for everyone if his fleece caught fire because he wanted to bite my hands."

All the sheep constantly tried to bite Leleen, a problem forestfolk frequently encountered. Avo had worn heavy mitts when working with the sheep. Nobody really knew why the sheep were inclined to nibble on forestfolk, as no other animals, not even the goats, seemed to bother.

After Avo left for Skyskape, it had fallen to Duun to care for the animals full time. Of all the sheep's names, Bigby's had proven to be appropriate. It was difficult to get arms around the substantial fleece on the fluffiest member of the family, but Duun did his best and managed to save his sister from the heavy fuzzball. He determined that he would take time to shear off some of Bigby's excess wool, but not so much to leave the creature shivering when the worst of winter began.

Leleen approached the opposite side of the table with a cup of green tea. She maintained a wide variety of trees and other plants behind the house that yielded a remarkable bounty depending upon the season. Because of her gifts, the trees were well kept, and the products of her efforts were superior to any goods not tended by forestfolk. Her tea was unrivaled.

She treated the trees like friends. From time to time, Duun could swear he heard her talking to them. He wasn't sure if this came with being a forestfolk or simply because she was lonely, but as funny as he found it, he didn't tease her about it. Avo, on the other hand, had always taken great joy in poking fun at Leleen. On one occasion, he claimed to have heard her cheering a bean sprout, encouraging it to grow strong, and thereafter called her "Leleen the Bean Queen." Avo had been oddly afflicted with the spins after eating them one night. Leleen had smiled slyly and dubbed Avo "King of the Latrine." After that, Duun never troubled Leleen. There was no telling how the plants would exact their revenge.

She handed Duun his cup of tea and he took a sip. He agreed—Leleen's tea was the best. Duun generally preferred his tea to be of a greener variety, but this one was not bitter. It had a slight sweetness that followed on the heels of an initial leafy flavor. Leleen had found the perfect temperature for tea—her preparations were such that it was ever so close to too hot, but the drinker was not required to sip it and then wait another two minutes.

"So, what did you two do today?" their mother asked. Duun dreaded the question, but Leleen picked up the slack for him and answered first. "Saved an apple tree deep in the woods. I think we will get a curious harvest from it when it bears fruit next year. I don't believe I have an apple tree like it in the orchard."

"How does an apple tree need saving?" their mother asked. The mysteries of forestfolk intrigued her. Her eldest brother had been one of them, but he had died at the start of the War of Kalamity and had been notoriously terrible at explaining things anyway.

"Well, it got overstimulated—perhaps during the warm weather we had last week—and blossomed too soon."

"Uh, huh." Although Duun's mother had been responsible for the animals when she was younger, her curiosity didn't mean she understood

Leleen's explanations, but at least this one made some semblance of sense. Her brother Norry's words, however, had been the stuff of riddles. She still wondered what he meant by the expression "oven of the tree." She wasn't alone—everyone wondered, even Avo and Leleen.

"What about you, Duun? See anything interesting today?"

Duun still wasn't ready to answer.

"Duun was telling me about the goats up on the cliffside," Leleen said as she tried to intercept the question, but Duun shook his head at her. He knew there was no point in dragging things out any longer.

His voice was flat—he tried to suppress some of the sting of the news. "Some soldiers came into town, and they said Avo did some bad things," he said.

Their mother drank her tea all in one swig and then set the cup on the table. "Do you think he did these things?" she asked.

"I don't know. Why would he?"

The mother sat upright and picked up her knitting. She had been working on a sweater for Leleen. Her housework included the responsibility of turning raw materials into more useful products and instructing the children of the community how to do so. Holding it to the light of the fireplace, she revealed one side of the intricate patterns she had woven.

"What do you think of this side? Is it nice?"

"It is," Duun said. All of her children had learned under her tutelage, but there were patterns she kept to herself as her own form of expression. She turned the weaving around.

"What about this side?" she asked. The other side of the knitwork looked messy and confusing. Duun shook his head and frowned and his mother nodded in response.

"Everyone we encounter has more than one side," she said. "Past choices or experiences are kept to themselves that nobody ever gets to see. They aren't always pretty. Sometimes if we saw this side," she said, pointing to the underside of the weaving, "we would wonder what is it that keeps them together. But it is *those* experiences and choices that shape and define the side of us everyone sees. The only people who ever see the wrong sides of our knitwork are the people who make them, and the people who own them, but they wear them all the same." She paused. "People admire the patterns for what they are, not how they're put together. Avo is your brother, and whether you know it or not, you've both had a role in making him who he is. Certainly, he's had experiences you two have not, but you've seen sides of him that no one else has. Who do you think knows your brother better—his own kin, or some strange soldiers?"

Leleen placed her hands around her teacup. Duun ran Bigby's wool between his fingers. For a lady who let sheep run through her house, their mother had the occasional pearl to impart. Before the siblings could respond, their mother got up and opened the door to the resting room.

"Well, I've had a long day making potato knishes. Remember to put out the fire before you go to bed. I'll be taking Bigby off your hands, Duun. Don't stay up too late, and we'll greet tomorrow refreshed and ready for whatever waits."

She waved some sort of bauble tied to her wrist around at Bigby, and the large sheep got up and followed. Leleen took a closer look at the bracelet."Is that some of my hair?"

"A small price to pay for not getting chewed on by a lamb all night. When you wake up undisturbed by the sheep, you'll thank me. Good night, you two."

Leleen sat speechless. "Unbelievable," she said. Duun couldn't help but chuckle. His sister shot a glare at him, and he stopped laughing and went back to drinking tea. He dared not make the next cup give him stomach cramps. He thanked Leleen for the tea and then put out the fire.

Leleen's green shone as a bright hue of blue for a moment that filled the room with a cool light. When in the dark, she caused the green in her skin to illuminate so she wouldn't accidentally trip over the sparse furnishings or the sheep.

"Avo will need our help," said Duun.

"And we will help him," replied Leleen. "But first we need our rest. You can't do anybody any good if you can't get any rest."

Leleen smiled as her light faded into dark. Duun sat for a long time, thinking of Avo deep into the night. Finally, he mustered the strength to go to his own bed. He hadn't the endurance to stay up and continue planning. He would leave that to the morning.

Chapter 5

Duun woke in the morning at five o'clock, as his body demanded. He would've loved to go back to sleep, but the needs of the animals couldn't be left to wait. Leleen continued to sleep because trees didn't run the risk of wetting themselves or getting covered in dirt in the stables.

Avo doesn't know how lucky he is to have a little brother to help with these chores, thought Duun, as he put on outer layers of clothes, filled his flax satchel with potato knishes, and opened the door to the pastures. Bigby the sheep charged forth to chow down on the clover in the fields. Duun picked a handful of the weed on his way to the stable to open the pens and release the rest of the sheep. Thunderburgh needed a bit more of a push than others but, upon seeing the green in the fields, followed them.

Next up came the chickens, who were eager to get out of their coop as fast as possible. As soon as Duun opened it, a flood of poultry raced to eat the seed he had placed in the trough. While they stuffed their beaks, Duun collected the eggs and placed them one by one in a basket with care and then carried the basket to a storeroom where they would be safe.

Once done with the eggs, he checked all the fences to ensure there was no breach where the foxes he had seen could get in. Avo had a host of dirty names for the vulpine menace, but Duun had had no trouble with the foxes. Perhaps the foxes perceived Duun to be kin, a covert agent among the forestfolk.

Done eating, the chickens cleared out from the trough and explored their surroundings as if they were seeing the yard for the first time. Careful to watch for "presents" left by the sheep, Duun took a seat in the pasture.

It was his job to watch the sheep and make sure none got too far from the herd. He removed balls of yarn from his satchel—he would work on his knitting while watching the flock. Wasteful living was frowned upon within the Knot Kovenant, so he aimed to make the most of his time with such pursuits. Casting on loops of woolen yarn, he knitted mittens that were not colorful but would be functional when the air grew colder. Time passed in an uneventful fashion, although there was an occasional need for him to relocate a wandering sheep and to keep Tippy and Floppy from falling over on their sides.

When the sun was directly overhead, he set aside his craft and reached into his satchel to pull out a potato knish. The breaded ball fit neatly in his left hand. As he nibbled, he tasted the tang of caramelized cabbage and onion cooked and surrounded by the soft starchy potatoes inside.

Meats cooked any way one could imagine were the cornerstone of the Tarrkavian diet, driven by the meatpacking industry and large fisheries in the urban centers. While the tenets of the Knot Kovenant did not forbid eating meat or killing animals with cause, it did require the act to be done only in service of one's nutrition and never for profit.

No such restriction was placed on farmers. Fruits, vegetables, nuts, seeds, and grains, and dairy and eggs were permitted to be sold as long as it was done with care, so members of the Knot Kovenant gravitated toward agrarian living. The work of forestfolk helped prevent the overtaxing of the land, so the Kovenant's religious kin lived in balance with nature.

There were many foods Duun had never tasted but he didn't fret about it. He mused that if he was ever so curious as to discover, for instance, how bacon tasted, he knew he could probably barter for a pig and do what needed to be done. Still, he had been told that some pigs dug up mushrooms they smelled underground, and this seemed like a better use for the creature. He'd also heard these pigs would *eat* the mushrooms before they could be collected and pigs had jaws that could easily chew through fingers. Perhaps I'll not get a pig, he thought.

About three in the afternoon, while he walked through the field with a pair of shears, touching up the sheeps' fleece, he heard a curious hum from the sky. At first notice, he thought the sound to be coming from the engines of the plane that had arrived the day before. But, as he continued to listen, the sound became louder than that he had heard the previous day.

He stood and turned his attention to the sky. Three small airplanes, followed by one much larger plane, passed through a brief break in the clouds. He looked back at the sheep and when he was content they wouldn't venture far, he followed the curious formation of planes. From the edge of town, he could see a throng of people also staring toward the skies.

Then, abruptly, the sound changed. Somewhere above the heavy stratus clouds, a buzzing engine rose in pitch, giving way to a loud screech that resounded off the wide canyon walls. One of the small planes shot down through the clouds and, just as it seemed to be flying headfirst into the river, swung upward and ran parallel. As it pulled up, something fell from the plane onto the roof of the post office. An explosion tore through the air and engulfed the building in a firestorm. In the midst of the malaise, the other two planes fired a hail of bullets at the streets. People screamed and ran indoors as the screeching of the planes continued overhead.

What made the curious screech? Duun could not say, but he set aside his curiosity and ran toward home for safety. He turned back to make sure the planes weren't chasing him, only to see small black objects fall and swarm from the larger plane on the other side of the river. Rising in a fanned-out pattern, they leveled most of the houses and businesses below.

When he reached the edge of the pasture, he found the sheep running about in panic. At first, he completely missed the sight of Leleen, who, with their mother, ran down the path calling to him.

"Get down!" Leleen screamed. As they all dropped to the ground behind the stone wall at the edge of the pasture, a storm of bullets bounced up the hillside, blasting the roof of their house and tearing through the shutters. Once past, the plane flew up and disappeared once more in the clouds.

Duun jumped from his crouch and ran to his family's side. He feared the worst, but as he reached them, he found both well, save for a few bumps and scrapes. "We need to get to the woods. We will be safe in the woods," he said.

Leleen stared at him. "Safe? Those bullets tore through our house in moments!"

"They have bombs too. We've no time to argue. We go now!" The family fled as best they could with no time to look back into the forest below the canyon's side.

Once more, Duun heard the plane pitch upward, preparing to strafe the area again. Even as they ran through the first sparse trees, they heard the zipping of bullets tearing through the brush and crashing into the ground ahead of them. Woodchips showered the ground in fearful cracks. Even a branch fell here and there.

Judging by the debris, Duun inferred the caliber of the bullets to be quite large. If even one bullet managed to hit one of them, it would spell a life-threatening injury. Whoever had flown this plane seemed determined to kill his family. And for what? Nobody in the family had done anything to make an enemy of anyone.

Duun could not say how safe they were in the forest, but he spotted a herd of goats fleeing up toward the side of the canyon. Goats did not understand the workings of machinery or firearms, but all creatures had an awareness of danger, and Duun believed these beasts would lead them to a safer shelter.

"We need to follow the goats," Duun said. Leleen nodded and she and their mother hurried as best they could uphill, but they hadn't the skills of climbing that Duun possessed. Keeping pace with the goats, he watched as they bounded toward a small cave within the cliffside. He signaled to Leleen and the family hurried to the cave.

Just as Duun's mother and Leleen entered, the plane made its presence known again. It flew just above the tree line but pulled up when it approached the canyon wall. A last second effort of the pilot was wasted as clouds obscured the top of the canyon wall, and in a thunderous crash, the plane was blown to pieces against nature's fortification.

A wing slammed deep into the ground just outside the cave and the ceiling began to shake as rocks were loosened from above. Duun was frightened for them all. If more debris fell, the cave would soon become a death trap. He grabbed Leleen's hand and pulled her with him out of the cave. They broke forth into the light of the outdoors and, in a brief moment of focus, he saw the image he had seen on the commander's sleeve again—an oval with two white featureless circles. It reminded Duun of an owl's head. In the tales and traditions passed down through the forestfolk, a screeching owl signified death's approach.

Duun was called back to attention when a crash was heard from behind. The cave ceiling had given way and stones had crashed down, entrapping their mother's legs. Caught as in a vise, she screamed in pain.

Each of the stones was too large to move without assistance. Duun was unable to pull her free and his mind raced. Leleen looked to Duun. "If we can't lift the stones, what options do we have?"

"I don't know!" said Duun. The attack had happened too fast. Today might have been like any other day, but instead, mystery raiders had gone on the offensive against Baron Blau's domain. The baron would know what to do—but his mansion was too far in the other direction for them to run to.

"The plane is gone," said Leleen. "Mom's not dying, but she is in a lot of pain. I'll do what I can to keep her from going into shock, but you need to think. Use that mind of yours. What options do we have?"

Duun took a deep breath and looked toward their mother, fearful that her injuries were like a scrape that felt so awful that you dared not look at it for fear of the worst. But he needed to be rational. He saw tears streaming down her face, the stones caught her legs but stopped just above her knees.

There were gaps between the stones. He had seen someone in the town lift a heavy cart that had lost its wheel using a small stone and a beam as a lever. Perhaps something similar could be employed in this situation.

"Leleen, can you make that tree grow a long branch?"

"I'll do what I can," she said. Trading places with Duun, she walked to a nearby tree and placed her hand on it. A branch extended downward. Once it reached a sufficient length, she caused the branch to dry and become brittle. When she pulled down on the branch, it snapped free and she passed it to Duun. He placed it in one of the gaps near the injury.

"What now?" she asked.

"When I say pull, you need to reach for Mom's hands and pull her out. I can't guarantee I can hold the stones up for long."

"Ok," Leleen said. "Stay with me, Mom. Duun's going to get you out of there."

As Leleen grabbed her mother's hands, Duun inserted the lever just over a rock. As it became securely planted under the stone that lay on her legs, Duun pulled down on the lever to raise the rock. It did not immediately lift but as he poured the full force of his body into the lever, the stone began to shift. "Pull!" Duun said, and Leleen dragged their mother free of the stones.

The siblings collapsed and sighed with relief. "What now?" Leleen asked.

"Stay here, stay with her. I'll go find the baron. He'll know what to do."

Duun ran like the wind. He had far to go and there was not a second to waste. With the rush of adrenaline firing through his heart, he did not pause or feel the fatigue and soreness of his movement. As he ran through the pastures where he had tended to his chores, he saw the carnage of a few sheep shot in the strafing. Their house had collapsed.

When Duun reached the baron's mansion, he saw smoke rising from one side of the building. He feared the worst, but as he beheld the scene from a distance, he saw Blau's plane soaring among the clouds. The large plane that had destroyed the town had fallen from the sky in flames and crashed into the river below. The others had broken off and fled beyond view.

Baron Blau landed his plane on his airstrip, and Duun drew near enough to be seen. Blau, huffing with anger at the damage that had been done by the marauders, spied him. "Are you all right?" he said, as he ran toward Duun. "Where is your family?"

The boy's eyes grew heavy…and he fainted.

Chapter 6

The heaviness of smoke lingered in the air when Duun returned to consciousness. The room in which he found himself was spacious and warm—as large as his entire house. He sat up, remembering that the cottage had been destroyed and the danger his family was in.

He had been too young, only two years old, to recall the War of Kalamity. Maybe a word or phrase said in passing came back to him from those dark days—a glimpse of the plane that carried them from the community in Ulkirn. A detail of the garden around their family home. He had no recollection of his father's face—his mother said they were too poor to afford a photograph. Sometimes Leleen mentioned things she remembered about him.

These memories pushed Duun into action. He strove to pull himself out of bed and found himself dressed in the most peculiar fashion, in a long shirt that covered his whole body and cotton socks upon his feet. He found the cord he used to tie his hair back on a square piece of furniture at the side of the bed. With his long hair out of his face, he rose and placed one foot before the other. When he was confident his feet would hold him up, he took a few steps.

The floor seemed to be made of a hard wood. Duun hadn't seen anything quite like it in all his time in the forests. He wanted to run to find his family, but he remembered the words of Leleen—he needed to be cautious and careful. Observations would be beneficial. He needed to consider what he knew, because knowing what happened around him would guide him to what he would need to do next. To the door of the room he went, and through it, he saw large hallways with high arched ceilings.

A woman in a deep blue dress and white apron saw Duun ease open the door. The maid approached him with brisk steps and offered a hand to keep him upright. "Are you well, boy? The baron said you took a nasty fall when you got here. By my best diagnosis, you got yourself worked up to the point of exhaustion. It's been a rather serious set of circumstances since you've been out. The baron is away looking for survivors in the town, but he will want to speak with you when he returns."

"Where's my family?" Duun asked.

"Yes, that's what I need to tell you about right now. Your sister is as lucky as she is green. Little more than what I can only assume are bruises. Baron Blau told me she was green, but I didn't think she would be…well, she's *really* green."

"Do you not leave this place often?" Duun asked.

"There's nothing out there that interests me all that much. I've got books to read and people to patch up. From time to time, I even play violin when I fancy the mood." She paused. "But that's not important right now. Your mother's situation *is*. Your sister told me what you managed to do to get her out from the rocks. She has broken bones and torn tendons. I don't think she will be able to walk again."

Duun's mind retreated inward. It had been his idea to hide his family in the cave and follow the goats. It seemed sensible by his understanding of nature, but what did goats know of airplanes and explosives?

"I know that look," said the woman in the blue dress. "Don't blame yourself. A lot of people aren't alive right now because they didn't have someone like you to steer them to safety. You're downright heroic. Your mother's awake, and we've been monitoring her situation since you've been out. Your sister did a lot to slow the bleeding and your mother should survive if she stays in our care." She paused, smiling. "We tried to get your mother to rest but that lady has been knitting without end since we've brought her here. I imagine we'll have a set of duvets for every bed in the house before the end of the week."

"Can you take me to my mother, ma'am?"

"Natalie. I'm not old enough to be called a ma'am. And yes, right this way. Follow me."

Natalie led Duun down the hall past scores of paintings of Blaus of generations past. Pictures of coasts and countrysides were interspersed among the portraits. One that stood out to Duun was a large citadel on a peninsula overlooking the sea. Words were written on a gold plate below the painting, but Duun he did not know what they said. He had not yet learned to read.

Toward the end of the hall was a photograph of a young Baron Blau standing by an old plane outside of a series of tents on a rocky field of battle. He wore a wide smile while the other pilots near him were more reserved. Duun's impression of Blau was that there was no one else in all of Tarrkaven quite like him. The boy wondered if standing out like Blau did actually make the world better or just made him a bigger target. He did not know much about the world beyond this canyon community and had little information by which to draw a conclusion of his own.

Natalie opened the door to the room where his mother stayed. Leleen waited by their mother's side, who worked frantically with her needles. There, in the middle of the room, was Bigby.

The maid frowned. "Who brought this sheep in here?"

"He follows me everywhere," said Leleen. "I think he's the only one from our flock that survived. I'll take him outside—Duun?"

Leleen ran to her brother and Bigby followed with quick little bounds along the floor. Natalie quickly reached for a broom and dustpan in the corner of the room and set to clean up the wisps of fluff that follow bouncing sheep.

"Leelee," Duun said, "I heard the news. Mom, I'm sorry I couldn't do more."

Leleen was grave. "We'll survive, Duun, but it's not going to be easy going forward. Our house is gone. All our sheep except Bigby are dead, and many of our chickens have run away. Only three are left."

"What about your trees?"

"They're for the most part unscathed, but it won't be easy to tend to them without a place to stay nearby." She put her arm around her brother. "Baron Blau said he wanted to speak with you when you woke up. He has a proposition of sorts, he said."

"Did he tell you about it?"

"No, and I did ask about it, but he said he wanted you to be awake first."

"There were soldiers staying here. Are they still here?"

He looked to Natalie, who continued to sweep behind Bigby no matter which angle he took to try and get to Leleen.

"Not anymore," she said. "They were here but were killed by a stray bomb, likely one intended for the baron. There was a fire, but it's now out. The raid did quite a number. It's going to take all month to get the scent of smoke out of everything."

"Duun," their mother said, seeing his fear. "You're safe."

"I'm going to step outside so Bigby can get some exercise," Leleen said. She gave Duun a hug and stepped out the door, followed by the sheep, followed by Natalie. The door closed leaving Duun by his mother's side.

"I'm sorry, Mom."

"Don't be sorry, you were brave. Be proud of what you did."

It didn't matter how much he heard these words or who he heard them from. In the end, Duun couldn't get past the dread that there was something he could've done differently. The home she had given him and his siblings was gone. No amount of rational thought eased his sorrow.

"I can't Mom. I should've done more. If there was something else I could do…"

"What you can do is rest and feel sad. We're all sad, but it's what we need most of all in times like this. Sadness means we still care. You care for your family, and that's what's most important."

"I'll give us a home again, and I'll find Avo somehow."

His mother smiled warmly. "We have a home, Duun. You don't need to do anything else. Just be here for me and your sister. Avo will be back." She stopped and looked around. "Goodness, what time is it? I'm going to get some rest. I'll see you in the morning. Talk to the baron when he comes back."

She leaned back and immediately drifted into restful sleep, her hands twitching every now and then with the knitting needles between her fingers.

Duun took the needles and set them by the square furniture next to the bed. The door opened and Natalie returned, wiping her brow. She placed the broom back in the corner. "Oh good, she's finally getting some sleep. She didn't sleep a wink until just now. I don't know how she does it." She glanced at Duun, who was crouching beside his mother's bed. "There's nothing to worry about now, I'll take care of her. Baron Blau is still busy. Find something to occupy yourself until then. I would suggest something, but I'm not sure what it is you folk do. Do you read?"

"We don't own any books outside of the Tenets of the Knot Kovenant."

"Not allowed to?"

"Can't afford to."

"Can you read?"

Duun shook his head. "I can't."

"Well, that certainly limits your options." She thought for a moment and her face brightened. "Tell you what. Baron Blau has some books of pictures from his travels. Follow me, and I'll take you to the library."

"Thank you, I appreciate it."

Natalie walked with Duun down the stairs and hung a right toward the wing where the fight had broken out. "There is some damage to the collection, but thankfully only records of production and expenses from past years across the Barony were destroyed. That's still bad, but they aren't exactly page-turners, so that won't affect you or me."

She glanced across the shelves. "There are quite a few books of Blau's photographs, so I'll grab a few and let you look through those so you won't be overwhelmed." She slid the ladder along the bookshelf up to a top shelf of leather-bound books.

"Oh, I don't know that I can use them if they're bound in leather," Duun said.

"The baron said you might say something like that. He said to tell you not to worry. Books are the inverse of wasteful consumption—if they are cared for, they can be used by thousands of people for thousands of years."

Duun considered what she said and felt the explanation to be acceptable explanation. The spirit of the law was to let no life or death go to waste. If books could be kept for as long as the baron suggested, then it would be a greater waste to *not* use them.

He reached out for a book from the pile Natalie was handing him. It had such a heft to it that Duun almost lost his balance and he realized that he was still a bit weak. He planted his feet for the second, third, and fourth time and walked the books one by one to a table in the center of the library.

He sat down at the table and placed the first book in front of him.

"If you'd like, I can start a fire for you," said Natalie. "The heat vents took some damage."

"That would be nice, but you don't need to go out of your way for my sake."

"Nonsense, this is my job. Seems like you understand what it means to earn one's keep. Look through those books, and the baron will see you as soon as he comes back."

"All right, then, and thank you."

Duun placed his hand upon the leather cover. He wondered how old the book was and how many other hands had held it. If it was of the baron's own creation, he thought, perhaps not as many hands as some of the other books in this place.

Still, he wondered what history the book had experienced. Opening the cover, he saw some written words. Duun could only guess at what they said, so he turned to the next page. The pictures Natalie had promised appeared.

The first picture was of the citadel upon the peninsula. Four large towers conjoined by walls were surrounded by cliffs overlooking crashing waves. All four towers connected to one another but also to a central spire like the spokes of a wheel.

Duun flipped to another page. All the photographs had been taken from an aerial view. Between the spokes were sports pitches and gardens. On the space that most directly faced the land were roads that led into and out of a gate. Along this land were more lengthy gardens lining the path before branching off into two roads. One led farther away, perhaps to a town or port, and the other to an expansive airfield.

The volume of planes in the picture was staggering—fighters, biplanes, bombers, passenger planes, and cargo planes. Upon further inspection of the building with the central spire, Duun saw what looked to be radio towers and windows that overlooked the entire area. Another tower, nowhere near as tall as the one in the citadel's center, was closer to the airfield. It featured radio antennae and a variety of lights and lines pointed in all directions. Was this Skyskape?

Further flipping through the pages of photos led to an image of Baron Blau arriving at the school in his own personal plane. He stood by its side and wore a scarf around his neck, with a pattern of repeating diamonds going up its length. Duun's mother had knitted these patterns into her work in the past—she called it an intarsia pattern, dark diamonds against a brighter background.

The next picture was of Blau once more, but with a familiar face by his side—Avo! His scarf's intarsia pattern was a reversed palette of white X's distinct against a dark canvas. Both the Baron and Avo looked happy. Avo looked young. Maybe just a little older than Duun was now.

Duun turned through the pages of the book in search of more pictures of Avo. He found one and sat gazing at it.

"Do you remember the day Avo went to Skyskape?" said a voice behind him.

Chapter 7

"What can you tell me about my brother?" asked Duun.

Baron Blau took a seat beside him at the table and opened another of the photo albums. He flipped through a few pages and then turned the book toward the boy.

"Your brother impresses me even as a legendary flying ace. Despite coming from a culture that employs very little modern technology in day to day life, he took to flying sooner even than I did. One day he sneaked onto my mansion grounds—past all of my guards—just to see me land my plane upon the green." The baron examined Duun's face. "He must've been around your age when he did that. He asked me why I fly, and I told him I did so because I wanted to do what no one else had ever done and go where no one had ever gone. Do you remember that day?"

Duun nodded. "I do. He had the biggest smile on his face when he came home. He went to Mom and Leleen and talked about how he wanted to learn how to fly a plane. Leleen wasn't so sure, and neither was Mom, at first. However, they couldn't keep Avo from his enthusiasm for long. Mom finally conceded to let him go to Skyskape."

The baron mused about what Duun had said. "I don't want to speak ill of your sister. Unlike many in this kingdom, I have a greater appreciation for the ways of the Knot Kovenant than you may realize. Certainly, I have my disagreements with some of the tenets, and a person in my position cannot realistically abide by all the commands of the Kovenant.

"But I appreciate that the followers of the Kovenant are survivors who have endured great persecution to refine and polish their truth. Your brother, in many ways, represents the best of your ideas, even if he doesn't reflect all of them—as your sister would like."

Duun nodded. "Leleen says the tenets are infallible and unchanging. Avo has always had doubts about that."

"Well, Avo is correct. Here, I have something that may help you understand." Blau stood up and walked behind a large shelf of books. He came back with two—one old and the other ancient. He set them out on the table before Duun. "I believe you recognize this one," he said, pointing to the old book.

"Of course, these are the Tenets of the Kovenant."

"Have you read it?"

"I cannot read."

"Well, for now, let me read you this passage." Blau turned a few pages and then slid a finger under the words as he read aloud. "'None under the Kovenant shall kill man nor beast without cause.' You recognize these words?"

"Of course," said Duun.

Blau then opened the book of cracked leather and turned to another passage. Running his fingers along a passage that seemed nearly identical, he read aloud again. "'None under the Kovenant shall kill man nor beast.' Period."

Duun looked at the passages more closely. He didn't know exactly what the words said, but he couldn't deny that some were missing in the older text. He looked to the baron in disbelief. "It's not the same. The first one says it's not okay to kill men or beasts unless there's a good reason. The second says it's not okay at all. "

Blau smiled at the boy. "Exactly. Just a few words missing changes the whole meaning from a moral *relative* to a moral *imperative.* A matter of personal judgment to an iron law." He pointed to one of the books. "This first copy was saved from Ulkirn during the War of Kalamity. It is why you recognize the text. This other text was claimed from a university in the city-state of Savissia, which is closer to the place of origin of the Knot Kovenant. Now, both were translated from the original language, and stemmed from a variety of manuscripts in between, but meaning is lost and gained in both places. So, my young friend, which is correct? One with or without the addition?"

Duun was confused. He had known only of one edition of the Tenets of the Kovenant. He wanted to say the one he was familiar with was correct, but then he wondered if it had simply prescribed an easier path to take.

Baron Blau closed both books. "Don't beat yourself up over it. The Knot Kovenant doesn't recognize a deity like the Faith of the Four does, nor do you have to contend with what the after life has in store for you. These words were written by gurus and mystics who lived in oases—who through migrations and exile ended up in villages and forests.

"A forest cannot be understood in the same way an oasis can. Eras can vary just the same as places and people can. This is why the Faith of the Four possesses an established body of pastors and priests to sort these affairs out as times and customs change. It's not to say one book is right and the one wrong, but rather that each deals with struggles that the other does not."

"So is Avo right or Leleen?" Duun asked. He tried to draw attention away from the fact he didn't know what an oasis or an era was. In truth, this matter of which the baron spoke far exceeded his understanding on many levels.

Baron Blau smiled warmly. "Leleen's not wrong. Though I do wish the secrets of the creation of forestfolk were shared with the common folk. A lot of good could come from sharing abilities like that with people across the kingdom. Avo just has a bigger picture of things. The sort of view one gets from being up high and seeing the world below."

"Do you think Avo is mixed up in the things those soldiers mentioned?"

"The question is not *whether* he is but *why* he is. Avo has principles—maybe not the same as yours or your sister's—but principles that he wouldn't betray. Until we can ask him what his intentions are, we can only guess at them."

"What if we sought him out?"

"Followed the trail?" A brightness appeared in the Baron's eyes.

"We don't know where he is, though," said Duun.

"But we *do* know where he's been," Blau said as he placed his hand on the photo albums.

"We've got a trail, then," said Duun.

The baron nodded. "And it leads straight to Skyskape Akademy. There is one small problem, though. The soldiers told me that because of Avo's actions, the new headmaster has forbidden the admission of any more students who aren't natural-born Tarrkavians. Due to certain programs implemented by the monarchy, they can't remove the current Knot Kovenant students or risk being called before a royal judge, but it is within their charter to bar the admission of new students under reasonable suspicion of danger. Two things are against you. Not only are you not a natural-born Tarrkavian—you're also the brother of the person responsible for these new rules."

Duun's heart sank. Just as soon as he had been handed a map to a clear path to learn the truth, the walls of the law, the soldiers' judgments, and the raiders' violence came crashing down in front of him once more. He was powerless once again in the face of those who dwelled in the courts of justice.

A hint of mischief appeared on the baron's face. "Although…if you could pretend to be someone else, you'd get in without any trouble whatsoever."

"Pretend to be someone else? How could I do that? People from Ulkirn have a distinct look and those of us of the Kovenant have practices that wouldn't go unnoticed."

The baron shrugged his shoulders. "You will find the people in this country tend to be quite vain. A wide array of cosmetics exists to change one's appearance so that even someone like you, with fox hair, could be made to pass as a noble-born upstanding member of Tarrkavian society."

"Noble-born? I can't even read."

"Not yet, but we can remedy that. Here's what I'm getting at, Duun. If we want to get you into Skyskape Akademy, I could pass you off as my legitimized bastard."

Duun's eyes widened. "Your what?"

The word "bastard" had little weight in Kovenant society. When two people loved each other in the Knot Kovenant, they just settled down together and started a family. There were no weddings or fanfare of any kind—as long as individuals possessed honest intentions and nobody ran off and lived a secret life with an entirely separate family, nobody disputed a pairing. If somebody had been deceitful in such a matter, they would be driven out of the community. And if they were forestfolk, they would be fed a poison that turned them a smoky grey and prevented them from using their special gifts of speaking to plants.

The Baron cleared his throat. "There's something you need to know about the sorts of people who run this country. A lot of them are greedy, indecent, dishonest folk. They get married for convenience, and then they run around with all sorts of people for fun. Some are understanding, and some are not.

"I have never married and I have never engaged in such libertine behavior. However, for the sake of discovering the truth, I'll say whatever I have to. I can't help but feel this attack from the raiders is connected in some way to Avo's disappearance. It's all too convenient to be a mere coincidence." He placed his hand on Duun's shoulder. "The youngest you can be to attend Skyskape is fifteen. How old are you now?"

"Fourteen," Duun said. "I'll be fifteen just before the springtime comes again."

"Then we'll work through the months to teach you everything you need to know to be believable as a noble's son. To be honest, I've never had to teach somebody how to read before, not to mention the basics of flying a plane, courtly manners, and a whole litany of other skills, but we're talking destiny here. If you can manage this, you will be following in the footsteps of those who walked the path of adversity to better serve your people and your family. You will be able to do what you could never do before. How's that sound?"

Duun thought about it. It wouldn't be easy. But he did want to be more capable, at the very least so that he could prevent an attack like the one that had just happened to their home from happening again. If Baron Blau could clear away the debris that blocked the path to his goal, it would be foolish to ignore it, but there was a matter of great importance left to settle.

"What about my sister and mother? I do a lot to help them from day to day, and Mom has suffered severe injuries."

"Don't worry. Look at who you're talking to. I'm the baron not just of *this* land but also of the counts whose domains are down the river and in the steel hills to the west. Supporting two women, given how capable Leleen is, will be a small matter for me and my staff. See it as a courtesy for doing your part to keep your people and my lands safe."

"I will need to talk this over with my family."

"Of course," Baron Blau said. "I can respect that. But don't delay. If we don't do this, our odds of finding what happened to Avo will become almost nonexistent, and the lives lost to the bandits will be unavenged. It is a lot to ask of you, but I cannot force your hand."

Chapter 8

Duun returned to his mother's room with one of the photo albums under his arm. Their mother still slept, but Leleen stood by her side.

"Did you find a place to put Bigby?" Duun asked.

"Yeah, some of the stable-hands offered to take him. I still have fingers, and he's got a nice spacious warm stable. Everybody's happy."

"Do you think Bigby's sad since all the other sheep were killed?"

Leleen pursed her lips. "Well, Bigby's not very smart," she said. "Maybe if he makes new sheep friends he won't know the difference."

"Really?" Duun said. He struggled to hide a hint of contempt in his tone.

"It's just an idea. Anyway, what did Baron Blau want with you?"

"He's got a plan. To investigate Avo's disappearance and determine who were those raiders who came after us. I'm going to enroll at Skyskape Akademy and follow the clues left by Avo in this book."

"Since when can you read?"

"I can't. It's a picture book."

"Let me get this straight. You can't read, and you're going to enroll in a prestigious and competitive flight academy?"

"Well, the baron is going to teach me—and I'll learn courtly skills."

Leleen's eyes narrowed. "What business does a Knot Kovenant shepherd have in knowing courtly skills?"

"Well, that's the thing. People of Ulkirn are forbidden from attending. I'll be going under a disguise—as Baron Blau's legitimized bastard."

Leleen took a step toward Duun and tripped. She caught herself on the side of their mother's bed and she sat down. "Are you pulling my leg?"

"Beg your pardon?" said Duun.

"What you're saying is that you're going to go to a school for snooty rich folk disguised as the legitimized son of an unwed noble…to go looking for clues that will be at least several months old by the time you get there, based on something you looked at in a picture book since you can't read. A school, may I remind you, for pilots flying planes—despite the fact you've never flown a plane yourself." Leleen stared at him as if he were an alien.

Duun sighed. When she put it like that, the whole idea did sound stupid. However, he was also sure that his sister underestimated what Baron Blau could do to teach him. The baron, after all, was a legend, and there was no doubt in Duun's heart that Blau knew exactly how to prepare him for the task. Also, as the baron had reminded him, if he didn't follow the plan they'd discussed, it would be almost impossible to find Avo. Leleen knew a great deal, he thought, but this time around, she didn't know everything.

"I'm not going to do this alone," he said. "Baron Blau is going to help me and he's going to help you two while I'm away. I'm going to learn how to read and fly a plane and when this whole matter is done, I'll bring Avo home."

Leleen looked sympathetically at her younger brother. "I know you want to find Avo, but this isn't going to be easy. What you're planning would be difficult for even an ordinary person. We are of the Knot Kovenant, and whether you pretend otherwise or not, if you are found out, you could die." She took a deep breath. "I heard more about that business with the soldiers. You have no way of knowing where they would've taken you to question you—to their plane, to Blakmarrow Island—places not kind to the Knot Kovenant. You've lived your life cautiously, but you haven't done it with bright green skin. A lot of people don't get us and hate us because we don't see the world they do."

She paused before continuing. "I get it, Duun. You've suffered a lot of hardship all at once. We've lost our home, Mom can't walk, and Avo's missing—and it's scary. But there isn't always something that can be done. Trying to chase after something and leaving behind what you already have can get you more lost than ever. Are you sure you want to risk that?"

Duun thought for a while. At first, he had no response because, in his heart, he was scared, and he knew his sister was, too. The overt caution he felt in these new circumstances nearly got the better of him, but then he thought about the matter from a different angle. "Avo would do it for us if our roles were reversed," he said.

It was Leleen's turn not to know what to say. On one hand, Duun was correct. On the other, there was no telling what Avo had gotten himself wrapped up in. *She* wasn't willing to pursue this course that Duun seemed to want to take, but even if it wasn't her choice, she knew that for the sake of the family, her younger brother would never give up. "You've grown up so much," Leleen admitted. "When Mom wakes up, you can tell her what your plan is. I'll do my best to keep things sane here. See what I can do about finding more sheep friends for Bigby. I'm sure they'll come from miles around if I stand on a hill high enough." She conjured up a smile. "Good luck with your plan."

"I'm not going yet," Duun said.

"No…no you're not, but when you go, don't forget we're waiting for you here." Leleen stood, placed her verdant hand on Duun's shoulder, and left their mother's room.

It was some time before his mother finally roused from her sleep and opened her eyes. Duun was quite tired himself, but had remained awake to speak to her. "Mom, there's something I need to tell you," he said.

"I know. You're going to go to Skyskape to try and find Avo."

"Were you listening to our whole conversation?"

"Yes," she said.

"That was hours ago! Why didn't you say anything beforehand?"

"I was really enjoying my sleep, and you two were having such a serious conversation, it wasn't my place to butt in." She gazed at her son. "You're just like Avo when he left here." She raised herself up in the bed. "I will admit I think the baron's plan is a bit farfetched. You'll find it's very hard to pretend to be someone you're not when you know deep down who you are. Even so, I think your heart's in the right place, and if you stay true to that, there will be people out there who will stand by your side and help you, despite those who will oppose you. The truth doesn't always make us popular, but it does tell us who we can count on."

Duun lowered his head. "Thanks, Mom," he said.

She curled her worn and wrinkled fingers around the edge of the blanket and looked at Duun with an expression that seemed to come from a deep aching portion of her heart. She pulled the blanket over her and, deep in thought, retreated beneath it.

Duun's mother saw in her younger son what she had seen in both Avo and her husband—a profound sense of purpose and a willingness to risk life for the safety of their family. Such purpose stood out striking and bold, like a note played out of place.

Duun should've had a humble home with a father and all his siblings together, safe and free from the horrors of war and greed, she thought. He shouldn't have been faced with finding his brother. When he left, as she knew he would, she would only have Leleen. Deep within, she feared that she would never see either of her sons again, even as the pain of her lost love still lingered from the war. She drove the fear down, instead stoking the hearth of her heart to have faith in Duun—as he had always put his faith in her. She looked deeply into her son's eyes. "Get some rest, dear," she finally said. "I've had plenty, but you need to get what sleep you can. And know I will love you always."

"I will," he said, "and I love you too, Mom."

When Duun retired that night, he was restless. He lay on his side and stared out the window at the night sky. The clouds were clearing and stars could be seen above. He heard the screech of an owl outside and his thoughts meandered to the planes that had destroyed their home. *Who were those pilots? Had they had some part to play in what happened to Avo? How did all of this fit into the bigger picture?* He thrashed about, fearful that he would never catch a minute's sleep.

He had heard once of a strategy for going to sleep. He'd never before needed to use the skill, as sleep had come readily to him in the past. But in this moment, he imagined himself as a series of knots over a frame of an effigy of himself. Starting from the top of his body and scanning down his face and neck through his shoulders and chest and the rest of his body to his toes, he imagined untying the knots one by one. He looked up at the sky in his mind and, seeing birds fly by, detached from attention or judgment. Soon after, his eyes became heavy, and he was greeted by sleep.

Chapter 9

For Duun, the next months were met with rigorous training. The baron tackled everything from his illiteracy to how to walk, dress, and wear one's hair to identifying features of a cockpit. He even had light hands-on practice in controlling a plane on the ground.

Some of the endeavors were more successful than others. Duun learned the controls of the cockpit with remarkable speed. The years of leaping, climbing, and knitting had given him incredible coordination and accuracy. He made mistakes here and there at the start, but nothing too damaging to person or plane alike. As soon as his muscle memory engaged, Duun proved he had the same or even more potential to handle machinery than Avo.

Learning to read, however, presented more hurdles. Although Duun grasped the concepts of basic grammar, vocabulary proved to be a bridge too far. At the very least, he grasped all 25 letters of the Tarrkavian alphabet, but those which made multiple sounds or different sounds when put together with other letters consistently gave him trouble. Nor could he master the inflections of Tarrkavian nobility. Instead, he sounded as if he were making a mockery of the aristocracy.

Natalie took great joy in the impression, but Baron Blau felt it would be best if Duun spoke in his own words. At least the boy possessed excellent penmanship.

One thing was even more difficult to work with than his reading—his hair. Noble fashion for men involved wearing one's hair short and, when appropriate, combed back and straight. Duun's hair grew fast, thick, and in multiple colors.

Both Natalie and Blau played at being fashionistas throughout the months, but the only solution they found—beyond his wearing a hood at all times—was dyeing the white hair that grew from the temples a shade of red that matched the rest. No scissors in Blau's possession were capable of taming Duun's hair, so the baron finally conceded that, as his bastard, they could get away with his longer hair.

He would not, however, be able to get away with the name Duun Howl. "You'll need a strong, proper Tarrkavian name," Blau said. "Thanks to Avo, Howl will draw unwanted attention, and everyone will spell Duun wrong." He gestured to the maid-turned-teacher. "Natalie, what's a good name for him that sounds close enough to Duun Howl that he won't forget it but different enough so as to not arouse suspicion."

"Dewey Wool?"

Blau rolled his eyes. "No, that sounds stupid."

Natalie tried again. "Uh, hmmm…how about Uun Howell?"

This time Blau frowned. "Did you honestly say 'Uun?' How many Uuns do you know?"

"I'm sorry, Your Lordship. Naming things is difficult for me. Do you know what I call all my violin music? Composition Numbers 1, 2, 3, all the way up to 65. This is exactly why most people name their children after their parents or characters from radio dramas. It's too difficult to make something original that doesn't also sound stupid."

The baron thought for a moment. "Natalie, what's your father's name?"

"Daniel."

"Then Daniel it is," said the baron.

Natalie made a face. "Daniel Blau doesn't really roll off the tongue without the title attached," she said. "Gets stuck right at the end."

"Well…then…how about Daniel *Hardy*?" said the baron. "That was my mother's maiden name." He stopped and said it to himself a few times. "Yes, I think Daniel Hardy will do well."

Duun said the name out loud. "Daniel Hardy. My name is Daniel Hardy. I'm Daniel Hardy." He repeated it a few more times with different inflections to remind himself so that it wouldn't sound as strange to someone else as it did to him. Then he practiced writing it and spelling it out loud. At the very least, he should be able to spell his own alias properly.

The time for learning was coming to an end and, of all the new things Duun had practiced and rehearsed those months, changing his name had not been one of them. He was more afraid of slipping up with the name change than just about anything else. He asked his family to practice calling him Daniel instead of Duun so he could avoid mistakes, but they messed up more often than he. The baron, however, used the alias correctly and Natalie, who had never really managed to get the hang of his *real* name, liked the change.

In the week leading up to his orientation at Skyskape Akademy, Duun completed the metamorphosis—as well as he could—to Daniel Hardy, the now legitimized son of Baron Blau. He wore all new clothes that met the standards set by Tarrkavian nobility and had even managed to make himself an aviator's jacket, using leather from a cow that had grown too weak at the end of its years. He had simultaneously cured, stretched, cut, fitted, and tailored the jacket for Daniel Hardy, while still operating by the ethics of Duun Howl. Finally, he'd sewn a soft but warm fleece interior into the coat and had hidden a cloth map of the continent inside a seam so in the event of trouble in a plane he flew, he would have the means to orient himself to his surroundings within the country.

When the day finally came for him to depart with the baron for Skyskape, he visited his mother and Leleen for the last time. Many of the trees from their old home had been transplanted to Baron Blau's estate to save Leleen the trouble of traveling so far each day. It was here among the trees that Duun found his sister, talking to them in whispers.

She was surprised to see his transformation. "I'm tickled green," she said. "They actually managed to change you into the perfect agent in just a few months."

"Told you it wasn't impossible."

"Well, you've got me there. Now, what is it I am supposed to start calling you again?"

"You can still call me Duun."

She gestured toward him with both hands. "Sorry, but I can't call *this* Duun." She was quiet for a moment but finally spoke again.

"Daniel, right, yes, Daniel. Well, Daniel, I hope you find Avo, but when you do, make sure that *both* of my brothers return." Duun's heart sank a bit. He didn't want this whole matter to drive a wedge between himself and his sister.

"We'll come back together," he said. "You'll see."

Leleen stepped toward him. "Can I still hug you or will I wrinkle your fancy outfit?"

"I'm about to be cooped up on a plane. I don't imagine one hug will mess me up any more than turbulence."

The two siblings held each other close, then Leleen held him away from her. "Write if you can," she said.

"I'll try," he said.

"I know." She laughed. "You're still not that good at it, so just try."

"Okay, really? You pick on me now?"

"Yep, you're still Duun in there somewhere." She smiled, and her skin lit with a bluish hue. "Be sure to say goodbye to Mom before you go. I think she's sleeping right now, but, as you know, she may be faking it. Either way, I'm sure she'll appreciate it."

Duun went into the mansion and found his mother asleep in her wheelchair by the fireplace. He grasped her hand between his two and squeezed tightly. "I'm going to Skyskape, Mom, but I'll be back, even if I don't find Avo right away. I will return before the year is done. I swear."

Her eyes opened, her face lit up and she smiled a peaceful smile. She patted his hands with her free hand. "I've got something for you, before you go." Reaching around the other side, she pulled out a solid-colored sweater.

"I made it out of Bigby's wool. Something to keep your dear friend close while you're up there in the sky. I've heard it gets cold, so think about your big round sheep when you're all alone in the sky."

When Duun stepped onto the airfield, he saw Blau's plane and hurried toward it. Baron Blau greeted him with a smile. "You're doing a great job, Daniel. Now all that's left is getting there. I'll fly. I figure you'll need as much time as possible to prep yourself for your new life."

Duun looked back toward Tarkkavian, thinking that by leaving, he was erasing parts of himself that he might never get back. And then he boarded the plane. Duun, for now, was gone. He was Daniel now.

Once inside, he perused the space. Outfitted with bedrooms and a nice sitting area, it was deluxe in terms of comfort for long flights, again far more than he and his family had ever experienced.

Leleen stood looking out the window. When she saw the plane leave the airstrip, she went up to see her mother. As she crossed through the doorway, she saw the emotions long held back for her brother's sake flowing freely down upon her mother's needlework.

Tears streamed down Leleen's face as well. They were united in grief.

Chapter 10

When Daniel determined, after staring at the ceiling and listening to the growl of propellers cutting through the air for three hours, that sleep would not come to him, he decided it would be a better use of his time to review all the pictures of Avo from all the photo albums, to look for common threads between them.

In several of the photographs, classmates were with him. Judging by their identical scarves, it appeared that many of the classmates had been with Avo all four years at the academy. As the years went on, younger students began appearing with him. Since Avo was supposed to have graduated just before he disappeared, it was safe to assume the people in the earlier photos had long since graduated too. Daniel grunted to himself. This meant the odds of finding people who had known Avo well were poor.

One boy in the photographs, however, wore a scarf unlike Avo's but identical to the one Blau had worn. Upon further inspection, Duun realized that across all the scarves, there were patterns of X's, diamonds, circles, and four-pointed crowns. Some had a single X marked with a K, a Q, an A, or a J. The students wearing each of the different symbols were as different as the scarves themselves, but those who wore the X's were the most varied of all.

Daniel moved pictures of Avo to a single photo album and made his way to the cockpit. Baron Blau sat in silence in the pilot seat. "Your Lordship, is there any significance to these scarves?" asked the boy.

The baron didn't answer. Duun worried he might've annoyed him, but when he stepped farther forward, he saw that the baron's mouth was agape and his eyes closed. A loud snore erupted from his sleeping mentor just as Duun slipped into the empty co-pilot's seat.

From behind the cockpit, the baron's assistant, Parker, spoke, startling Duun. "Do you wish to speak with his lordship?"

The boy gestured toward the snoring baron. "Is it safe for him to be sleeping like that?"

Parker smiled. "His lordship has everything well under control, and if he doesn't, then I am here. He has trouble sleeping most nights, so it is my job to handle his sedation. If you wish to speak with him, I can awaken him."

Duun nodded timidly. "If it's not too much trouble."

Parker reached for a small brown bottle in a doctor's bag at his feet and poured two drops into the baron's open mouth. Soon after, the baron roused from his seat. With an almost compulsive check of his hair, he turned to his helper.

"Are we there already?"

"Not yet, but we will be soon," said Parker.

"Ugh, all right, might as well get myself together before we get there," Blau said.

"Were you asleep at the yoke?" asked Daniel.

Baron Blau smiled at the boy. "Yeah, just for a little bit. Why? Are we off course?"

"No, Your Lordship," said Parker.

"Something you wanted to ask, Daniel? You seem like there's something you want to ask."

"How can you be so sure?" Daniel asked.

"Well, you've got your own cabin, but instead you're here in the cockpit."

"Oh, well, yes, sorry. I had a question about the images on the scarves."

The baron nodded. "Ah, yes, the scarves of the estates."

"The what?"

"By now, Daniel, you know there are four towers surrounding the citadel. In each of those four towers are the dormitories for students from the four estates. Korona Red, Diamond Blue, Doubloon Gold, and Krossbone Brown. Your goal is to be in Diamond Blue."

“How do they choose who goes where?”

“There’s a written test. Your performance will decide which of the four estates you will be in.”

“Are there any differences between the estates?”

“Yes, they are all completely different,” Blau explained. “Korona Red is reserved for the students who achieve the highest scores and settle all matters of command and administration from the tower. They handle intelligence, strategy, and communications with the pilots in the air. Students may choose their estate if they score high enough on the entrance exam, but you don’t want Korona Red.”

“Why not?”

“Because if you’re a Korona Red, unless you’re personally flying the king or his family somewhere, you don’t fly the planes. You spend your time almost exclusively reading and writing charts.”

“No, I don’t want that.”

“Right. Doubloon Gold is the engineering and design group. Again, more reading and writing. They make planes and munitions, but they don’t fly missions. The only two estates whose students consistently fly are Diamond Blue and Krossbone Brown. Blue flies the fighters—Brown holds the bombers together. But you don’t want to end up in Krossbone Brown.”

“Why?”

“When you see the bombers, you’ll know that Krossbone Brown is underfunded, and since they realistically serve only one purpose, very little interest is put in doing anything more for them than the bare minimum.”

“Wouldn’t it be easier to find Avo if I was in Krossbone Brown like he was?”

“No, I can guarantee you’ll be better off in Diamond Blue.” The baron glanced at Daniel. “Just do me a favor and remember to keep your hair touched up. Do not let your white spots show.”

“All right, I won’t, I won’t.” Daniel grew apprehensive at just what sort of place he was getting himself into. What did Avo get involved in and what exactly was the baron trying to warn him about?

“Relax,” Blau said, “no sense getting worked up before your first day. There’s going to be a lot of good kids just like you at Skyskape.”

"You're telling me there will be many kids at this school who are secretly refugees pretending at being nobility to locate lost family members with bright green sisters and a pet sheep who became the sole survivor of an air raid?"

"Well, maybe not *exactly* like you. But those are just your *circumstances*—not who you are. You'll find people who are observant, thoughtful, cautious, and brave—and people who are none of those things. Keep an open mind and smile when you meet anyone new. If they turn out to be awful, then just steer clear of them. It's a big citadel—you won't be glued to them all hours of the day."

"What about food?" Daniel asked.

"You're going to have to bite the bullet on that one. If you're ever in doubt about what you need to do or how you should act just remember to ask "'What would Daniel do?'"

"What if I ask myself what Duun would do?'"

"That would be okay. However difficult, Duun knows that every struggle he encounters makes him better equipped for finding his brother."

Daniel thought this over and decided that, in the short term, Blau's advice would be best followed—at least until he was familiar with his surroundings and comfortable in his routine. It was the change to entirely new horizons from what he had always known that frightened him most of all. Even while he learned under the tutelage of the baron and Natalie, his life had still been in the presence of his family and the surrounding countryside. He didn't know where to begin with this new life ahead of him, but he would do his best to stay out of trouble and, when his brother was found, that would be the end of it.

"I think I can manage that," he said.

"Good, looks like we're coming up on Skyskape. Parker, get us clearance to land the plane."

Parker turned to a radio communication console and began speaking to someone in the tower. Daniel looked out the window—in front of him was the view of the citadel he'd seen in the photographs along the walls of Blau's estate. It was like seeing the masterpiece of an artist brought to life or a tree bursting forth into brilliant color with the arrival of spring.

The waves of the Topazali Sea crashed upon the stones of the cliffside in mighty bursts of foam. The towers stood decorated with vibrant banners that hung down from the windows. The central spire glowed in eclipse, the light of the setting sun behind it.

In the fields between the gardens stood magnificent varieties of trees in full bloom. The pitches for sports were empty, but all manner of people filled the wide courtyard that led to the entrance of the academy. On the road leading into the academy lines of automobiles moved toward the school. Some came from the airfield, where the school's planes were kept; others came along the winding road from town. They reminded Daniel of beetles crawling on branches in his beloved forest. He understood why everyone who saw it took photographs of the view and yet, nothing could compare to seeing it in person.

Parker returned the microphone to its cradle. "Your Lordship, we will be landing at Runway 28, just outside of Landskape."

"Oh, good. We can show Daniel a little of the town before we go to the school."

"What's Landskape like?" Daniel asked.

The baron rubbed his chin. "People from all over the kingdom set up shop there to capitalize on the best and brightest students the nation has to offer. The town has it all—movie houses, foreign cuisine, dance halls, night clubs, parks, tourist shops for people who want to pretend they go to Skyskape, supplies and official equipment for people who actually go there. Anything you could imagine is waiting for you right down there."

"What are half of those things you just mentioned?"

"Things you will just have to learn for yourself."

The baron pulled back on the yoke and began their descent. After a couple of passes, the plane landed on Runway 28. Daniel had learned from Baron Blau that the runways at the airport were situated in terms of the degrees of compasses, beginning with Runway 1 and running until 36. As the wheels of the plane touched down, the sun set below the ocean horizon and the lighthouse transformed into a beacon for passing vessels.

Baron Blau unbuckled his seat belt and stood, stretching his arms above his head. He groaned as he removed his jacket and hung it on the back of the pilot's chair. "Here's some more advice. Don't grow old. People will tell you that every stage of life has its advantages. They are liars." He turned to Parker. Get the trunks. We're going to have company here soon." *Trunks?* thought Daniel, confused. *I only have one trunk.* The baron had designed it so that some of his belongings as Duun were in a compartment underneath.

As they stepped from the plane, Baron Blau approached a man in a deep blue uniform standing by an automobile. Daniel felt a quick snap of worry at the sight of a soldier, but then his fears were quickly assuaged when Blau approached and shook the man's hand.

"I would've never have guessed that the Blue Blitz would be putting his own student through Skyskape," said the man, smiling. "Last I heard, you still weren't seeing anybody, but that was a long time ago. Where does the time go, mate?"

"Well, the seasons change and so must we," said the baron. "Daniel, I want you to meet your geometry instructor, Professor Gerald Thompson."

Daniel's voice said, "Good to meet you," but his mind was trying to untangle what geometry was. Muscle memory took hold, and he gave what he could assume was an appropriate handshake. Perhaps he was not as prepared for this mission as he had hoped, but he could at least give off an air of confidence. The rest could fall into place later.

"We're seeking to get accustomed with the surroundings since we've just arrived. Is there still a Barnesworth on Mercer Street?" Blau asked.

"Nah, it closed down a while back. There's a Darlington's where it used to be."

"Darlington's? Minah's gotten into the department store business now?"

The professor nodded. "Minah Darlington's getting into just about any business you can think of. You didn't hear it from me, but she's got a daughter going to Skyskape this year." He glanced at Daniel. "I imagine you'll see her in some of your classes. How about that, Danny boy?"

Blau was surprised. "Minah Darlington has a daughter? How similar is she to her mother?"

"I don't know, but I have stocked up on aspirin just in case."

A noise was heard over head and Blau looked upward. "You wouldn't happen to have any of that aspirin with you now, would you?"

A plane flew low and fast overhead. Both Daniel and the professor dropped to the ground. Parker stood next to an empty dolly—trunks blown around by the force of the plane were scattered along the pavement. Blau stood as an unfailing obsidian pillar. When the plane touched down on a perpendicular runway, a look of contempt crawled across his face.

Thompson helped Daniel up and the two looked in the direction of the plane. When the cockpit door opened, a woman of dark complexion descended the stairs, yanked off her helmet, and spiked it against the ground with an enthusiastic whoop. Her hair, full of energy, frizzed over her brow like a black cloud. She strode toward the baron, took his hand, and shook it with vigor.

"Orson Blau, how've ya been?"

"Ms. Darlington, always a pleasure," Baron Blau said, mustering composure from some hidden reserve.

Daniel watched the woman closely. Minah Darlington moved like a comet—dazzling, direct, and so quick one might miss what she would do next. She seemed about five years older than the baron, but her energetic attitude rivaled that of Leleen's in early spring. Perhaps even Bigby would appear docile in the face of this enterprising mover. Her crew tried to keep pace with her, but there was no telling where Minah would be next. She appeared in front of Daniel, her hand outstretched.

"You must be the baby baron." She looked him up and down. "Not too shabby, if a bit too shaggy. Although, I must say, red hair? Ooh, I bet your mother's a feisty one. I doubt you get that from your old man. I can just see the fire in your eyes, waiting at any moment just to burst forth. I doubt even you've seen it, but don't worry, a Darlington has an eye for potential often overlooked by others. Your old man Orson may not know how lucky he is to have a lad like you. We'll be watching your endeavors with care and certainty. Yes, we will."

"We?" Daniel managed to say before Minah bolted around him and Blau and wrapped her arms around them both. She leaned forward with excitement.

"Here she comes," said Minah. "My very own flesh and blood. Sharp and sweet, like a paradoxical slice of cheese."

Down a ramp at the back of the plane rolled a roofless automobile driven by the smallest old lady Daniel had ever laid eyes on. Her white hair was tied into a bun just behind her head. He decided she had to sit on a tortoiseshell to look over the steering wheel. How she pressed the pedals remained a mystery.

"Hmm," Minah said, "*that's* not my flesh and blood—that's Ms. Booke driving my latest and greatest vehicle. Rest assured, the transport is not made of flesh and blood. That would be terrifying."

"Or a horse," Daniel said.

Minah stopped in her tracks and looked to the sky. A great big smile spread across her face, starting at her eyes. "Oh, Baby Baron, you are a genius. What if we could make a faster horse? All the power of an automobile with the intelligence and biological needs of a living creature. Orson, I may have to steal this one from you when you're not looking."

"Over my dead body," Blau said.

"Oh, Orson, let's not be so macabre. You've raised a remarkable specimen." Minah leaned toward Daniel and spoke in a low voice. "But don't think for a moment you can underestimate me or my daughter. We play for keeps in this family."

"Yes, ma'am," Daniel said, feeling terror at her sudden shift in tone.

"Great!" Minah switched back to her jubilant cadence and waltzed in the direction of the plane. "I'm going to see what's keeping her and then go to my store in town. We've got sandwich counters and sodas and shakes so thick you need a spoon. I'll catch you there!" She disappeared up the ramp into the plane.

Blau glanced at Daniel. "She's a human tornado," he said. "One of the biggest movers and shakers in Tarrkavian society—with no shortage of moving or shaking—and a legendary inventor, but I wouldn't be surprised if she tied a lightning rod to her back as an alternative to sleep. We might just want to skip going to Darlington's and go straight to the school. What do you say?"

"Did anyone else notice she didn't mention me at all?" Professor Thompson said.

"Consider yourself honored," Baron Blau replied. "Let's run."

CHAPTER II

The drive through downtown Landskape proved to be the first of many experiences that inspired and excited Daniel about the future. On this one road, there were brilliant light bulbs illuminating storefronts and billboards with magnificent splendor. People walked about here and there dressed in fancy outfits for such an occasion as hitting the town just before the start of the new school year. Several of them were Daniel's age or perhaps a bit older.

A positive energy ran through the people on the street, the same sort Duun might have expected from the chickens leaving their coop to partake in the feed of a new day. Or perhaps he was among fireflies—but without the serenity of the glowing bugs dancing through the woods on a summer night.

Once they were past Darlington's, Baron Blau happened upon a silent and empty diner called the Wave's Break. "Ever have coffee before, Daniel?"

"No, what is it?"

Blau laughed. "Bean water that keeps you awake."

"Lifeblood for old codgers like us," Professor Thompson said.

"I'm having no trouble staying awake," Daniel said. It was going to sleep that was most often trouble for him.

"We'll stop for a cup or two," said Blau. "You don't have to get anything if you don't want."

"Okay, then," Daniel said.

The trio stepped out of Professor Thompson's car, and then decided it would be best if Parker took the car and its luggage to the hotel to shake off Minah Darlington. As he drove away, the trio went into the diner and found seats in a booth away from the windows.

Not another soul dwelled in the diner save a couple in their fifties behind the counter. The man with a white apron pulled pastries from the oven. His hair was short and he wore a matching white hat. The woman, with short silver hair and a lithe frame, tended to a coffee pot between the counter and the booth.

"Welcome to the Wave's Break," said the man when they chose a booth. "I'm Hunter and she's Jaki." Daniel was unsure if they were a couple, but he thought it might be rude to ask. Natalie and Blau had made sure to hammer into his head that Tarrkavians had many hangups that wouldn't even be thought of in the Knot Kovenant.

Three mugs of darkness steamed a roasted fragrance into the light that hung above the booth. Professor Thompson selected the four most cubical sugar lumps from a bowl on the table and placed them into his mug. He stirred them out of existence in the abyssal liquid. The baron leaned back and waited for his to cool without even so much as an attempt to drink it. Daniel stared down into his mug and saw nothing but the halo of the light above reflecting back. He made a naive attempt to drink the coffee as it first came out.

"Gah!" Daniel said.

"Careful there," Blau said. "You gotta let it cool off first."

"Sorry, my sis—" Daniel stopped when he saw Blau's eyes widen. The baron subtly shook his head.

Daniel had wondered where and when his first blunder might be. Thankfully, it had happened with somebody who could still keep him in check. Professor Thompson was still too occupied in stirring his coffee to notice.

"My sensibilities aren't accustomed to this drink yet," said Daniel. He wasn't sure that his words made sense, but they sounded intelligent and informed and he was willing to roll with it. Blau gave silent approval for the save and then directed his attention to the front windows to make sure Minah was not looking for them.

Daniel noticed that the lights from outside refracted through the windows in a curious manner. As they sat there without a word, a shiny black telephone rang on the counter. Hunter picked it up, listened to a few words, and pointed the receiver toward Blau. "It's for you," he said. The baron went to the counter with his coffee, took the receiver, and put it to his ear.

"Blau speaking," he answered. He stood in silence a while, saying nothing, and sipping from his coffee. Thompson's coffee had almost turned to caramel. Daniels' cup remained untouched as though it were a black hound that had just bitten the boy.

"All right, I'll be right there." Baron Blau drank his entire mug in one go, and turned to the professor. "Jerry, will you keep an eye on Daniel for me? Some responsibilities have come up that I must attend to."

"You got it, Your Lordship," the professor said.

Blau put three coins on the counter and walked out the door. The professor turned to Daniel. "Your old man's a rather guarded sort, isn't he?"

"How do you mean?" Daniel asked. He realized that he would have to guard his words now that the buffer for his blunders had left. He aimed to keep his questions and answers as vague as possible. The baron had taught him most people like to speak and will make up all sorts of things to believe themselves if you don't guide their thoughts.

"Well," said Thompson, "back during the War of Kalamity, he seemed to appear from nowhere. House Blau served at the foot of the king, but after going and winning battle after battle, dropping fiend after fiend after fiend and halting Buldwikk's territorial expansions, he settled for a barony still on the central axis of the country but far from the capital at the source of the river."

"What exactly do you mean by fiends?" Daniel asked. The War of Kalamity had happened when he had been young. He knew little of the military might of Buldwikk. He knew the Buldwikk terror came from sorcery and not from technology, but that was all he had ever gleaned from his family. His family had suffered when the war had come to Ulkirn, and they had been separated from Duun's father, so he never brought it up at length to Avo, Leleen, or their mother.

The professor gazed at Daniel. "Figures Blau wouldn't tell you what you're up against." He paused, thinking. "I know a professor who can explain it a lot better than I can. She has insider knowledge—if you catch my meaning—but instead of tanks and planes and battleships, the sorcerers of Buldwikk cobble together giant monsters through the ritual gathering of the dead in great cauldrons and kilns. Things that swim, trample, devour, and destroy, and in the wake of the casualties, their sinister acolytes gather up bodies from the battlefields to fuel greater and more terrible monsters. Even the largest beasts and most terrible reptiles pale in comparison to the kytinfiend." He paused again. "As a veteran, I find them terrifying; as a man of the Four, I find them blasphemous; and, as a mathematician, I think they're a pain in the ass. Don't tell the baron I said that, but our science has given us the edge as the first and final line of defense against them. If Tarrkaven falls, then the whole of the world is damned to follow."

The radio in the diner had stopped playing music and crackled with dead air and Daniel froze. Professor Thompson threw another lump of sugar into his coffee and shrugged. "You're the baron's boy, so you've probably got it covered if it comes to that. Probably won't. Buldwikk hasn't done anything in thirteen years. Visolia has probably shown them the joys of movie houses, blue jeans, and big bands. At least they're good at something, but building planes is not one of them."

The professor sipped his coffee. "I'm not being mean, that's just the truth. If it takes starlets and swing music to keep Buldwikk from cleansing the world of life, then I guess Visolia is good for something."

With these words, Professor Thompson stood up and placed his mug on the counter. "I'm going to go and relieve myself. Don't catch on fire or anything while I'm gone."

Daniel really didn't want to be alone, but even Duun knew it would be strange to follow someone to the restroom and do nothing. So he sat, paralyzed, imagining what manner of beasts Buldwikk might send. Duun had heard of a beast that lived above the canyon overlooking the baron's domain and every once in a while, he'd found the occasional ball of fur and bear bones dropped down the side of the canyon. The fear of such a beast had kept him from ever venturing up the cliffside. The goats knew how high to climb to get salt, but the dumbest among them would climb higher and never be seen again.

Who could say? Had the beast of the canyon destroyed the plane that had attacked the village?

Daniel looked around. Darkness had fallen and the night had a funny quality to it, a sense of danger lurking around every corner. Never mind that they were now miles away from the canyon. After the professor's story, Daniel imagined the beast of the canyon waltzing right out of a movie house to snatch him away in a bag of bear fur. He would probably wear a hat too. Everybody seemed to wear hats in this town. Maybe he'd tip it to a lady as he passed.

The image in Daniel's mind grew more stupid with each addition. He was saved from his fright by sound of the diner door opening and the sight of Baron Blau.

"Where's Professor Thompson?" asked the baron.

"In the bathroom," Daniel said.

"When he returns, we're going to get you to the hotel."

Chapter 12

As Daniel had come to expect in the world in which Baron Blau lived, even the hotel suite was bigger than the house in which Duun had grown up. It had three rooms, each with its own bathrooms—one for the baron, one for Daniel, one for Parker. Daniel barely slept a wink.

When morning finally came, the staff of the hotel brought platters with breakfast. On Daniel's platter were eggs on toasted bread, a glass of orange juice, and a sliced tomato along with grilled baked beans, sauteed mushrooms, and fried, diced potatoes. After eating his fill, Daniel donned an outfit of trousers, a button-down shirt, and a sport coat, and then joined the others in the common room.

The baron greeted Daniel with a box. "Good, you wore long sleeves. You'll need them for what I'm about to give you."

Daniel took the box and opened it. Inside was a knit sleeve that ran the length of his arm. It held five different shades of blue that varied in no immediately perceivable pattern. Daniel gave it a quizzical lookover.

"As I mentioned on the plane," said the baron, "placement into an estate at Skyskape is based on a written examination. In my opinion, that is rubbish—circling letters doesn't prove that you can fly a plane. But, since you struggled with reading and writing, I had this sleeve made for you. The lightest shade is A, and each shade darker corresponds to the letters B, K, D, and E. The first five rows are a reminder—all the rows afterward correspond to the answers of the test. Don't draw any attention to yourself—make sure the sleeve remains hidden."

"Wait, so I'm cheating my way in?"

"Don't think of it as cheating. Think of it as removing barriers to our operation. I'm sure other students will be doing the same thing. Just remember that our goal isn't necessarily for you to be a pilot but rather to help you find Avo. Whatever you have to do to achieve this goal is irrelevant, because the goal is what matters."

"What if it keeps somebody else out of the program they want?" Daniel asked.

"They're not trying to solve a mystery where the entire safety of the kingdom is at stake. *You* are. We can't afford any mistakes, and we need to employ every resource in our possession to achieve our ends."

"What if I get found out?"

"You won't be found out. If you were able to read better than you can, we wouldn't have to rely on these methods. There's no shame in taking an easy road if it achieves the desired outcome. In the end, Avo's not going to care whether you passed the test truthfully. In the grand scheme of things, nobody else is going to lose sleep over it, either."

"*I* will," Daniel said.

The baron scanned Daniel's face. "You won't when you find Avo. I don't want to hear any more of this—you need to take this test, ace it, and when you've done so, you will be allowed your choice of estate. Pick Diamond Blue. If you're placed in any of the others, it will slow down our investigation, and then Avo may be lost forever."

"Fine," said Daniel. "I'll do what I have to do."

"Good. I'll make it up to you, and you'll thank me later."

Daniel wasn't so sure about that, but he decided if horrific monsters couldn't move the baron, neither could a poor illiterate shepherd. He pulled the sleeve onto his arm underneath his coat, and then followed the baron to the car.

When they arrived in the lobby of the hotel, Parker met them, frowning. "Sir, our automobile has happened upon a flat. The valet was bit overzealous when he took it to get parked."

"Of course, he was," Baron Blau groaned. "All right, new plan. Daniel, I'm going to get you on a bus to go to the campus while I have a word with the hotel staff. Parker and I will meet you there once we know what estate you've been placed in and where you'll be staying." He placed his hand on Daniel's shoulder. "I'm counting on you…and so is Avo."

"Yes, sir," Daniel said.

He and the baron stepped out of the lobby. In the plaza outside, they encountered Minah Darlington with a young woman in tow who couldn't have been much older than Daniel. She didn't have the same frizzy hair as Minah, but wore her short black hair in a bob. The girl leaned the side of her face against her hand. Pink manicured nails peeked through the slight waves of her hair. She sat in silence as Minah hopped over the side of the car.

"Hello again, Baby Blau! I figured you and ol' Orson were probably staying here. There aren't many other places a person of principle would stay. I managed to find my flesh and blood and I would be delighted if you would say hello. This is my very own daughter Johanna. JoJo, this is Baron Blau's boy, Daniel Hardy."

She looked around. "Where is the baron?"

"He's got trouble with something called a valet," Daniel said.

Minah assumed a nervous expression for the flash of a second and then returned to smiles. "Tell you what, Danny dearest. You escort JoJo to the campus so that you don't miss your entrance exam. If you'll just sit back there with Johanna, Ms. Booke will get you where you need to be. I'll get this whole mess sorted and then Baron Blau and his automobile will be right as rain. Nothing the best engineer in all of Tarrkaven can't handle. Have fun, you two!"

Before Daniel could say anything, Minah whisked past him and entered the revolving door. He shrugged his shoulders. He did, after all, have an exam to catch, and talking to someone his age couldn't be that bad. He walked over to the car and introduced himself.

"Hi, I'm Daniel. Your name is Johanna?"

"It is," the girl said with a dulcet tranquility. She avoided making eye contact. He climbed into the seat next to her and noticed her hands fidgeting in her lap atop the pleated skirt she wore.

Ms. Booke pulled away and Daniel continued to try and make conversation. "Nice to meet you," he said. "Are you nervous? I'm having a little bit of trouble keeping my head above water myself. I've never been in a town quite like this one. It's a little intimidating."

"Oh? Do you not travel with the baron?" asked the girl.

"Well, he doesn't leave home often, and I've not seen outside of the canyon before. How about you? Do you travel often?"

"Mom takes me everywhere. I even help her at work." Ms. Booke took a sudden turn and Johanna gripped the handle on her car door.

"Do you help her build the planes?"

"I do, but she's having me attend school here so I can be a proper administrator before I step back into her business."

"I see. She's not coming to school with you, is she?"

Johanna's eyes widened and she shook her head. Daniel was getting used to being far away from his family, but he had appeared to weather the change better than she. "It's neat that you help build airplanes. I'm not even that sure I can read, but I think I could be a pretty good pilot, y'know?"

"You can't *read*?"

"Well, I wouldn't say it quite like that, but I'm not the best at it. Still, I'm hoping to give it my all for the baron's sake."

"Are you familiar with what this test involves?" Johanna asked.

"I heard it's multiple choice. So, when all else fails, I'll just use the process of elimination."

"Forgive me for asking, but why exactly are you attending this school?"

Daniel thought about the question. Naturally, he couldn't tell her the true reason he was here, but he could give an answer that was more or less true. Avo had always said something about flying a plane that inspired awe in Daniel. He recited it from memory.

"Being behind the stick of a plane is like having a view of the whole world from the eyes of birds and angels. All the things that stress us out are so far below, and we are given the privilege sought for centuries to see the whole world made small and quiet while moving like no other living creature on the face of the earth. It's like being the energetic dragonfly bounding through the reeds over the still waters of a pond undisturbed."

"You think so?" Johanna asked.

"That's why it's so cool to me that you work on planes. You are giving people a gift—to see what no one else can," Daniel said.

The girl sighed. "That's certainly very hopeful."

"I'm going to get into Diamond Blue so that I can fly the fighter planes. I take it you're going to be in Doubloon Gold? Baron Blau described it, and that sounds like what you do."

"Mom wants me to aim for Korona Red, I think, because she wants me to help organize and lead the business side of the company. I'd rather do what I've been doing and choose Doubloon Gold. I think I'm at the start of a breakthrough that could be of service to both Doubloon Gold and Korona Red—a machine that will track the movements of Buldwikk's monsters and help better organize our own military actions. And that's just the beginning."

"That's incredible. A machine can do that?" Outside of airplanes and the steamboats that traveled up and down the river, Daniel had not been exposed to a lot of machinery. There had been a textile mill in the town, but it had been ruined by the bombers. He had never been inside of it.

Johanna nodded. "That and more, but I guess it will have to wait for another time."

"Because your mother says so?"

"She's the smartest person in all of Tarrkaven, and I guess I'd just be playing second fiddle, so maybe she's right."

Daniel leaned back in his seat and saw that they were approaching the gates of the school. Johanna seemed to be conflicted and he thought of his own predicament and what the baron had asked of him. Like her mother, the baron was probably right. He wouldn't have to rely on cheating if he had had a better background in reading. Perhaps he was being selfish not taking the gift he'd been given in order to find Avo. However, he thought, this wasn't Baron Blau's call. Daniel Hardy was a blank slate, and how he behaved on campus depended on Duun. Even if Daniel Hardy was a lie, he didn't have to be a liar.

"This may seem strange, but I had never heard your family's name until yesterday," Daniel said. "It seems like your mom has done some neat things for the kingdom. But this is *your* school year, and it's your call. The baron has done some neat stuff too, but I don't want to do things the way he did it. Better or worse, it won't feel right if I don't do it my way."

Daniel self-consciously combed hair over his temples and Johanna turned and looked at him. A small smile crept upon her face. "That's an interesting way of looking at it. I think I needed to hear that." She paused for a moment. "There's something you need to know. If you don't perform well on this test, you may end up in Krossbone Brown."

"Yeah, the baron mentioned that. I would like to fly the fighters, but if that doesn't turn out, then I guess the kingdom needs bombers too." Baron Blau had warned that being in Krossbone Brown would be a hard learned lesson if Daniel chose not to cheat. He'd also acted like it wouldn't guarantee his being able to find his brother. Still, Avo had endured it, and if being in Krossbone Brown meant he could still find Avo, even if it was harder, he would do it.

"How about this then, Daniel," Johanna said. "Let's both aim for what we want without worrying about what anyone else has to say. No regrets."

"Yeah, no regrets," Daniel said.

***

When Ms. Booke parked the car and Johanna climbed out, Daniel did a double-take. The girl stood above six feet tall. The way she had shrunk down in the back of the car in the presence of her mother had obscured this fact. This train of thought was interrupted when Ms. Booke shooed him out of the car.

Professor Thompson greeted Daniel and led him to the central tower and up the stairs to the lecture hall where the test would be administered. The boy took a seat at the end of a row in the very back of the hall. If his convictions would make him crash and burn, he'd rather no one was there to see it. He saw Johanna enter the lecture hall and take a seat on the other end of the same row. Other students continued to file in until finally, the whole lecture hall was packed to the brim.

"All right," Professor Thompson said. "I'm going to pass out the tests. Keep them turned over until everyone has one." He walked down the aisle nearest to Daniel and passed a stack of tests to each student at the start of each row. Daniel took his and passed the rest to the next student.

When the passing out of tests was complete, Professor Thompson glanced across the room. "Did everyone get one?"

Johanna raised her hand. "I didn't," she said.

"What's this paper then?" said the student next to her.

"I brought scratch paper. It says on the board that I can," she replied.

The professor nodded his head. "Ah, good to see someone is extra prepared. My mistake," he said, and he walked down the outer aisle. "Here's another one coming your way."

When Johanna received her test, the professor turned back to the rest of the group. "This test is timed. But don't panic. We just want to see what you can do. We have a place for everyone at Skyskape, but we want to make sure the hardest workers get the first pick. Everyone do your best and pick your choices wisely. Any questions?"

No questions were asked.

"Right, begin."

The rustle of papers turning over sounded the beginning of the examination. As soon as Daniel viewed the questions, he knew he was doomed. The first question read, "How do ptarmigans differ as the seasons khange?" The next was "When did the krown implement the first kounsil of barons?"

None of the questions had anything to do with aviation—or anything Daniel had experience with. He began to sweat, and he placed his fingers over the temple to guard himself against the horror of what unfolded before him. Then he thought of the sleeve wrapped around his arm. It would offer all the solutions he would need and save him from Baron Blau's anger. He glanced to the far end of the row—Johanna was working diligently to finish the test. How could he stand by what he had told her if he used the cheat sheet?

With a deep breath—and a resigned will to fail in a spectacular manner—Daniel circled "B" for every answer. He thought of Natalie back at the baron's estate. 'Even a broken clock is right twice a day,' she'd once said. Maybe this is what she'd meant. If Baron Blau was so intent on finding

Avo his own way, he'd do it himself. Daniel wouldn't let this test break his nerve, and he wouldn't let Krossbone Brown break him either.

When Professor Thompson called time, he asked that the students write their names at the top of their tests and pass them to the opposite end of the row. When his test reached Johanna, he saw her run her finger along the corner of the page and then stack the tests on top of what he'd assumed was her scratch paper. When Professor Thompson came around to collect the tests, Johanna handed him the stack and then crumpled her scratch paper and tossed it into a nearby bin.

The professor smiled. "Okay, students, if you will be patient, we'll get these tests graded and come back with the results. Sit tight for just a bit."

He walked out of the classroom, and a strange woman with graying lavender hair replaced him. She took a seat and watched the class intently. For a second, Daniel felt certain she was staring directly at him. She then gave a knowing smile when the door opened, and Professor Thompson returned.

"Thank you, Dr. Violite," he said as he turned to face the occupants of the lecture hall. "This is shaping up to be an interesting school year. We have some impressive students this year. There were two perfect scores." He gestured toward the back of the auditorium. "Please give it up for Johanna Darlington and Daniel Hardy."

Chapter 13

Daniel awoke to a dark room. His internal clock remained unaltered despite the late evening from before.

As he rose from the bed, he felt along the wall in search of a window, bumping his knee against what he could only assume were the myriad trunks with which Parker had filled the room. Finally, he determined he had brought himself all the way back around the room to the bed, where he'd begun. There was no window in the room.

Starting again, he moved toward the center of the room. Once there, a cord hanging from above him brushed his face. He pulled on it and a single light bulb filled the room with pale cold light.

As he'd suspected, the room was cluttered with trunks and yesterday's clothes. There *was* a door, however, and after putting on the clothes similar to those he'd worn the day before, he stepped out into what seemed to be a central hallway.

Daniel wasn't sure what had happened with the exam. He felt fairly certain that every answer on the test had not been "B." Some other power had seemed to intercede to ensure he stayed the course. As the baron had said, he'd been offered a place in each of the four estates but had settled on Diamond Blue to prevent friction with his "father."

Baron Blau had gone home but, upon seeing Daniel after the exam, had expressed his obvious delight. He believed, of course, that the boy had relied on his sleeve of stolen answers. When he'd given the sleeve back to the baron, he'd known that something—or someone—had changed his answers. Someone, he decided, and he had a hunch he knew who.

Within the hallway, the tower began to take on a more defined character—a carpeted runner and framed landscapes adorned hardwood floors and paneled walls. The hall curved toward a central commons area Daniel remembered passing through the night before. Within this dwelling area, students sat and talked amongst themselves. Daniel steered clear of any other students—his primary objective was to find Johanna. Making new friends could wait.

The other Diamond Blues seemed engrossed in their conversations about the states of their rooms and being forced to use a hall toilet. Daniel chuckled to himself. Prior to entering the baron's home, Daniel had had no concept of indoor plumbing, let alone showers or toilets that flushed. There were so many new things, he knew that to truly survive this ordeal, he would need to wait and watch before saying anything. He had only begun to understand how different the life he had lived for almost fifteen years differed from that of these noble-borns. Almost all of the students in Diamond Blue were the sons and daughters of barons and baronesses, dukes and duchesses, counts and countesses.

It had been late into the evening before his business with the baron had finished, so there was no opportunity to meet with the other students or visit the other estates. Venturing out the tower door, and checking his hair as he went, Daniel went in search of Johanna.

At a table in the courtyard immediately outside the Diamond Blue tower was the strange woman who'd waited with the students while the exams were being scored. She wore a long black dress with lavender locks spilling from the back of her head. Dark bags drooped under her eyes and she rested her head in her hands. Two skulls on a pendant hung around her neck—one a cat's and the other a small bird's. She appeared to be about the same age as Minah Darlington, but Daniel wasn't sure.

She reached for a pack of licorice gum and then caught sight of Daniel. "Hey boy, have you come over here to register? You're a first year?"

"Yes, I am," Daniel said. "My name is…Daniel Hardy."

"Dr. Violite," she said. "I'm the professor in charge of your class. I'll also be teaching tactics and strategy. Are you looking at my skulls?"

"Yes," Daniel said. His honesty got the better of him again.

"They're my cat and my canary. The cat ate the canary, so I ate the cat." The two froze in silence for a moment that did not cease soon enough for Daniel. "They make for much better companions now," she continued.

Waving her hand over the pendant, thick black smoke rose took shape in her hand and she moved it over the table. The small black chitinous body of a cat appeared with the head of a canary head. In the center of its skull, a large red stone seemed to hum and give off a red light. Once settled, the creature groomed its beetle-like plating.

"It sheds a lot less than a real cat," said Dr. Violite. "Keeps the house clean." She glanced up at Daniel, who was staring at her, a hint of a smile on her face. "If you've heard anything about a sorceress of Buldwikk on staff, that would be me. Rest assured, I harbor no ill will toward Tarrkaven and hold no love for Buldwikk. I met a strapping young pilot early in the war, and never looked back."

She gazed into Daniel's eyes. "You don't care about any of that, do you? Right, well, here's your orientation information. In this packet right here. There's a map, and a compass, and a…you have eyes. Just be ready for the opening convocation at ten. Here also is your scarf. Since you're an initiate at this point, there's nothing fancy. You'll get your diamonds once you get up in the air, but until then, this will at least show people which estate you belong to. It's also how the porters will identify you, so don't lose it. In fairness, though, the porters probably won't be up and about at this hour. I'm honestly surprised *anyone* is up this early."

"Thank you, I guess," said Daniel.

"That's why I'm here." She poked the cat creature in the crest with a long pale finger.

When Daniel didn't leave, the woman frowned. "Is there something else?"

"Do you know where I could find a Johanna Darlington?"

"The industrialist's daughter? That girl is stupid tall, isn't she? I thought I saw you looking at her yesterday. Hate to say it, but she's out of your league. Regardless, just walk toward the tower with the big golden banners on it. If she's out and about, I figure you won't have much trouble finding her. Just don't go poking around the girl's dorms. School rules and all that. Those are in the envelope too. Really, you should look through that envelope. I'd tell you about it myself, but I don't want to."

"How long have you taught here?"

"Since the war ended. I have royal tenure."

"I don't know what that is," Daniel said.

"You'll find out soon enough. Off you go."

Daniel turned to leave. This time the woman at the table called him back. "Hold on," she said as she stopped midway drawing a line through Daniel's name. "Orson Blau is your father?"

"That is correct," Daniel replied.

She shook her head. "Huh, and you think you know a guy," she said to herself. "Anyway, have a good school year. Don't crash a plane or do anything nefarious. Maybe go grab some breakfast before you go see your not so little friend. By the way, women don't like a man who's clingy," she said. She looked down at the table and chastised the catbird. "Don't scratch up the table, Lusille."

Having survived yet another encounter with the strange sorceress, Daniel continued forth guided by the map. Breakfast would have to wait—he needed answers first. To his relief, the words on the map were fairly simple. The layout of the academy and its grounds were also simple, but the airfield's map was an absolute nightmare to decipher. Perhaps, that one could be addressed with time.

Finding a large tower with golden banners on it proved an easy task. Daniel walked along the circular path until he was just below the golden tower. In this courtyard was an expansive garden.

Daniel thought of Leleen. He knew his sister would have the time of her life among so many different types of plants. Of course, she would probably introduce herself to each and every one. If the plants spoke back, what would they say? Would they know what happened to Avo? The garden beckoned to Daniel. Duun much preferred the fresh scent of flowers to the smell of exhaust in Landskape.

He continued toward the Doubloon tower, and mere moments before he reached it, the door flew open. He stepped quickly to one side. Maybe the sorceress had been on to something about grabbing breakfast first.

"JoJo dear, I know you love science and technology, but I think it would be good if you broaden your horizons a bit."

Minah Darlington stood with her arm holding the door wide open before him. "Well, hello, little baron!" she said. Behind her was Johanna, whose face was flushed with red.

"Hello, Ms. Darlington," Daniel said.

"JoJo says you're going to be a top rate pilot in Diamond Blue. I'll bet you'll give ol' Orson a run for his money."

"How do you do, Daniel?" Johanna said, her face masklike. Although her expression was polite and formal, beneath the visage Daniel detected a warmth.

Minah glanced at her daughter and then back at Daniel. "She's shy, but she's a good girl. I hope you two will be fast friends. They'll tell you some mullarkey about how the students of your estate will be your closest friends, but that's just the tired old thoughts of the kings of old. The future will be built on what you can do, not whose blood is in your veins." She paused. "Make no mistake, Mr. Hardy. I think Orson is a fine man, but it was his flying that made the legend, not his heritage."

She glanced around the quad. "Looks to me that Thompson fellow isn't even here yet. Typical. Sleep is for the weak. You're already up, Daniel. I'm looking forward to your continued success! When you graduate, consider coming to work for me!"

As soon as she finished speaking, Minah quickly made her way down the path. Johanna still stood at the doorway leaning against the frame. The stone visage dropped away to reveal exhaustion.

"Did you just wake up?" asked Daniel.

"More or less," Johanna said.

"Should you be awake?"

Johanna yawned and then covered her mouth with a hint of embarrassment at having given herself away.

"Ah, fair enough. I have something I want to ask, but it can wait."

"No reason to wait. Yes, I *did* replace your test."

Although he'd suspected it, Daniel was stunned. "Why?"

"I want you to stay around. I think I'm doing the right thing, but Mom, well, you heard her. I'd hate to get to choose my own path and you not have that same choice."

"Are you sure that won't get us into trouble?"

"If it comes to that, I'll take full blame."

"I don't want anyone getting in trouble for my sake."

"Don't worry, it won't happen again. See you at convocation?"

"Yes, of course. Get some sleep," said Daniel. Johanna gave a thumbs up and went back inside her dorm. Daniel still didn't understand fully why she would've done such a thing for him. He'd only met her the day before and she didn't know about the scheme.

Daniel decided that breakfast could wait a bit longer and went back to his own dorm. Upon reentering his room in the Diamond Blue tower, he first located the trunk that contained his school clothes, as well as notepads and fountain pens. In the secret compartment beneath, he found the photo album of Avo's pictures and some needles and balls of yarn—courtesy of Bigby. He was about to drag another one of the trunks over as a makeshift seat on which to knit when he heard something rattle inside. Out of curiosity, he opened to find it was empty, but upon closer inspection found there was a false bottom in the trunk. Inside, he found a folder that contained a five-by-five grid with the colors white, red, green, yellow, and blue along both sides. Within the boxes were the twenty-five letters of the Tarrkavian alphabet. Below them was a note that read, "yarn kode talk, expekting gifts, work on spelling - BB."

The other trunks yielded many more balls of yarn—not all from Bigby. That poor sheep certainly had abundant fleece, but this was too much even for him to muster.

Each ball of yarn was dyed in one of the colors of the code. He was surprised by the trunks' contents, but remembered that his first responsibility was as the baron's spy and his second as a student. If he intended to complete the investigation, he would need to keep his grades up. He grabbed a ball of yarn and his needles and set to work on a message:

"FOUND YARN, WILL RITE SOON."

Chapter 14

When he had finished knitting the message, Daniel returned to the common area to find twelve other students gathered, their numbers divided evenly between boys and girls. The boys all bore the same courtly appearance the baron described—hair cut short or combed back close to their scalps. The girls all wore their hair at shoulder length.

What stood out to Daniel was the small size of the class of first years. When Daniel had first seen the citadel, he had assumed it would be filled with students from all across the kingdom. Among twelve other students, all of whom had existed before in some capacity within courtly life, hiding oneself would not be as easy as he'd thought. He would need to keep up his guard.

It wasn't long before he was noticed. "Well, I'll be, Blau does have an heir after all," said a boy with ice blue eyes.

"Doesn't look a thing like him," said another boy with a wide frame and small ears.

"Of course not. Blau flies as one who came from the heavens above and has never needed to walk along the ground. This one's just like the rest of us. Only human."

"He got a perfect score on the test. That's pretty impressive."

"Unless he cheated."

"Still, that hair is a wild red. Tell us, Skinny, where's your mother from? A cathouse?"

Daniel didn't know what to expect from other students. He wasn't entirely sure what a cathouse was, either, but he assumed it wasn't a house full of cats. Some cats were known to have red hair—perhaps it could be viewed literally.

Laughter interrupted his thinking. He hadn't anticipated becoming the subject of ridicule so quickly. However, he decided, he could take the flak as long as his real identity remained unknown. Daniel was a fantasy, and any scathing comments against Daniel could be easily discarded. Using his alias as a shield, Daniel shrugged. If the blows landed on Daniel, then Duun was safe.

"Wow, did your mom beat you or something?" An icy gaze curled the lips of the speaker into a devilish grin.

"Nah, didn't know her. She died in the war," Daniel said. His words came out, distant and impersonal—he and Blau hadn't developed this part of his false identity. Duun felt dirty because he'd told yet another lie.

The student's blue eyes widened, and he seemed to shift his weight onto the back foot. "Oh, well, isn't that a shame," he said. "By the way, I'm Jensen. This is Isaak and Martin. We're nobleborn and nobleblood, but I don't think the same can be said for you."

"Don't talk such rot," said a girl with long black hair. Bangs hung down to her eyebrows, and her eyes were almost as dark as her hair. Her lips, as red as dried blood, provided sharp contrast. "Nobility is a way of life. Just because you came from the seed of great men and women doesn't mean you're great yourself, Jensen."

The boy took a half-step back as if to bow. "Baroness," he said.

"Lukka," the girl corrected. "You're not my subject. Don't posture to get into my good graces."

"Ugh…Lukka," Jensen stammered. "Yes, well, perhaps I was too quick to judge him. It's just he doesn't seem much like the baron, and I thought it was strange."

"Not all of us are lockstep with our folks. It's shortsighted to ridicule someone for not being like their parents, don't you think?"

"Yes, Lukka, of course."

The girl spun on a heel toward Daniel. "And you…" she said. "You lost your mother in the war? I'd think Baron Blau would've mentioned losing a wife in the war. He lost a father and a brother, and he mentioned that at length when he took the role of baron. Seems suspicious he wouldn't have mentioned a wife and certainly not their only son. Wouldn't you agree?"

Daniel said nothing. Just like that, Duun felt his guard slipping. What was this girl talking about? Baron Blau lost a brother and his father in the war? He knew Blau's father was dead, but the baron had never said it was during the war. And a brother? If this was public knowledge, wouldn't he have told him in advance?

Daniel tried to break gaze with the girl, but she paralyzed him with her glare. A shiver ran down his spine—he scrambled for something to say but was saved by an unlikely ally. "Lukka, Baron Blau didn't have a brother," said Jensen.

"All right, then," said Lukka, backing away but keeping her eyes on Daniel. "I just can't shake this feeling you're hiding something. Liars always have tells—and every fiber of you is saying you're hiding something."

Jensen offered a defense. "Maybe he's just nervous that you're like a few inches from his face. Most people would be."

"I don't remember asking your opinion," Lukka shot back.

"Right, okay," Jensen said.

Lukka turned and strode toward the door. "We have a convocation to go to. If we're done lollygagging, we should head to the front lawn." She opened the door and stepped through. The door slammed shut, leaving a speechless group of classmates behind it.

"Well, I guess we better follow the baroness," said Jensen. He looked at Daniel. "For your sake, shrimp, I hope you're not hiding anything. She's got a keen sense for people and will not hesitate to have you executed if you did cheat. The youngest baroness in all of Tarrkaven may be a shrew, but she's no joke. Between you and me, you didn't sneak in here, did you? Not one of those weird limes, are you?"

"Look at me. I don't have green eyes," Daniel said.

"Good," replied Jensen. "You don't look like some godless heathen, but you never can tell these days. I'm sure we'll be fast friends," Jensen said. "See you at the convocation."

Jensen walked out with the other students with whom he'd been chatting before, and they laughed about something in hushed voices. Other students who had been bystanders followed suit. Daniel put some time between their exit and his own and then headed out. Were these scarves set in stone? Could he change his decision after it had been made? Perhaps it wasn't too late to join Johanna in Doubloon Gold. If he was there, he would at least know someone at this school was genuine—and safe. Unless, of course, she had been playing at some charade with him in a power play against her mother.

Daniel hated having to think like this about others, but his mind moved this way out of fear of his surroundings and a need for security. In any case, his mission was more important than his feelings, but once more, he doubted the baron's plan to put him in Diamond Blue. How could Doubloon Gold or Krossbone Brown be worse?

Daniel walked down a pathway he believed would lead him to the courtyard, but he didn't see any of the other Blues. As he continued, he saw another student in the corner of his eye. He took the other's presence as reassurance that he was going the right direction and continued forth at a confident pace, but his confidence deflated when he ran headlong into a custodian's shed.

He turned to find the other student behind him, a boy dressed in a motley medley of colors that seemed tailor-made but chaotic. Like a harlequin, he wore a light tweed jacket with a forest green shirt underneath and burgundy trousers over white tennis shoes. To complete the look, he wore the burgundy scarf as an initiate of the Korona Red estate and a bright blue tam.

"Well, well," said the student, "It would appear we've found a shed."

"Yeah, well, it won't help us get to convocation," Daniel responded. It was clear that neither of them knew where they were going.

"Oh, tut, tut," said the strange boy. "Not with that attitude. Idle workshops are the Shadow's hands. That's what the priests say, right?"

Daniel wasn't sure what to say. He wasn't familiar enough with the Four's religious doctrine because Blau hadn't thought it important, but this sounded similar to something someone in his home village had once said. To his dismissive response, the fellow's face lit up. He walked past Daniel, caught his arm and turned him back toward the shed.

"We're going to be fast friends. C'mon, let's peek inside. I'll bet there are keys to all sorts of goodies in there."

"We need to get to the convocation," Daniel said.

"Look, everybody is gonna be there. We can slide in the back. Besides, who's to say this won't take us right there?"

"It doesn't look attached to anything."

"This place served as a fortress in the wars of yestercentury. I'm sure there's a hidden path somewhere in there."

"You think so?"

"Of course, my guy. Err, you got a name?"

"Dan…"

"No! Don't tell me. I want to guess. Andrew?"

"No."

"Amos?"

"Nothing that starts with an A."

"Bob."

"No!" said Daniel, exasperated.

"I'll resume this, but it would appear the shed is locked. Lucky for you, I am quite handy at getting myself into places."

"Or…we could go somewhere else."

"Nah, this will get us where we need to go. I'm going to open this door, but you can't look. If you do, then you'll know my tricks, and then I'd have to sue you." Daniel didn't know what that was supposed to mean, but since this boy was the only person besides Johanna who had given him the time of day without cruel mockery or judgment, he decided to play along. He turned his back to the door.

A cacophony soon followed. Daniel turned around to see this boy's foot sticking through the door just above the handle. "Yeah, I thought it looked like some weak wood. Seeing as you've seen my tricks."

"I *heard* your tricks."

"Tomato, tomahto. If you'll help me free my foot, I swear on the crown that I won't sue you."

Extracting the other fellow's foot from the door took some effort. The boy couldn't stand still long enough for Daniel to easily get his foot free, but after he tried different angles, he was able to pull the stranger out of the door. The boy then reached his hand through the hole and unlocked the shed.

"Simple enough, Karl?"

"Wrong again," Daniel said.

"Ah, I'll get it eventually. Let's take a look inside." Pushing open the door, he waltzed in like a ballroom dancer with a pulled groin. Sunlight poured into the shed, revealing a variety of tools that glistened as though they had been recently purchased.

"Man, oh, man, they don't spare expense around here!" said the strange young man. "I'll decide if it's money well spent when I see the planes." He glanced around and grabbed something from the edge of a table. "Jackpot! Here's a key-ring." The boy swung it around on his finger until it spun off and hit the ground.

Daniel grabbed it—eager to return it to its place. Causing trouble would lead to serious repercussions—he would not be able to find Avo if he was sent home. "We should get out of here," he said, tugging at his pilfering companion's tweed jacket.

"Nah, I think I found the real prize. Oh, hoh! There's a flare gun under this blanket. Oof, it's kinda coarse for a blanket. And, look, there's a design on it." The boy threw it over his shoulder and stepped out to show Daniel.

Daniel looked at the sash and shivered. The purple band bore the image of an owl's head with empty eyes.

Chapter 15

Daniel froze in horror at the sight of the emblem of the owl. It jerked him back to the day of terror—the fiery blast when the plane struck the canyon wall, the sound of falling stones and his family's horrible cries amidst the swirl of dust. Bile rose in his throat at the memory of the smell of blood from the sheep in the pastures.

Why was the emblem before him within the custodian's shed? He couldn't say, but the concern on his face was detected by his colorful companion.

"Whoa, buddy, you all right?" said the strange young man.

Daniel pointed at the emblem. "What's that doing here?

"Hmmm, my guess is the custodian either confiscated it from a student, or he is accessorizing. Maybe occult chic is in this season." He gave a wide smile as though he hoped it would lighten Daniel's dour mood, but the smile drooped when it was clear it had not. "Does this symbol mean anything to you?"

Daniel stopped to think. Was there a way he could discuss it without revealing his identity? He could try, but what good would telling this stranger do him? Still, Baron Blau said he would need friends. He would have to say something.

"There were these pirates with planes who attacked Baron Blau's home and the town in our barony. The planes bore this symbol."

The boy removed the cloth from his shoulder. "Oh," he said. "So we're looking at some sort of terrorism threat? Against the crown?"

Daniel nodded. "And against the Knot Kovenant refugees."

"The who? What now?" The boy's face shifted from confusion to recognition. "Oh, the limes? Whoa, that's wild. I mean, I know people don't like them for whatever reason, but it seems kinda asinine go use military equipment against some farmers and stuff, don't you think? Like they're not going to share their farm tricks if they're all riddled with bullets, right? Heh, farm tricks."

Daniel's face showed an anger that he couldn't hide. The other guy noticed this too. "You all right there, bud? Did I say something? Did I do something? Well, other than what I'm doing right now? Wait, is it about the limes? Do you have lime friends?"

"I have Knot friends, yes," said Daniel.

"I've never heard that before. Is that what they're called? I'll be honest I don't know too many, uh, Knots. In the capital, everyone just uses the little green citrus fruits on trees to describe them. Is it rude to call them limes? That's on me. Sorry about that."

"Just stop talking," Daniel said. "We're wasting time, we may be in danger, and we're not where we're supposed to be."

"Right, right, sorry again. I'm not exactly the picture of grace under fire. Okay, shutting up," he said, all the while folding the cloak into a big purple bundle.

Daniel's expression softened when he saw his new companion so distraught. There had been a time when he had been ignorant of the way people viewed the Knot Kovenant. He hadn't considered the same could be seen in the opposite direction.

The boy walked ahead and rounded a corner and then suddenly bolted back. "Good news. We've got security coming this way. We can tell them about the cloak, put the custodian behind bars, be lauded as heroes and forgiven for not being at convocation—which has almost certainly started by now."

"We don't know that they aren't in league with the custodian."

The wheels in the strange boy's head turned. When this realization clicked, he nodded. "Okay. New plan." He threw the cloak into Daniel's hands and shoved him into a nearby hedge. "Get on out of the garden. You have the keys and the cloak. I'll run interference. Find a broom closet or boiler room. Lock the door from the outside and get yourself trapped within. If you can hold onto the keys, that's a plus. If not, don't worry about it, we'll find more. No matter how bad it looks, don't make a peep. You got all that, my guy? Good deal. Now shoosh."

Daniel wasn't sure where this whole plan was going, but he didn't like the sound of "no matter how bad it looks." Even so, he needed a lesson in keeping his head down and this seemed as good a chance to practice as any. As the guards rounded the corner, his unknown companion leaned on the wall opposite the hedge. He dusted off the shoulders of his tweed coat.

"How do you do, good sirs? Keeping the peace, I hope?"

The head of the guards frowned. "Your father said you might try something like this. I didn't expect it would happen on the first day. You need to come with us."

"When did Pops say this? It's not like *he* had the decency to show up," the boy said.

"Rigel, your father has important business," said the guard. Daniel reasoned that the man was familiar with the boy since he knew his name, but that seemed strange given that…Rigel…was a first year just like him.

While Rigel bought him time, he hurried close to the hedge until he found a doorway back into one of the surrounding towers. Still hugging the wall, Daniel kept his ears open for the sound of footsteps.

The tension of the moment stretched to feel like hours, but before long he found a boiler room. As he moved toward it, he heard the sound of footsteps on a fast approach to his location. He shoved the key into the door, gave it a twist, and then stowed the keys deep down into a coat pocket. The loud jangling noise shot a fiery bolt of adrenaline through his heart.

Before he could disappear into the boiler room, the steps rounded the corner. Some kind of watchdog barked and zoomed toward him. Even with the whites of his hair dyed, Daniel felt like a fox hounded for meddling with chickens.

Instinct took hold and he threw the ring of keys at a wall behind the dog. In the time the dog slowed and glanced toward the sound, Daniel slipped through the door and locked himself in. The dog pounded its paws on the door and barked and growled to any who would listen.

Daniel's mind spun with the uncertainty of what would happen now. Of course, a dog couldn't exactly explain that his prey had locked himself in the boiler room. He had to rely on Rigel to sort the matter out. He only hoped his new "friend" was present when he was discovered.

The waiting dragged on. Although there was little need for a boiler at this time of year, the enclosed space and thundering of his heartbeat made Daniel sweat all over. He removed his scarf and coat and hid the purple cloak under his coat. He wiped his brow with his sleeve, and heard the sound of keys at the door and voices outside. The door opened and the elder guard looked at Daniel and let out an exasperated sigh.

"Rigel, do you know who this is?"

"Yeah, a dweeb."

"Show some respect, even for your station. This is Baron Blau's only boy. Now, the poor lad's missed the whole convocation because of this prank you pulled. We'll be sure to notify your father about this."

"Whatever you say," said Rigel. "When he gets back to you in the next century or so when he's done dedicating orphanages or slaughterhouses or something of the sort, tell him school's going great and I would've loved for him to be here."

"Your father has a greater duty than anyone else in this kingdom."

"Yeah, buying fancy new dinner tables and building bowling lanes in the palace."

"Why can't you be more like your brother?"

"Because you've got my brother and, to be quite frank, I don't see what's so special about him that you'd want two of us."

"You haven't heard the last of this, Prinse Rigel."

Daniel gulped.

"Oh, I don't imagine I have," said Rigel. "It's going to be a fun year, wouldn't you say, Billiam Brown?"

"*William* Brown."

"Then where does the B come from when Pops calls you Bill?" Daniel had to admit he had often wondered about this name swap too, but perhaps it was a question nobody could answer.

The guard's face reddened. "Never mind all that. You need to apologize to Daniel here. You're lucky that we aren't going to tell the baron about your stunt."

"Last I checked, Baron Blau swears fealty to the crown. So, I think I can get away with ruffling his feathers now and then."

"Apologize to the boy," said Brown, more forcefully this time.

"Fine," Rigel said. "The boy, I apologize." A mischievous smile flashed across his face as he patted Daniel on the shoulder. He turned back to face the guards and, with an arm behind his back, gave Daniel a thumbs up.

"There, my heart pours out for all my subjects now. Happy?"

"This better not happen again."

"Nah, it won't. It's no fun now."

"You'd best get to the cafeteria and return to your class tables. Are you uninjured, Daniel Hardy?"

Daniel nodded his head up and down. "I'm good. I'm fine." He looked at the dog now standing by the guards on a leash, and it gazed with a glare that could kill. The guards seemed none the wiser.

"Good, hopefully, your classmates will fill you in on everything you missed. We'll show you two to the cafeteria."

"Ah, yes, once I arrive, my bootlickers and asskissers of a class will have a proper meal. What'll it be? Coronation rump roast? Good thinking, men," Rigel said.

The guard shook his head in annoyance. "Quiet, your grace."

The two were led from the Krossbone Brown tower to the cafeteria in the central tower. A single place was set at the Diamond Blue table just for Daniel. Everyone at the table—indeed, everyone in the cafeteria—looked up from what they were doing when they saw him enter with Rigel. Daniel grimaced at the attention. I was better off back in the boiler room, he thought.

When he sat down at his place at the table, he looked around. Jensen was seated to his right and Lukka was across from him. Perfect. He stared at a plate covered with marinated beef over a bed of fried rice. He thought he could make out onions somewhere in the midst of it and decided his stomach would have to keep its protests to itself.

"Hey, Dannyboy," Jensen said. "You get lost?"

Daniel didn't answer.

Lukka leaned in. "Just a word of warning. You'd do best to steer clear of Prinse Rigel. The Klown Prinse is a blight upon this kingdom. If he had been born poor, his quick lip and pranks would've had him killed him ages ago. Eat up before it gets cold."

Daniel picked up a spoon and tried his best to extract the rice from under the beef. His stomach's protests finally won out and, soon enough only the beef remained. He prodded at the beef with his spoon.

Jensen looked at Daniel with amazement. "What? You're too much a manlet to be a picky eater. It's meat. Eat up."

Daniel thought of Blau's words regarding the Tenets of the Knot Kovenant. Had the forestfolk of old known such circumstances would exist in this era, perhaps they would have forgiven him. He had dodged the exam and kept his values intact, but he wouldn't be able to dodge this hurdle forever. Defying the words of the Kovenant felt like a betrayal to his community, but he reached for his fork and stabbed a piece of meat.

This is for Avo, he thought as he inserted it into his mouth.

Chapter 16

For perhaps the first time in his life, Daniel slept in following the events of the previous day. By the time he roused from his slumber, his heart leapt in his chest. Was he missing a class of some sort? Not sure yet what his schedule looked like or whether there'd be repercussions for tardiness, he hurriedly dressed and went to the door. Once he had made it to the commons area, he found the other Diamond Blues gathered about in their usual socially exclusive merriment. Jensen looked up and saw Daniel's panicked expression.

"Whoa, slow down there, Dannyboy. Where are you off to?"

"Don't we have class today?" Daniel asked.

"Oh, right," said Jensen. "You missed the convocation. No, we don't start until tomorrow. It's time for freshers. It's all explained on that bulletin board over there."

"Freshers?"

"Yeah, where students get settled in and accustomed to the town and school grounds. Go on, check out the bulletin. You can read, can't you? Maybe try taming that mane when you're done with it. Don't wanna go out on the town looking like you live in a burrow or something."

Daniel stepped over to the bulletin board and looked it over. He read the words in slow, careful silence, but his efforts gave him some certainty of how he would be forced to endure the arrogant Diamond Blues. The other houses would also be going out, and he could use the opportunity to meet with Johanna or even Rigel. In the meantime, he could get to work arranging his pictures of Avo and identifying which ones lined up with locations around the campus.

He gathered some towels from his room and went to the shared washroom in the hall. There were two showers and two toilets in separate chambers. He cleaned himself up and checked his hair for patches that might've slipped through the dye. By the time he finished, dressed in his weekend clothes, and returned to the common area, his other classmates were gone. He smiled to himself—he was free to investigate what actually mattered to him.

He was headed back to his room when he heard the door to the women's hall open on the opposite end of the common area. Short steps that didn't tarry stopped suddenly behind him. "Where do you think you're going?" asked Lukka.

Daniel prepared for the inevitable interrogation. "I'm going to put on a pot of tea and knit a hat. Aren't you going to follow the rest of our class?"

She stepped over to the bulletin board and then stepped back so fast Daniel refused to believe she had actually read it. "I'd rather not waste my time with them. They are children."

"So are you and I."

"I gave up such silly notions when I became a baroness of Tarrkaven. I am here as long as I need to be so that I may defend the fatherland from our enemies on all fronts and from the dangers within our borders—especially those left ignored by the crown in these times."

"Okay, but even Baron Blau takes time out to do other stuff besides just fly and fight all day."

"What *does* Baron Blau do?" she asked. She leaned against the back of a mahogany sofa, her hands resting on it.

How could Daniel answer this? Blau had played a role in his basic education, but he wasn't sure he could talk about that. Since the baron had spent most of his time fabricating the role of Daniel as his heir, he hadn't shared much about what he actually did. He thought about the stories that Avo had told him. Very close to the baron, his brother had been privy to the going-ons of the baron's estate.

He met dignitaries from other baronies and countries, made contracts and leased land to business owners, hosted social gatherings within his great estate, and invited important travelers to stay as he had with the soldiers on that fateful day. When the need arose, he would talk with other nobles about what military action Buldwikk was taking and what could be done to reinforce the border. Bits of conversations Daniel had overheard suggested that the baron tended to relate to people being dissatisfied with every parcel and scrap of land they did or didn't own.

Before he had begun his studies, Daniel had never thought of any of that to be work, but he knew now that work could be a lot more complicated than herding sheep and feeding chickens. Sheep seemed oblivious to the world around them most days, but chickens could be a bit more temperamental.

Daniel shrugged his shoulders. "I guess he referees rich people who argue over what they do or don't deserve."

"Oh, that doesn't go away, does it?" said Lukka. "I've had to deal with some of that with my castellan's supervision. I had hoped he would do more of that once I had finished my time at the flight academy. I guess I am a child after all."

Daniel didn't know why he was indulging in this conversation with Lukka—he felt certain she hated him just like the others. But he continued anyway. "You say that like it's a bad thing."

"Isn't it?" she answered. "There's a whole world out there, a dangerous world that is coming apart at the seams and they are laughing and playing and mocking you like nothing out there matters."

"You didn't need to say that last part," Daniel said. He knew they were making fun of him, but it still hurt to hear it. "But it's true what you say. We're dealing with some sort of mysterious pirates who attacked our land a while back. It's hard to be playful when you know how much is wrong with the world."

"Did you say pirates? Did they take anything?"

"Lives mostly. They wiped out our town on the riverside and over a hundred of the subjects of Tarrbly—not to mention several of the Knot Kovenant."

"Sound more like marauders than pirates. And, oh, right, the tree people."

Daniel tried to remain nonchalant. "Why does everybody hate the Knot Kovenant? It's not like they hurt anybody."

"You don't know?" asked Lukka, and then she answered her own question. "Of course, you don't. The baron harbors them for some reason." She paused and looked at him. "Well, if you can get past their blatant disbelief in the Four and the fact one of them stole a plane from here last year, you still can't forget what they did to the crops in Ulkirn. Those green people made all the crops lethal over there under orders from no one and when the Buldwikk soldiers ate them and died, Buldwikk retaliated by using their dead to make gigantic and terrible kytinfiends that ravaged and ruined the country. Not to mention the fact that those very crops cross-pollinated plants across the countryside and wiped out many other citizens of Ulkirn. Who could trust people like that?"

Daniel knew little about what had happened in the war, but he also didn't understand the sway his sister Leleen held over the flora of their fields. The prank she'd pulled on Avo back in their childhood seemed similar to what Lukka described, but it had been trivial compared to the widespread horror apparently caused by this catastrophic attack. Perhaps this was why forestfolk exercised judgment on those who acted out of accordance of the Tenets. Those who were not forestfolk followed the Tenets in preservation of the culture and respect to the world around them. It was the glue that held the surroundings together.

Daniel sought a way to defend his people without outing himself. "Baron Blau trusts them. The Knot Kovenant never did anything of that sort in our barony."

Lukka gazed at him. "Baron Blau is strong and brave and likes just about everyone, but I think you're naive to assume he trusts them. I think he keeps them close so that if they try anything, he'll be able to put his foot down all at once. Don't you think it's curious that he would have them all live in a barony enclosed in a box canyon filled with forests nearest to his personal arsenal? It's like he wants to see them try something so he can deal with it at once."

Daniel was angered by this, but inside, he was curious. What Lukka said *did* sound like the careful planning of a killer. Still, the baron had shown compassion to the Knot Kovenant, and Daniel had never seen Lukka interact with the baron before.

Who was this girl to make baseless accusations of him?

Lukka must've noticed the expression on his face, but she interpreted it as anger. "I'm sorry," she said. "He *is* your father, and it's not good to accuse anyone of treachery without facts. I'm not good with the whole trust thing, because trust makes it hurt all the more when you're wrong. Did you just say you were going to knit?"

"Don't just change the subject like that."

The door flew open and in walked Rigel. "Hey, friend! I saw you didn't go with your class to the bus stop, so I figured I'd ditch my class to find you." Then he saw Lukka. "Aha! The Baroness of Briars. I should've known you were holding him up. He's got nothing to do with the fiasco yesterday. That was all yours truly."

"Well, if it isn't the Klown Prinse," said Lukka. You're not supposed to be here."

"Klown Prinse? Do people call me that?" Rigel grinned. "I love it. I'm going to put that on all my stationery from now on. Anywhoodle, red-maned friend, I'm going into town. I figured you'd probably want to tag along too. I know where all the fun stuff is."

"The guards will take you away for being in the wrong dorm," Lukka said.

"Uh, what's the point of having a kingdom if I can't go wherever I want in it? Divine right outweighs the gripes of a stodgy old headmaster."

Lukka proceeded to correct him and then stopped herself. "Oh, right, you weren't at the convocation either. Stop trying to rope Daniel into all your hijinks."

"Okay, point taken," said Rigel. "Counterpoint. It'd be more fun to rope Daniel *and* you into my hijinks."

"No!" Lukka said.

"We're going to play hide and seek. Everywhere the light touches is fair game, because, well, divine right. Daniel, I deputize you with my divine right. If Lukka here can't catch us before sundown, then we win and she's gotta go with you or myself on a date."

"My grace, you are repulsive," the baroness growled.

"Yeah, yeah. If you win, I get in trouble."

"What makes you think I'll play along?" Lukka asked.

"Pullease…you know who I am. You know what I'm capable of. Leaving me to my own devices when you know what I could do basically makes you guilty by association. If I get caught, then I'll let everyone know that I told you how I was going to steal that creepy cat thing from Dr. Violite and how you could've stopped me but didn't. Daniel, you're on my team. Come with me. Without further ado. Tick tock, tick tock."

Grabbing Daniel by the arm he bolted out the door. Lukka straggled along behind. Before she caught up with them, Rigel took Daniel into the same hedges as before.

"All right, friend. I'll keep her distracted. You go back to that tool shed and find more goodies. I found more keys to help you get in there." He glanced around for Lukka. "If you find anything, come get me. We need to find a good meeting point. Preferably somewhere we won't get in trouble, because I don't want to waste my freshers having to explain myself to these klowns."

"Well, there's a nice diner in town that's pretty sleepy. I went there the day I arrived."

Rigel smiled and nodded. "The one next to Darlington's. I know the place. I'll see you there!"

Daniel grabbed the keys from Rigel and broke up the path to the custodian's shed. Rigel headed another way and Lukka continued her pursuit of him.

When Daniel reached the door of the shed, he loosened his scarf and felt a weight had been lifted.

Chapter 17

Daniel rounded the hedges and made a beeline straight to the custodian's shed. He made certain to mind his surroundings as he approached. When he circled around the perimeter of the shed and felt confident no one was watching, he went to the door—which remained unrepaired.

Easing it open, he stepped inside and looked around for anything worth picking up. Sure enough, the tools Rigel had described were first rate, but they wouldn't help him find Avo. He glanced where he'd found the cloak and noticed a box in the back.

With careful hands, he unfastened the latch. When he peeked inside, he saw a metallic wheel with letters written at its center: MRLDRGNFLY B-ROLL. He didn't know what these letters meant, but he felt like the device must point to something. Carefully refastening the latch, he picked up the box and hightailed it out the door and back through the hedges to the dormitory.

When he arrived at his room, he placed the box in the trunk that also now held the cloak and flare gun. Once the box was secured, he buried it in balls of yarn. Although his room full of luggage wasn't much to look at and could be frustrating to navigate in the dark, it did give him ample places to hide any clues he gathered.

Just as he fastened the trunk, he saw a shadow under the door of his room. Daniel held his breath. Had somebody seen him in the shed after all?

He scanned the room for a means to defend himself but found nothing. There were knitting needles, but he lacked the imagination and temperament to employ these as weapons of self-defense. He would've liked to have had his shepherd's staff, but he knew that he couldn't keep up the disguise of a baron's heir and walk around with an old piece of wood. Finally, his eyes fell on the flare gun. It hadn't any charges, but perhaps he could pretend that it did. He gripped the gun by his side and approached the door.

"Who's there?"

"Who else? It's me…Lukka."

"Oh, have you found Rigel?"

"No, I haven't. Do you know where he could've gone?"

"We're not allowed in other estate's towers. Maybe he went back to his."

"You're probably right, but this *is* Rigel. For him, being told not to be somewhere is reason enough to be there," Lukka said.

Daniel thought for a moment. "Well, on the bright side, Dr. Violite probably isn't there right now."

"She's probably gone to town with our classmates. Which is probably where he will go next. Come on! We've got to get him!"

"Why do *I* have to come along?"

"Don't think I didn't notice you ran off with him despite my warnings not to get involved with him. I'm keeping an eye on you to make sure you don't try anything." She paused. "He's not hiding in *there*, is he?"

"He's not."

"You better not be lying."

"What's it going to take to prove to you I'm not a liar?"Daniel felt terrible because since he'd come to the campus, he'd lied many times, but with respect to this particular matter, he wasn't lying.

"Let me check to make sure he's not in there."

"Okay…"

"Don't think it's because I want to see your room."

"I never said that." Silence emanated from the other side. "I'm opening the door," Daniel said finally, tossing the empty flare gun behind the luggage.

The door creaked open and Lukka rose up on her toes, straining to see over Daniel's shoulder. He stepped back and presented the room to her, waving his hand and bowing.

Lukka scanned the room. There were many chests and yarn balls, but no sign of Rigel. Satisfied, she turned away.

"You sure you don't want to come in and look for him?" Daniel said

"No."

"He's probably going into town."

"Right, then let's go."

"Right now?"

"Do I look like someone who likes repeating herself?"

"Right, right now then," said Daniel.

He and Lukka hurried out of the dorm and ran toward the the bus stop. When crossed the courtyard, the bus was waiting, and sure enough, there was Rigel hopping aboard. Lukka broke into a sprint but before she could get there, the doors closed and the bus continued down the lane. Rigel smiled and waved to them from the back window.

Daniel sat down on the bench while Lukka paced, alternately looking at the posted bus schedule and glaring down the street. She walked in even steps like a cat feigning disinterest in the affections of its owner, but her pace remained brisk. Her hands twitched at erratic intervals.

Within a few minutes, a swarm of thirteen students, all wearing golden scarves appeared at the bus stop. Looming above them was Johanna, who awkwardly kept to herself at the back of the group. She kept her eyes down until she saw Lukka wearing out the sidewalk and Daniel sitting on the bench, appearing to be as nonchalant as he could.

Upon seeing him, Johanna's countenance brightened. She sat down next to him while the rest of her class talked among themselves. It was apparent given where the majority gathered that they were all a little afraid of Lukka.

"Off to see the town?" said Daniel.

Johanna nodded. "There's actually something in particular I'd like to see."

"What's that?"

"A film. The Fingers of the Woods. We filmed it several months back, and I want to see it all put together now that it's out."

Daniel did not comprehend the word "film." Was this a noun or a verb? He couldn't say. He was confident Johanna wouldn't think of him too harshly if he revealed his confusion.

"Film?"

"Oh, do you not have movie houses in Baron Blau's lands?"

"Movie?"

Johanna smiled brightly. "You should definitely tag along then! Unless you need to get somewhere with…" She gestured timidly toward the pacing girl.

"Oh," said Daniel, "that's just Lukka. We're in the same class. She's waiting for the bus."

Johanna glanced at Lukka surreptitiously. "What's she going to do to the bus when it gets here?"

"Probably ride it, but she's looking for Prinse Rigel."

"Oh, yes, our prince. He reminds me of Mom. They get along famously."

"They've met?"

"Yes. I met him too…once. It was enlightening. Almost every student in the houses outside of Krossbone Brown have met before. You are a noteworthy exception. But I can't say I'm familiar with her either."

"Prinse Rigel called her something else. The Baroness of Briars."

Johanna looked at Lukka. "You mean she's real?" Johanna sniffed. "She's shorter than I expected. I know that isn't saying much considering…" She waved a hand across her own lengthy figure. Daniel made a point not to stare at her for too long.

"Still," said Johanna, "if *she's* here, then you're in for some tough competition."

"Competition?" asked Daniel.

"Class placements. They mentioned it at length in the convocation yesterday."

"Oh, yeah, I got derailed from that. The *monarchy* needed me."

Johanna grinned. "That doesn't surprise me. Anyway, your skill and prowess in the air in executing some specialized skills determine how many pips are on your scarf."

Seeing Daniel's continued confusion, she explained. "Basically, the class is arranged like playing cards with the deuce being the worst and the ace being the best. The king calls the shots, the queen manages the flights, and the jack is the utility player of the sky.

"These roles break down into different functions depending upon the house, so my hope is to be King of Doubloon Gold so I can suggest our project for next year. Of course, Mom used her influence to still get me a place in the flight tower as a sort of operations advisor. I guess we can call it a compromise. After the stunt I pulled by choosing my own house, she made her move. It was as if she knew what I'd do."

She stole a glance at Daniel. "Sorry. Am I just unloading all of this on you?"

"You say that like you're not allowed to be human," Daniel said. It was a little too much information, perhaps, but he was happy to get Johanna talking again after their previous encounter. Between Baroness Lukka who might hate him and wish harm upon others and a prince who seemed to actively want to get him into trouble, it was nice to know someone out there who just needed a friend.

Johanna shook her head. "Yeah, I don't know. Life's just different in the capital. Business magnates and barons and royals live so high above the black waters of Tarrkaven in penthouses and skyscrapers that it's easy to begin to believe everyone who runs this country is gilded. Is life different where you're from?"

Daniel shrugged but said nothing. A shepherd can only keep the charade of being a baron's heir going for so long. A noncommittal answer seemed like a safe response.

"Right. I suppose you probably have a pretty limited frame of reference," Johanna said.

Just then, a bus pulled up to the stop. Lukka quickly walked over and gave two quick but gentle taps to Daniel's knee with what looked like a nightstick. "Come now, Daniel, keep your eyes peeled."

He frowned up at her. "Where did you get that?"

"I always have this with me when I leave home. Courtesy of years' worth of self-defense classes."

He almost prodded further but stopped when he recalled he had wished for his shepherd staff just hours before.

Johanna and Daniel stood and climbed the steps into the bus. Johanna took an aisle seat due to her height, and Daniel took the window so he could see outside and assist the baroness in her search for the wayward prince. Lukka sat opposite the pair and placed her nightstick in the seat beside her. The bus pulled away. As it reached the crest of the hill, Daniel looked longingly in the direction of the school's airfield.

"They tightened security tenfold since last year, I'm told," Lukka said as though she sensed what he was thinking. "Some Knot student went AWOL and caused a huge mess. Thankfully, nobody died." She paused. "They've got the works now. Watchtowers, machine guns, more anti-aircraft batteries, and a squad of fighters on standby to be airborne at a moment's notice."

She followed his gaze. "We're not even going to touch the planes until summertime. I think the stormy spring weather plays a larger role than trouble with malcontents, but that Knot student is why Krossbone Brown will be under careful scrutiny this year. Only people with a familiar track record or with trustworthy parents made it in this year."

Daniel glanced over at her. "Why is it called Krossbone Brown?" It certainly doesn't fit with the shimmering motif of the previous three estates, he thought. Nor does it instill confidence in one's chances of surviving getting in a plane.

"How familiar are you with the history of playing cards?"

Daniel was surprised. He didn't realize people kept up with that sort of thing. Who had time for such trivial information?

"I can answer that," said Johanna. "The four suits represent the four estates of Tarrkavian feudal society. Crowns for royalty, diamonds for nobility—previously clergy, doubloons for merchants and tradesfolk, and crossbones for immigrants who traditionally handled burials. It was considered sacrilegious in the Faith of the Four to knowingly touch the bones of the dead. It also just so happens the four estates correlate to the Four themselves—Father for the Krown, Mother for the Diamond, Sion for the Doubloon, and Shadow for the Krossbone."

Daniel raised his eyebrows. Apparently, *she* had time for such trivial information.

"I play a lot of cards at home," she said.

Lukka picked up where Johanna had left off. "So the Krossbones exist as a sort of branch by royal creed to allow immigrants and refugees a shot at full citizenship. They mostly man the bombers, but the Ace and Jack can fly as fighters with those of higher standing. That is, until last year's graduating Ace up and became a terrorist."

Daniel refrained from commenting as Lukka raked his brother's name through the coals. Duun felt a bit of pride to understand that his brother had risen against all odds to fly among the best of the other estates. It also gave him confidence that Avo was still out there free and unharmed.

The bus finally arrived in town. Johanna set out toward the movie house. Daniel followed suit, intent on discovering more about this phenomenon known as film.

Lukka grabbed the back of his sleeve. "The town is far more sprawling than I thought. I need your help finding Rigel."

"He could be anywhere," Daniel protested. "He could even be on the bus going back to the academy."

"We will find him if we fan out and cover more ground," said Lukka.

Johanna, overhearing the conversation, turned back. "Your ladyship," she said, "nothing will frustrate his highness more than ignoring him."

Lukka rotated the nightstick between her small, neatly manicured hands and then a hint of a smile appeared on her face. "What's this movie about?"

***

THE UNLIKELY TRIO sat at the back of the theater watching a tale of horror. A creature from the woods preyed upon an expedition of explorers on an island among the misty, unexplored portion of the planet called the "Veil of the World."

Daniel thought it all looked hokey. The monster looked like a large nasty green sheep on two legs. His mind wandered. Is this how Leleen views Bigby? At one point the sheep monster trapped someone inside a rapidly growing tree. Johanna smiled with glee, but Lukka curled into a shaking ball. Caught between two polar opposite reactions, Daniel wasn't really sure which camp to side with.

When the movie finally concluded and the credits rolled, Johanna described how she knew each person involved and little facts about how they liked their sandwiches or how many kids they had. Lukka loosened up, but she had an air of caution. She feared some greater horror lurked in the stylized texts of names and roles.

Johanna stood first, followed by Daniel, and the two of them together helped Lukka back to her feet.

"You will speak of this to no one," Lukka said.

Daniel wasn't sure anyone would believe him if he did, but both he and Johanna insisted they wouldn't.

Lukka was adamant. "I need to find Rigel."

"It's gotten pretty late," Johanna said. "But we've still got time before we have to head back."

"He's at the diner near Darlington's," Daniel said. "He wanted to meet there when the day was over."

"I don't know whose side you're on, and that concerns me, but I won't let this information go to waste," Lukka said.

"That's okay. I don't know what side I'm on either."

"You're only digging yourself a deeper hole," Lukka said before spotting a playbill outside of the box office of the theater. She looked at Johanna. "Wait, what's *this* film?"

The playbill featured a masked hero wearing a strange green suit with a cape that draped over his shoulders. He stood by a painted image of an airplane that waited on a runway below a sky filled with fire. The title read "The Emerald Dragonfly: Coming to the theater in summer."

"Oh, yes," said Johanna, "this is one Mom was so excited about. She personally directed it. Something about a hero she made up to get people excited about the pilots of Tarrkaven. It all sounds like military propaganda to me, but I can see how people would think something like this is cool."

"I'd certainly like to see it," Lukka said.

"I'll just stick to monster movies," Johanna replied.

Daniel couldn't get a read on Lukka. One moment she was brandishing a bat looking to hunt down a prince, the next she was scared of sheep monsters, and then she was enthused over visual narratives about mysterious heroes. This girl was strange and unpredictable, but Daniel thought she was tolerable when she let herself open up to others.

The trio arrived at the Wave's Break to find Rigel seated at a booth. His expression betrayed that Johanna had been right. As the three entered, Rigel looked up—there were light scratch marks on his face and hands.

"Let the record show I still won because you didn't catch me before sundown," Rigel said.

"Okay, then, where's Dr. Violite's pendant?" demanded Lukka.

"Her cat bird thing was on me before I could lay hands on it. I got away with my life."

"Shame," Lukka said.

"Daniel," Rigel said in a pout, "don't tell me you spent the whole day with pretty girls. I needed you. I trusted you."

Daniel rolled his eyes. "Can we stay out of trouble at least until classes start?"

"Yeah, I guess," said Rigel. "I suppose catching those purple cloaks will have to wait too."

Lukka looked up. "What purple cloaks?"

Chapter 18

Rigel and Daniel froze as if they'd been caught in the midst of a capering heist. Johanna was clearly confused, but Lukka's eyes pierced through the prince. He looked to Daniel and then Lukka looked at Daniel too. Daniel had not intended to be the subject of this interrogation, but it appeared he had no other choice.

The diner remained largely empty but Daniel kept his voice low. "I have reason to believe Skyskape has been infiltrated by a dangerous terrorist group. The same that devastated the Baron's lands."

Johanna lifted her head as though the purple cloaks had some meaning to her. Lukka's eyes prodded Daniel to keep talking. Despite this, Rigel spoke first.

"Yeah, we found a purple cloak with the symbol of these guys and a flare gun in the custodian's shed. Daniel was supposed to go look for more stuff while I was leading you on a wild goose chase." He stared at Daniel. "So, did you find anything?"

Daniel made a mental note not to trust Rigel with any damning secrets.

"I found a box containing some sort of metal disc. It had letters written on it, but—" he stopped, realizing that if he made it apparent that he didn't know what it said, Lukka and Rigel would know that he couldn't read. That would create a problem for both him and Johanna. How could he have received a perfect score on the entrance exam?

"I don't really remember what was written on it."

"Hold on," Johanna said. "What do you mean? A terrorist group devastated Baron Blau's lands? Why didn't I hear about this? It would've been in the papers and on the radio. Are you being serious?" Daniel had little knowledge of these modern means of communication, but now that she mentioned it, it was strange that news of this attack had never left Baron Blau's domain.

"Yes, I am. I don't know why it wasn't reported, but it *did* happen."

"Back to the shed," said Lukka. "What did you do with all the things you found?"

"They're in my room."

Lukka glared at Daniel. "Didn't you say you were going to knit?"

"I had planned on it," he said.

"You knit?" said Rigel. "Could you make me gloves? I'd really like some gloves."

Johanna smirked. "At this time of year?"

"Never mind that," Lukka said, impatiently. "You found a metal disc and a cloak and your conclusion is terrorists?"

"And a flare gun," interjected Rigel.

Lukka rolled her eyes. "A flare gun isn't strange. When a plane goes down and a pilot or crewman has to bail from the vehicle, they typically have a flare gun—to signify their location so they can be picked up. That's a tool you'd expect to see in a tool shed at a flight school. We're looking at circumstantial evidence at best."

"And a devastating terrorist attack," Daniel said.

"Yes," said Lukka, "one that didn't get reported in any of the many news outlets this kingdom has to offer."

"What symbol was on the cloak?" Johanna asked.

"An oval shaped like an owl's head with two dots in it like eyes. I saw it on the planes that attacked my people, on the cloak Rigel found, and on the cuff of one of the soldiers that went to Baron Blau to report a missing person."

Johanna frowned. "I know that symbol." She reached behind her ear and pulled out a fountain pen—and drew a symbol on a napkin. "Did it look something like this?"

Daniel's eyes were wide. "Yes, exactly like that," he said.

Rigel looked at Johanna curiously. "Did you have that pen behind your ear the whole time?"

"Never mind that. I *know* this symbol. The movie Mom is working on, *The Emerald Dragonfly Strikes Again*, features this symbol as the sign of the antagonistic Twilight Parliament. They're supposed to be some sort of generic army of evil for the Emerald Dragonfly to fight against. They're fiction."

Lukka's frustration mounted. "Are you kidding me?" She turned to Daniel. "That's a disgusting thing to joke about. You came all this way to a military flight academy to play at being a soldier in some made-up silver-screen war, and you're trying to recruit people to take part in your playtime? I expect this from the Klown Prinse, but I would've thought better of Baron Blau's heir. There are real dangers in this world, real enemies at our borders, and you're crying wolf? You're lower than Rigel."

"Knock it off," said Rigel. "What reason would Daniel have to lie about something like that?"

Lukka glared at the prince. "Because he's in a new environment where he needed a way to seem significant or special and get people to like him. Wanted to feel important to get out of the shadow of his father. Those aren't outlandish reasons."

Daniel was devastated. "What can I do to make you understand I'm telling the truth?"

"You can stop lying. There are no movie bogeyman evil armies dwelling in Tarrkaven. When you're ready to act like a grown-up, I'll take you seriously. Until then, stay out of my way." Lukka got up from the booth, stormed out the door, and continued down the road in the direction of the bus stop.

"The nerve of her," Rigel said. He pressed a hand to his temple as though to relieve a headache.

"Well, she *is* the Baroness of Briars," Johanna said. "There's no room for nonsense in her life. She's been through a lot, and honestly, it's more than any of us could know."

"What has she been through?" Daniel asked.

"It's not my place to say," Johanna said.

Rigel crossed his arms. "Well, no matter what she's been through, it's no excuse for her to be so vicious." He turned back to Daniel. "Just so we're clear, and not that I don't trust you, but this whole Twilight Parliament devastating Baron Blau's lands is real, right? I'm not usually the person people pull pranks on, so if this is all some long con, I'm impressed. If it's true, then I'll help however I can."

"It's the whole reason I'm at this school," Daniel said. "I'm not a liar." Every day, he thought, I fall a little deeper into a hole I'm digging myself.

"Good enough for me," Rigel said. "What about you, Johanna?"

Johanna looked at Daniel and paused before answering. "It is highly unlikely that such an attack by a militant group, based on the villains of a movie, would occur without anyone hearing about it. But you don't seem like the sort of person who would lie, Daniel. If you say they're a danger, and they're at the school, then I'll do what I can to help out. Don't let Lukka bother you. When we find more tangible evidence, I'm sure she'll come around."

Rigel waved a dismissive hand at the door through which Lukka had departed. "Never mind that. We can do this with just the three of us. It's probably better that way. Daniel's a good reliable noble, better than an uppity baroness. Good to know Blau's got such a worthy successor."

"Right," Daniel said.

With Lukka gone, he felt like he should tell the two of them the truth of his identity. But what would that accomplish? Rigel had mocked the Knot Kovenant. And how would Johanna respond if she realized he had been lying to her? He decided it was too much of a bombshell to place upon them at this moment.

"What we know is that the members of this Twilight Parliament could be students or faculty. I'm not saying we should be guarded, but we should exercise caution in talking about these matters on school grounds," he said.

"That's the other thing," Johanna said. "We are all in different houses. It will be difficult for the three of us to be in the same place together at a moment's notice." She looked at Daniel. "Rigel and I will probably see each other more than you will see us."

Then, her face brightened. "Unless you could bring that metal disc to the library. Was there a tape coming out of it? If so, it's probably a film reel. I could get us a projector."

Daniel didn't know how to answer Johanna's question, so he changed the subject. "The library might have too many eyes and ears. How about we meet here? It's quiet—and there's never anyone here. It won't arouse suspicion if the three of us go out for coffee on weekends."

"I can't think of a better place. If we had window booths at court, everyone would speak more freely," Rigel said.

"We're like proper spies," Johanna said.

"Or detectives," Rigel added.

Daniel shook his head. "Whatever we are, remember we're not going to talk about this anywhere but here."

The other two gave their assurance they would not. Then Rigel put his hand in the center of the table. "All in." Johanna and Daniel stared at the prince who wore a wide smile full of expectation.

Rigel's eyes bounced between the two. Neither of his friends knew how to respond. Undeterred, he tapped the table twice again with his hand.

Johanna and Daniel looked at each other and then tapped the table in front of them twice. "All in," they said.

Rigel sighed. "We really need to get you two out more."

***

THE BUS ARRIVED BACK at the school, and the trio departed along their separate paths back to their towers. Daniel stopped at the foot of the Diamond Blue tower and braced himself for a cold reception.

Gripping the door, he pulled it open, dreading the inescapable presence of Lukka. To his surprise, she was not in the foyer. No one, in fact, was within—and Daniel took quick advantage of the opportunity to go to his room undisturbed.

Once there, he quietly closed his bedroom door and locked it. Taking the metal disc from the trunk where he'd hidden it, he carefully examined it. Johanna was right—a fine bronze, semi-opaque tape was wrapped around the disc.

He carefully returned the disc to the trunk and lay down on his bed. He still dreaded his lack of preparedness for what was to come, but today he was calmer—he had made two allies and, better still, two friends. Two people he wouldn't have to compete with at this school who could assist him in following the trail to the Twilight Parliament.

But where to begin? He thought for a moment. With the film reel, no doubt. He closed his eyes, turning the reel over and over in his mind until, finally, he fell asleep, ready to greet the morning beyond.

Chapter 19

Daniel woke in the morning, cleaned himself up in the bathroom, and made sure to check whether his hair needed to be colored again. As content with his appearance as anyone starting education in their teen years can be, he sallied forth to the cafeteria with a pack of tea leaves from home. There he was met with the breakfast all proper Tarrkavian people enjoyed: fried eggs over a bed of rice along with grilled tomatoes, mushrooms, and baked beans. A butter-based sauce containing a variety of mild spices covered the eggs and mixed with the rice.

Filling a mug with hot water and the tea leaves, Daniel found this food to be far more palatable and far less guilt-inducing than the meal he'd eaten before.

Daniel's classmates seemed largely absorbed in their own little worlds. They guffawed at the same pompous critiques of anyone who wasn't in their "group," but Daniel seemed of little interest to them.

Lukka, on the other hand, still managed to sit directly across from him, but she paid no more attention to him than she had in their previous few encounters. Daniel committed to himself to do nothing that might irritate the baroness, and breakfast went by uneventfully, although he was a bit uncomfortable.

Finally, with a full stomach and a clearer conscience than usual, Daniel ascended the stairs of the central tower along with the rest of his classmates. On the second floor were two large lecture halls and a host of smaller classrooms that rose along the heights of the main spire. Offices and workspaces populated the levels above.

For the more general subjects for first year students, the large lecture halls best suited them. Students from all four estates could fit within a single one—although they were required to sit among their own peers. This was a pleasant surprise to Daniel, who had assumed he would be attending classes among strangers. Knowing that Rigel and Johanna were also present brightened his mood further.

The first subject of the day was geometry. Professor Thompson, who he'd met on that first day, taught with exuberance, drawing shapes and explaining distances as though he had just made the discovery for the first time. Daniel found math to be far more accessible than writing—there were no large words to reveal his lack of education. He kept records of the numbered angles of regular polygons and could already make some sense of how the lines connected into attack vectors within a three-dimensional space of air. With each line drawn on the board, he could envision an airplane zooming into the range of another. He could also envision—from the angles—how a plane landed upon a runway, though matters of mass and velocity were left for a future class. Daniel found Professor Thompson to be a good teacher, not too technical, but not overly intent on being comedic.

The next class was geography. Dr. Pollins, who presided over Korona Red, taught this class. With an air of noble upbringing, he spoke with an accent Daniel had not heard before. He later learned this was the way people born and raised in the capital among high society spoke—he recognized aspects of Johanna and Rigel's speech that matched the professor's.

In the class, they examined maps of Tarrkaven and its surrounding neighbors as they'd been before the War of Kalamity and after, with its present borders and disputed territory.

Daniel looked closely at the maps. Skyskape Akademy sat tucked away in a safe corner of the landmass upon a peninsula overlooking the stormy northern seas. He quickly found the large river that ran down the length of the country before ending at the star denoting the capital somewhere along the southern ocean—and saw the dot that marked Blau's domain. He assumed the letters around it spelled something comparable to the name of his home.

The warmth of Professor Thompson's voice was lacking in Dr. Pollins' demeanor. Daniel assumed that the explanation of current affairs carried a greater degree of seriousness than the subject matter of the math teacher. The lessons Dr. Pollins taught represented the most real threat to the country's future, and the professor didn't dare downplay the serious nature of the conflict—even in its present stalemate.

Toward the end of the lesson, Daniel leaned his head on his hand and looked down the row to where Rigel sat. His strange new friend appeared to be doodling cartoons. Daniel heard a barely audible scoff from the throat of Lukka, who was seated right behind him.

He was growing irritated that this girl—who seemed to be making every effort to ignore him—was glued to his hip. He turned back toward the professor and thought about one of the lessons he—as Duun—had learned as a boy. A fundamental belief of the Knot Kovenant stemmed from the principle that all life that coexists within a close space exists to benefit and support the other. Foxes ate rabbits to thin the population that would encroach upon the sheep's pastures, but the rabbit's excrement helped enrich the soil so the grass could grow to support the sheep's diet.

Clearly, whatever force kept Lukka in his presence was the rabbit poop of this scenario. Grinning to himself, Daniel decided his analogy had finally broken down. He would devote his attention elsewhere. While he'd been lost in his thoughts, Dr. Pollins had concluded his lecture, and the third teacher of the day made his task somewhat easier.

Through the doorway walked the figure of Dr. Violite with her long lavender hair and a black velvet gown that drifted along the floor in puddles of cloth. In both of her pale thin hands, she carried two chicken wings. Hanging from around her wrist was a small cauldron and a pendant of skulls was draped about her neck. Daniel surmised that the shadow under her eyes probably stemmed from sleep deprivation rather than day-old mascara.

"Well, hello, hello, class," she said as she crossed the lecture hall toward the lectern. "Some of you know me, and some of you will *get* to know me. I am Dr. Violite." She paused when she reached the lectern. "I am a former Buldwikk sorceress, and if you have any complaints, know that I have royal tenure and burning your parents' letters is more pleasureable to me than morning coffee."

"I'm here to teach you a thing or two about the foes you will be facing on the battlefield. But before I get to that, let me tell you more about myself. I won Miss Buldwikk fifteen years prior and would've won the year before had nepotism not been at play that year. I'm married to the magnificent and, dare I say, spicy Vikar Nostram, and up until this year, I was the representative professor for Krossbone Brown. I was moved to Diamond Blue following my predecessor's unfortunate injuries.

"Third-degree burns are no joke, kids. Thankfully, he wasn't in a plane when it happened, so don't feel traumatized about getting into a plane after I tell you that. Does anyone have any questions?"

Daniel was afraid of even considering where to start with questions. He read the faces in the rest of the room and it appeared everyone else was too. Although Rigel was still doodling, he raised his hand first. "Hi, Teach, why did Pops give you royal tenure?"

Dr. Violite narrowed her eyes. "My knowledge of Buldwikk sorcery helped bring the war to the present pause we are experiencing. Unraveling the techniques and powers of my people allowed the engineers of this country to develop and employ proper weapons to stop the unstoppable. That said, engineering only goes so far against tormented husks of the dessicated. That's where spirited pilots make up the difference."

"Why not just teach us how to make the shadow beasts of Buldwikk then?" another student asked. It was Martin from among Jensen's cronies.

"Oh, you can't be taught how to do that. This is something that isn't understood in a kingdom that excels in technology and is second only to Visolia in industry. Magicians of all sorts—be they Buldwikk sorcerers or Ulkirn Knot Kovenant faithful or what have you—must pay a costly price before they even get a shot at casting spells."

She glanced around the room. "I recognize all of you come from affluent homes and are too young to understand costs outside of the payment of coin. I'm talking about a payment of body, mind, or soul. I sold my mind for Buldwikk, and after one thing led to another, I became your teacher." She let out a soft chuckle that nobody in the hall found to be too funny.

"Anyway, enough about that. Most soldiers of Buldwikk don't bother with swords or guns or bombs or anything of that newfangled tech we build in this country. We summon our kytinfiends from among the dead and bind them in the dark of the Shadow."

Doctor Violite removed her pendant and dropped it into the cauldron. Next, she tossed in the two chicken wings and waved a marked palm over the cauldron. A deep burning red shone from within. Slowly, out of the dark smoke that billowed from its surface, rose the half-cat half-bird creature Daniel had seen when he'd met her days earlier. This time, however, it possessed wings where its front legs had been before. The creature hissed through its beak, and the red stone flickered with a fiery glow as a warning to the students present.

"Who wants to take a guess where you need to hit the beast to dissipate it?" Violite asked. When no one immediately responded, she pursed her lips. "Here's a tip. Answer the first question quickly if you don't plan on answering any more questions today because my first questions are usually the easiest."

Daniel heard Johanna's voice from a far corner at the back of the lecture hall. "The big red stone?"

"Rightarooney," said Dr. Violite. "Of course, if it were that easy then it wouldn't be a terror to the world. Kytinfiends are merely echoes of the creatures they once were, guided with the less-than-stable hands of their creators. However, they recognize where they are most vulnerable and react to keep themselves safe. The small ones are agile and vicious on an infantry level, and the big ones are sturdy and powerful, entirely capable of leveling cities on their own." She paused. "Make no mistake—no amount of firepower anywhere outside the red stone will kill these fiends, but a sufficient enough blast will stagger them. When Buldwikk finally amassed the death tolls to unleash the largest of their forces onto the battlefield, the military of Tarrkaven relied upon heavy artillery barrages to try and hit the red stone. These were costly and desperate attacks when successful and disastrous when the target was missed.

"However, the leaps and bounds made in aviation turned what began as a recon craft into an effective countermeasure against the Buldwikk forces. The amount of ammunition expended in attempting to hit the red stone made it difficult to justify the existence of these weapons. That's when the up and coming engineering prodigy Minah Darlington introduced the guided rocket. Using a combination of wire guides, weighted wheels, and propulsion to slice through the air with considerable accuracy, pilots found they could break the stones with a single well-placed shot and fly out of harm's way, thus turning the tide of the battlefield."

She walked over to the cauldron, which continued to spill out black smoke and what looked to be a thick tar. She gave it a pat on the side, which caused the tar rising out of the top to shift and run down.

"Now, the one challenge," she continued, "is that a kytinfiend can always come back to life if its bonekiln remains intact. Personal ones are about the size of this one, but the ones used for the most gargantuan terrors can be built into large agrarian fields. Guided rockets won't do much against these, and that's where our bombers come into play. Not as glamorous as fighters to be sure, but they are equally crucial to success on the battlefield. Drop the payload within and the risk of kytinfiends coming back is erased permanently."

Dr. Violite punctuated this comment by reaching up her sleeve and procuring a grenade. She pulled the pin and dunked it down into the pot. The whole class dove under their tables and Dr. Violite laughed maniacally. Then the sound of a ringing alarm clock rattled from inside the cauldron.

"Relax, boys and girls, it's a dummy grenade. Oh, the looks on your faces! The first time I did this trick, about twenty soldiers came in and pointed their guns at me. Don't worry, though. No matter how many times I do this, royal tenure preserves me again and again. Now, of course, if someone actually was hurt, then tenure wouldn't save me from the law. Hence the slight deception.

"That's it for my class today. If you have any questions or need additional tutoring, my office hours are posted upstairs. Please pick up a syllabus before you leave for today and review it before tomorrow. Toodles!" Violite whisked away the shadowy creature in a puff of smoke with her marked hand and picked up her cauldron. As she exited, she passed another professor coming in. Most, including Daniel, raised their heads over their desks to see who would take Dr. Violite's place.

"She did the grenade thing again, didn't she?" said Professor Auberdine.

Chapter 20

Professor Auberdine taught history, but spent most of his first day trying to put the students at ease after Dr. Violite's display with the cauldron. Fortunately, Auberdine was a down-to-earth soul who contrasted with Dr. Pollin's propensity for the dire and Dr. Violite's bombastic lunacy.

To Professor Auberdine, the history of the kingdom was best displayed through discussion of the people who had lived in different ages from the beginning until present day. Daniel decided that history was his favorite course, but he much preferred listening to the professor as he lectured to attempting the reading assignments.

Daniel, Johanna, and Rigel agreed to meet midweek in the library for study time together. The three friends thought it would pair nicely with their planned weekend meetings to be focused on finding a solution to the mystery of the Twilight Parliament. About halfway through the first week of classes, Daniel made his way to the library, where he found Johanna. She had saved him a seat at her table.

"Will his highness be joining us?" asked Johanna. Daniel watched as she arranged her notes by subject and date in nice even piles.

"Yeah…just…you know how he is," Daniel said with a polite smile.

As if on cue, Rigel marched in with a large stack of papers—and not a book to be seen. Seating himself beside Daniel, he greeted Johanna and propped his feet on the vacant chair next to her.

"Comfortable?" Johanna asked, with a mild measure of snark.

Rigel crossed his hands into a "T" so as to pause the conversation. He reached into the bright green coat he wore and pulled out a tin of mints.

Popping one in his mouth, he set the tin on the table as an offering to his companions. "Hit it," he said.

Johanna rolled her eyes. "All right. I think everyone here understood the math pretty well. Are there any questions or concerns before we continue to the next subject?"

"Yeah, I got one," Rigel said. "You are really tall."

"That's not a question," Johanna answered.

"Nah, but it begs the question. Why are you so tall?"

Daniel hated to interrupt, but he felt the question was out of line. Perhaps Rigel didn't intend for it to be, but it bordered on being as curt as Jensen's interrogation that Daniel endured on the day of the convocation.

Johanna opted to answer the question all the same. "I take after my father. I understand he's quite tall. Taller than me, perhaps. I can only assume it's one more way Mom intended for me to stand out in a crowd."

"Oh," Rigel said, penitent. "I didn't mean to pry if your father's not around anymore. I may blab more than I intend."

"Well, he's not *dead*, if that's what you mean. He's just never been in the picture. I don't know if that was by choice or by command." Daniel wasn't sure what Johanna meant by this, and judging by Rigel's face, he wasn't sure either.

"Your mom didn't want your dad around?" said Rigel.

"Something like that. She had a litany of criteria for who her partner would be in an effort to select the best traits. Tall, intelligent, straight hair. I guess when the matter was settled, he had expended his usefulness. When I was born, I was given over to governesses and tutors."

"At the risk of sounding like a jerk again," Rigel said, "are you saying your mom foaled you like a horse?"

Johanna made a face. "Everything's an experiment with her—or an attempt to make a better and brighter model. I guess in her mind I'm just the latest variation on her original design. I worry sometimes that if I don't meet her expectations she'll conspire to have another child to replace me. Am I terrible for thinking that?"

Rigel shrugged. "Secondborn princes are just insurance policies—I'm probably here only in case my brother pushes up daisies. It's hard to say how the parents of the elite and famous view their children. That said, perhaps your mother does see you as a daughter and my father sees me as a son. They're both rather complicated individuals, and in a position few really understand." He gestured at Daniel. "*He's* lucky, though. Seems like he's a chip off the old block. Well, except the hair, which I gotta say I am wicked envious of. We'll get along just fine, though, I think—the three of us."

"Could've been the four of us," Daniel said.

"Oh, don't dwell on Lukka, Daniel," Rigel said. "She's not acting that way as anything personal to you. She just doesn't trust anyone. You can't win them all. Just ask my brother what he makes of me." Rigel looked around the table at the others. "We really got off on the wrong foot, didn't we?"

"*You* got us off on the wrong foot," Daniel said.

"That I did," he said, changing the subject. "Well, let us compare notes on geography."

Daniel unfolded his notes and pressed them against the table to keep them flat. Johanna moved the stack of other notes to the side and focused simply upon the three pages of geography notes she had taken over the past few days. They were a work of art, combining detailed descriptions from the classroom discussion with Johanna's own commentary and observations.

Daniel had no doubt Johanna had had considerable practice taking notes since she worked under the close eye of her mother—among the greatest minds of the Darlington Corporation. He assumed this, though, because Johanna's handle of written language far exceeded his own comprehension and was thus beautifully indecipherable. He handed her *his* notes.

Johanna looked over them and handed them back to him. "I say this as your friend, Daniel, but I have no idea what any of this says. Can you tell me what you wrote so I can help fill in the details you missed and correct your spelling?"

Daniel looked at his notes, and as he began to try and remember what had been said as he wrote them, he determined they were largely a lost cause. He wasn't even sure about his own spelling. He was sure he had misspelled Ulkirn—the country in which he'd been born—at least three different ways.

"Rigel, do you have anything to contribute?" Johanna asked.

"As a matter of fact, I do," he said. His notes consisted of cartoon drawings of each professor talking about their subject. Simple words in word balloons depicted how the countries related to one another and described how Violite made her kytinfiend by throwing the chicken wings into the cauldron (which also appeared to be alive as it churned with a big happy face planted on the front). As Rigel flipped through the pages, the caricatures bounded about and explained information.

Both Daniel and Johanna picked up the cartoon drawings and looked through them with expressions of awe. Rigel wore a smug grin when the two looked back to him.

"I can actually follow this," Daniel said.

"How are these so comprehensive?" Johanna asked. "I've seen films less in-depth than these."

Rigel smiled. "Well, I have a pretty good sense for people and what they say and do. I took to doing this when Pops was holding court, decreeing laws of the realm. Drawing cartoon depictions of the people with requests sometimes frames them in a different light. That and certain words or phrases suggest intentions that aren't always evident. Of course, Pops doesn't make time to look at them and my brother thinks they are frivolous and useless. That's why I only share them with people I like. You are most certainly welcome."

"You are a hero among heroes," Daniel said.

Johanna glanced at Daniel with a playful smirk. "Okay, now, isn't that laying it on a bit thick?"

Rigel grinned even more. "Bask in my glory, peasants," he said.

Daniel broke into a thunderous applause. The librarian shot a nasty glance at him and he dropped it into a golfer's clap. Johanna fought to hold back her laughter.

"So whose notes should I add to my own?" Daniel asked.

"Whichever works best," answered Johanna. "Just work hard to glean your own observations in the classroom."

Daniel nodded. "I'll write both so that I can work up to your level, Johanna."

He set out two pieces of paper and pulled out two pens, holding one in each hand. At the same time, he transcribed Rigel's notes with his left hand and Johanna's with his right, each on separate pieces of paper. When he finished, he looked up at his friends. Rigel and Johanna both stared slack-jawed at him.

"Did I do something wrong?" Daniel asked.

"I didn't know you were ambidextrous," Johanna said.

"Ambuh what now?"

"There's a royal guard who can shave both sides of his face at the same time," Rigel said. "But this is something entirely different. Why didn't you tell us you were a golden god among men, Daniel?"

"Do people not write with both hands? We knit with both hands. We climb trees with both hands. Doesn't seem like that much of a leap."

"I've got cousins who knit, Daniel," Rigel said, "but not like that. Speaking of which, could you bring your needles to the library some time? I'd like to learn, but my brother says it's improper for a man to do."

"Why would he say that?" Johanna asked.

"He's old fashioned. Got a tall tower shoved right up where the sun doesn't shine. Anyway, for a second, I was worried he was right." He looked at Daniel. "Do you have any work to show? I'd be interested in seeing it."

"Not yet, but I'll have something soon," Daniel said.

Johanna picked up the copy Daniel had made from her notes. Upon closer inspection, she saw that they weren't as perfect as she had previously envisioned. While a great improvement upon what Daniel had written on his own, she had one observation that she couldn't ignore.

"Daniel, your handwriting is a work of art, but your spelling is atrocious. If you don't mind, I can help you with spelling."

"Is it that big of a deal if I can't spell?" Daniel asked.

"No, not to me, and I don't think Rigel cares that much either."

"Nah," Rigel said. "Kinda impressed you managed to misspell something that is spelled correctly right in front of you, though."

Johanna thought for a moment. "That aside, spelling will more than likely matter to the professors and anyone of authority you run into later on in life. Not to mention your housemates aren't exactly understanding folks."

"I see that is true," Daniel said. Anything he did that didn't fit into the gold standard of Baron Blau would arouse scorn—and more importantly, suspicion. Reading and writing were skills most noble-born students had acquired by this point, and it would seem unlike a noble to continue with bad spelling.

Before, he had only learned what he could from Natalie and the baron, but Johanna and Rigel had skills that could help him frame the lessons in a new light, and he figured if he could trust them with this matter. Later, perhaps, there might come a time when he could trust them with the truth of his identity. He agreed to their offer of assistance with his spelling for the time being.

While the three friends engaged in their self-assigned learning community, where Johanna and Daniel sought to make the grade and Rigel sought to earn their adoration, Lukka listened to their merriment from behind a bookshelf.

Finally, she picked up her things slipped out of the library. Daniel caught a glimpse of her leaving and wanted to say something, but instead held his tongue. Despite their differences, he felt a phantom pain because of Lukka's absence, and this kept her on his mind.

Why did she matter to him?

He didn't know.

Chapter 21

Professor Auberdine waited on a bench for a bus. With no particular interest in his surroundings, the professor watched the bus as it approached from far down along the road. His glasses rested on top of a leatherbound book with a deep purple ribbon poking out from the bottom of its pages. He checked the watch worn from a chain that stemmed like a gold vine from a pocket of his dark grey vest.

When the weekend had come, Daniel felt relief at having survived his first ventures into the classroom. He wrapped the wooden box in the purple cloak and then tied a cord he had knitted to practice Blau's code, around the box. It read simply THE EVIDENSE KOLLEKTED IN FIRST MONTH. He double-checked the spelling to make sure it was accurate, and when he was satisfied, took the wrapped items and headed to the meeting with his friends at the Wave's Break.

When Daniel reached the bus stop and saw the professor, he felt an instinctive need to leave the teacher undisturbed. In an attempt to appear casual, he stood by the bus schedule holding the wrapped purple package with awkward shifting hands.

Professor Auberdine looked up at him. "Y'know, I am a human being, and benches are built to accommodate multiple people. If it was Dr. Violite, it'd be a different story, but you don't have to do all of that."

"Right. Of course," Daniel said, and took a seat on the bench.

The professor smiled. "You're Daniel Hardy, Baron Blau's boy? How are you liking Skyskape so far?"

"Fine. It's fine," Daniel said. How else was he supposed to answer that question? Baron Blau had told him people who complain upon first meetings seldom had many friends, so Daniel aimed to be pleasant, but he'd begun to think that everyone is a little dishonest from time to time.

"Are you going to see some friends?" asked the professor.

"Yeuhs," Daniel uttered in a confused stumble of sounds. "Yes, I am," he clarified. "Rigel and Johanna."

"Wow! Those two are polar opposites, but that's good to hear. I can't help but notice you don't talk to your fellow Diamond Blue students that much. They aren't giving you trouble, are they?"

"Not as much right now," Daniel said.

"Well, as long as you've got your two friends, then you should be good. It's easy to think the quantity of people who like you is the measure of how good a person you are, but it's not. Lots of people like the king, but he hasn't exactly done much good for the kingdom on the whole. I know divine right puts him in charge of the country, but his extravagant lifestyle has leeched more and more authority away from the crown." He paused. "Baron Blau is a pretty fair ruler, but many barons and dukes follow the king's example of self-interest before state. Oops, there I go, talking politics. You've probably got no interest in any of that."

"Actually," Daniel said, "I do." A part of him regretted beginning this train of thought, but the words had already escaped his lips before he could stop. "What're your thoughts on the Knot Kovenant?"

Professor Auberdine placed his glasses and his book by his side. "So we're clear, are we talking about the people of Ulkirn or just the Knot Kovenant?"

"The Knot Kovenant," Daniel said.

"Well," Professor Auberdine said. "I'm a follower of the Four and believe them to be a divine and infallible authority. I don't necessarily love the Knot Kovenant's idea that the gods are dependent upon their followers to exist. I don't trust magic because so much of it is in the Shadow's domain. The Tarrkavian in me shrinks away from uncorking the bottle on powers beyond our control. The Sion's light doesn't exist outside the law of the Father or the love of the Mother." He paused.

"However, I also know that sometimes justice lies beneath the Shadow's shroud. The Knot Kovenant and the forestfolk may be druids and magicians, but they live governed by law and that's better than most magic. I worry that bringing them here to this land will lead to others who seek to profit off that power to seek out their secrets. History reports some forestfolk being created well after birth, and if the wrong person receives that power, it could erode the foundations of Knot Kovenant law and then natural law.

"We've already seen that with Buldwikk sorcery. Lettings these forces run unbridled across the world will do more damage than any war of bullets and bombs. When Ulkirn is liberated, I think the Knot Kovenant should be made to return—for their own safety as well as the safety of Tarrkaven. If Ulkirn cannot be restored, then a new home must be sought out."

Daniel didn't know what to make of the idea of the Knot Kovenant being sent back to Ulkirn. He had been born in Ulkirn, but the only life he had known had been in Tarrkaven. "What about the Knot Kovenant born in Tarrkaven?" Daniel asked. "Many of them have a life here."

Professor Auberdine thought for a moment. "Well, in a perfect world, laws would be passed to protect the rights of the Kovenant. The Knot Kovenant exists in many other countries, and it is the protection of law or, at least, tolerance of the masses that allows them to coexist. The way Tarrkaven stands at present, I cannot guarantee such concessions could be made."

"Tarrkaven can change though, can't it?"

"It can, but it may take time. One person cannot make that sort of change overnight. It may take lifetimes for the Knot Kovenant to be accepted in Tarrkaven and, all the while, there will be the uphill battle of the desire to exploit their power."

The bus pulled up and the door swung open. Professor Auberdine picked up his glasses and book and stood up. "I'm glad there are students who are interested in the state of the kingdom. I'm sure you'll make a great baron someday."

Daniel had no idea how to respond to this last part. He *couldn't* be a baron. He was just a shepherd. This charade would come to an end at some point, wouldn't it? Yet, based on what the professor had said, if he continued to exist as Daniel Hardy, would the world allow him to become

Duun Howl again? He had never thought about it, but he couldn't ignore the question. When this job was over, would he just disappear from Johanna and Rigel's lives? Did Duun Howl die so Daniel Hardy could live?

"Hey, you all right there?" Professor Auberdine asked. "I hope I didn't just put too much pressure on you. You're still young, and you won't have to be baron right away. Anyway, that's a real colorful gift you've got there. I hope whoever the lucky person you're sending it to likes it."

Daniel snapped back to the present and got up to board the bus as well. "Right! Thank you!"

The professor smiled. "All right, then. I won't trouble you any further. I'm looking forward to your input in class. And, if you're interested in more Tarrkavian history, you should come by the Historik Research Society room. The upperclassmen are good kids. You'd like them. Have a good one."

"Yes, I will. Have a good one, that is," Daniel said and then decided he needed to stop talking. He got on the bus and sat alone by the window. When the bus stopped in the town, he stepped off and walked to the Wave's Break. Johanna stood talking with Hunter and Jaki. Rigel wasn't yet there.

Hunter frowned at Johanna. "You want to do what now?"

"If you don't mind, I've got a projector and a screen to shine up on the wall. It may take some time, and we will need to wait for it to get dark out."

"Uh, huh," Hunter said. "Why can't you just do this back at the school?"

"Oh, well, it's for a special school project, and we don't want wandering eyes seeing what we've been working on."

Hunter looked at the wrap-around windows of the diner. "Do you mind if the whole town sees it? I can draw the blinds, but this is a business, and it's gonna turn heads if we close up early."

"Will it, though?" said Rigel, who had appeared behind Daniel. "Seems like the Darlington next door is doing more to disrupt business than the Darlington in front of you."

"Listen, your princeliness," Hunter said. "Our business was around before Darlington's, and our food is better by far."

"What about the Visolia lime pie?" Rigel said.

"Our Visolia lime is world's better," Hunter chortled.

"I'll be the judge of that," said Rigel.

"Nice try," said Hunter. "No free food for you."

"Worth a shot," Rigel said.

Johanna steered the conversation back to the equipment. "I can compensate your business for your time," she said. "If we can't show the film in here, then is there somewhere more private we could watch it?"

"My office will do nicely," Jaki said. "But you'll need to wash your hands." She looked at Daniel. "And your red-headed friend is going to have to wear his hair up if he's coming back here."

Daniel realized that both Rigel and Johanna wore hats. Rigel turned around, looked Daniel up and down, and then yanked the blue tam off his head and slapped it down on Daniel's head. Reaching into his coat, he procured a beanie cap which he then placed upon his own brow.

"Have you been carrying that around this whole time?" Johanna asked.

"Yeah, it's a little too drab for my liking though."

Johanna's eyebrow twitched as though some critical system was failing in her mind, but then she closed her eyes, took a breath, and mumbled to herself. "Not your circus, JoJo."

Rigel made a frame with his hands and beheld Daniel in the tam. "Y'know what? Just keep that hat, Daniel."

Once inside, after everyone had washed their hands and Johanna set up the projector in Jaki's office, Daniel unwrapped the cloak and cord from around the box and opened it. There sat the tin. Johanna reached in and looked it over. "This is a B-roll for Mom's movie."

"A what now?" Rigel asked.

"In movies, there's the scenes in between the story stuff that establishes locations, clarifies actions, or frames the shot a different way. That's the B-roll. I wonder how this managed to get here. This cloak looks like it was made for the film set, though. I wouldn't worry too much."

Daniel's heart sank as he began to worry the evidence accumulated would paint him an idiot who believed movies were real. How could he prove Blau's lands had been attacked after such a debacle? Would Rigel and Johanna even be his friends?

"Hey now, let's still watch this film," Rigel said. "We've got a small little theater in here. Let's not waste it."

"A B-roll may not be very exciting, so we may as well get settled in," Johanna said.

The trio sat in silent attention on the floor as they watched a screen that displayed monochrome images of beachfronts, city skylines, cars driving along roads, crowds of people meandering about their daily lives on the streets, planes filling the air among the clouds.

In its own way, it held Rigel's attention, who likened it to a sort of visual art project during the first fifteen minutes, but afterward, his interest waned and he watched with the vacant expression of a koi in a block of ice. Johanna's attention proved even shorter—she dozed off between the two boys and leaned her head on the back of Ms. Jaki's desk.

Only Daniel watched with fierce scrutiny, because his foothold on the investigation wavered with each passing frame. After about the fifth instance of street cars, Daniel got up to attempt to switch off the projector. He stared at the controls, attempting to deduce what would turn off the bulb.

Just then, the screen changed from the carousel of humdrum images to a dark interior. What appeared to be a fortress built into a cavern danced through flickering frames upon the screen. The large banners of the Twilight Parliament hung from watchtowers and barracks within the fortress. The jagged movements of the camera's view suggested it was being carried on foot by a clandestine agent.

The view then shifted to show soldiers in helmets that covered their faces. The helmets had large eyeholes and two sharp points like a horned owl's—and short, flat beaks that covered their mouths and noses.

Behind them were individuals in chains, marching at gunpoint. When one would fall over, though the video was without sound, Daniel could see the soldiers fiercely chastise him and drag him back to his feet, shoving him back into line. The chained people were led to a cargo boat and placed in cages.

Daniel was surprised at how well lit the people were, and he suspected this was due to some form of studio lighting. But, then, he realized from the shadows cast at the feet of the soldiers that the light stemmed from the people! When a woman walked by with flowers in her hair, it all became clear. *These were forestfolk.*

The scene shifted again to the ship's deck. An individual wearing an outfit identical to the Emerald Dragonfly's stepped into view and struggled with one of the helmeted soldiers. After wrestling a rifle from the soldier's hand, the Dragonfly drove its bayonet through the soldier's chest. The soldier reeled from the stab and blood flowed from the wound. The soldier tipped over the ship's railing and into the sea.

The Dragonfly disappeared from view but before, for a brief moment, it looked to the camera. It was then Daniel noticed something that had not been on the movie poster from before—the Dragonfly wore a scarf of erratically colored lines. Bands of varying width lined the scarf. No discernible pattern was evident except that it resembled that of the coded cord he had knitted.

Then, it dawned on him. The Emerald Dragonfly in the film used the same code Baron Blau had taught him. He was sending a message!

"Johanna, Rigel, look!" Daniel said.

"I'm awake!" Rigel said as he bolted up. Johanna rubbed her eyes and stared at the screen.

Daniel was frantic. "Don't tell me you missed the Emerald Dragonfly stabbing a guy!"

"The who did what now?" Johanna asked.

"Dammit, Daniel, I was having a good dream," Rigel said.

"Johanna, how do I play this back?" asked Daniel.

"Hang on, let me see it," Johanna said. Going to the projector and reversing the playback, she saw the man roll out from over the deck as the blood returned to his chest and the Emerald Dragonfly struggled with the soldier. It continued to roll back to the forestfolk being dragged in chains onto the ship and into the underground fortress.

Johanna viewed the footage, paralyzed at the revelation. "This isn't from the movie. Mom wouldn't make a movie about this."

"Uh," said Rigel, "she *was* making a war movie. Maybe it's like really good special effects or something."

"I mean the soldier who got stabbed. Mom faints when she sees blood."

"Wait," Daniel said. "She faints when she sees blood?"

"Yes," Johanna said.

"In any instance?"

"Um, yes, under any circumstance," Johanna answered in a quieter tone.

"That's kinda inconvenient, isn't it?" Daniel asked.

"Yeah," said Rigel. "She owns factories and stuff, and accidents are bound to happen all the time, right?"

They were enthusiastically interrupted by Johanna, who decided now was not the day to introduce Rigel to the ways of the world. "In any case! Like in factories, yes, that's correct. She can't stand the sight of blood and won't put blood in her films as a result. This footage is legitimate."

She paused, thinking. "I'm beginning to think you're onto something, Daniel. Good work with your persistence. Bravo. This is not from Mom's film. It's from somewhere else. Which suggests the Twilight Parliament is either real or somebody is acting as this fictional entity to traffic forestfolk."

"So how did the footage end up at the school?" Rigel asked.

"Well, there are two possibilities as I see it," Johanna said. "Option A is that this Twilight Parliament confiscated the video footage and reviewed it until they grew weary of seeing routine filler footage. That seems a bit unlikely. Then there's Option B. Whoever is opposing the Twilight Parliament was using the custodian's shed as a place to hide valuable evidence of their operation."

"Do you think it's the custodian?" Rigel asked. "I mean, besides me, who else would go poking around the custodian's shed?"

"Well, the duties of the custodian are handled by students. So, it may not be easy to immediately determine who put it in the shed. Also, it's entirely possible they've already graduated. Let's keep our eyes open and our ear to the ground and see whatever else comes up."

"So whaddya know, Daniel. You were right all along," Rigel said.

Daniel thought of the forestfolk in chains. Being right was not at all what he wanted.

Chapter 22

The months of spring carried on in the classroom while stormy weather dominated the skies over the citadel. Daniel met with Rigel and Johanna in the library in the afternoons and when the weekends arrived, at the Wave's Break as they could. The storms were terrible throughout the season, turning the roads into deep muddy bogs, so there were several weekends when the friends did not meet.

They'd been unable to gather more evidence after the discovery of the video footage. While there were certainly leads to be followed, many obstacles presented themselves. Finding out, for example, who were the previous year's student groundskeepers proved nigh impossible as there were no formal records—responsibility was given to anyone who volunteered on an as-needed basis.

They couldn't dare show the footage to anybody else without arousing suspicion. Above all, they hadn't identified the cove fortress in the film—it could've been in any number of locations. The borders of Tarrkaven spanned both a northern and southern coast with rocky capes, cliffs, and inlets, many of which hadn't been documented by the Tarrkavian Geographik Society.

The only reliable lead was the Emerald Dragonfly's scarf, but getting a completed record of the colors of the scarf proved challenging. Only one tail of the scarf appeared in the shot long enough for them to determine a pattern, and the delicate nature of the film meant that, if they dwelled on the shot for too long at a time, the cells might melt.

But, with time between viewings, they were able to get multiple views of the footage. Watching the scene of the soldier killed again and again made each of them uncomfortable, but after all their efforts, the single tail of the scarf was differentiated into dark and light shades. The light shades were either white or yellow and the dark either red or blue. Depending upon how the shadows were cast, green could appear as either light or dark.

Daniel taught the code to Rigel and Johanna and together they worked out possible combinations. However, in the presence of so many possible variations of colors, the translations proved an arduous task.

Above all else, the commitment of the trio to keeping up with classes stifled many of these endeavors. Daniel's grades didn't matter as much to him as his mission was a personal one, but he knew he wouldn't be able to stay at Skyskape if he failed. Since he operated at a disadvantage due to his poor reading skills, the first quarter of the year had been consumed with his efforts to secure a foothold at the academy.

The challenges he faced in finding more information about his brother Avo stifled even minor progress in his mission. The photos he had of Avo seemed to include just friends and students from the school year. At this point, all had already graduated or were gone. In addition, the locations of the photographs had no real correlations, at least that Daniel could see. Perhaps the pictures were simply the excited recollections of an Ulkirn boy in a much larger world.

Duun was happy, however, to see that Avo had had friends in the pictures—just like the ones he had made on his own. Of course, Avo's friends knew him as Avo, and he couldn't reveal that Avo was his brother while he continued to pretend to be Daniel Hardy.

After months of the subterfuge, he felt as if he had left Duun back at home. He went to the cafeteria without any gripes and ate whatever was served. At Skyskape, there were none of the great forests of his home to climb and explore, and the hedges and flowers of the gardens made for poor climbing material. He wondered what the flowers might reveal to Leleen if she were at the school in his place, but to him, they were silent.

His other classmates in Diamond Blue had ceased to give Daniel trouble. He'd done well enough in the classroom to be seen as a middle-of-the-road student. Despite Dr. Auberdine's request, Daniel made no effort to ask more questions in class. However, his reading and writing had steadily improved as the quarter went on. Even Baron Blau noticed, remarking about it within their correspondences.

Over the months, Daniel worked away at his knitted secret messages. In the beginning, he'd knitted a scarf, but toward the end of spring, the scarf became separate swatches that simply reported that there was nothing new to report. He had reported to Blau what he had found about the Twilight Parliament and whether he believed there to be some connection of Avo's disappearance. Blau had written back through yarnwork transcribed by Natalie in the code they relied upon. Diagonal markings in black yarn indicated the ends of sentences:

"THIS TWILIGHT PARLIAMENT IS DANGEROUS / IF THEY ARE AT SKYSKAPE FIND NAMES AND HIDEOUT / YOUR FAMILY IS WELL AND I HAVE REBUILT THEIR HOUSE / PARKER PROKURED MORE SHEEP TO ASSIST IN OUR KOMMUNICATION / SEVERAL KNOT KOVENANT SURVIVORS HAVE GONE TO ASSIST THEM IN YOUR ABSENSE / WHEN YOU FIND MORE ABOUT THE KNOT KOVENANT BE IT STUDENT OR STAFF DO NOT HESITATE TO WRITE ME / I WILL ASK MINAH ABOUT EMERALD DRAGONFLY / KEEP YOUR HAIR DYED / BLAU"

With all the studying and working Daniel did, he had nearly forgotten to dye his hair on one occasion. Thankfully, he'd noticed the white spot in class before anyone else did and managed to pull it under the tam Rigel had given him.

When spring ended and summer began, the moment many students had eagerly anticipated arrived. "Well then, class," Dr. Violite began in an address to the Diamond Blue students, "today the weather's cleared up enough for us to get all of you up in the air today. All we'll be doing is seeing if you can get up in the air and back down without significant damage to school property or yourselves. However, your performance will be evaluated to determine your placement come autumn, so take them seriously.

"Or don't. Honestly, it's no skin off my back if you fly or not. I'm just the one who will be throwing stuff at you in a couple weeks' time. Looking forward to it, e-heh-heh." She walked out the door and the sound of her laughter trailed behind her. A twitch of worry about what she had meant rumbled through the classroom, but it was soon set aside by the enthusiastic anticipation of finally being able to fly.

In class in the weeks before, they had covered the functions of a cockpit so that they wouldn't be complete strangers when they reached the airfield. There were the pedals that controlled the rudder, the stick that governed the pitch and roll of the plane, and the throttle that governed the plane's speed. Johanna's mother Minah had even developed cockpit simulators that were attached to a board of lights. Green or red lights flashed to signal correct or incorrect inputs by the student.

Because of Daniel's practice with Blau, he was already familiar with each function, and between the class lectures and Rigel's colorful illustrations, the results of his efforts allowed him to far exceed expectations. His teachers praised that he took after his father, and the rest of Diamond Blue's indifference turned to scorn when they realized they would have to compete with what they saw as a younger Baron Blau. Of the Diamond Blue compatriots, only Lukka performed better than Daniel. The cockpits greatly resembled ones flown by her subordinates in her home barony, she said.

Meanwhile, Rigel's class had reviewed the proper terminology for communications from the tower, how to coordinate radio communication, landing and takeoff protocols, and identifying the layout of the airfield. When they spoke about it at the library, Daniel took that to be a confusing mess, and Rigel told him not to worry about it.

Johanna had dealt with the greatest volume of work. In her engineering program, she had studied physics, ballistics, and aerodynamics as well as the electrical and analog systems of the aircraft and abbreviated lessons about what Rigel was learning in his classes. Despite the immense workload, she had taken it in stride, but she had relied upon Rigel's drawings from time to time for assistance.

Diamond Blue students were first to travel to the airfield. The students of Krossbone Brown would get their turns the following day.

Daniel tapped his foot in apprehension about what waited ahead. As much as he knew the material and what needed to be done to fly, he couldn't help but worry that he would make a critical error due to an overexcited twitch or a mechanical failure. He had been told the best way to combat these preflight nerves was a checklist and he looked through the notes he had rapidly put together.

In the back of the bus, Lukka sat in composed silence. Her feet moved as though she was pressing pedals and her hand moved by her side as though she was operating the throttle. One of the other students had the audacity to whisper a jest about it, only to be stopped cold by Lukka's dark eyes, which opened and pierced like steel straight through their foolish smiles with the same coldblooded attention as when a reptile's eyes open when disturbed from its rest.

When the bus arrived at the airfield, planes were lined up outside the hangar and prepped for flight. A soldier approached Professor Thompson, who stood off to the side. "Where the hell *is* he?"

Daniel recognized the soldier immediately. It was none other than William Brown, the soldier who had accosted Rigel on the day of orientation.

"His majesty is famous for being difficult," said Thompson. "We just need to be patient. He must be around here somewhere."

"He better be. Go ahead and get these students ready to fly while we find him."

Daniel glanced around nervously. Rigel was nowhere to be seen.

Professor Thompson turned and faced the students of Diamond Blue as they exited the bus, his smile betraying nervousness. Daniel understood—if they had lost sight of Rigel, he might be getting himself in all manner of trouble. Daniel decided not to dwell on it, because whatever Rigel was up to, he wouldn't do it without a reason.

"Hello Diamond Blue and Dr. Violite," said Professor Thompson. "We'll be having you take off two at a time. Remember you're just going to get up in the air, take a lap, and get back onto the ground. If you've been paying attention in class, you should be fine. If you are feeling nervous, that's natural, but before long you'll feel more in control than you would with your feet on the ground. I guarantee it."

Daniel remembered how Blau had fallen asleep in the cockpit on their way to Skyskape. He probably wouldn't be able to manage that level of calm in a fighter, but it did instill confidence.

Thirteen planes were lined up on the runway one after another. Students were guided to board them from nearest to farthest. Lukka was among the first to get into a plane on the opposite end of the field, and from there each of the Diamond Blues followed suit.

Daniel looked for Rigel again when he reached the last plane. With no sign of the prince, he climbed into the cockpit, calmed his nerves, and began his checklist. Going through each system and making certain everything operated as intended, he found his mind put more at ease by the function of each instrument. He switched on the radio to the tower and heard Johanna giving instructions under the supervision of a teacher. It was reassuring to hear the voice of a friend.

Judging by their callsigns, the first two planes would be piloted by Lukka and Jensen. As the two planes took to the sky, Daniel couldn't help but marvel at the grace of the Libertys rising from the ground and into the air. Their long flat wings moved like albatrosses rising upon the wind, their propellers turning so fast so as to be almost unseen to the eye.

"Move into position, Daniel…err…Diamond Thirteen. Over." Johanna said.

Daniel smiled and started the engine. It clicked three times and whistled out heated air as the propeller began its rotations. As the engine fired and sang its energetic melody, the hum of the propeller boosted the sounds with a deep and beautiful bassline.

The wheels turned along the asphalt ground beneath the wings and Daniel closed the glass canopy overhead. Once the cockpit was secured, he sat on the runway, his propeller turning in anticipation—a goose beating its wings in hope of rising into its home in the sky.

"You're clear to take off, Diamond Thirteen. Sion guide you. Over." Johanna said.

Daniel pushed the throttle and the plane began its gradual approach before breaking into a charge. Hearing the rise of the engine's energy, he pulled back on the stick and the plane began its climb into the great clear sky above him. Pressed into his seat by the pitch of the plane, Daniel smiled as the land disappeared from his view and the great blue sky surrounded him. The air rushed around the canopy as he found himself climbing beyond the earth and he looked around. The other students of Diamond Blue soared through the sky with him.

As they took a lap—across the sky, around the town below, and finally, the campus spire—he smiled broadly. Up here in the sky, he was a part of something greater—above the petty prejudices of the kingdom, above the classes and assignments and worrying about grades, beyond the anxieties of the machinations of terrorists or conquering nations. Cozy within the cockpit, Daniel felt he had finally gained a view of the tapestry that spun together from the knots of all living things, woven together in peaceful quiet below him. Here above came a freedom even beyond that he had known in the forests of his home. A world without complication, a dream of the sky, a road into the great blue.

Chapter 23

Daniel turned the plane around toward the spire of the academy. Planes were already ahead of him, and the first among his class was already turning back toward the airfield. While over the ocean, he looked down at the waves crashing on the rocky cliffs below.

The first plane approached the citadel spire when, reflected in the sun's light, Daniel saw a stream of liquid flow from it. He realized by the way it evaporated in the air that the fluid was fuel—a fuel line had ruptured and begun spilling out over the ocean. He heard Johanna's voice over the radio to the plane.

"Diamond One, remain calm and return to the airfield, over." Diamond One, thought Daniel. That's Lukka!

"Roger that, over," Lukka replied. Her voice did not register alarm. Then, a second and third leak ruptured from beneath the wings and with a cough of smoke, the propeller stopped rotating.

"The engine's dead," said Lukka over the radio, now with a hint of tension in her voice.

"Stay calm, Diamond One. Eject, and we will send out search and rescue," Johanna said. "Ugh…over," she added, as if she had forgotten under the mounting stress.

"If I eject the plane will hit the schoolyard. I'm going to try and steer it in, over," Lukka said.

"There's no time for that, the building can take the impact, you need to get to safety first. Eject and pull your chute. Repeat. Eject and pull your chute."

Daniel remained in formation, but his full attention was focused on the conversation on the radio.

"The canopy's stuck," Lukka said.

Daniel could see that her cockpit was clouded in a heavy black outpouring of smoke. He doubted she could see through the glass.

Joanna spoke again. "Lukka, you'll need to break the glass. Use your pick and pry the canopy open."

Daniel shook his head as if to say no. If Lukka broke the glass, she would be bombarded with smoke. She wouldn't be able to bail if she passed out before getting clear of the cockpit. Something was definitely wrong—this was more than an ordinary mechanical failure.

He watched as the plane teetered but continued to fly toward the citadel. There were still no signs of an ejection from the plane, and it grew closer to the tower with each passing moment.

"Diamond One, do you copy? Lukka, do you copy? Steer the plane away from the spire," Johanna yelled.

Daniel pushed hard on the throttle to full and began to drop in altitude to reach her. Immediately, a woman's voice he didn't recognize broke through the silence. "Diamond Thirteen, do *not* break formation." It was not that of one of his teachers. He reached and flipped off the radio.

Daniel's plane shook as his velocity strained against the pull of gravity. According to his instruments, he was pushing just below three hundred miles per hour. He had one shot at what he intended to do—any attempt to slow the plane might result in a collision with Lukka.

He buzzed straight past the Diamond Blue tower, flipped the plane around, and hung upside down in his seat as he cleared the wall around the citadel. With a sudden push of the brakes and a pulling back of the stick, the tail of his plane swatted Lukka's fuselage like an uppercutting fist. He heard the screech of metal on metal.

For a moment, Daniel was worried that his plane had exploded, but as his muscles pushed forward and he turned the stick back around, he found himself just over the ocean. Wow, he thought, if I was any lower, I'd have a clear view of the fish.

He yanked the stick back and the plane began to rise again as the slipstream ripped across the ocean below. He then tilted the plane and swung back around toward land. As he turned, he saw Lukka's plane. It had crashed in a field outside of the school near the road between the citadel and the airfield. Already fire crews and an ambulance were in position to retrieve her. Most of the plane's fuel had been lost in the descent and the plane looked to still be in one piece.

He was too high to see if Lukka was all right. As he neared the airfield, he flipped on the radio. He needed it, come hell or high water. "Diamond Thirteen, land your plane and get back to the citadel ASAP," said the older feminine voice. "Over and out." The curtness of the voice's tone didn't spell well for Daniel, but he would not apologize for what he had done. He lined up with the runway and began his descent.

Daniel figured his plane had suffered hull damage from the impact, but he imagined the difficulties he might have in landing would be minor in comparison to what awaited him back on the ground. When he finally touched down and brought the craft to a stop, he opened the canopy and climbed out of the cockpit on legs that made him feel like Flopsy with a wooly coat too heavy on one side. Soldiers quickly approached and guided him to a canvased truck which drove him back to the citadel.

***

Two soldiers accompanied Daniel to the top of the central tower and led him down a hall. Rigel sat in a chair outside an office. He wore an uncharacteristically serious expression, and when Daniel glanced at him, he mouthed the words, "Meet me at midnight." Another door opened and Daniel was pushed into the headmaster's office, which overlooked the entire campus.

The headmaster sat at a desk facing him. She appeared much younger than Daniel had imagined—younger even than Baron Blau, he thought—but more than likely on the cusp of thirty. She could hardly have the experience to lead a flight academy, and he might have said so except that he wasn't in a position to make such observations.

Rigel, though, would've said it, he thought.

The voice he had heard in his headphones spoke. "Daniel Hardy, you defied my direct orders."

"Yes, headmaster," he said.

"You nearly endangered the life of a fellow student."

"Yes, headmaster."

"Had anything gone wrong with your little stunt, both of you would've been killed. It is a miracle of the Four that you're even here."

Daniel silently concurred with a nod.

The headmaster gestured toward the door. "I'm going to have words with the joker outside in a moment. Unfortunately, there is very little I can do to him," she said. Daniel thought it curious that she wasn't even going to attempt to deny that she had no control over Rigel. But, she continued, "As for you, I'm grounding you indefinitely and will meet with the baron to discuss your fate."

Daniel felt a large lump rise in his throat. Despite the fact that he had tried to do the right thing, it would be ironic that, after all his efforts, he might still have found a way to get kicked from Skyskape. He wondered if Avo had been in a similar position. Maybe people like Avo and him weren't cut out for a world of strictly-enforced rules. Perhaps people of nature had no place among the ivory towers, stone walls, and paved roads of Tarrkavian law.

He remembered a phrase that the baron had taught him to say. "Permission to speak freely."

"Granted," said the headmaster.

"Did the baroness survive?"

Daniel thought he saw a twitch of the headmaster's face.

"She's a bit shaken, but Lukka will be fine."

It was at this moment that Daniel noticed a resemblance between Lukka and the woman in front of him. They had to be related somehow, he decided, but the headmaster seemed too young to be Lukka's mother—that is, if Lukka still had a mother.

"Thank you," Daniel said.

"If there's nothing else, you may return to your dorm. Do not leave the estate tower until we have decided what will be done with you. Food will be brought to you from the dining hall three times a day. Baron Blau is on his way here as we speak."

"Yes, headmaster. Thank you." Daniel stood and turned to leave. As he walked through the door, Rigel bumped straight into him.

"Oops, sorry plebe," Rigel said. His balled fist reached into Daniel's pocket as he faced the headmaster. "Gonna show you how a real troublemaker raises hell. Ain't that right, Miss Strauss?"

"Your highness, please take a seat and shut up," the headmaster said.

The door closed behind Rigel and Daniel found himself standing alone in the hallway. A heavy weight dragged him down into the earth as he descended the stairs of the tower. He would've taken the elevator, but he could see the scornful looks of William Brown and his squad of soldiers through the metal doors. Daniel guessed that anyone who readily disobeyed commands earned the ire of the men and women of arms.

About halfway down the stairs, on a lower floor, he saw the infirmary. and sneaked to the door. Through the glass, he saw Lukka, who sat in a bed being tended to by nurses. Not a single person from Diamond Blue had come to wish her well. He pushed open the door and then saw Johanna standing beside her bed, so he stood in place, examining the baroness from afar.

Her bangs hid bandages drawn around her skull. Her dark eyes were noticeably shaken but her lips were fixed in their usual stoic expression. One arm hung in a sling over her shoulder. The tiny fingers in view turned and trembled as she pantomimed to Johanna what she could have done differently. It amazed Daniel how, even in the face of certain death, Lukka was still thinking through problems and searching for solutions. She made eye contact with Daniel, but for only a moment, before swiftly turning back to Johanna.

Daniel decided to let her rest and continued his descent for a few more flights. He took a seat at the foot of the stairs and, remembering Rigel's hand in his pocket, removed a wadded note. On it was one of Rigel's cartoons.

Two figures tampered with an airplane, one Daniel assumed was the one Lukka had flown. Both figures wore cloaks with the image of the owl upon them. Below the cartoon was a message. "See me at midnight tonight. I'll get Johanna."

That night as he lay in his bed, waiting for time to pass, Daniel thought about the possibility of his being expelled. It was its own sort of cruelty to finally make progress only to face expulsion for the crime of saving a life, but he was still resolute. He closed his eyes and the image of sheep and pastures and the forests near his true home. Duun knew what needed to be done in the face of a crisis and was still right there by his side.

As midnight approached, Daniel realized that Rigel hadn't said *where* the three friends would meet. It wouldn't be at the Wave's Break—the buses didn't run, and it was past curfew.

Just then, his door swung open and in walked Rigel and Johanna. Rigel scanned the room and made a face. "You don't have a window?"

"How did you get through my door?" Daniel asked.

Rigel smiled and spun a keyring around his finger. It flew off and Johanna reached out and caught it.

"Huh," Johanna said, "he really *doesn't* have any windows."

Daniel looked at his friends. "Do you both have windows?"

"Yeah, mine faces the garden," Johanna said.

"Mine faces the coast," Rigel said.

Daniel asked again. "How did you get into the building? It's past curfew."

"We crawled through Lukka's window," Rigel said.

"Are you kidding me?" said Daniel, thinking of Lukka's apparent opinion of Rigel.

"Hey now," Rigel said. "Don't get upset. You've got luck where it counts. Room placement apparently isn't where it counts. Anyway, we need to update you on what we know."

Johanna ignored Rigel and launched in. "Lukka was in the plane you were supposed to fly. Somebody with access to the list didn't realize Diamond Blue pilots choose their own planes."

"Somebody must really want the Baroness of Briars dead," Rigel said.

Johanna looked at him and shook her head in disgust. "No, Rigel, this doesn't have to do with Lukka. Someone wants *Daniel* dead and Lukka accidentally got in the way."

Daniel sat up. "Why would somebody want *me* dead?" He was sure there were several Diamond Blue students who might want it, but they wouldn't have had the means to tamper with an airplane. Had he made a mistake in the investigation? Had he let a loose end slip?

Johanna looked at Daniel. "What matters is Lukka is alive and so are you."

Daniel thought for a moment. "Johanna, when you were talking to Lukka in the infirmary, were you asking her to join in our investigation?"

Johanna seemed surprised. "Oh, you saw that? No, I wasn't. I felt like it wouldn't be a good thing to spring on someone after a brush with death. I just didn't want her to be alone. She wanted me to review what could've gone wrong with the plane. Always thinking, that one."

"The way I see it," Rigel said, "is that we shouldn't bring anyone else in. Whoever's out there is playing for keeps now. Those guys I saw on the airfield were serious business. Armor, rifles, and those owl cloaks, and not a single person noticed or tried to stop them."

Daniel shook his head. "Rigel, our investigation put Lukka in danger. This is going to endanger others regardless of whether we bring someone else in or not."

"I don't disagree with you," said Johanna. "However, Lukka's in rough shape right now. She doesn't need the stress of looking for terrorists on campus."

"How about after she heals?" Daniel asked.

"Let's cross that bridge when we get to it," Johanna said. "We don't know where we'll be on the investigation when she's better."

"Which may bring us to the next complication," Rigel said. "In light of my disappearing trick, Pops sent a telegram to the headmaster's office."

"A what?" Daniel asked.

Rigel smirked. "He's old fashioned. And…I've been put on gardening duties through the summer until I learn some sense." He made quotation marks in the air with his fingers as he spoke the last words.

"Maybe that could help us find who was storing the evidence in the shed." Daniel said.

"Probably," said Rigel, "but the point is I won't be able to meet with you two in the library in the meantime."

Daniel frowned. "Won't that be a problem for our investigation?"

"Only if we're not meeting at the Wave's Break anymore," Rigel said.

"Why wouldn't we?" Daniel asked.

"Rigel and I were thinking," Johanna said, "that we don't know if it's safe to meet there anyway. It's a rather public venue, and it's possible that if they're after *you*, they could be onto the rest of us."

"I don't see what the big deal is," Rigel said. "It's not like they know anything about our involvement. Daniel was the target. Perhaps they're specifically after Baron Blau. He got attacked before."

Johanna leaned against one of the many trunks in the room. "That's a possibility, but I think a cautious solution is better for the safety of all of us."

Daniel looked back and forth at his two friends as he weighed the options of each of their positions. He knew it would fall to him to cast the tiebreaker vote in this arrangement. They'd obviously discussed all this ahead of time and reached an impasse.

While he may have been the target, Lukka had still been put in danger—but the investigation had been the whole reason he came to this school in the first place. "I do think safety is important, but I think we can be safe and continue the investigation too. Let's lay low for a month or two, and in that time we will each make an attempt to decipher the scarf. There are six possible color combinations that make up the image, so if we each take two and attempt to make sense of them in our own time, we can reach a conclusion. All the while, our assailant will believe us scared straight. How about it?"

"I mean, it *is* an idea," Rigel said with resigned acceptance.

Johanna smirked at the prince. "You're just jealous you didn't think of it."

Daniel ignored his friends. "In two months' time, it will be back to normal."

"Yeah, I suppose it will, but don't you think it might be easier for them to pick us off if we're apart?" Rigel asked. "If they were bold enough to attempt an attack on Daniel, then who's to say they won't go after Johanna or me? Assuming what you suggest is true, of course, and they are on to all three of us."

"We can't know for certain, but let's be careful just in case," Daniel said.

"If you say so," Rigel said.

Chapter 24

Daniel waited in his room and worked in feverish fury with his needles. He was unable to be gentle, however, and left loops of yarn too tight to get his needles through. Frustrated, he finally set the project down. The knitting wasn't a message or code—just an attempt to keep his mind off of his precarious position.

A dinner of coronation chicken sandwiches, black tea, and some sort of sliced potatoes the others called chips was brought around to his room. He sighed. After months of following the routine, doing well at being an alter ego and making friends, it might all be brought to an end too soon. He was no closer to Avo, and enemies waited around every corner unknown to him and his friends.

He thought about Rigel's drawing and wondered about the cloaked figures. How had they gotten through to the airfield? Were they students? This was doubtful, as the only class members out there had been Diamond Blue and most of them had been in the air. Teachers? Possible, but if Professor Thompson had known something was wrong with the plane, wouldn't he have stopped Lukka from getting into it? Strangers to the campus wouldn't be able to get past the guards, so that ruled them out.

A glimmer rose in Daniel's mind. What if the people tending to the airfield were part of the Twilight Parliament? That would make sense. They would have access to the planes, could operate without the watchful eye of teachers or the crown, and might have facilities for secret meetings entirely separate from the campus. What made no sense was why they would want Lukka dead, yet they may have determined from callsigns which student would get in what plane. Unless they had made a mistake and sabotaged a plane on the wrong side of the airfield. He shivered—in that case, as Johanna said, the plane they had wanted to go down was his. He shook his head, trying to clear his mind. None of this would matter in a few hours, and yet he couldn't stop trying to make sense of it all.

Around eight o'clock, a guard returned to Daniel's room. "Baron Blau has requested your presence in the headmaster's office," he said.

This outcome was worse than Daniel had anticipated. He wasn't ready to be scolded by both of them at the same time. He had expected to get a lecture from the baron on the plane back home.

He crossed the green, entered the central spire, and ascended through the elevator. After a slow walk down the hallway, he arrived at the headmaster's office. Natalie sat in a chair by the door, alongside Parker, who kept his eyes on his pocket watch. The young woman ran to Daniel and threw her arms around him.

"I heard your plane collided with another plane," she said. "Are you okay?"

"I'm fine, just shaken," Daniel said. He was surprised at the reception. He hadn't expected the baron to bring the retinue for a parent-teacher meeting.

"Oh, bless you, dear. Are you eating well? Have you eaten yet?"

"I ate dinner a few hours ago."

Natalie frowned. "By the Four, it's not right for them to treat you like a prisoner here."

"It's nothing, really. Is the baron here?"

"Yes, he's in the office waiting for you."

"Is he angry?"

"Well, you know the baron," she said.

Daniel interpreted this to mean that he would likely be scolded for endangering the mission. Which meant he was in for two lectures—one each for Daniel and Duun. He straightened himself up in a nearby mirror and checked to make sure the white strands of his hair weren't showing, and then stepped forward into the office.

Baron Blau sat in a chair. He seemed at ease—his fingers steepled before him and his elbows planted on the armrests.

"Hello, son, how are classes going?"

"Good…well…they are well," said Daniel.

Was Baron Blau always so casual before roasting people who displeased him? Daniel remembered the soldiers who had come with word of Avo's disappearance and crimes. The baron had torn them asunder with his cutting sarcasm.

There was tension in the atmosphere, but it didn't appear to be directed toward him. "Have a seat. We won't be long. I had a discussion with the headmaster here, and she told me a bit about the situation. Did you know your flight was being filmed?"

"Filmed?" Daniel asked. "Like a movie?"

"That's right. The headmaster showed me the video of your flight. Would you care to watch it? You'll find something you may not have noticed from the cockpit."

Daniel remained standing. "I guess."

Baron Blau pointed to a chair and nodded at the soldier by the projector. The soldier turned off the lights in the office and shone the film on a screen on the opposite wall. In flickering black and white, Daniel saw Lukka's plane smoking and sailing downward toward the central spire. In a split second so quick that it could easily be missed, Daniel's plane jumped into frame and struck Lukka's plane from below, causing it to turn and clear the tower with inches to spare. The film then ended.

"First of all," said the baron, "that was a gutsy move that nobody else would've made."

The headmaster frowned. "Because the odds were that it would almost certainly wouldn't have worked."

"Except…" drawled the baron, "it *did.* And by his action, my boy here managed to save your younger sister and, by default, you. A girl, I might add, who happens to match my rank. And you thank him by having him grounded and expelled?"

"I understand all of that," the headmaster said, leaning in.

The baron gazed at her. "So you're telling me the boy who saved the only family you have left, who prevented a disastrous accident that would've affected many nobles of note and your own life is being repaid by being expelled for taking a risk that paid off?"

"I respect your opinions, Baron Blau. However, we cannot tolerate such recklessness in our flight program."

"For Four's sake, it's a school! A school is a place of learning, and you can't teach someone if you expel them for doing something, dare I say, heroic—even if a bit reckless. If mechanical failure is a possibility, perhaps you shouldn't fly your students out over the ocean. Maybe you should have instructors up in the air with them. Maybe there should be instruction about maneuvers and formations for guiding a damaged plane back to a safe landing space." He paused, his expression more serious. "Don't make a scapegoat of Daniel for *your* mistakes."

"Well, it *was* a risk—we just couldn't take keeping him around," the headmaster answered. "After the last boy you sponsored, we didn't want a repeat."

Baron Blau abruptly stood at the mention of Avo. He spoke in a calm, but cold, voice. "How long have you been headmaster, Marley? Four months? Maybe you were a top-notch instructor, but by being an administrator you have stepped into the political arena of this nation. You should've thought of that before pawning your role of baroness off on your younger sister.

"Now, I could bring all of this before the crown and the House of Lords. A leader of a school who endangers kin, citizenry, and the crown—had Prinse Rigel been in the tower—who is in above her head in a role she's possessed for four months, alleged by a baron who has been a hero of this country for the past thirteen years…I'll let you take a minute to do the math and see the only way that would turn out."

It took fewer than ten seconds for the headmaster to respond. "Fine. Daniel will not be expelled and his grounding will be lifted." She smirked. "Is this to your liking, your lordship?"

"Yes, I believe it is. Now, if you will excuse us, I will take Daniel back to his dorm. Thank you for your time. Have a good rest of your evening."

Baron Blau opened the door and gestured for Daniel to walk through ahead of him. The boy felt confused and a bit dirty from being present at what had just taken place. While he still didn't regret the maneuver he'd pulled off, he did acknowledge that he had been in the wrong for turning off his radio and defying orders. However, watching the baron strongarm the headmaster into submission reminded Daniel of when he had been ordered to cheat. He wondered if he really knew the sort of man the baron was.

Once outside, the baron directed Natalie and Parker to take the elevator down. "Daniel and I will take the stairs. I'd like to know more about his first solo flight."

"Yes, sir. Of course, sir," Natalie answered. Both she and Parker quickly headed toward the elevator while Baron Blau opened the door to the stairs. When the door closed, Daniel turned to the baron. "Don't you think that was a bit excessive?"

Baron Blau descended in silence for a moment. "Maybe a little bit, but don't dwell on it. I'm fighting fire with fire. She took a hatchet to a situation that needed a suture. If you're aware of where you were at fault, then there's no need for such hostile disciplinary measures. There's nothing to learn from it."

"I suppose you're right," Daniel answered.

"It sounds like you're making all sorts of friends. Friends with Prinse Rigel and Minah Darlington's daughter?"

"Yes, that's correct."

"Good. Friends in high places are good to have. Avo still eludes us, and that's unfortunate. Did you learn anything new about our other investigation?"

"I did. Rather, a friend gave me a tip. The plane that crashed had been tampered with by the Twilight Parliament. Prinse Rigel saw two people in owl cloaks working on the plane, but we're still not sure how deep this whole thing goes. He kept his mouth shut until I ran into him outside the headmaster's office."

"Well, it sounds like you've made the Klown Prinse a powerful ally. I can respect that. Few have managed to achieve anything like that."

"Rigel's not just an ally—he's my friend."

"Those *aren't* mutually exclusive," Baron Blau replied. "Same reason I associate with Minah Darlington despite our many differences of taste and personality. She's a powerful industrialist who is making all the best breakthroughs in Tarrkavian engineering. Not to mention she's got the king in her pocket."

The baron paused. "That's the way of the elite, Daniel. As well as we treat each other, we expect to be treated well in return, because it is unity that makes us stronger."

"How do *you* benefit from me being here?" Daniel asked. The question sounded harsher than he intended.

"Well Daniel, if I'm being honest, being such a public hero often paralyzes my hands from doing what needs to be done. I can't hunt down mysterious organizations that threaten the kingdom or my own people in my spare time. *You,* however, can, and somebody with that sort of skill and opportunity is wasted living a whole life herding sheep."

The baron paused again. "You know the ways of the Knot Kovenant—everything is connected and everyone is intertwined with those around them. In nature, you see that spiders undo and rebuild their webs every night, changing the knots in their design. Each time they rebuild the web, they make it better. Think of this whole ordeal like that. Placing you here puts you somewhere more advantageous for you, for me, for the school, and the kingdom—if we're being honest. Do you think your little friends would be friends if you kept herding sheep?"

"I don't suppose so."

"Exactly. Now, I was able to help you this time, but I don't think I'm going to be able to manage it a second time. So, knowing what you know now and how the brass thinks at this school, try to stay out of trouble. Your little prince friend seems to have immunity to most trouble, so I'd consider relying on that more if I were you. Keep your hands clean and make the most of the pieces you have in the game. The tenets of the Knot Kovenant have been realized in a new way—in a reconstruction of the web."

The baron smiled. "Now, if that's all, I have to say that was a remarkable maneuver you pulled off…even if it *was* dangerous. It reminds me of my time back during the war. Those planes were held together with wood and steel cable. The way you spun the plane and swatted the baroness was like a sidewinder."

"A sidewinder? Like the snake?"

"Yeah, it's got a nice ring to it. You should make it your call sign."

"I'm Diamond Thirteen."

"Oh, that's just temporary. You get to pick your call sign for your placement."

When the two reached the bottom of the stairs, the whole of Diamond Blue had gathered except for Lukka, who was still in the infirmary.

"It really *is* Baron Blau!" Jensen said.

The crowd swarmed around, thrilled to see the war hero descend from the stairs like a divine god coming down to greet his people.

The baron's face broke into a wide smile. "Well, if it isn't the boys and girls of Diamond Blue. I used to fly for Diamond Blue. Have you met my son, Daniel Hardy? He's the Sidewinder of Diamond Blue. Turns out he's way more useful than all of you."

He glanced around the common room. "I'm ashamed to even call you Diamond Blues. Better pull your own weight, because when Buldwikk comes knocking, they won't care what your titles are. Daniel acted when none of you did, and that's what it takes to be a hero." He turned to Daniel and placed his hand on his shoulder. "Well, I've got business to attend to. I'd better see some major improvements before fall. It's past your bedtime, anyway."

Baron Blau stepped through the crowd and out the door, leaving the Diamond Blues staring at Daniel with what he could only think was hatred.

Chapter 25

After Lukka's crash, the students of Diamond Blue spent more time out of the classroom and in the cockpits. Daniel's ambidextrous handling of throttle and stick presented him with a significant edge over the other students and, in secret, the voices that had once mocked Lukka earnestly wished her a swift recovery so that she could put him "in his place."

After only a few days, the Baroness of Briars was upright and back in the classroom, but she still wore her splint and a few bandages along her brow. Even though she hadn't been back in the cockpit flying with her class, she still ran circles around Daniel in classroom studies.

However, although Johanna hadn't had as much time to dedicate to Daniel's tutoring, he made great strides toward improving his performance. He avoided Johanna and Rigel in the classroom, as their coursework became more focused on mechanics and tactics, but he still helped Johanna at the hangar to better familiarize himself with the Liberty's systems.

On days when Johanna wasn't at the hangar, Daniel assisted Rigel with his gardening—that was an enlightening experience too. In all the years that Duun had lived in nature, tending to the trees and gardens, he had only ever seen forestfolk work with plants. The poetry of movements and the gentle and encouraging praise Leleen gave all of her little flower babies was nothing like the fierce frustration displayed by the flamboyant prince.

Rigel struck his fists against the earth in a grand royal spectacle. "I've watered you. I've fertilized you. I've checked the pH in the soil. Why are you so wilty?"

Daniel smiled to himself and then pointed to the ground. "There's chickweed all over the flowerbed, Rigel. It's probably hogging all the nutrients from the marigolds."

"For Four's sake!" said Rigel, as he pulled a bunch of weeds from the ground. "Get out of the flowerbed, you little bottom feeders."

Daniel chuckled and changed the subject. "Have you figured anything out on the scarf code?"

"Yeah, I worked through it with the code you gave me, and all I got was gibberish. What about you?"

"Well, I'm not too confident in what I got."

"You got gibberish too, didn't you?"

"I *did* get gibberish."

"Bollocks, well, then that leaves Johanna. Surely she came up with something."

"She had some business up in the tower today. I can go catch her if you want."

"But the chickweed…" whined Rigel.

"Don't worry, chickweed comes out of the ground easily."

"But there's a lot of it and my hands are sore," Rigel said, his hands pitifully dangling in front of him.

"That's easy. Next time, don't bang your hands against the earth."

"I trusted you, Dan, my man," said Rigel.

"This matter is more important."

Rigel made a face. "What has the kingdom come to these days? Every man for himself. How is a prince supposed to rule a land of independent thinkers?"

"Make an example of the chickweed, and then maybe I'll consider it," Daniel said.

Rigel waved his hand majestically. "Yes, off with their heads!"

Daniel stepped into the central tower with his notes in tow. As he walked up the stairs, he heard a commotion in the hallway and the voices of girls from his class in a medley of mocking sneers. He stopped to listen.

"Shadow's light, how's a tall girl like you ever going to find a husband? I didn't know they let ostriches into this school."

"Oh, Edwina, she's got the Klown Prinse and the Sidewinder wrapped around her little finger. I'll bet they do whatever she says. Her mother practically runs the country."

Daniel rounded the corner toward the voices to see three of the girls standing in a circle around Johanna, who was on the floor with her papers and books strewn about. Her knees were reddened as though she had been tripped. One of them noticed him coming into view. "Oh, look, there's the Sidewinder now. Coming to JoJo's rescue?"

A fury swept over Daniel that he had never felt before. His hands clenched tight into fists, but he dared not raise them from his sides. "Back off, you three," he said.

"Look," said Edwina. "The Sidewinder's shaking." She turned to Daniel. "You should tell your girlfriend to watch her step. She nearly dropped those books on us, and if she had fallen on us, I might've died."

"The headmaster will find out about this," Daniel said.

"If you blab, Sidewinder, we'll say *you* attacked us. It's us three against you."

"Ugh," spoke a new voice, "Is *everyone* at this school a liar and a fiend?"

Daniel turned in the direction the sound had come from. Lukka blew past him and placed herself between Johanna and her three attackers. She still wore her splint, but she assumed a stance with evenly grounded feet as though she stood before a hurricane. In her free hand, she held a nightstick. "You come near Johanna again, and I'll put you three little hens in neck braces. You hear me?"

Edwina raised her eyebrows in mockery. "Well, isn't this fun? Is the Klown Prinse going to crawl out of a little car any second now?"

Lukka cocked her head. "You think I can't introduce you to a world of pain just because my arm's in a splint?"

"How are you planning on swinging that thing with one arm? If the authorities hear that you hit us with that stick, then you're sure to be out of this school."

"Who said I was going to *hit* you with it?" Lukka asked.

"There must be some reason you carry it around like a dung beetle guarding its heap."

"There is, actually," said Lukka, "and if you don't take your little powdered noses and teach them to mind their own business, you'll be intimately acquainted with the bat's purpose."

"Well, little Miss Baroness, I would've thought your parents would've shown you where to keep your nose, but I guess they're too busy pushing up daisies to raise a proper daughter."

Lukka bit her lip and took a long, drawn out breath. "Here's why I carry the baton." She chucked the stick overhead and gave a swift kick, her foot disappearing into Edwina's abdomen. Then, just as swiftly, she withdrew her foot and planted it back on the ground. Lukka reached up and caught the bat as it fell. "I use it to measure out how fast I can kick your clueless ass."

Edwina moved her mouth as if to respond and then suddenly wretched in pain and dropped to her knees. Placing her hands on the ground in front of her, she hurled the day's meals in a grotesque and humiliating display. The other two with Edwina dared not go near her for fear of getting their hands dirty or facing the swift rage of the baroness. They bolted away down the hall and Edwina climbed to her feet to stagger after them.

As they disappeared, Lukka called out behind them. "Lay a hand on her again, and I'll make it come out the other end. Are we clear?"

"Hey, what's going on out here?"

Around the corner came the flowing shape of Dr. Violite. "Why did three girls go running away, one of them covered in sick?"

"I did it," Lukka said, honest even in the face of certain judgment.

"Heh, nice. Did you also say the part about it coming out the other end? I mean, not to get too graphic, but my sleep medication ties my insides in wads and, if you offer that sort of relief, I could make it worth your while."

"That's all right, I'll pass," Lukka said, unable to hide her disgust.

"Give it some thought?" Violite asked.

"I already have."

"Ok, sure, sure, just wait until you're older. Then you'll understand."

Lukka jerked her head toward Daniel. "Do you have anything useful to contribute here? If not, I suggest you get Johanna back to her dorm."

"Right, sure," he said, scrambling to help Johanna rescue her papers.

He walked with Johanna as far as he could to the dorm tower. At the door, he cleared his throat. "Johanna," he said, "I wouldn't be at this school if it wasn't for you. You were my first friend and you're a great friend."

"Do you think I'm too tall?" Johanna asked.

Daniel thought about it. "You *are* tall, but not *too* tall. That's just who you are. You are my friend. Edwina and the others are not. Also, if they're only going to be cruel to people, who cares what they think?"

Johanna passed Daniel the crumpled heap of her notes. "I couldn't make sense of the scarf. I tried. I swear I did."

"We all did, and none of us could get it," Daniel said. "Maybe if we put all the attempts together, we can figure something out. How's that sound?"

Johanna wordlessly reached into the pile and pulled out the cipher. Daniel looked it over and gave a puzzled expression when she suddenly blinked away her tears. She snatched the paper back from Daniel and stared hard at the back.

"What if the colors don't strictly follow the pattern given to you? Like 'A' could be Blue-Blue instead of White-White. It will be more work for us, but we could be able to find a message if the colors are related to different letters than the one on this code."

Daniel thought about what she'd said and something stirred in his head. "So, in other words, a person who knew the system might not be able to find the answer using the established patterns."

He broke into a grin. "Johanna, that's brilliant." He grabbed her arm and pulled her back toward the front of the tower. "Let's get Rigel and go to the gardener's shed. We'll crack this code yet."

Chapter 26

Inside the gardener's shed, Rigel and Daniel sat across from Johanna. Each looked through the color patterns in the scarf, trying to identify them. Even though none at first had anything to say, a spirit of relief rested over the space as the friends had finally been reunited. Rigel looked up, perplexed. "The colors of the code don't correspond to what we have."

Johanna shook her head. "I'm afraid not. Whoever put this scarf together did so with the anticipation of somebody knowing the system but looking for a different color combination." She looked to Daniel. "Did you say Baron Blau taught you the code?"

"That is correct," Daniel said. Up until now, he had secretly wondered if the person in the film reel had been Avo, but there was no guarantee that Avo had been tasked with doing the same work Baron Blau had assigned to him. In any case, Daniel reasoned that the colors had been altered by Baron Blau to avoid anyone familiar with the system from making any determinations.

"There are a few different ways the code could be altered to be hidden from people who recognize the system," continued Johanna. "Perhaps all the colors were shifted to the next one over. In this case, A could change from white-white to blue-blue or red-red. Another possibility is that one color was shifted in one direction and others in another. In that case, A could be red-blue, or red-yellow or any variation of the five colors."

Rigel groaned. "So what you're saying is this is going to be a lot more work than we thought?"

"It doesn't have to be. This recording was made *for* somebody. If I were to guess, I would say it was for somebody on Mom's payroll."

"What if the person is working for your mother herself?"

"Again, it's doubtful. She hates blood," Johanna said.

Daniel thought for a moment. "Maybe it was just interspersed with the B-roll footage for the movie. If that were true, we could assume it was somebody making this Emerald Dragonfly movie. Is that right?"

"It's a safe bet," Johanna said.

Rigel perked up. "Could you ask your mother for a list of everyone working on this film?"

"She's going to want to know why," Johanna said. "And she'll flip if she finds out I'm looking for a terrorist organization."

"She would?" Rigel asked.

"Never mind the devil-may-care airs she puts on in public. She's a bit overprotective in the face of certain dangers against me."

"I would've never guessed that," Rigel said.

"Well, a rather specific circumstance caused it," Johanna said as she gripped her right shoulder. "I had an accident a few years ago that nearly killed me and left me with a dreadful scar."

"Can we see it?" Rigel asked.

"No, it's hideous," Johanna said.

"C'mon, you can trust us," Rigel said.

"It's not really somewhere I can comfortably share with others," Johanna said.

"Now I *really* want to see it," Rigel said. "Daniel, back me up here."

Daniel ignored the prince's banter. "Where could we see who would work on this film?"

"Well," Johanna said, "over the break between terms, a premiere will be held in the capital. I could get us seats for the showing. How's that sound?"

"That's still quite a ways off," Daniel said.

"Well, we've waited already for quite a while to get this far. What's a little while longer?" Rigel said.

Daniel frowned. "Knot Kovenant people are being put in chains and taken on boats to somewhere. More people could be hurt in the meantime."

"Oh…right…your Knot friends," Rigel said. "Hmmm, well, there's a good chance whoever made this code didn't just pull it out of nowhere.

As long as written language and textiles have existed, I'm sure this code could've been employed for any length of time. So how about that Dr. Auberdine? I bet if you presented something related to the code without its actually *being* the code that he could offer some pointers."

"Can't we all go together?" Daniel asked. "Wasn't it your idea to stick together as a group?"

"Oh, I would, but y'know, gardening. Johanna could still tag along."

"If we do," Johanna said, "then I think we need to consider bringing in someone else to help us out. If there's trouble, I'm not much of one for fighting and Daniel can't exactly get into a plane to settle the score."

Rigel clenched his hands into fists and waved them around. "C'mon, Daniel, don't you know how to put 'em up?"

"Conflict isn't really in my nature," Daniel said.

"Ugh," said Rigel, "you two are the worst freedom fighters ever."

"Do you fight, Your Highness?" Johanna asked.

"Uh, I'm royalty. In chess, the king doesn't do any fighting. It sorta just sits back and covers its ass."

"So, you're equally useless," Johanna said.

"Uh, rude," Rigel said. "So, who *is* this mysterious warrior you're thinking about bringing in? And it best not be Lukka."

"It *is* Lukka," Daniel and Johanna said in unison.

"Isn't she like super injured right now?" Rigel asked.

Johanna and Daniel looked to each other with expressions of uncertainty. How could they even describe what they had seen with Edwina? There was a chance what she'd done was magic of its own, and since there were no official schools of magic in Tarrkaven, that would raise questions of where she had learned it and whether it should be shared with a royal as graceless in his handling of secrets as Rigel was. The two had a silent conversation with their eyes.

Rigel cradled his head on his hands. He was not about to be excluded from this exchange. "I'm right, aren't I?" said Rigel, with a smug smile.

"Yes, you're right," said Johanna, "she's injured. She's probably busy preparing for the flight exam anyway." Her eyes told Daniel to ask Lukka anyway.

"Didn't you catch the part where I said she was injured?" Rigel asked.

"I don't think she's going to let that stop her. Flying means the world to her. There's a reason she's called the Baroness of Briars," Johanna said.

"I assumed it was because of her winning personality."

"No, she flies as a rear gunner in defense of her island home. Occasionally, there are pirates and raiders who try to pick fights with ships along the southern coast. She accompanies her pilots into battle. She got the name because of the riddled holes in the planes of those who've made the mistake of tangling with her. She's a deadly gunner, maybe the deadliest."

"I'm going to be testing against that?" Daniel asked.

Rigel grinned. "Anywhoodle, sounds like Daniel's got another challenge on his hands. So, Danny boy, can you brave the briars?"

"Ugh..."

"Good man, your service to king and country is regarded and appreciated," said Rigel. "May the Sion guide you or the Shadow welcome you to her warm embrace." He turned to Johanna. "Let's get some seats to that premiere and see what we can't figure out about this Emerald Dragonfly."

"I have a question," Daniel asked. "Why do they call the Emerald Dragonfly emerald that if there's no color in the movie?"

"The Emerald Dragonfly comes from the wetlands west of the capital. It's not exactly easy to land a plane there, but apparently the Dragonfly can do it."

"So he himself isn't green?"

"Doesn't show business fly in the face of the church of the lime?" Rigel asked. Then he remembered who he was talking to and that Daniel got strangely touchy when the subject came up. "Wait. My bad. I meant the Knot Kovenant."

"I don't know about that," Johanna said. "I don't think he's a forestfolk if that's what you're asking. I don't know him, though—those films really aren't my favorite. So predictable, so formulaic."

It would be ridiculous for Avo to be a movie star, thought Daniel. If he was hiding and trying to prove he wasn't a terrorist, then the silver screen was no place to stay hidden. "Well, then, I guess we've got our work cut out for us," Daniel said.

"At least you and I do," Johanna said, cutting her eyes toward Rigel.

"Rude, Johanna," Rigel said, "but I'll tell you what. When I wear my gardening stuff, I'm basically invisible. I'll keep an eye out for whoever our secret Twilight Parliament goons are. How's that sound?" Before Johanna could respond, Rigel added, "I'm not going to get involved if I see anything. I'm just going to watch."

"Well, I guess that's better than nothing," Johanna said.

"Johanna bringing the burn. I don't know where this is coming from, but two can play at this game."

Daniel noticed that Johanna didn't seem anywhere near as shy when she bantered with Rigel. It was a nice change of pace to see this from the girl who tried to hide away from the view of all around her.

Rigel seemed to bring that out of people. Even if he was a bit insensitive, he rolled with punches well and took as well as he dished. In some small part, Daniel was happy to have this camaraderie again.

Rigel picked up his gardening trough, left the shed, and resumed his scourge of the chickweeds. Daniel turned to Johanna. "Where can I find Lukka this time of day?"

"I think she goes to the chapel a lot. You should try checking that out first. Are you religious, or do you take after your father?"

You have no idea, Daniel thought.

Chapter 27

On the campus of Skyskape is a chapel built to the Four Divines. Whether in the mightiest of cathedrals or an icon hanging on the wall of a grandmother's cottage, certain features exist across all the celebrations of the faith.

Dominating the view from the doorway into the chapel is the great rhombus, which overlooks a vestibule divided into the images of the gods. The Father and the Mother, the keepers of wisdom and passion, respectively, stand in the sides of the images. The Father stands upon the solid earth, a testament to the firm foundation of law and governance over the people of the world. The Mother pilots a vessel at sea, navigating to the bountiful fortunes that await all who would take the leap into the turbulence of the waves. Above is the one the parents hold most in reverence—the Sion.

Though depictions vary—and are inconclusive as to whether the Sion is a son or daughter—the faithful know they all exist to represent the spirit of invention and curiosity, to light the skies above and bring inspiration to mankind. They stand in the light of the sun and shine down upon the world with radiant splendor. The Sion is the gift of the divine Mother and Father to all of humanity. But, in the light of the Sion, there exists his counterpart, the Shadow.

Some mistake the Shadow to be a bogeyman who deals only in death and darkness. While the Shadow *does* govern death and the dark, she is not a being of malevolence. She is the master of secrets and of that which has yet to be revealed. There can be no wisdom, no passion, no curiosity without uncertainty. One cannot make a decision—no matter how inspired or driven—without the uncertainty that it may not come to be. If everything is understood, curiosity has no object. Thus, while often the most overlooked of the Four, the Shadow moves on her own—as wind through the barren branches at the bottom of a desolate canyon. She remains unseen and unknown, but her presence is never wholly forgotten.

The interpretations of the omnipotent and omnipresent powers that govern all the kingdoms of the world may vary among the different sects and faiths. However, there are few kingdoms that cannot trace their roots back to the ecclesiocracy, a continental government that exists largely for ceremony in the present era, but once served as a unified yet decentralized government for the continent.

The buildings that served the Four had the same general layout—a brazier of fire at the front, a pulpit at the left, a pot of offerings at the right, and a confessional at the back.

In all of Daniel's time at the academy, he had had no cause to come to this chapel. While the Knot Kovenant didn't deny the existence of the Four, it did *not* adhere to the creed that the Four were omnipresent or omnipotent. Omnipotence implied the Four could exist without relying on any other life—and omnipresence suggested the presence of the Four appeared more directly in the world than the Faith characterized it. When he entered the chapel, Daniel wasn't sure whether he was being watched by either a divine presence or whatever clergy was present, but he knew that the baron maintained no such chapel at the mansion.

On the pews within, a few students of varying years and estates gathered here and there, but what stood out to Daniel first and foremost was Lukka's familiar shoulder-length black hair and blue initiate scarf. Although he found himself alone on this mission, he admitted it wouldn't be so bad. He was only going to talk to the girl who carried a blackjack everywhere she went, could reach through people and make them vomit, and suspected that he was keeping secrets.

Lukka sat in the back silently scanning the backs of the heads of everyone else within the chapel. Daniel rounded the pew where she was sitting and approached to see the nightstick sitting by her side. Rigel would've been the authority on the topic, but Daniel was pretty sure there was a rule that said she couldn't bring a weapon into the chapel. Regardless, he would take his chances and, if need be, his lumps.

As Daniel seated himself, he was met with Lukka's steely dark irises, cast from the corners of her eyes. She didn't reach for the stick, and he felt her lack of action in this regard was as warm an invitation as he was going to get.

He turned toward the front but was unsure where to direct his attention. Was he supposed to stare at the rhombus overlooking the chamber or the burning fire? Was he was supposed to look at the vicar speaking from the pulpit at the side of the room? Since everyone's attention seemed to be fixated on the fire, he decided that was the appropriate thing to do.

The fire itself was hidden behind the silhouettes of other students, but as the smoke rose as a thick white cloud it disappeared so as not to hide the Father, the Mother, and Sion. Did it wholly disappear? Or did it dissipate across the chamber? Daniel couldn't say.

The vicar spoke in a language unfamiliar to Daniel. He wasn't sure if it was expected that people know this language or not, so he decided the best course of action was not to comment. The only downside was that he wouldn't know when the service ended, so he sat and waited with Lukka.

At some point, about fifteen minutes after Daniel had joined Lukka, the vicar switched from this unknown tongue to more familiar speech. "Now let us stand for the blessing of the Four."

As if by instinct, Daniel stood at attention in an instant. From the back of the chapel, it became immediately apparent nobody else had done so. Daniel felt a small hand loop around the bend of his left arm. With a gentle tug, Lukka pulled Daniel back down to his seat. The vicar continued. "Turn in the psalm book to the two hundred-eightieth page."

Lukka reached for the book that rested in the back of the pew and deftly flipped to the appropriate page. Then she stood, signaling to Daniel to join her, and held the book between them. Daniel saw lyrics written beneath some musical notation. His only real experience with music had come from Natalie's violin playing, most of which she played from the heart.

Daniel had only just begun to get a handle on words and didn't know what any of the markings meant. Determined not to let anyone down, however, he decided to raise his volume when the notes went up and quiet his voice when the notes went down. As he took his first impassioned deep breath, Lukka snapped the book closed.

The harpist beneath the pulpit began playing a soft melody of high notes that descended into a sleepy tune of soft spiritual music. The other students sang a tune from the psalms. Lukka sang along by memory. Recognizing the folly from which he'd been saved, Daniel stood in silence and listened intently to the tune, the lyrics for which were now back in the unintelligible language.

Daniel waited in patience for the song to end, doing nothing until he was positive there was no other way he could make a mistake. When he perceived they had reached an ending point, everyone sang again a second, third, and final fourth verse before the song actually came to a close. Then, when the song was finally over, he felt the gentle tug of Lukka on his arm and seated himself. The vicar said a few more words and then everyone stood up again and dispersed.

Lukka turned to Daniel. "What do you want?" Her words carried some bite.

"Have your wounds healed?" Daniel asked.

"Well enough. Are you suddenly discovering the need for religion or is there something else on your mind?"

"Uh, I'll get back to you on that. We need your protection with the bat or whatever else that is."

"From the bullies or the Twilight Parliament? Either way you can count me out. I don't have time for children or childish games."

"You keep saying that like you're not fifteen yourself."

"I *am* fifteen, but I haven't been a kid since I was nine."

"That's kinda sad."

"The world's a sad place. You can cry about it, or you can deal with it."

"Is that what they teach you here when they speak the gibberish?" Daniel asked. He considered that it might not have been a good idea to say that while he was still in the chapel, but when he didn't spontaneously combust, he rolled with it.

"I believe The Four govern all things. Everything that happens happens for a reason," Lukka said.

"So the world's sad because it has to be?" Daniel asked. This was not how he had intended this exchange to play out, but still, if it meant he could somehow turn it around to win her allegiance, he would bound forward into the furnace.

"The Shadow doesn't reveal why, but yes, there is a purpose to sorrow."

"What is *your* purpose then? Why are you here if all you do is cast shade upon everyone and everything that crosses your path? Is it because your sister is here?"

"She's no sister to me," Lukka said.

"Really? You two seem cut from the same cloth."

"Yeah? Maybe we were, but she chose to run away and be a teacher."

"I fail to see how that matters. What's wrong with wanting a career?"

"We needed a baroness, an administrator of our home, a watchful guardian. She chose to be none of those things. She just passed them off onto me, and I've had to pick up the pieces since."

"Then what do *you* want? Why are you actually here?"

"I don't have to tell you," Lukka said.

"You're just going to keep hiding?"

"You're the one who's hiding," Lukka said. "I can tell there's something you haven't even told the others. Something you're ashamed to admit. Why are your hands tanned and calloused like a stableboy's? Why don't you know a thing about the faith of the Four? Why do you meet with those two to discuss this whole conspiracy thing that you won't entrust to the authorities if it is serious business and not a children's game?"

"Would *you* trust the authorities?"

"On my island, I *am* the authority, and I'd rather handle it than rope two other so-called friends into this crusade of yours without telling them whatever it is you're not telling them. Start with that, and maybe, just maybe, I'll indulge in curiosity into whatever little game you're going on about."

"It's not a game. In that B-roll footage, we saw that the Twilight Parliament is kidnapping forestfolk and that the Emerald Dragonfly is fighting a one-man war against them. He stabbed one of their soldiers on a boat. Johanna said that her mother would never put a scene like that in the film because she passes out at the sight of blood."

"You can confirm that?"

"It's been the only clue we've had for months. That and the scarf the Emerald Dragonfly wore in the shot. I think it's a code."

"Pentakromatic," Lukka answered.

"Who…what now?"

"It's a system of communication used by monks of the Way of the Empty Fist. They use it to identify their own while disguised. The Emerald Dragonfly studied under them. You call yourself a fan and you don't know that?"

"I knew it was a code, but I didn't know all of that. Its five colors are white, red, yellow, blue, and green, right?"

"Depends on the dojo. The Emerald Dragonfly didn't go to the Righteous Karp school."

"That's not a real thing," Daniel said.

"And yet you know their colors? You're just a mountain of secrets, aren't you?"

"What if I am?" Daniel said. He knew he had passed the point of no return. Lukka would, without a doubt, suspect something. It was a gamble, but perhaps that's what he had needed to do from the start. "It doesn't change the fact that they tried to kill me.

A quizzical expression appeared in Lukka's eyes. "What do you mean by that?"

"You and I unknowingly swapped our planes at the last second," said Daniel. "Rigel found the roster for who was supposed to fly each plane. You were in the air before anything could be done."

"So, either somebody wanted me dead or somebody wanted you alive and didn't mind me getting killed," Lukka said, her words fading as she finished the sentence.

"Hey," Daniel said. "It doesn't matter. You are alive. One way or another you have a shot at finding whoever's responsible for this and dragging them out into the light. Twilight Parliament or otherwise. Isn't that cause enough to fight back?" Daniel's voice softened. "These guys are real killers.

They may be students or faculty or anyone. Johanna trusts you, and we've got a plan to find out more information, but it will be very dangerous unless we have you backing us up."

"What am I going to be doing?"

"Johanna and I saw you fight or whatever that business was back in the hall. I suspect you can do more than make people lose their lunch. That may be helpful if we get cornered. Up until now, we've had to play it safe because none of us can really fight."

"Not at all?" Lukka asked.

"I mean, I'm not bad with a staff, but violence isn't really in my nature."

"Are you serious? Why are you in the fighter program then?"

"That's another secret," Daniel said.

"Forget a mountain of secrets. You live in a *kingdom* of secrets."

"You have no idea."

Lukka turned this over in her mind and slid her hand down Daniel's arm to his wrist. "I'll do it under one condition."

"What's that?"

"At the end of this week, we've got our target practice exam. If you score higher than me, then I'll come back and join your little gang of heroes. If I score higher than you, then you're going to tell me all your secrets."

Daniel was silent for a moment. He had told a lot of lies, and if anyone found out it could doom everything he had worked toward at this point. Of course, he could just lie to her again when he claimed to be telling the truth. Although, if she knew he was lying to begin with, he was sure she'd figure it out again. He would have to risk it all.

"All right, it's a deal."

"Then may the best pilot win."

Chapter 28

In the toolshed after class, Daniel told Rigel and Johanna about his agreement with Lukka, but omitted the part about what would happen if he lost. Rigel patted his hands on the gardener's workbench and let out a deep breath, while Johanna fidgeted with her notes. Daniel shot a glance first at one and then the other.

"Hey, what's that supposed to mean?"

"Uh, we didn't say anything," Rigel said.

"Seems like you two are saying a whole lot for not saying anything."

"Well, I mean, she's a natural-born fighter. Don't take this the wrong way, but she's got years more experience than you," Johanna said.

"Are you ready to face the briars, Daniel?" Rigel made a menacing gesture with his hands in Daniel's direction.

A thought about Bigby getting stuck in the occasional patch of thorns flashed into his mind. He thought his fluffy friend should count his lucky stars that he didn't meet the fate that thorns could apparently do in this kingdom. "Okay, so she shoots a lot," he said.

"*And* she shoots accurately," Johanna added.

"That shouldn't be a problem. I can fly really well."

"Unless you've shot machine guns at some point with Baron Blau, I think you'll find you're in for a surprise," Johanna said.

"You've got to hit the target with the guns before you hit it with the plane. And the guns aren't under the crosshairs," said Rigel. "They're on the wings."

"I think I should be able to manage that."

"Have you ever fired a gun ever? At all?" Rigel asked.

"Well, no," said Daniel, "but I can control a plane, and a gun only fires in one direction, so how hard can it be?"

***

"All right, Diamond Blue, a heads up. We've got some strong winds over the practice field. The target balloons will be a little all over the place today. So, to risk any serious danger of planes colliding with each other, we've determined the best course of action is to send up two closest-ranked students at a time to compete against one another."

Jensen raised his hand. "Professor Thompson, will this affect the rankings among students?"

"Well, if you were slacking off until now, then you've got no one to blame but yourself. Coincidentally, you'll be going up first, Jensen. You'll be up against the best Krossbone Brown has to offer. That's what happens when you are at the bottom of a group of odd numbers. Then we will work our way upward two by two until we end with our two top contenders: Lukka Strauss and Daniel Hardy. Since they'll be going last and will have the most time to prepare, we have an extra special challenge for them to contend with."

"Why do *they* get preferential treatment?" asked one of Jensen's cronies.

"Because they can handle it. Any more stupid questions?"

Somebody yelled from the back of Jensen's squad. "Is the world flat?" When silence descended over the class, the same person said, "What? He offered."

"Well, Jensen, you let that rank ahead of you," Professor Thompson continued. "Let's go over the ground rules. No firing upon your opponent in the air. It does no one any good if you shoot down your own wingmen. If you hit a balloon with your plane, you're disqualified. Daniel here was incredibly lucky last time, but that was a one-in-a-million maneuver. It won't work in the future. Lastly, and perhaps most obviously, whoever hits the most targets wins against their opponent."

When Professor Thompson mentioned the collision. Daniel could swear he heard a click in Lukka's throat and he saw her shift her footing. He had no intention of crashing his plane into anything else. He remembered Baron Blau's warning. He would be on his own if he did it again.

Professor Thompson continued. "There is one more matter. In the past, you had fellow students manning the tower. We have chosen staff to handle the role this time. We will also have upperclassmen from different estates observing from various spots across the field to communicate with the control tower and report the scores." He paused. "Does anyone have any further questions?"

Lukka raised her hand. "Will we have access to the wire-guided rockets for this exercise?"

"Excellent question," Professor Thompson said. "You will have two. I would recommend not relying on them too heavily, but it's best you get used to employing them. Use them wisely, and you will be fine. Anything else?" Nobody had anything else to ask and so with that, Jensen went to take the first plane up into the air against the Krossbone Brown student.

Daniel knew little about the students of Krossbone Brown. He remembered from Avo that the best in their class had a chance to fly outside of the bomber as a sort of vanguard, but he had no way of knowing how they compared to Diamond Blue fighters. The difference in ability between the two proved staggering as the student who had fought to the top of Krossbone Brown greatly outperformed Jensen.

Daniel couldn't help but notice how the two pilots differed in their use of ammunition. Jensen would take long pulls of the trigger to catch balloons. While he initially cut down many more balloons than his opponent, he also ran out of ammunition faster. His opponent had been far more conservative on the trigger and aimed to line up the shots before rupturing the balloons. Once Jensen was out of ammunition, he attempted to rely upon the rocket to try and take out the balloons in tight groups. Relying too heavily on the controllable nature of the weapons, he fired the first rocket at a crowd of three balloons and, not recognizing the force of the wind, made the rockets turn too fast and detonate far from the cluster. The display of the explosion was quite impressive from the ground.

However, even with the curved shot, they achieved a range far removed from the plane itself. It appeared Jensen had forgotten to manually detach the wire after the explosion, and so they hung below the plane, producing greater drag that slowed his plane down.

Daniel saw Lukka's gloved hands counting the number of seconds between the launch, the detachment, and the detonation. When the first round was over, the student from Krossbone Brown touched down and was hailed the winner.

As the pilots landed, the next duo went up into the air and flew over the practice field. Weather balloons took to the sky and the next round began. The planes varied in color for the crews on the ground to identify who was whom. Boards were updated on the ground to calculate the scores of each person as reported through radio at the tent where the classes waited.

Over and over, groups went up, took the exam, and then came down. As the rounds went on, each group became more cautious in their uses of the rockets and relied more heavily upon the cannon fire to make short work of the balloons. The differences in scores between competitors became more and more narrow.

At last, it was Lukka's and Daniel's turn. Getting into the planes and rising into the air, the duo prepared to try and outmatch each other in the blue field above. As soon as the planes left the runway behind, the balloons began to rise as they strafed from equal distances. Lukka immediately dropped her plane down to catch the first balloons rising up from the ground. Daniel had feared this would be her strategy. As he had learned in the classroom, targets were easiest to hit when they were getting off the ground. Whoever made contact with their opponent first was sure to claim victory.

Daniel had predicted that Lukka would not be able to shake the fear of nearly crashing before, but over this wide-open field, all fears of a collision or engine failure had gone away. He would need to take that same daring attitude to keep up.

Of the forty balloons, Lukka had already taken five to Daniel's two. The balloons moved both apart and together from where they launched in the harsh and turbulent wind currents. Daniel felt the strong gusts pushing and shaking his wings from underneath, but he held the stick firm and kept his interceptions tight against the balloons. He tried his best to focus on the targets and not his opponent, but he couldn't help but see how

Lukka fought whenever she passed into view. Her barrages lasted longer than Daniel's did. She would run out of ammunition sooner than he would. However, she did puncture more balloons per barrage.

At fifteen minutes, Lukka had broken ten balloons to Daniel's eight.

A new cluster of balloons rose together and Daniel moved in to attack them. Lukka thundered above him at a higher speed. Daniel counted on this and launched his rocket. At the angle he flew, the rocket shot toward the ground, but then using the smaller stick on top his flight stick which he placed his right hand upon leaving the throttle unattended, he caused the rocket to twist back upward and strike the cluster of balloons before Lukka could reach them.

When the explosion cleared, Daniel looked up through the canopy to see that it hadn't been as direct a hit as he'd hoped. Two balloons from the group remained. By the time he turned his plane skyward, Lukka had cleaned up the other two. But, he had managed to close the gap with his maneuver as the duo fought neck and neck. Lukka 12, Daniel 11.

The next round of four balloons rose out over the coastline from below a cliff. Lukka spun her plane around and began to drop toward the ground hard and fast. Daniel followed suit, cursing himself for not seeing the balloons before her. However, he recognized her trajectory would have had her slamming into the cliffside before she pulled up to reach the balloons.

He started to lean toward two other balloons rising toward the sky but his concern couldn't stop him from glancing back in Lukka's direction. She stormed toward the cliff and just before she made contact, she fired off a rocket and blasted away the stones from the ground. In a huge, heated puff of debris, the heat created an updraft that pushed her upward and let her take all four balloons in a sweeping storm of bullets.

Daniel wondered whether she wanted to be the best or whether she was determined to learn his secrets. Either way, she seemed willing to risk anything for the goal. When he claimed his balloons, the gap in the number of balloons burst had widened to three.

"Lukka, do keep in mind there are students launching those balloons. I think a few of our upperclassmen will need a change of pants after that maneuver," Professor Thompson said through the radio.

Lukka's maneuver had allowed her to pull ahead for the moment, but it put her far on the edges of the range of the operation. As the next five balloons rose, Daniel managed to shoot down four before one of them got carried away in the wind, and pulled ahead of her. Daniel 17, Lukka 16. Lukka caught up to the last one and shot it to pieces, but even against the single balloon, she still held the cannons a little too long.

Daniel could only wonder what went through Lukka's mind in the cockpit of a Liberty. Did she keep that same cool composure in the air she had when she sat in class or in the chapel or at the cafeteria? The way she curved and dove through the air was like the wild coils of large brambles. However, a sidewinder could turn more suddenly and erratically than briars on a vine and, as five more balloons rose, the two pilots charged toward the center to gun them down.

With the ever-shifting slipstreams of the planes, the maneuvers they pulled over one another nearly drove the clusters of balloons apart. Carving the skies to shreds with bullets, Lukka brought the score even at nineteen.

The final two balloons rose at opposite ends of the field. Daniel thought this was strange since if both opponents pursued a different balloon, the test would end in a tie. He shot his balloon and she shot her balloon, and then came a new voice over the radios.

"Hello, my little sweeties," said a very tired voice. "It's your very own favorite teacher. So nice of you to make it this far, but now let's kick her up a notch and give this final round a little more excitement. While you were getting those balloons, we cleared the fields of all the upperclassmen. You're going to face off against a very special friend of mine. Someone you should know quite well by now."

A storm of dark clouds emerged from a central point on the ground. Rising over the field beneath stormy clouds was a massive 700-foot beast with the lower body of a cat, the wings of a chicken, and the giant head of a canary with a magnificent ruby red stone on top.

Dr. Violite laughed with her usual "heh-heh-heh." "This one's for all the marbles."

Chapter 29

Daniel felt a rush of cold air in the cockpit as the giant kytinfiend took shape. It opened its giant beak and sang its discordant melody, beating its wings to create winds akin to a hurricane. The winds' sheer force sent Daniel's plane into a near tailspin.

As he fought to get control of his aircraft, he caught a momentary view of Lukka, who had used the opportunity to rise higher and higher into the air. While 700 feet was impressive from the ground, it paled in comparison to the altitudes achieved by the Liberty.

Daniel brought his attention back to his own situation. Being caught in the maelstrom would spell a quick and terrible end if he could not get clear. He had almost cleared the gusts when the monster lifted and shifted a hind leg and kept batting some more. The plane spun again, and Daniel knew that as long as these conditions continued, he would not be able to escape the cockpit.

The fury of the wind stopped when bullets suddenly picked apart the feathers of one of the kytinfiend's wings from behind, giving Daniel the respite he needed to correct his plane's flight. He pushed hard on the throttle and took flight upward once more into the sky.

He turned his attention back to the monster. Gaps had been cut through its left wing. Flying up the back of the kytinfiend was Lukka. She'd risen high above the creature and then downward to shoot. It would be a hollow victory for Lukka if he died before he had a chance to divulge his secrets.

Dr. Violite crackled through the headsets. "Hey kiddos, before anyone thinks to complain that I made the monster too big this year, I would like to remind you that this kytinfiend is a product of the generous donations from the cafeteria from all the poultry slain to fill your plates. In truth, you have no one else to blame but yourselves and your classmates. Use that information how you will.

"Imagine how much harder this would be if the whole thing was a giant chicken. My stupid cat's big hind legs aren't suited for this sort of upper body. So while quite helpful for a exam, this kytinfiend would not be viable for combat on the battlefield. Still, you can see what sort of threat a giant wingspan of this sort poses. Let this be a good learning opportunity."

Daniel now understood why the radio had an off switch. Having learned his lesson from the last time, he loosened the headset from his ears. He glanced up to see that Lukka was struggling in an attempt at a pass at the gem on the beast's head. A finicky creature with the monocular vision of a canary, it constantly shifted its head forward and backward to take in its surroundings. He drew near to the beast but saw that Lukka had finally drawn near enough to fire a rocket at the beast's stone. Daniel saw the flash of the rocket as it departed from beneath the wing, but as it took flight near the stone, the kytinfiend's two large cat legs pushed off the ground and the whole beast shot into the air. In any other circumstance, he thought, it would have looked silly, but with its size magnified substantially it was something of a horror.

The rocket crashed somewhere into the beast's lower back. It recoiled and twisted in the air, just missing Lukka with its tail. As the kytinfiend came crashing down from the dark clouds it had created overhead, it slammed into the ocean. The water that crashed outward rippled high and wide into the stony shore. Water exploded up the side of the cliff, rising up to the beast's large round abdomen.

The monster, displeased to be in water, stomped its hind legs with exaggerated steps and rose from the sea, shaking the earth with each footfall. Lukka, now with no rockets, fast approached one of the beast's wings. Daniel repaid her favor and, squeezing his stick tight, sent an onslaught of gunfire that ripped the creature's undamaged wing to shreds. Large crimson metallic feathers sliced through the air and crashed onto the fields below.

Now Daniel was out of bullets. Lukka was out of rockets. There was no telling how many bullets she had left, but he knew it wasn't many. Did she have enough to crack the big red stone?

Unsure he could get close enough to the stone to hit it with a rocket, there was one chance to finish the thing before risking a move that could get one of them killed. He switched the frequency of his radio to open air. "Lukka," he said, "it's me. I've got an idea, but I need however much ammunition you have left to pull it off."

"I've not yet begun to fight," said Lukka.

"I know you want to win, but this might be a bit more than we can chew. So, tell you what—if you use the last of your ammo to shoot off the kytinfiend's tail, I'll let you ask one question that I must answer."

The beast began its wild discordant melody again and Lukka spoke back through the radio. "Two questions, and you've got a deal."

"Fine. Two. Let's stop this thing before anyone gets hurt."

The radio crackled and Lukka spoke again, this time with a focused tone. "On the attack, I'll let you know when the tail's clear. Keep clear until then."

"Got it," said Daniel. He pushed the stick back and ascended with violent energy toward the dark clouds that swarmed above the beast. He looked for Lukka and, in an instant, saw the muzzle flares of her cannons and the flashing heated shells of bullets rattling off the monstrous tail. The tail came loose and landed flat on the ground.

With the realization that it had been assaulted from behind, the beast aimed to spin about on its back legs. However, its great size was too much to manage without its tail for balance and the kytinfiend tumbled backward, revealing the red stone. Daniel loosened his final rocket and aimed it at the beast's massive head. The bright red stone shattered in the explosion and as its body melted away like cold magma back into the earth, Daniel pulled up and leveled himself about ten feet shy of the ground. The skies began to clear and the bright light of the setting sun shone through.

Professor Thompson whooped through the radio as Daniel and Lukka flew into formation. "I'm going to refrain from using teacher talk to say that was one hell of a finish. A gutsy move on both pilots' part and just a damn fine example of squad tactics. You're both clear to touch down on the runway. Sion be with you."

The two Liberties touched down at the airbase. Students of all four estates cheered with exuberance. As Daniel climbed out of the cockpit, he jumped down to the wing and then to the ground to look for Johanna and Rigel. Rigel pounced on Daniel and, with both arms wrapped tightly around him, lifted him up over his shoulder. Daniel smiled a sheepish smile as he came face to face with Johanna. She threw her arms around both of them.

"Shadow's light!" yelled Rigel. "I was sure that thing was going to kill one of you. I am so glad I'm not going to have to fight those things." He lowered Daniel to the ground and then said with some concern, "We are not going to be doing that, right?"

"Don't hold your breath, little prince," Dr. Violite said, appearing from nowhere. "Buldwikk has many more terrible monsters than my little chunkster. Maybe not this year, but your time will come all the same. Daniel, that was almost not terrible and as a student in my class, I am just almost proud."

"Thanks, I guess, Dr. Violite," Daniel said.

"Now if you'll excuse me, I'll be thinking about what to make for my next exam beast. I shiver in anticipation, he-he-heh."

Violite disappeared from view, and Rigel turned with caution back to his friends. "Could you imagine what it must be like to be her children?"

"She doesn't have kids," Johanna said.

"Well, that's probably a good thing."

Daniel interrupted their banter. "Anyone see Lukka?"

Johanna glanced toward the planes and pointed. "There she is." They all watched as Lukka stepped down from her plane and strode toward them.

Removing her helmet and shaking out her hair, she placed her helmet firmly in Daniel's hands. "Two questions. Respect our deal."

"Uh, hold on BB," Rigel said. "Daniel won so you can save your questions for when you join us at the Wave's Break."

"BB?" Lukka asked.

"Briar Baroness. I thought about calling you BoB, Baroness of Briars, but then you'd have to have a bobcut and Jo's already got that covered. Didn't want to step on her style."

"Ok, I get it," Lukka said, rolling her eyes. She looked back at Daniel. "Two questions."

"Right now? Daniel asked.

"No, at the Wave's Break. I need to think about them. Tonight, seven o'clock. Don't be late."

"Wouldn't miss it for the world," Daniel said.

Lukka turned and walked away. Rigel gave a quick glance between Daniel and Lukka and back to Daniel. "So is something going on between you two?"

"We made a deal," Daniel said.

"Yeah, and she lost," Rigel said.

Daniel thought for a moment. Rigel and Johanna were bound to find out sooner than later if Lukka was going to join the gang. "We made another deal while we were up in the air."

"Like a cool deal? Like a date deal? What sort of deal?"

Johanna stepped in. "Rigel…"

"I mean, like it's cool," said the prince. "That's what we should be doing in school. Especially if Buldwikk rolls up and certain death awaits us afterward. I just sorta got the impression she hated you. Anyone else think that?"

"Rigel," Johanna repeated.

"All right, all right, let's get you out of your flight equipment. It's a little warm out to be wearing all of this in the summer. Johanna, avert your eyes. I'm going to help Daniel get all put away."

"I'll catch you guys by the bus stop?"

"Sure thing, Jo," Rigel said.

Johanna gave Daniel one more hug and then ran along to the bus stop near the airfield. Daniel tossed Rigel Lukka's helmet and they both went into the hangar.

"Ugh, you think she'd put up her own helmet."

"Yeah, I don't know," Daniel said and then paused. "I don't think she's that bad. She's all by her lonesome wherever she's from. Her sister runs the school. Her parents are gone. I feel bad for her."

"While I'm putting away her helmet, I can put away your helmet too."

"Yep, you got it," Daniel said. He yanked his helmet off and his hair was tossed upward. For a flash of a few seconds, the long white tails of his hair sprang up into Rigel's field of vision. Rigel froze at the sight of the hair, and the helmet that Daniel tossed to him flew over his shoulder.

"Hey, uh, Daniel, buddy…there's something wrong with your hair."

Daniel ran his hand through his hair and found the white tails. He frantically tried tying them back behind the rest of his red hair, but to no avail. Rigel picked up the helmet and quickly slapped the helmet back down on Daniel's head. "Looks like I have a couple questions too."

The two met Johanna at the bus stop as they'd promised. "Hey, Daniel, I think you forgot something," she said, grinning. She jokingly held her hands around her head like she was removing a helmet.

"Yeah, Daniel," said Rigel in an uncharacteristically direct tone. "I think you sure did forget something."

"What happened?" asked Johanna.

Rigel turned to Daniel and raised his eyebrows. "Well, Daniel, how about you finally tell *us* the truth?"

Chapter 30

The crammed bus ride into town proved tense and heated. Johanna sat between the two boys, wondering what quarrel could have erupted in the time between her seeing them off to the equipment lockers and them coming back to the bus stop. Were all guys as temperamental as the display she was seeing here? Rigel looked like Daniel had run over his dog, and Daniel looked like the dog. Was this what it was like to have siblings? What would be the responsible thing to do? Better still? Why did *she* have to be the responsible one? Her mom wasn't very responsible, come to think of it. Maybe these were the cards the Father dealt her. If she could get them to the Wave's Break without anyone dying, she would count that as a victory.

When the bus finally stopped, the trio got out from the back and walked down the street to the Wave's Break. As they entered and turned to their usual booth, Lukka sat waiting for the three of them with a cup of tea and a plate of shortbread cookies.

If this had been a normal day, Rigel would have wondered why he had not known there were shortbread cookies on the menu, but his mind was otherwise occupied. Daniel sat across from Lukka and Johanna sat by Daniel's side.

Rigel turned to Hunter and asked if they could shut the blinds around the diner.

"Havin' a witch's gathering?" Hunter said.

"Nah, you missed that about thirty minutes ago," Rigel said. "We just need privacy."

"Ah, well then I'll give ya boys and girls the VIP treatment." The heavy older man went around drawing all the blinds before switching the open sign to closed. He stepped into the back and yelled to his wife. "Jaki, the monarchy's havin' clandestine meetings in our diner."

"Again?" she said from the back.

"Again," he answered.

Rigel took his seat by Lukka's side and wasted no time. "How many questions did he promise you, Lukka?"

"Two," she answered, confused by the serious tone of the boy she knew to be a perpetual jokester.

"Here's a freebie," said Rigel, who reached across the table and yanked the helmet off Daniel's head. His white tails fell into view. "Who *are* you? *Really*."

Johanna turned to look at Rigel and instantly noted the strange feature of Daniel's hair. Lukka dropped the shortbread cookie she had just picked up a moment before.

"Rigel," Daniel said in a weak voice.

"I'm serious, Daniel—if you *are* Daniel Hardy. Who are you really? Because I think I don't know what an Ulkirn refugee is doing at this school. Only citizens get to fly in Diamond Blue."

"You're a Knot Kovenant," Lukka said, the truth dawning on her. "*That's* why you didn't know the liturgy at the chapel. *That's* why you have hands like a stable boy."

"That's why you couldn't read and write well," Rigel said.

"And the food at the cafeteria…you wouldn't eat it the first day," Lukka said. "I just thought you were picky, but you weren't supposed to."

Daniel felt his vocal cords tighten. "You are right," he said. "I'm not… Daniel Hardy." His eyes were warm and wet and his fingers trembled. "My name is Duun. Duun Howl."

"Ahhh," said Johanna quietly. "Like *Avo* Howl." The others looked at her quizzically. "Those were the letters I came up with from the adjusted code of the scarf. I thought they were gibberish, but that was the name written on the scarf. Is Avo Howl your brother?"

Lukka stared at Duun. "The terrorist?"

Duun shook his head. "He's not a terrorist. He's missing, and he might have been hunted by the Twilight Parliament." He took a deep breath. "Shortly after the soldiers came to tell us Avo had abandoned the school, the Twilight Parliament came in screaming purple planes. They attacked Baron Blau, and they attacked our people. They tried to kill my mother and sister and succeeded in killing our sheep, destroying our home, and killing our neighbors. My mother can't walk anymore because of them." No one said a word.

"Baron Blau came to me and asked me to be part of his plan to find Avo and the Twilight Parliament. I didn't want to lie about who I was, but it was the only way Baron Blau would allow me to attend this academy."

"Will Baron Blau confirm this?" Johanna asked.

"No," Duun said. "I can't let him know anyone found out who I am. He wanted me to keep this all a secret from the start. He expected me to disregard my religion for the sake of the greater good, and to an extent I have done just that. That's why I answered the test honestly. Because, if my life was going to be a lie, then I wanted to still be me after it all. I just wanted someone here I could trust."

"You wanted a friend…same as me," Johanna said.

Rigel swallowed. "What am *I* to you then?"

"I am the same person I've always been," Duun answered.

"Yeah, well, *my* friend is a noble son of Baron Blau. Not a lazy machine-hating, freeloading Knot Kovenant tree-hugger."

Johanna frowned. "Rigel, does a lazy person rise to the top of their class?"

Rigel shifted in his seat. "Well, no."

"Does a lazy person learn how to read and write over the course of a few months?"

"No, a lazy person doesn't do that either."

"Does a lazy person go above and beyond risking everything to protect their loved ones at the risk of expulsion, incarceration, or execution?"

Rigel held up his hands and glanced across the table at Daniel.

"Okay, look, I get it, but why didn't I get to know? We were pals, man. You and I taking on whatever those chumps put us through."

"Probably because he knew you'd respond the way you did," Johanna said.

"C'mon, Jo. You must feel a little cheated," Rigel said.

"No, I don't. Daniel or Duun, he's still been by our side from the start."

"But why couldn't he just tell us? Even just tell us that he had something he couldn't tell us everything about, but that he trusted us to trust him."

Johanna got up from the booth and turned her back to her three companions at the table. She brought her hands up to her collar. Hunter walked in with a pot of coffee and said "Hey, you kids need anything or—" He stopped cold at the sight of Johanna. "Sion's light! She's disrobing." He turned a 180 and went back into the kitchen.

"Here, Rigel, do you see this?" Johanna dropped her blouse and exposed her bare back to her friends. A massive scar like the scattering branches of a tree spread from her shoulder down both her triceps and across her entire back. "I was struck by lightning when I was twelve. Mom was parading me around for years as her little prodigy and, at a golf tournament, she insisted we go forward on a stormy day. I got struck while in mid-swing." She paused. "Lightning burns the skin underneath. It damages the nerves. It left me with all of this, and it keeps going further down. I think you get the idea, so I won't show you that. My mother's perfect experiment marred by the Shadow's judgment for her hubris. You wanted to see it, so here it is."

She pulled her blouse back up over her shoulders and turned around. "We've all got things we hide. We don't do it because we hate our friends or think less of their ability to understand. We do it because we're not ready to admit it to ourselves, or we can't—in case someone else gets hurt. Either way, we have to believe in our friends—not because they owe us, but because friends don't keep score."

Johanna sat back down and the three of Duun's compatriots sat in silence. Lukka reached for a shortbread cookie and put it in her mouth before anything else happened that took her by surprise.

"Daniel, ugh, Duun…Johanna," Rigel answered slowly. "This is a lot to take in. I want to be able to say I'm good. I want to say I can forgive or that I'm sorry I see it this way, but I can't do that. Maybe I'm a bastard for thinking it, but I do. I need to take some time by myself to make sense of it. Until then, bye, I guess."

With that, Rigel got up from the table and headed for the door. Just before he cleared it, Duun spoke.

"I'm sorry, Rigel," he said.

"Yeah, me too." And with that, he was gone.

Silence dominated the table. Lukka felt particularly awkward upon witnessing the dissolution of a friendship. However, attention fell to her in the silence. She felt as exposed as Johanna had been.

"Lukka, you've been quiet," Duun said. "I promised you the truth, and you still have two questions."

Lukka sipped her tea to hide the catch in her throat. "I have just one question." She turned to look him straight in the eye. "You promised you would tell me the absolute and total truth."

"Of course," Duun said.

"Duun Howl," Lukka said, correctly pronouncing his name on the first try. "Have you or will you ever conspire to hurt anyone in the Kingdom of Tarrkaven?"

"I haven't…and I will never," Duun said with strength in his words and spirit in his lungs.

"Then that's all I need to know," Lukka said. She turned and smiled at Johanna. "I'm looking forward to working with you two."

Duun nodded his head, relief washing over him. "Thank you," he said. "So, what happens now?"

"Now we go on semester break for a month," Johanna said.

"A whole month?" Duun said.

"Yes, but we still have two tasks. One is to go to the Tarrkavian Historik Sosiety to seek answers on the Twilight Parliament and to find potential hidden bases along the coast. That will have to wait until we come back. The other is to attend the premiere for Mom's movie to find out what we can about the identity of the Emerald Dragonfly. I managed to get tickets, but I guess you can have Rigel's ticket, Lukka."

"Tickets to the new Emerald Dragonfly premiere?" Lukka said. She tried to mask the exuberance in her voice but failed.

A hint of a smile appeared on Duun's face. "I thought you said that was all kid stuff."

"Uh, I'm allowed to like something and not let it dominate my life.

Although, it sounds like the Twilight Parliament might also be real if they sabotaged my plane. It looks like this is a matter to be taken seriously. I'll see about getting my responsibilities handled at home for the premiere."

"Where is the premiere being held?" asked Duun.

"The capital city," said Johanna.

"There's a matter I need to tend to," Duun said. He thought about how long it had been since he last saw Leleen and his mother. Of course, if what Johanna said was true, and the cracked code did identify the pilot as Avo Howl, then going to this premiere could be his best shot at finding his brother. He couldn't let this chance slip by. "If I can make it happen, I will."

"Okay, if not, Lukka and I will see what we can do. I hope you can make it, though," Johanna said.

"Me too," said Duun.

***

When the trio returned to campus, Lukka offered to walk Johanna back to her tower. Duun headed for his room, taking care that nobody saw him in the helmet or his white locks. As he entered the common room, he heard a solitary voice and ducked around the corner. It didn't take Duun long to recognize the voice as Jensen's.

"Look, it was windy today," he said. His voice seemed more hollow than usual. "No, but Dad—"

Duun heard something like a buzz coming from the phone. He could almost make out words. If Jensen's dad was on the phone with him, and his voice could be heard from the receiver, then Daniel could only wonder how loud he was speaking. Duun's experience with telephones was minimal, but when any other student sat in this common area, he never heard so much as a squeak from the handset.

After more interrupted protests and stammers, he heard Jensen dialing. "Hello sir," Jensen said to someone obviously new. "What do you need me to do?" He paused, trying to get his voice under control. "I'm not upset," he lied. "I want to meet up. Will the ship be waiting at the usual place?" He listened in silence and then spoke again. "By plane? That's impossible. I'm not afraid, but you can't land a plane in the cove. You'd fly into a wall. Right, sorry, I'm good. If it's possible, then I suppose it'd be easier to transport the limes without incident. I'll see you there, sir."

Daniel waited in a cranny just inside the door until the phone call ended. Then he heard Jensen approach and slipped back out the door.

Jensen sensed that someone was there. "Wait, who's there?" He looked out through the door into a garden devoid of onlookers. Daniel sat deep within the hedges, just as he had when he'd first met Rigel.

Here he was, once again, with a dangerous discovery, one he must keep all to himself.

Chapter 31

When Daniel woke in his dorm room the following morning, he heard the sound of someone rustling about—moving objects and picking things up. His mind immediately turned to the fear of a raid and as he bolted up in his bed, he found himself viewing the ambling and disinterested figure of Parker packing his luggage.

"Oh, Master Hardy, sorry to startle you," Parker said. "The baron is on a tight schedule and would like you to meet him in the courtyard post haste."

"Is anything wrong?"

"No, sir, quite the opposite. The baron has located a surgeon to operate on your mother's injuries. There may be a chance she can walk again."

"That's excellent news," Daniel said. He hadn't thought such a thing possible, but he hadn't come to Skyskape to study medicine. He wondered if Johanna knew anything about the science of it, but perhaps if this was a new procedure, it would be beyond her understanding.

"There is one small matter," Parker said. "Your sister has forbidden the operation, and your mother is in agreement with her."

"Why?"

"It is not my place to pry in such matters. The baron felt it would be best you spoke with them about it."

Daniel was confused. "I mean…I don't see what's the problem. I'll talk it over with the baron and my family and see what to make of it."

"Very well. Now, if you will go to the courtyard, Baron Blau will meet you. Some of the school security has offered to assist with the moving of your luggage to the airfield."

"I don't have time to say any farewells, do I?" Daniel asked.

"Perhaps if you make them on the way to the courtyard. By the way, Master Hardy, do you have some means of hiding your hair? It would appear you have been negligent in keeping up with your secret identity."

"Oh, right, yes. I have a hat. I've been wearing it." Daniel had almost entirely forgotten to hide away the white streaks of his hair, even after the fiasco of the day before. He went to get a hat, but realized all he had was Rigel's blue tam, which didn't adequately cover all of his head. It would certainly draw attention if he walked around with one hand on the side of his head, and he was sure to hear an earful from the baron if word got out that he hadn't dyed his hair and had been found out. He would do what he could to hide the side of his head as he went past the campus security assisting Parker, but he hoped it was early enough that none of the rest of his classmates were up.

Walking past William and the security with him, he reached the common area. He was worried that he would see Jensen at the phone. Instead, he found Lukka sitting and waiting there.

"You're up early," she said.

"Yeah, I've got family business back up the Tarrbly River," he answered.

Lukka looked him up and down. "You're not going out there looking like that. C'mon, I have something that will help." She took his hand and walked him back to her room. Sitting him down on a stool, she opened a box and drew out some shears.

"Are those sheep shears?" Daniel asked.

"Right, you're a shepherd. I guess they're comparable. I'm surprised you didn't think to try something like this on your little farmer homestead."

"Well, the homestead was in ruins when last I saw it."

"Right, sorry about that," Lukka said softly. "You've lost people too."

"Well, I never knew my father—my real father that is. Baron Blau is the closest I've had."

"It sounds to me like you're more his spy than his son. There's nothing wrong with that, but don't get it confused."

"He's done a lot of good for my family," Daniel said.

"Because you can do a lot of good for him," Lukka said.

She cut away at the long white hairs growing from his temples. "I don't mean to sow seeds of dissent. However, I'm in a position where I don't trust anyone right away."

"Because your trust was abused when you were nine?"

Lukka paused and put the shears down on the table. "Right," she said.

Daniel wondered if there was more to her parents' death than he knew. "You say you're not a child anymore, but you *were* a child then. Don't beat yourself up for your sister's decision. It's not your fault if you believe in others and they turn that belief against you. That's on them."

"Right, yes," Lukka said. She lowered her voice as if to evade the subject.

He looked in the mirror. "Wow, that made a pretty big difference already." He shifted his head. "Still need to get the other side, though."

"Oh, right, Daniel..." Lukka said. "Or, I guess...Duun."

"Daniel's fine."

"Don't tell Baron Blau any more about where Avo is."

"He's going to expect that."

"I know he is, but if Avo didn't return to his own family, I think he must've had a pretty good reason not to. Give that some thought."

Daniel nodded. "All right, I will."

When Lukka finished cutting away the white streak from Daniel's hair, she held it up to her own temple and looked in the mirror. Then she frowned.

"I look like a skunk," she said.

"That's all right," said Daniel. "I look like a fox."

"Foxes are cute."

"So are skunks as long as you respect their boundaries. That's pretty much the rule with most animals, foxes included."

"Aren't foxes like little dogs?"

"They are," Daniel said, grinning, "if they're dogs possessed by cat demons."

Lukka stifled a laugh. "Oh, yeah, that makes sense." She looked at her handiwork. "You probably shouldn't go out into the hall. Somebody will notice and then people will talk."

"I guess I'll use the window," Daniel said. "I see you have one."

"Do you not have a window?"

"I do not," Daniel said.

"Oh, Mother bless you. I'm sure I'd go mad if I had no windows."

"Yep. Thanks for noticing."

Lukka held out the shears. "Here. You could probably get more use out of them than me." Daniel realized his hair had a great deal more volume than hers. Leleen had taught him long ago that this wasn't something to comment on, especially to a girl, so he took the shears with a smile.

"Thank you, Lukka. See you at the premiere."

***

Daniel, now relieved of most of his incriminating hair, still wore the tam as he went to the courtyard. Baron Blau stood waiting out front by his roadster. "Hi, hello, we need to move."

Daniel hurried to the passenger side of the car, and once he was in, the baron floored it. It was not characteristic of Baron Blau to lack composure. "What's the hurry?" asked Daniel.

"I received a threatening message today. It was written in the code I gave Avo, which is different from the one I gave you."

"Right. It's a means of communication from a martial arts school. I learned about that."

"Daniel, I think we need to begin thinking that Avo *did* have something to do with the attack on your family and my town," Baron Blau said.

"Don't be ridiculous," Daniel said. "Why would Avo do that? He's not a killer." He thought of the footage of the Emerald Dragonfly stabbing the Twilight Parliament soldier. If Avo *was* the Emerald Dragonfly as Johanna suspected, then would it make sense for him to be attacking a Twilight Parliament soldier?

Baron Blau kept his eyes on the road. "Those scarves serve a lot of purposes beyond identification. They can also be used to carefully relay a mark among assassins."

"A what?"

"A target. I received one with my name on it in the code I taught Avo."

"OK, but you're forgetting that during that attack, one of the bombers went after my homestead and my family."

"I don't know that all the pilots would know who was and wasn't supposed to be attacked. I'll bet one of them saw you going up the lane and figured it would be necessary to wipe out any surviving witnesses. The Knot Kovenant on my land were not harmed—it was the other people who lived in the town. Perhaps Avo coordinated an assault against *me* for revenge."

"Why in the Shadow's name would Avo want revenge against you?"

"Avo was keeping a secret and I discovered it. It would appear somebody else discovered it too, which prompted Avo to flee. It's entirely possible he believes I'm the one who spilled this secret of his."

"What secret?" Daniel had to wonder what secrets Avo could possibly possess that he wouldn't know about. He had known his brother his entire life. Then he remembered what Johanna had said to Rigel the night before. Some people aren't ready or willing to share parts of their lives with the people they are closest to for fear of consequence. Daniel retracted his question. "Never mind, don't tell me."

Baron Blau answered anyway. "Avo is fraternizing with a Buldwikk sorcerer."

Daniel was stunned. There were many angles from which this revelation could be approached, but he had no idea where to start. "Huh?"

"I sent Avo to Skyskape for a reason similar to why I sent you. To investigate an influx of new students from neighboring countries and to report back to me about any that might possibly be serving as double agents for Visolia or Buldwikk. It would appear he made contact and then got too close. I wrote to him that I knew what he was doing. Shortly thereafter, I learned that somebody else had made this discovery too. I suspect Avo believes I'm the one who told *that* person."

"Why didn't you tell me this from the start?"

"I didn't want you to believe your brother had turned traitor unless you found that answer for yourself. It seems the time has come at last for you to know."

Daniel remained stubbornly loyal to his brother. "I refuse to believe that, and I'm going to find Avo before this school year's over."

"Do you even know where to start?" Baron Blau asked.

Daniel almost mentioned the movie premiere, but then he remembered what Lukka had warned. A part of him told him to resist telling Baron Blau what he knew, so he feigned ignorance. "When I know where to start, I will."

The baron's face softened. "Okay. I recognize a lot has probably happened throughout the first term. You've been busy. I might've assumed you were too much like Avo to get it all done upon arriving at Skyskape. I apologize for that. You should take it easy this break." He glanced at Daniel and smiled. "I've actually got some good news for you, but you may want to talk it over with your family."

Daniel nodded. "Parker told me. My mother's surgery. I want to say I support it, but I want to hear the reasons for her reluctance first."

"Right, of course," Baron Blau said. "I suppose your sister and mother are worried about the anesthesia. It's a big decision. I will wait until we're back to go over all the details. We're going to drive right onto the plane and then take off."

"What about Parker?"

"He'll meet up with us later. For now, it's very important we get into the air."

"What is the matter really? You're not acting like yourself, at all," Daniel said.

"I think my plane was followed on the way here, and I fear we may have to fight our way back home."

Chapter 32

Daniel found himself seated in the cockpit of the plane. Baron Blau climbed into a rear turret situated behind where the loading ramp carried the car onto the plane.

"Just take off," said the baron. "Fly like there's no problem and keep an eye out. The seas over the ocean are especially foggy today. They could come out of anywhere."

"Shouldn't we radio the tower to let them know we may be attacked on our way out?" Daniel asked.

"No, the less known the better. It's possible our enemies will intercept our transmission, and then we could endanger more pilots. Our best course of action is to handle this on our own. Also, they aren't going to meet us in the skies over the cape. They're more likely to attack over the sea where rescue is not guaranteed. Just keep calm. You've flown several times by now, and I understand you've faced off against a kytinfiend. It's the same business. I'll handle the shooting—you just focus on keeping an eye out and not getting shot."

"As you wish," Daniel said. With the matter settled, he received the confirmation from the tower to take off, and a few short moments later he was in the air. He immediately noticed that the baron's plane did not handle as well as the Liberty did, but its overall velocity was comparable enough. "Baron, I'm not a hundred percent certain how to get home from here. Any pointers?"

"Don't worry about that now. I'll take care of that once we're safe. Just fly along the coastline for now. It's clear skies above despite the fog below.

So, there's a chance they'll see us before we see them."

"Shouldn't I take the plane lower then?"

"No, I want them to see us first. They can get the drop on us if we don't have enough time to react."

Daniel had learned in the classroom that the first plane spotted tended to be the first plane to go down in combat. However, Baron Blau knew his plane and had strategies beyond what he had learned so far. Blau's abilities were refined on the battlefield, and for every rule, there were always exceptions.

However, he felt certain Blau wasn't telling him everything. There was no room for second-guessing while they were in the air, so he decided that despite his uncertainties about the baron, his concerns should be set aside until they were out of the apparent reaches of danger. He struggled to keep an eye on the coastline while keeping the plane parallel with the horizon. Under ordinary circumstances, on a craft of this size, this was the role of a navigator, but at present, he would need to listen to Baron Blau's orders from the back of the plane.

As soon as the plane was out of the reach of communications with Landskape, the baron barked a command. "We've got three of those planes with the purple markings coming up from below to join us. On my orders, I need you to drop altitude. I'll do what I can to scare off our challengers."

"Roger that," Daniel said, as if by instinct. Casual conversation went out the window when he was focused on his responsibilities as a pilot. It was hard for Daniel to hear the other planes over the hum of the propellers on either side of him, but after only a couple minutes, Baron Blau gave him the order to dive.

Daniel thrust the yoke forward and turned the plane toward the sea and downward. A smattering thunder of machine-gun fire fell from the rear of the ship.

"Turn her upward," yelled the baron, "and prepare to bank right. I don't imagine they suspected that."

Daniel affirmed this order and followed through. He knew how the move would've felt had they been in a Liberty, and the difference between the two planes took him by surprise. Even so, he turned the baron's plane with ponderous difficulty, and the baron was ready to fire again. Daniel caught sight of a purple plane spiraling down toward the fog with fuel streaming from its wing. Moments later, a pilot bailed from the cockpit and opened a parachute.

"Looks like that one got out okay," said Daniel.

"Yeah, but that'll only do so much for him. There's nothing but sea below him."

"So, do you think these planes just came from the sea?"

"No, I'm betting they came from an airfield somewhere along the coast, but where there might be one is beyond me." The baron paused and then barked out another order. "Stay sharp. Looks like his friends are coming back around."

Without a word, Daniel turned the plane to place the incoming planes in view of Baron Blau's cannons, but just as he turned, he caught sight of another plane entering the battlefield. This plane was unmistakably a Liberty, but across its fuselage and wings grew a fine coat of moss that colored the craft with a bright green hue.

This plane moved faster than any Liberty Daniel had seen on the campus and maneuvered upward to join the other planes that threatened them. Then, the green plane took two quick—almost imperceptible—shots at the pursuing purple planes and dove hard, disappearing into the fog below.

Baron Blau yelled from the back. "Something strange is happening to our attackers. They're breaking off."

Daniel turned the plane upward and saw the two purple planes descending as vines and moss sprouted across their fuselage, tangling the propellers and sending the planes into nose-dives. Daniel wasn't sure if Baron Blau had seen the mysterious savior, but he was convinced who the Liberty's pilot had been. He opened his mouth to comment but remembered Lukka's words.

When the planes disappeared into the fog below, the baron came forward to the cockpit. "I think that was the last of them," he said. "I'll take the yoke from here. Did you see what happened to those planes?"

"Some sort of engine trouble, I think," Daniel said.

"Seems to be a lot of that around you."

"What do you mean by that?"

"Well, it happened to Baroness Strauss, didn't it? Somebody must be looking out for you. Unless you're secretly hiding some special ability of your own." The baron squinted at him. "Are you?"

Daniel shook his head. "Just ambidexterity. Nothing special beyond that."

Blau thought for a moment. "I don't think that would cause enemy planes to stall. Anyway, good flying."

As Daniel moved from the pilot's seat and took up responsibility for navigating, thoughts raced through his head. Could Avo be alive and well after all? He had suspected that his brother was the Emerald Dragonfly all along, but this encounter had all but confirmed it. He was eager to see his friends again so he could tell them, but his first priority was going home and settling the apparent disagreement between his family and the baron about the surgery.

***

The managing of maps and measuring of angles and distances traveled had been a major part of Daniel's mathematics education at Skyskape. He plotted the quickest course but the flight would still take the better part of the day. As evening arrived and the plane was finally ready to touch down on the mansion's private airstrip, Daniel noticed many noteworthy changes that had been made in his absence. It had been just short of a year since the bombers had come and destroyed the town, but he recognized from the sky that great progress had been made in rebuilding the surrounding area. He also saw that the farms and homesteads that had belonged to the families of the Knot Kovenant had seemed to migrate closer toward where the town had been. Many structures, no doubt assembled with assistance of the forestfolk, already rose up along the shores. Great gardens of moss and flowers grew over the ruins of the old buildings.

"Since you've been gone, Tarrbly has become a model for a new type of town," Baron Blau said. "I've been working with local leaders in the community to reimagine and redefine the impact that the Knot Kovenant could have in the kingdom as a whole. We've also reorganized agriculture to be more efficient. A lot of lands were freed up after the attack, so we took great strides to reorganize and revitalize the area. We're producing more crops and providing a greater quality of life for our residents than anywhere else in Tarrkaven—even better than some parts of the capital itself. Word's traveled far and a lot of people have been looking to move into the area, but I've done the best I can to stymie such efforts until all repairs have been made to the town. Pretty impressive, wouldn't you say?"

"Without a doubt," Daniel answered. "Did Leleen play a large part in all of this?"

Baron Blau glanced at Daniel. "Leleen has been Leleen about it. She's not too keen to play along with the changes taking place," he said. "That's fine. Not everyone will be on board with radical reinvention, but change can be good. She'll come to realize how much more can be gained by what is going on here. Anyway, I know she and your mother will be happy to see you again. I had them wait at the mansion for when we came home. Natalie has been keeping them company."

"Parker didn't come back with us on the plane. Will he be safe?"

"He's coming back via another route, albeit a slower one. There wasn't anything in your luggage that you really needed besides all that yarn and the photographs, right?"

"Not particularly."

The plane touched down and the baron brought it to a smooth stop. "Then there's no need to worry. Parker can handle himself. Go ahead and see your family. I'm going to put the plane back in the hangar."

Daniel stepped off the plane and walked toward the estate. There were lights in many of the windows. As Daniel entered into the foyer, he was greeted by Natalie. "Oh, Duun, it's so good to see you again. Leleen and your mother are in the dining hall. They've been looking forward to seeing you and would've been down here except that your mother is frightfully difficult to transport these days."

"Has her condition worsened?" Duun pondered how long it had been since he'd last seen his mother and sister. Not being able to talk about them or to them while maintaining the charade of being Daniel Hardy had never meant they were far from his thoughts.

"I was told her condition is at a bit of a crossroad," Natalie said. "I'll let them explain it to you, and I will get refreshments while you talk it over." She led Duun to the dining room where he saw his emaciated mother seated in a wheelchair. Her eyes appeared largely vacant, and she seemed to not realize he had entered the room. Leleen sat by her side holding her mother's hands as if she were looking for a sign of life. When she heard them enter, she stood and greeted her brother. Natalie excused herself and left the room.

"Duun, there you are," Leleen said.

"Leelee, what's wrong with Mom?" Duun asked.

"The doctors said she's developed an infection where she was wounded. Untreated, it is eating away at the muscle fibers. It saps a lot of her strength and has taken quite a toll on her sleep patterns. Recently, she's often been vacant like this."

"Why didn't I know about this sooner?"

"I would've done everything in my power to send a message, but Parker told us Baron Blau had forbidden it so as to not endanger your cover."

"He could've just sent a message through his code," Duun said.

"You're right. He could've sent the message through his code, but he didn't." Leleen glanced around to make sure she wouldn't be overheard and spoke in a quieter voice. "I don't know that I trust Baron Blau."

Duun nodded. "Parker said there was a procedure that could be done to halt the infection and repair Mom's walking."

"Is that what he said? Yes, but it's at quite a price. There is all manner of medicine that will halt the infection, and I don't have a problem with that approach. However, her tendon will be repaired at the expense of one taken from a calf."

Duun gazed at his sister. Now he understood her resistance. "Cows are slaughtered across Tarrkaven. Using a calf's tendon would just be using a part that would otherwise be wasted."

"Duun," said Leleen, "that's not how slaughterhouses work. They don't just take organs for medicine and then take the leftovers to the deli. The meatpacking practices in the kingdom are wasteful."

Duun cocked his head. "How would you know if you never leave Tarrbly?"

"I *did* leave. I went with the baron a couple months back to meet with the doctor and went exploring on my own. I saw it myself. It's a veritable abomination."

"But isn't it worth Mom walking again?"

"We can't kill in the name of convenience, Duun. It goes against who we are as Knots within this living order."

"You say that like the Tarrkavians aren't somehow also a part of this order."

"They forget that they are, and they upset the balance more every day."

"I still don't see why you are refusing this kindness."

"Because the baron is unwilling to investigate alternatives."

Duun felt his perspective shift. Leleen's words changed the matter and, between Lukka and now Leleen, he understood his family's concern about putting so much faith in the baron.

"Why would he do that?"

"I don't think Blau sees people as people," said Leleen. "I think he only sees what is useful and has no tolerance for anything or anyone that cannot produce to suit his aims. I can't imagine you'd understand that since he's given you all the keys to the kingdom while you've been gone."

"Wait," Duun said. "Leelee, the baron hasn't helped me any more than once since I've been at Skyskape. I've had other helpers, and they've pointed me in the direction to Avo. I think I even saw Avo on our way back here, but my friends told me to be cautious about telling the baron any details.

"I think Avo will appear in the capital, and I need to get there. I'm going to make Blau reconsider this matter, and I will get to the hospital in the capital and get Mom some other kind of help while I find Avo. How's that?"

"Blau doesn't reconsider. I don't think there's anyone in the world who could make that happen."

"I can," said Daniel, "because as you said, I'm useful. He's not going to jeopardize that if he knows I know where Avo is."

"Do you know where Avo is for sure?"

"Not exactly," Duun said. "But, at the very least, I know more than Blau does, and that is enough."

Chapter 33

The next day, Baron Blau took Daniel in person down into the village to see all the progress that had been made in the reconstruction of Tarrbly. The Knot Kovenant people lived in the old town rebuilt and reinvigorated by the magic of the forestfolk to introduce strong foundations and vibrant foliage that instilled the river basin with clean air and colorful buildings. Many Knot Kovenant took on roles that didn't violate the tenets but were not part of the old ways before the attack had taken place.

As they ventured farther out into the countryside, Daniel saw that a great many sheep had taken to the hills where his family's once paltry few had been terrorized. The countryside had seemed to take on a new life, even as more of the Knot Kovenant moved toward the town's center.

However, there seemed one difference in the whole of this agrarian township. Under the more careful control of the baron, everything in the basin seemed more planned and more purposeful than it had been before. The lands of farmers were no longer boundless and unfiltered but now carefully plotted and partitioned from one another. The forests that had surrounded the canyon walls had been carved away to secure more lumber for reconstruction and future building efforts in the community. The mountain goats that had once lived on the cliffsides had been tamed for farming, and the foxes had been driven from view. Where once there was a community living surrounded by nature, the bounds of civilization encroached farther along the edges of the canyon.

Daniel knew that all the advances were good for the lives of the people and without question made life more comfortable. He had benefited from the comforts of life at the academy even in his spartan windowless room. He knew the town's condition had improved drastically over where it had been when he had left the canyon, but it seemed to have become a world apart. It was as though his return had not been a return at all but a trip to a different exotic locale.

While they drove through the countryside, Daniel turned to Blau. "Who's been tending the sheep in my absence?"

Blau shifted the gears in his car. "Oh, well, I've had some farmhands and herdsmen come from other parts of Tarrkaven. I assure you they're all Knot Kovenant. I've also had researchers of animal husbandry come to consult with the local community to reach a better understanding of how to increase our yield from the creatures."

"That's incredible," said Daniel. "I didn't realize there were other populations of Knot Kovenant looking to come here."

"Our successes have changed a lot of perspectives on how Knot Kovenant can live in a kingdom like Tarrkaven. Refugees from Ulkirn, as well as a few from other parts of the continent, came looking for sanctuary from Buldwikk's conquests. Tarrbly has become a sort of laboratory for the Knot Kovenant's future."

"What about the subjects of Tarrkaven?" Daniel asked. "Nothing the Knot Kovenant may learn about integrating into Tarrkavian society will matter if the Tarrkavians won't accept them."

"I don't think the Tarrkavians' apprehensions of the Knot Kovenant are truly directed at its people," said the baron, "but rather at its magic. The sorcery of Buldwikk has made everything that can't be explained by science seem dangerous to Tarrkavians. However, I think all of that will change when they see the forestfolk can benefit all parties."

Daniel rode silently for a few minutes, thinking. Based on what he'd heard said about the Kovenant by his fellow Diamond Blues and by Rigel the night after the exam, he wasn't sure what Blau had said was a perfect answer. He remembered, too, what Dr. Violite had said—that Tarrkavians only want what they can buy with money or power and not what they can sacrifice as the price of magic. Then his mind turned to the filmed footage of forestfolk being stolen away by the Twilight Parliament. He turned to the baron. "I don't suppose you've heard about the kidnapping of forestfolk, have you?"

"I have," Baron Blau said. "Which is why if the Knot Kovenant can be brought into my domain in greater numbers, then they can be guaranteed safety."

"Yes," Daniel said. "But it is the responsibility of the Knot Kovenant to spread across the entire world and not to be sequestered in one space forever."

"Oh, don't worry, Daniel," Baron Blau answered. "This isn't a permanent arrangement. It's a temporary precaution until we can figure out who is actually capturing forestfolk. When we find these assailants, then we can spread the Knot Kovenant out across the kingdom with a new understanding of how to make the most of our lands while also letting the Knot Kovenant tend to its noble calling. *You* understand."

"I do, but you'll understand if some stick to the old ways. Like my sister and mother."

"I've already said that they'll come around."

"They may not. Our values aren't a matter of preference. Mom won't go through with the surgery you suggested because she values those beliefs more than her own life," Duun said. "I thought from Parker's optimism that she'd be at least in the same condition as when I left, but she's become very sick while I was gone."

Baron Blau saw the concern in the boy's eyes and pulled over to the side of the road. "Duun, I don't understand why your mother's condition has worsened as suddenly as it has. Parker's assured me she's taken her medicine as the doctor recommended. I understand that the solution isn't perfect, but what is one calf to your mother's life? If we search for alternatives, we may be wasting precious time when a solution is right in front of us."

"I understand that you feel this is a kindness," Daniel said. "And I appreciate everything you've done for my family in my absence. However, our ideals are more valuable than our own lives. If she has chosen not to go through with the operation, then I can't change her mind. Her ideals are also mine. You believe in certain truths that are core to your being, things that you wouldn't change because they are central to your whole identity as the hero of Tarrkaven. You know that some people can't just ignore their core principles even if the outcome would be perceived as a good."

"Then it would appear we've reached an impasse," Baron Blau said with a hint of disappointment.

"Not exactly," Daniel said, ready to risk his last bargaining chip. "I believe I have information that could be beneficial to you, but I need to be confident that you will find another way to help my mother until she fights off this infection."

"Do you know where Avo is?"

"I don't know exactly where he is, but I do know where he might be."

"Ah, so your hopes are all riding on a perhaps?"

Daniel turned to his benefactor. "Have you heard about the film *The Emerald Dragonfly*?"

"I'm not much of one for the movies or really any passive entertainment. I'm a doer, and I don't have time to sit still."

"Well, I think the franchise is a cover for Avo. Apparently, the Emerald Dragonfly is a pilot who fights against a mysterious shadow army called the Twilight Parliament."

Blau's eyes narrowed. "Well, that does add up in part. A group of owls is called a parliament, and I *did* notice the planes that attacked Tarrbly bore the markings of an owl."

"Right," said Daniel, "and I think Avo may be who the movie is portraying. The Emerald Dragonfly will be at the movie premiere in the capital this month. If we go to it, we may be able to catch up with him."

"If it *is* Avo," Baron Blau said. "There's no guarantee he's this so-called Emerald Dragonfly."

"There's something else you should know," Daniel said. For his mother's sake, he would risk his latest discovery. "When we fought the raiders in the skies on our way back home, I saw another plane covered in a fine green moss that matched the ones we used at the school. It didn't make much noise and fired only two shots at our attackers—but two shots were all that were needed. I believe its bullets were coated with flora—plant life with properties only a forestfolk could have given it. That's the only way I know that a plane could look—or operate—like that."

Blau's curiosity overcame his skepticism. "This plane appeared in our dogfight?"

"I saw it only for a moment, but we of the Knot Kovenant know much about fostering the care of plants even in adverse environments. What's more adverse than an aircraft flying through skies of varying temperatures and wind conditions? No ordinary person could do that to a plane and still expect it to fly."

"What if that plane you saw is just an isolated incident?"

"Sir, it's too much of a coincidence to be ignored."

Blau leaned back in his seat. "I suppose you're right. I'll indulge this curiosity of yours if it means finding Avo, and in return, I will see to it that we seek out alternative treatments for your mother. You and your family will travel with me to the capital, and while we're there, you see about going to this premiere and looking for Avo."

"Do you think Mom is well enough to travel by plane?" Daniel asked.

"Oh, I wouldn't dare put her on a plane. Especially since the last time we flew we were attacked. No, we will take a riverboat down to the capital, a much safer and far less conspicuous means of getting her there. I must commend you, Daniel. You're negotiating, and that's good. It means you're thinking more like me."

"Well, I had a good teacher," Daniel said. Even so, he couldn't help but feel a bit of disgust at the way Baron Blau seemed to use people. He hadn't forgotten how Blau had strong-armed the headmaster into keeping him at the school, but if Blau's language was one of worth and value, then he would need to do his part to oblige. Though the mysteries of speaking to plants as Leleen and Avo did were lost to him, he felt certain they spoke more than words in their native tongues to the flora.

Perhaps in his own way, he was communicating with Baron Blau in a way their protector understood. If Blau cared about results more than anything else, then Daniel would do whatever it took to locate Avo. He only hoped the matter of Blau's accusation of Avo would have an explanation. "What is so dangerous about Avo befriending a Buldwikk sorcerer? Dr. Violite is a Buldwikk sorceress—sure she's strange, but as far as I know, she's not evil. "

"Attachments of all sorts make people do stupid things, Daniel. People can lose sight of what's really important and put themselves under the thumbs of others just because emotions can get in the way of what really matters. It's possible this snake that got into the kingdom turned Avo, and that's what resulted in the whole fiasco that followed. Buldwikk has been looking to get their hands on designs for aircraft for some time, but their sorcery cannot replicate the flight of birds. However, aircraft fly through industrial means. To sway a pilot to their side comes with the added benefit of discovering the secrets of our flight. It would spell disaster for the defense of our kingdom and the rest of the world if our technology fell into their hands."

"What if the sorcerer wanted a fresh start and had no allegiance to Buldwikk?"

"If sorcerers wanted a fresh start, I doubt they'd go and attend a military aviation academy that would send them back to the front lines. Neither of us will ever know unless we find Avo, because apparently everyone else involved is either missing or dead."

"How do you know that?"

"The defense of the kingdom is my business. The soldiers that came that day told me some of this. I've put together other information through my other sources."

"Like Parker?" Daniel asked.

"Like Parker and others," he said. "Fighting in the skies gave us peace but fighting in the shadows has maintained that peace." A hint of a smile appeared on Blau's face. "When did you figure out Parker is more than my assistant?"

Daniel shrugged his shoulders. "It makes sense looking at the bigger picture," he said.

"Your talents are wasted on being a shepherd. I hope you realize that."

Daniel had begun to suspect that the baron was correct.

Chapter 34

The riverboat that went down the Tarrbly to the capital appeared quaint and covert. Daniel had never been on a boat before that he recalled. Perhaps he had when he first came to Tarrkaven many years ago, but if so, he had no real memories of it.

As the baron had suspected, the skies weren't safe for him or Daniel as the mysterious fighting force seemed to hound them from the mists. While not quite on firm ground, Daniel took some joy in knowing his mother would not be taken to the capital via the sky. Flying was liberating, but today, it also felt chaotic.

He had never thought of his home life as chaotic, and the part of him that identified as Daniel didn't feel as though he belonged in that sort of life—just as Duun didn't seem to belong in the sky. He was happy about one thing, though. It appeared Baron Blau had kept his word. The new medicine Daniel's mother had received showed promising results.

Leleen, who sat inside the family's room on the boat, had little to say.

"Are you all right, Leelee? You're looking a bit green," Daniel said.

She rolled her eyes. "I expect jokes like those from Avo. School's been a bad influence on you."

"Well, when we get Avo back, I'll let him take care of the jokes from then on."

Leleen looked at her younger brother. "You're sure he's in the capital? Seems a bit public if he's a wanted fugitive."

"A place full of people is perfect for someone to hide."

"But, like I said, most folk aren't green."

"I'm sure even a green person can find somewhere to hide."

As the boat continued down the river, its occupants saw the water change from deep blue to a shale-colored black. The skies shifted from a cool shade of blue to a spirited gold, and on the horizon rose the towering skyscrapers of the capital city. Daniel had learned in his history classes that the coast upon which the capital had been built centuries before on the Tarrkasz Sea had always had black waters and gold skies and the first sailors that had come from beyond the edges of the world had named the kingdom for those characteristically dark waters. The Topazali Sea surrounding Skyskape was a bright blue like the river Tarrbly at its source. No one knew why the Tarrkasz Sea was black or why it had such a strange effect on the sky.

In any case, the great skyscrapers rose like a dark jungle of glimmering leaves and bright vines of electricity. Daniel had climbed trees throughout his life, but he grew excited at the thought of climbing a building. The cliffsides that surrounded Tarrbly had beckoned him to climb, but the presence of a great dark beast above its slopes kept him from attempting such a bold venture. It was in this city that Rigel lived, but on the heels of a thought of seeing him again, Daniel remembered his falling out with his strange friend.

The boat came to a halt at a wharf, and Baron Blau filed off with the Howl family in tow. As if by command, Parker appeared for the first time since he had been at the school to wake up Daniel. He drove the limousine to carry the family to a hotel. Once they reached the lobby and rose through the elevator, Daniel beheld the city from above as it stood against that golden sky. The view from the observation level of the central spire of Skyskape was an equally stunning vista, but it was a view of nature. The view from atop the hotel of the goldenrod clouds shining over the black metal buildings appeared as the landscape of a colony of insects hard at work, redefining their surroundings in vivid and energetic colors.

As time passed and their mother received more medication for the infection in her injured leg, the golden sky shifted first into a deep garnet and then faded into a dark maroon.

Finally, the time of the premiere approached. Daniel and the baron both dressed in formal attire.

Daniel was uncomfortable. "Is dressing up really necessary for a matter such as this?"

The baron nodded. "I've been told it's appropriate. I can't imagine we're going to get through this thing without running into Minah, so it's best not to be rude while we are her guests."

"Fair enough," Daniel said. Dressing certain ways for certain gatherings was a strange trait to Duun, and he took some amusement from high society having so many rules for appearances. Sheep didn't care what you looked like unless you were green—in which case they actively tried to eat you.

Baron Blau drove them to the theater in the limo. Parker agreed to stay behind and take care of Daniel's mother. Leleen also offered to stay behind as she felt it would do no good for Daniel's cover if he showed up to a public gathering with a green sister.

When they arrived at the premiere, they were immediately stunned by the swarm of camera flashes exploding in front of them. He could barely see what was in front of him, but a valet came up to take the limo away, and Baron Blau helped lead Daniel forward.

Once past the paparazzi, Daniel caught sight of a Liberty outside the theater. He saw no way in which it could've landed there, so he assumed it had been brought via truck to the spot. Although the Liberty was green, it did not bear the texture of a moss-covered plane like the one he had seen the day he and the baron had flown home from the school.

"Sion's light!" said a familiar voice. "I never thought I'd see the day ol' Orson went to the movies. Daniel, you have moved mountains today."

He looked up to see Johanna and her mother on the red carpet in front of them. Johanna wore a long deep green dress, courtesy of her mother.

"I didn't do anything," Daniel said. "He wanted to show up all on his own."

"Yes," said Baron Blau, his tone far less amused than Minah's. "I am curious about this Emerald Dragonfly of yours."

"Oh, I wager you must feel cut from the same cloth as him. He's already inside. You can't miss him." Minah looped her hand under Blau's arm and took him into the theater, leaving Daniel alone with Johanna. He felt relief of some tension in his shoulders as he now stood in the presence of a friend.

When Daniel drew near her, the two absconded into the theater and out of the eyes of the crowd. Daniel shook his head. "I think I just had a thousand pictures of me taken, and I don't think my eyes were open for a single one of them."

"Oh, yeah, don't worry about that. Mom doesn't let them take pictures of me anymore. Reminds me of the lightning."

"Is getting struck by lightning like that?"

"The light part, yes. Lightning is hotter, and then you also have the part where you wake up after the fact unsure of what smells like it's cooking and how long you've been on the ground."

"That's rough," Daniel said.

"Yeah, this is the part of showbiz I could do without. Give me production any day. Publicity is a beast of its own."

Daniel glanced around. "Is Lukka here?"

"And Rigel, but he's opting not to sit with our group for the time being."

"Ah, yeah, that's about what I thought he'd do. He was eager not to think about Rigel. "Where's Lukka now?"

"She's been looking for you. I managed to get us a box to watch the film from. Look, there she is now." Subtly, Johanna gestured in Lukka's direction.

In the light of the theater's foyer, Lukka's hair had a brightness and her dark eyes were softer than he'd ever seen in the well-lit classrooms at SkySkape. In a dress that captured her ephemeral beauty, she approached Daniel and Johanna—not in her usual choppy stride—but in an almost regal movements. In that moment, Daniel understood why the elite had so many other opportunities to dress in different ways. Johanna tried hard to hold back a laugh at his speechless expression.

Johanna spoke in a low volume. "I'm going to go talk to Rigel." As she stepped away, she said over her shoulder, "And don't forget to tell Lukka she looks nice." She left the shepherd to sink or swim on his own. The monarchy was being stubborn, but Rigel had at least shown up. She could work with that.

"Hello, Daniel," Lukka said, careful to use his alias. "Fancy meeting you in a place like this."

Daniel's mind ran in circles through his skull. He was suddenly panicked over what sort of a compliment would be appropriate. He didn't want to lay it on too thick, because she had only now begun to open up to him. Endangering that while he was short a friend would put him on a back foot during this mission. He also didn't want to seem disinterested, because that would be rude in its own way. Baron Blau had often told him that to earn people's trust, the best thing to do was to rephrase what a person said. With finesse, Daniel might've said something charming. Instead, what came out was, "You look fancy in a meeting place like this."

Lukka paused as if she processed the words. Turning them over in her mind, she decided she would play along with the shepherd boy, who now stood as nervous as a cat in a rocking chair factory. Standing by his side, she said, "Ms. Darlington got us passes to meet with the cast. Do you want to meet the Emerald Dragonfly?"

Daniel felt like she'd phrased it in the sort of way an older sister speaks to a younger brother she assumes is hopelessly stupid. But the mission was to make contact with the Emerald Dragonfly, so he nodded his head. "Okay, let's see him, then." The two Diamond Blue students walked together toward a VIP curtain manned by security. In front of them, an individual dressed as the Emerald Dragonfly waited to be admitted. Many of the wait staff were dressed in similar costumes, but none were so insistent to enter the VIP area.

"Sir," said the guard to the man, "we can't let you in here."

"Why not? I'm the Emerald Dragonfly,"

"I think we would know if you were, but Julius Goldman already came through a moment before. If you are a fan, you can wait for an autograph later."

"Okay, fine. You're right, I'm not Julius Goldman, but I *am* on the stunt crew. That has to count for something."

"Sorry, sir, only the principal cast through here. You can take a seat in general admission."

"General admission? It's a premiere! What counts for general admission when everyone here is invited?"

"Well, if that's not suitable for you; we can escort you off the premises."

"You're not going to get away with this," said the costumed man. "I'm getting through one way or another."

"We can take this up with our higher-ups," spoke the security man. "You may find walking away now to be preferable."

The Emerald Dragonfly impersonator stepped back and threw his hands up as if in disbelief. His motion seemed like a challenge, but then in the corner of his view he saw Lukka and Daniel.

"Oh, uh, sorry folks. Ye havin' a lovely night, and here I am causing trouble. It's no harm. I'll leave you two lovebirds be. Enjoy the show, thanks for coming out tonight. The real Emerald Dragonfly would be happy to meet with you. I'm going to hop along. Don't mind me."

"No problem," Daniel said, unfamiliar with the stranger's exaggerated accent. He noticed a small stain on the coat of this Emerald Dragonfly, one of a deep brown that had stubbornly stuck to the costume after many efforts to wash it clean. However, before he could inquire further, Lukka secured Daniel an entrance to the VIP section. The security man led them through the curtain and directed them up the stairs to a set of box seats. Up above, Lukka locked eyes with the star Julius Goldman.

Goldman had all the trappings of a film star. He was tall, even taller than Johanna. Daniel found it hard to believe that he could even fit in a plane. Yet, he wore a fine tailored suit pressed for such a night as this. When he saw the duo approach, he spoke with a suave voice made for the airwaves. However, Daniel immediately felt let down that he was not actually emerald and certainly wasn't his brother.

"You must be Lukka Strauss. Are you her plus one?"

"Daniel Hardy," Daniel said as if by instinct.

"Oh, Baron Blau's son. Is the baron here?"

"He's around," Daniel said.

"I'll be sure not to miss him."

Lukka spoke as though the Four themselves had manifested before her. "I'm a big fan of your work."

"I'm always happy to meet a fan," Julius said.

"How does it feel to act as the Emerald Dragonfly?" Lukka asked.

"Well, I have to say it's pretty daunting. Taking Ms. Darlington's vision for a hero for all of Tarrkaven from the radio and putting it on the screen. It's something else. I have to say our crew did fantastic work and gave us some exhilarating visuals, but a story's not a story without characters, and I hope everyone will see the Emerald Dragonfly and feel safer because of him."

"But he's fictional," Daniel said. He didn't want to seem a naysayer, but he felt the sideways glance of Lukka bore through him and decided maybe saying what's accurate was not necessarily what was appropriate. Julius laughed it off all the same.

"I suppose the Emerald Dragonfly *is* fictional, but you have to give him some credit. He inspires faith in the men and women who *do* protect our kingdom in the air every day. Ms. Darlington told me you two are cadets at Skyskape. As an alumnus, I can say I'm proud to call you defenders of our crown and people. This movie is for you."

"Well, we can't wait to see it," Lukka said with a smile as she took Daniel over to a seat in the next box down.

"He wasn't Avo," Daniel said.

"No. Did you think he would be?"

"I guess," Daniel said.

"The Emerald Dragonfly is a fictional hero."

"But the Twilight Parliament isn't a fictional threat," Daniel said. "And there is an Emerald Dragonfly who is actually fighting them."

"Maybe it is Julius Goldman. You don't know."

"Yeah, but Lukka, you must notice as a martial artist that he's too clean to be a fighter."

"Well, you don't have scars if you don't get hit," she said.

"You also don't get hit if you don't fight in the first place," Daniel added.

Lukka rested her hand on top of Daniel's. Her fingers were hardened as one who'd spent years training to fight. They felt a bit rough but compared to the calluses of his hands that had worked fields and climbed trees, there was a level of familiarity.

Still, her palms were soft and warm, and they carried a measure of reassurance. "I'm sorry it wasn't your brother. I really am. Even if he's not here, that doesn't mean he's not out there somewhere. I'll understand if you want to step outside."

Daniel *did* want to leave as he wasn't much for movies. As he scoped out the rest of the theater, he saw Rigel sitting in the box across from theirs with Johanna. Rigel made an attempt to not make eye contact with Daniel, and he did a particularly poor job of looking away whenever Daniel looked in his direction.

Throughout the theater, Daniel saw no signs of Baron Blau or Ms. Darlington. This didn't surprise him. The baron had told him he didn't care for movies…and Ms. Darlington was probably still outside working the crowd.

The night grew worse just when it was supposed to be the long-awaited answer to the mystery Daniel had hoped for. However, Baron Blau had imparted wisdom that one should never leave a friend or loved one unattended, especially if they were doing something they really wanted to do. To this end, he would stay because he had worked hard to win Lukka's trust, and he wasn't about to abandon her as she began to open up to him.

He leaned over to Lukka. "I wouldn't miss this for all of Tarrkaven," he said.

The lights dimmed over the theater as the projector shone upon the silver screen, counting down before the picture began. The crowd fell quiet. The fanfare of Darlington's film studio began to play before going to the opening credits in the foreground of clouds rolling through the sky.

When the credits ceased, ending on the starring credit of Julius Goldman as the Emerald Dragonfly, the film began with the eponymous owl-eye-marked planes of the Twilight Parliament flying onto the screen. Daniel knew that these planes didn't match the ones that he had now twice struggled with, but rather were some sort of approximation using whatever Minah Darlington had available.

A view came from the cockpits of the enemy fighters as they declared that a single green plane had entered their airfield. They all moved to engage when the film suddenly skipped and ceased. The audience was kept in darkness, but suddenly, in the light of the theater, the emblazoned sigil of the Twilight Parliament appeared on the screen. The declaration "Power over Privilege" flashed beneath it.

In the light of the screen, clouds of dark fog coalesced and amid the aisles of the audience emerged a dozen arachnid kytinfiends the size of hounds. With almost demonic speed, they bounded into the crowd and attacked people below. The first to fall among the crowd were the waitstaff—all dressed as Emerald Dragonflies.

Chapter 35

Panicked screams flew through the crowd and Daniel and Lukka jumped up from their seats. When they moved, one of the giant kytinfiend spiders jumped upward toward their box.

Lukka thrust her hand forward with a swift jab and punched through the spider's chest into its bright red orb. The orb shattered across its maroon body, and it melted away in a dark residue. Daniel stepped back and up, onto his seat. "Are you all right?" asked Lukka.

"Yes," he said.

The crowd below found themselves in a far more dire situation. The spiders bounced among the patrons, biting and piercing anyone who tried to escape. Had these been creatures of nature, they would've coagulated the blood of their prey and stopped when satiated, with a sufficient bounty. However, these spiders came from Buldwikk sorcery and existed only to kill with speed and efficiency.

Daniel looked across the theater. Johanna and Rigel were cornered in their box by four spiders moving up along the walls toward them. Johanna sat perfectly still but shouted across to the theater. "Everyone! These beasts are responding to movement! Stay still!"

Lukka spoke through clenched teeth. "There's no shortage of movement," she said. "Don't you think four creatures are excessive for our friends?"

"Perhaps they're being held hostage," Daniel said.

She thought for a moment and then nodded her head. "I suppose that means that whoever is controlling them is nearby. Otherwise, the kytinfiends would revert to their natures—or whatever is close enough to their nature. Remember Dr. Violite's monster?"

"Anyone in here could be the sorcerer," Daniel said.

"And we're looking at about twelve individuals. The coordination of the ones attacking our friends suggests the sorcerers are close together and have a view of the theater."

Still perfectly still, Daniel scanned the expansive room with his eyes, trying hard to push the screams of the crowd out of his mind. As his eyes reached the back of the theater, he saw the light of the projector. It had been taken over by the enemy. "I think they're in the projection room," he said.

"No doubt they've locked it," Lukka said. "If no one else will, then I'll have to fight these monsters."

"What happened to the security team?"

"They must be trapped outside the theater."

Daniel's heart jumped to his throat. "Please don't do anything rash."

"Do you have any better ideas?"

Daniel glanced toward the projection room again. An idea unbefitting Daniel Hardy came to him, but it was well within the capabilities of Duun Howl. "I've got one. You don't happen to have that bat of yours, do you?"

"Yes, always," said Lukka, eyeing the corner of the box.

"When did you bring that in here?"

"Before I went out to find you. What are you planning?"

"You'll see. Cover me while I go and talk with the light man."

Lukka looked confused but shrugged her shoulders. "Sure…"

Daniel grabbed the bat and swung out on the curtain.

A kytinfiend bounced toward Lukka and she quickly readied herself to fight. Grabbing its mandibles with one hand, she reached through to its red orb with her other and shattered the second spider. She threw its melting remains down by her feet and looked up to see Daniel now scaling the ornate decorations in the theater as though they were the branches of trees. He made good speed, but Lukka knew he would be attacked again soon enough by the spiders if she did not assist him. With careful strides, she went into the hall and made her way into the neighboring box.

The actor Julius Goldman sat on the floor, cowering beneath the railing. A spider in the box eyed him through the burning light of its orb. As the door swung open, the spider turned its back to him and leaped toward Lukka. Julius kicked at the spider's legs and its momentary stagger allowed Lukka time to drive her heel through the orb.

"Wh-wh-what d-d-did you do?" Julius stammered.

Lukka thought the question strange. In the image she had seen of the Emerald Dragonfly, he wore a scarf of the same martial schools she had trained from. She had assumed the actor in the Emerald Dragonfly movie would've been familiar with the concept, but Julius appeared to be in the dark. If he had attended Skyskape, she reasoned, he would have known it was a very different matter to fight a kytinfiend from a cockpit than to stare one down unarmed.

"I saved you and I'm helping *him*," said Lukka, looking up toward Daniel. "Keep quiet and don't move."

"Who?" Julius carefully glanced up in the direction Lukka was looking and saw the hands of the shepherd as he climbed toward the light room.

Lukka stole a quick glance at Johanna and Rigel. The spiders approaching their box were drawing nearer and Rigel appeared quite panicked. That is, until he spied Daniel climbing along the walls with Lukka's nightstick tucked beneath his belt. He watched with desperate attention as Daniel worked his way around to the projection room window.

When Daniel reached the far wall, he grabbed hold of a brass railing, pulled loose the bat, and swung it high above his head and swiftly through the glass of the window, striking the projector. The machine clattered onto the floor of the booth, sending the whole theater into chaotic darkness.

Those who still survived screamed louder in the shadows and Lukka rolled her eyes. *This is probably the worst rescue mission in the history of the kingdom,* she thought, but she remembered that everyone was improvising. Her primary goal, however, like Daniel's, was to save their friends above all else. "Stay right here and don't move," she said to Julius. "I'm going to do something useful."

She exited the box and rushed to the lower level of the auditorium just as Daniel squeezed himself through the projectionist's window. The remaining shards cut his suit and scratched his arms as he passed through to find cauldrons filled with a deep, ominous froth. A storm of footsteps moved toward him, and he leaped over the cauldrons, scooping one up and swinging it blindly behind him. Scalding ooze from the cauldron splashed on the face of one of his attackers and wails erupted. *Dr. Violite would be proud,* thought Daniel.

He could barely see, but he heard the cock of a gun. "Drop the kiln," said a stern voice. Instead, Daniel slung the cauldron in the direction of the voice and dove to the corner of the room. The remaining molten contents of the kiln spread across the exposed film of the projector's reel and fire exploded around the sorcerers within.

In the light of the fire, Daniel recognized the man with the gun as the security man who had escorted Lukka and him into the VIP section. He arched himself toward the door and threw open the lock. In the doorway stood a man dressed as the Emerald Dragonfly wielding a fire extinguisher and ready to strike the door. Minah Darlington stood by his side.

"How did Duun get in there?" asked the Dragonfly.

Daniel whipped his head around and stared. "*What* did you say?"

"Never mind," said the Dragonfly quickly. "Stand back, citizen."

With that, the costumed figure reached into a pouch and threw a spray of small pellets across the room. The pellets morphed into a wild tangle of vines. From the vines grew gourds that multiplied—squeezing, bending, and destroying the kilns. Inside the theater, the kytinfiends dissipated—the source of their power was now in ruins.

"Shadow's light!" Minah said. "Daniel, are you OK?" She threw her arms around him blotting out his vision in her embrace. "What happened in there? Is Johanna safe? What about the prince?"

"I don't know," Daniel said. "Never mind that. Who's with you?"

"Oh, this is the—" Minah turned to find her companion had vanished. "That's strange. He usually stays for the theatrics of his work." She turned back to Daniel. "That was the Emerald Dragonfly. The *real* one."

Daniel was stunned.

"I'll explain later," Minah said. "Quick, we need to get the people out of the theater." An immense squash blocked the door of the projector room and the two squeezed through a narrow passage into the hallway. Once outside, Minah looked back into the room. "He just never can clean up after himself, can he?"

"Ms. Darlington," Daniel said. "Johanna told me something about you that makes me think it wouldn't be a good idea for you to go in the theater."

"Nonsense, Baby Baron," Minah said as she walked toward the main floor of the establishment. "I own this theater, and it's my responsibility to answer for—" She opened the door and beheld the damage done by the sorcerers and immediately fell backward into Daniel's arms. He set her down lightly upon the floor.

The sight in front of him was sickening, but his threshold for disgust had risen the day the Twilight Parliament had bombed the innocent people of his town. Now a righteous fury burned within his heart. They would pay for their crimes.

Johanna, Lukka, and Rigel all came down the stairs from the balcony to find Daniel seething at the display, but a semblance of peace washed over him when he saw that his friends were all right. Julius Goldman followed along behind Lukka. "I'm finished," he said to the still unconscious Minah. "Find yourself another Emerald Dragonfly."

The group watched Goldman as he disappeared into the lobby, quite certain that Minah Darlington had already done just that.

Chapter 36

Cop cars, fire crews, and ambulances stormed into the theater to assist in cleaning up after the disaster. Johanna knew where exactly they could go to get away from all of the chaos—if only for a while. She and her friends lifted a still unconscious Minah and took her to the Darlington's across the street from the theater.

The Darlington Tower in the capital is among the tallest buildings in the kingdom—perhaps in the world—rivaled only by the towers of Visolia. On ordinary days, thousands of shoppers perused the department store housed in the lower levels.

The top of the tower is a marvel of engineering—designed to take in the expansive skyline of the urban center and draw people from all over the world to behold the beauty of Tarrkavian progress. A rotating restaurant gives diners a view of every aspect of the city from the sky above.

Today however, the most convenient feature was its proximity to the theater. The tower was one of only a few places where one could look away from the ruin below.

Daniel and his friends could not ignore what had happened, but it appeared to them now that the person with the answers they sought was still out.

As they stood waiting, Rigel turned to Daniel, slowly and shamefully. "Duun," he said, "I'm sorry."

"Shhh," said Daniel. "Can't this wait?"

"No, it can't. I was being an ass. Maybe you're not who I thought you were, but after tonight, I don't think I deserve who you really are. You went straight into action. I couldn't do a single thing to stop any of that from unfolding. You're an absolute hero."

Lukka forced a cough.

"Oh, and Lukka. I am honored to have a defender such as yourself. You are a worthy baroness of Tarrkaven."

A hint of a smile appeared on Lukka's face. "That's better."

Rigel shook his head. "I'm not a good friend. I've never had many. Well, apart from the people at court who are always sucking up to me. But that doesn't excuse the harmful things I said about you both."

"I appreciate the apology," Daniel said. "However, it seems like now we've found our enemy is a more terrible threat than we realized."

"Right, yeah, seriously," Rigel said. He looked down at Minah. "How much longer until she wakes up?"

Johanna counted down on one hand. When she reached the final second, she pointed to her mother, who roused with a startle.

"What happened?" Minah asked. She took in her surroundings and put the pieces together. She scanned the faces of the four teenagers gathered around her. "Oh, I see."

Johanna helped her mother stand. "Mom, who are the Twilight Parliament—really?"

"I guess I owe you the truth after tonight," Minah said. She took a deep breath. "The evil army from my movies isn't a fiction at all, but rather a tangible threat against Tarrkavian society. It's made up of radicals inspired by the government of Buldwikk who wish to see Tarrkaven rebuilt in Buldwikk's image."

"But those were Buldwikk sorcerers," Daniel said.

"No, they were *Tarrkavian*, but they used Buldwikk sorcery," Minah said.

Lukka frowned. "Buldwikk sorcery can't be learned by anyone who hasn't paid the price to become a sorcerer. At least, that's what Dr. Violite said."

"And Dr. Violite's correct," said Minah. "Somewhere in the kingdom an altar has been built that grants the Twilight Parliament's forces the ability to use Buldwikk sorcery."

"Why would anyone want Tarrkaven to become Buldwikk?" Rigel asked.

"Well, for starters, Buldwikk has no king. Tarrkaven is a country with a long and detailed history of many great families and legacies and individuals who are related to those great families and legacies that grant them power by association. In other words, if you want to be someone really special, it helps if you are related to someone else really special. If you're born on the streets or on a farm or anything that doesn't come with lands or titles, you will have a hell of a time making anything of your life, even if you are ambitious."

"*You* did," Johanna said.

Minah smiled at her daughter. "Yes, I did. I'm an exception to the rule. But if I hadn't made myself and my mind indispensable to the ruling elite, then I would still be fixing automobiles in my father's shop. I had to be so good that my genius could not be ignored. I had to be so charismatic and exciting that nobody would want to ignore me. It took a lot of work to build up the propaganda so that everyone would believe in Minah Darlington, but I couldn't have grown my empire to even a tenth of its size without convincing the king to look the other way on my practices and policies. It would seem that I came to believe I was unstoppable and lost sight of the people who were underneath my own company."

"So what are those words—Power over Privilege? asked Daniel.

"That's their motto. Tear away everything that wasn't earned and build a new country where those who *can* do and those who *cannot* die."

"Has it really come to that point?" Lukka asked. "Are people so dissatisfied with the state of the kingdom they would resort to attacking innocent people in a movie theater? Sure, there are problems in Tarrkaven, but the same could be said for anywhere, especially Buldwikk."

Mrs. Darlington sighed. "I've come to realize that when people are so willing to perform an attack as bold and terrible as this one, it's because we have failed them as leaders. I antagonized the Twilight Parliament in the radio dramas and had intended to do it again in the film, because I didn't understand them. If the people saw us and thought life in a land like Buldwikk was a better choice, then the leaders of this country need to do more for our people."

"We saw footage of forestfolk getting chained up and placed on ships," Daniel asked. "How did the forestfolk get dragged into this?"

"Well, the magic of the Knot Kovenant is particularly offensive to the Twilight Parliament. You don't have to do anything to be a forestfolk if I understand it correctly. You just have to be the firstborn of a Knot Kovenant family."

"So what?" Daniel asked. "Leelee and Avo had their responsibilities, and I had my own. They never lorded what they could do over me. We were equals." Almost instantly, he realized that his outrage had gotten the better of him and he had revealed a secret not everyone at the table was privy to. He and his friends looked wide-eyed at Ms. Darlington as she processed his words.

Finally, she spoke. "You're not actually the baron's boy, then, are you?"

"No," said Daniel. "I'm not."

"If you're related to Avo, then you must be Duun," Ms. Darlington said. "Duun Howl." Her eyes narrowed. "Wait, Duun Howl, Daniel Hardy. D.H. I'm an idiot."

"It doesn't matter," said Duun. "Now that you know, I need to know how Avo fits in all this."

Johanna nodded. "His name was on the Emerald Dragonfly's scarf in the footage we found. Is he the Dragonfly?"

"Yes," Minah said. "Avo had been working for Baron Blau for a while, but he also worked for me."

"What happened the day he was accused of being a terrorist?" Daniel asked.

"I could tell you what he told me but even as pressing as things are, I promised him I wouldn't tell anyone—even the baron—what really went on."

Daniel sat up. "Wait, Baron Blau…where was he when everything broke out?"

Minah shook her head. "I don't know. He escaped my grasp before the movie started," she said.

Lukka called time out with her hands. "What?"

"Oh, it's a running joke between myself and the baron," Minah said.

Lukka looked around at her friends. “No, that’s not what I mean. The baron escapes from Ms. Darlington and then the attack happens. Does anyone else find this suspicious?”

A new voice joined the party in the revolving restaurant. “I’m glad to hear that someone has good sense.”

Duun glanced up to see the man dressed as the Emerald Dragonfly—the one who had troubled the security officer, the one who had made the gourds grow in the projector room. The man pulled away his mask and helmet, and Duun saw the bedraggled, sweating, but algae-green face of Avo staring back at him with a tired but relieved smile. “Hello, little brother.”

“That’s your *brother*?” Lukka asked in a low voice.

“Yes, why?” Duun asked.

“Damn,” Rigel said.

“All right, c’mon now,” Daniel shot back.

Avo cocked his head. “Uh, am I interrupting something?”

“No, don’t mind me, go ahead,” Rigel said. “I’m the prince…Prinse Rigel. Hello.”

“Shoosh, you,” Johanna said.

“What? I’m grateful for his service.”

Avo backed away from Rigel’s chair and looked at Duun. “Should I come back when it’s just you?” He liked the attention, but the young royal seemed to give him a bit too much attention.

“No,” Daniel said. “You can trust my friends as much as you trust me.”

“Well, that’s good,” Avo said. “You’re just about the only person I trust anymore.”

“Excuse me?” said Minah.

“Yes, even you.”

“I’d like to hear later how you’ve been, Avo,” said Daniel. “But right now, I need to know why you fled and why you couldn’t come home. Baron Blau said things, but I want to hear from you first.”

“I’m sure he did. I’m not really sure I understand everything myself, but all I ask is that you listen to my side of the story.”

“We’re all ears,” said Duun.

Avo nodded and pulled up a chair.

Chapter 37

"When I began my study at Skyskape four years ago, it came at the sponsorship of Baron Blau. Officially, the refugees of Ulkirn are not citizens of Tarrkaven. The only opportunity to receive citizenship is to complete training at Skyskape and fly among the bombers against Buldwikk." He pointed to Duun and himself. "With Blau's sponsorship, I was going to learn how to fly so that I could go back to Ulkirn and find our father. However, I didn't consider that by being an Ulkirn immigrant, I would not be given a chance at the placement test and would be immediately placed in Krossbone Brown.

"That first year told me that I would certainly die if I got into one of the bombers. Tarrkaven's bombers are slow and brittle. In truth, they are second-hand cargo planes designed to drop as many bombs as they'll hold with a chance of hitting the kilns. If they go down too soon, they may take out Buldwikk's ground forces, but even if you survive the plane via parachute, capture on the ground means being cooked in the very kilns we were sent to destroy.

"The only escape from being trapped in a bomber is to be an escort pilot, but only the best from Krossbone Brown are chosen. I didn't have the background knowledge to manage such a feat, and since the air force is eager to fill the skies with bombers, they weren't intent on teaching me otherwise.

"Baron Blau had his own matters to attend to, as he received word that there was a rising number of kytinfiend attacks around the academy. His fear was that the sorcerers were hidden among the students in the academy.

The academy is outside the jurisdiction of the surrounding town due to an antiquated legal code established by the king. So, I reached a deal with Blau. He would teach me how to fly a fighter craft, and I would be his eyes and ears within Skyskape."

He looked around the restaurant and leaned back in his chair. "Blau knew many things about Buldwikk sorcerers, but not all. I learned a lot more from Dr. Violite. They keep their kilns at home, but they keep the effects of bones nearby so as to summon their kytinfiends. Most important of all, Buldwikk sorcerers require frequent prescriptions of sleeping medication to put them into a dreamless sleep. There's a price to pay in becoming a sorcerer—accepting the possibility of dying within one's nightmares.

"As Baron Blau taught me the identifying features of a sorcerer, he also taught me how to make the most out of the Liberty. The algae that runs through my skin oxygenates my blood so that I can perform more daring maneuvers than an ordinary pilot. Our ability to communicate with floral life means we can achieve greater awareness of an ordnance by coating it with a fine layer of moss and communicating with it. By using these abilities in ways never before seen, I earned Baron Blau's respect."

He shook his head. "But that was the biggest mistake I ever made. At the time I didn't realize it. I became a vanguard of Krossbone Brown and the best pilot the bastard class of Skyskape ever put in the air.

"The rise in status afforded me more opportunities to assist around campus. On Blau's advice, to try to identify sorcerers in our midst, I began assisting in the nurse's office to determine who among the students required more sleep medication than others. That proved tricky. Since eager first-year pilots are anxious to get into the cockpit, a lot of people need sleep medication before exams. However, in the lulls between exams, one particular student in Diamond Blue seemed to need a more regular fix. The name he called himself was Armand Mondago."

Avo glanced around the table. No one said a word, so he continued.

"How can I describe Armand? Quiet, but clever…quirky. But anyone who can be killed by their dreams and summon up shadows of the dead tends not to be ordinary in any other aspect of life. However, not all of them act like Dr. Violite. Many are more subtle in their eccentricities.

Armand only ate his meals in the garden and he collected bones from his meals in small amounts. He never made too big a to-do out of life, and as a pilot he was spectacularly…ordinary.

"It turns out that most folks will willfully ignore someone who makes it their business to be ignored. But not me. Even if I hadn't been looking for enemies of the kingdom, I've never been much of one to ignore those who wish to be ignored. So, I didn't.

"Approaching Armand wasn't easy at first. When somebody as green as a tree wants to talk to you, then suddenly everyone is interested in what the tree boy is saying. But I had to understand Armand on his level and I found out he spent a great deal of time in Dr. Auberdine's Tarrkavian Historik Sosiety. I went there and, at first, I don't think he was too keen to see me. However, I did my best to seem interested in the work that was done there. Before long, I managed to build a polite rapport with him. A polite rapport was something I could work with.

"Our connection became something else when I found out the other Diamond Blue students gave him trouble for his lackluster performance. At a certain point during the second year, they did team exercises, and while Armand isn't a good or bad pilot, he is abysmal at speaking up. His classmates were determined to get him to open up using tried and true methods that would work on anyone—trashing his room and beating him senseless.

"I overheard that they were going to attack him through the flowers in the garden, so I beat the Diamond Blue students to Armand's room by growing a vine up to the window. I offered him an escape, but instead of going down the path, he handed me his kiln. I knew exactly what it was after Dr. Violite had pretended to throw a grenade in hers that first week. I can only imagine he knew what it meant to me as a forestfolk. Since I had suspected for a while, it dulled the impact of the revelation. Perhaps he wanted me to throw it back in his face and face justice, but I'm probably the worst at ignoring injustice.

"So, I took it, and as they entered to mete out their punishment, I left the bulb of a devil-barb as a trap. It spat its poison at them as they entered. They quickly retreated—it acts as an irritant to skin.

"Afterward, Armand and I spoke a lot—about who he really was and why I became a pilot. We spent a lot more time together because we two were the most out of the ordinary. Yes, he was from Buldwikk, but he wasn't at Skyskape to steal secrets for military use. He'd grown up on a farm where kytinfiends were used as beasts of burden to plough fields and pick fruit from orchards. The war was overtaxing his family and their lands. He was part of a revolutionary faction that intended to study Tarrkavian government and science to reform and revitalize Buldwikk from the ground up. The former left much to be desired, but the latter proved of interest to him.

"He put his faith in me, and I in him, but somewhere along the way toward the end, he was discovered. Armand disappeared, and not long after, our friendship was revealed. Soon after, Baron Blau sent me a letter saying that he knew about us and that I'd been keeping secrets, and then the old codger of a headmaster sent me to Diamond Blue's Professor Harbottle for what I thought would be a routine errand. Dr. Harbottle knew about our friendship as well—and *he* was part of this Twilight Parliament.

"He was determined to punish me for what he called 'traitorous fraternizing'—not with a sorcerer of Buldwikk, but with one who *opposed* Buldwikk. I was stripped, beaten, and nearly taken away to wherever the Twilight Parliament sends their captive forestfolk, but in a moment's luck, I was able to grab a flare gun from the holster of one of the people in the room and fire it. It struck Dr. Harbottle and, as he burned, I fled in the chaos.

"Afterward, I tried to get dressed and flee with the kiln, but the security forces were upon me so fast that I could barely manage the former and failed spectacularly at the latter. Fleeing for my life, I managed to get to my plane and take off. I evaded capture for quite a while but, a raw bundle of anguished emotions, I was uncertain of where to go and my plane went down in a swamp in southern Tarrkaven. I thought it was a remote locale, but soon after, I found myself pursued by an armed force I hadn't seen before."

He looked at Minah. "That's when I ran into Ms. Darlington, here. I told her what I've told you, and with her own suspicions about Baron Blau and the Twilight Parliament and her interest in a reimagined Buldwikk, she agreed to assist me by making me her special operative. I've been about that ever since, studying martial arts and taking the fight to the Twilight Parliament."

Avo glanced around the room. "Any questions?"

No one said a word.

Chapter 38

Duun and his friends sat quietly for a moment. Then Rigel pointed to Avo. "Hold on, now. Didn't you say you worked with Ms. Darlington before your escape?"

Avo nodded. "It was for an internship as a test pilot which I did in the first half of my final year. As part of an employee enrichment program, I got to learn about martial arts. While I didn't know her well, my interactions with her gave me a strong enough sense that she could be trusted—somewhat. I trust her more now than then."

Duun looked at Ms. Darlington and back at Avo. "What do you know about the Twilight Parliament's activities?"

Minah shrugged. "We didn't expect what happened tonight, but it looks like we were lucky that you kids were there."

"Beyond that," said Avo, "we know that the trafficking of forestfolk has remained largely in the northern reaches of the kingdom. We suspect they have a hidden base out of view of the ground from which they launch their planes. How they manage this is beyond us at this point. The person who knows this region best of all is Auberdine, but after the stunt I pulled, I haven't been able to talk to him."

Duun thought for a moment. "I had a brief encounter outside the classroom with him. He *did* strike me as someone suspicious of magic, but I think he will understand that what you and Armand did was not out of wickedness. Surely he'd play his part to stop this injustice."

"I hope so," said Avo. "If there're any regrets I've had, one is that I didn't get the chance to settle matters before I left."

"Won't you get that chance if someone like my mother pleads your case?" Johanna asked.

Avo shifted back in his chair, his lips tight. Ms. Darlington reciprocated. A chef brought over a pie, and Avo cut off a slice and picked it apart with a fork. After eating a bite, he laid down the fork.

"It can't all be a misunderstanding. Armand didn't come to Skyskape legally and I did severely burn somebody with a flare. I think I would've been better off had I shot him with an actual gun. People aren't going to forget something like that so easily. Dr. Harbottle being a terrorist, notwithstanding."

"So, what's the plan?" Duun asked. "You're just going to wander around as a shadow the rest of your life unwilling to let anyone hear your side of the story?"

Avo started carved out a second slice of pie. "If I let my story get out there, then anyone anywhere can twist it to suit their needs. The Twilight Parliament was so bold as to attack my home and family and I *still* came out of it the bad guy. I am just one forestfolk in a kingdom that doesn't wholly trust people with magic. Even as the Emerald Dragonfly, Goldman did all the public appearances. I existed as an uncredited stuntman."

He glanced at Minah. "In a perfect world, I'd smash right through the door and declare myself protector of the kingdom and to the people yearning for freedom in Buldwikk. That's not the world we're living in. Our world is the one where a shadow army waits in every crowd, eager to cause havoc and carnage just because they don't like that our leader inherited the job."

"Won't you at least explain it to Mom and Leelee?" Daniel asked. "Mom's been fighting through a rough patch, and I think it would do her a lot of good to see you again."

"If I go to see them, I could risk putting them in danger," Avo said.

"*Not* going to see them already put them in danger. They're here in the city, and if we suspect Baron Blau is up to no good, then what better time is there to see them?"

Ms. Darlington turned to her aide Ms. Booke, who'd been standing off to the side. "Do we know where Orson is?"

Her assistant nodded. "I heard a report from the police chief that he's checking back into his hotel. A lot of police are on the streets tonight, given the attack. If the baron is trying anything, now would be the time to catch him in the act."

Duun turned to his brother. "What'll it be? I'm going to him whether you go or not. If there is further trouble, this could be your chance to clear things up with him. You can avoid your family all you want if you think it will keep them safe, but these enemies have been ruthless. They won't stop until they've gotten to you, even if you try to turn your back to it, and I'm not going to stop pursuing you until you come back."

Avo gazed at his brother. "There's no shaking you, is there? I don't remember you being this stubborn."

"I learned it from you."

"Well, I guess we could argue in circles until one of us dies, or I can tag along and face Baron Blau. Even so, Duun, you have to be prepared for the possibility this won't be the clean storybook solution you expect it to be."

"Storybook solution?" Rigel chimed in. "You know he couldn't read until a few months ago. I don't think he expected anything." Johanna elbowed him in the ribs. "Okay, shutting up now."

"Are your friends going to tag along with you?" Avo asked.

"Under the circumstances," Minah said. "The streets are too dangerous right now. I'll take the prince, the baroness, and Jojo to the palace. Ms. Booke can take you two to the hotel. Anyone disagree with that?"

"They could be walking into a trap," Lukka said. "I can help."

Minah placed a hand on Lukka's shoulder. "Dear, I know you've studied martial ways that serve well against kytinfiends, but our enemies also use guns like any other red-blooded Tarrkavian. So, unless you can catch bullets midair, I recommend you head to the palace with me."

"I haven't learned to catch bullets yet, but I might be able to tell if Baron Blau speaks the truth or not," Lukka said.

"Yeah," Rigel said. "She's like a walking lie detector. She knew Daniel was hiding stuff from the beginning. She's not the sort of person you should let go to waste."

"I respect your attempts to help, but if something goes wrong, I don't want to risk a baroness getting in danger. Also, if Baron Blau *is* up to something and you lock horns with him, there's a chance this whole affair could endanger the whole kingdom. Ol' Orson is slippery, and these are just the sort of circumstances he could spin to his favor."

"You said it yourself," Lukka said. "I'm a baroness. I outrank you."

"True," Minah conceded. "But I'm the one with the vehicles, so unless you're planning on walking, Ms. Booke will do as I ask—and you will do the same."

Lukka growled, but she saw she couldn't outmaneuver the business magnate. "Fine," she said. She turned to Duun. "You need to stay alive. I still have a question, and you still owe me an answer. If it turns out this situation is a greater danger than you realized, then you'd better do everything in your power to get back to us. Understand?"

He looked into her eyes and nodded gravely. "You've got it, Lukka," he said. "Stay safe, all of you. We'll meet again as soon as we can."

Avo and Duun stood up and Ms. Booke joined them. Minah turned to her assistant. "Do *not* stop for anyone or anything. If it turns out there's trouble, then you get the boys back to me in no time."

"You can trust me, Minah," responded Ms. Booke. "I am lightning."

"That's the spirit," Ms. Darlington said.

Avo and Duun followed Ms. Booke down the elevator to the underground garage. When she reached a black car with armored doors and windows, she waved the two brothers in and shut the door behind them. Getting into the driver seat, she turned the ignition, put the car in gear, and buried the gas pedal as far into the floor as her small boot could manage. Gliding the car around corners to the sound of squealing rubber, she stopped for no one and nothing to get back to the hotel.

"Uh, ma'am," Avo said. "It won't do my brother any good if we get killed before we reach the hotel."

"Dearie," Ms. Booke said as she turned around and looked back at Avo, "I won the Visolian Open twenty years ago in a car way less safe than this. We're going only a fraction of the speed a Liberty flies. Flyboys like you two should be used to this sort of thing."

Avo grinned. "Yeah, well there aren't fire hydrants and street lamps a few thousand feet in the air."

"Every party needs a pooper. That's why we invited you." Ms. Booke made the sound of a raspberry with her short, fat tongue.

After the eternal horror of their five-minute commute came to an end, Avo and Duun bailed from the vehicle. Ms. Booke flew off as soon as they were out, and Avo grabbed Duun by the hand and pulled him into the hotel lobby. As they entered the elevator together, they caught their breath as the elevator slowly ascended floor by floor.

"Duun, there's a chance we may have to fight and kill when we reach the room," Avo said. "Are you prepared to face that possibility?"

Duun had suspected this conversation would come up soon enough. "I'm not a fighter, Avo. I wasn't even expecting the film to combust in the projector."

"Right, that's what I thought you'd say," Avo said. "I'm not going to ask you to, but we may not have a choice. Fight if you can, but if you cannot, then get away however you can. Got it?" He gave his brother a reassuring pat. "I'm proud that you've still managed to keep the tenets of the Knot. It is a struggle in this kingdom—I am a shameful forestfolk."

"I haven't kept the tenets as well as I could've," Duun said. "I've eaten meat that I didn't kill myself."

"So do vultures and hyenas. Don't beat yourself up over that. It's not like you're profiting off the destruction of wildlife. Don't lose sleep over tenets like that—it's not what they were made for." Avo glanced at the lights in the elevator. "Is our stop coming up?"

"It will be here soon," Duun said.

"All right, stay sharp," said Avo. "Here we go."

The door to the elevator slid open. Avo took point and Duun followed behind. As Duun entered the suite, he saw Parker wave his hand to send a shadowy image of a ram toward Baron Blau. Leaping with the speed of a panther, the ram charged into the baron. Blau tumbled through the window and out into the city below.

Parker turned to the two brothers. "Right on cue," he said. Before either could act, he drew a pistol and shot Duun in the chest.

"You limes are coming with me," he said, "or your mother will be next."

Duun's head hit the ground but he felt nothing. His last memory was the vision of the shadow of a kytinfiend that looked an awful lot like Bigby with the cavernous eyes of an owl.

Avo raised his hands in surrender.

Chapter 39

Daniel roused among white linen curtains to the bright golden skies of morning over the capital. His ribs felt sore and his sides itched with the merciless agony of a tarantula's fur. He tried to scratch his sides but found both of his wrists restrained. His feet were similarly tied to what appeared to be a bell. As he tried to move his foot, the bell rang and a nurse rushed in to attend to him.

"Stay calm," she said. "Ms. Darlington will be here to see you. We'll need to change your bandages. The vines did quite a number on your ribs."

"What now?" Daniel asked.

"I don't know how you managed to get yourself tangled in dragon's glory in the middle of Tarrkaven, but you should count yourself lucky. The bullet would've severed your aorta clean in two. Dragon's glory isn't merciful, though. It squeezes tight, so several of your ribs are cracked and bruised. It's also quite poisonous, so you may feel the need to scratch your sides. Do not do that. We'll reapply the ointment. For now, it's very important that you don't struggle."

Daniel looked first to the restraints on his hands and then to those on his feet. "You've got it."

The nurse went about her work, and as soon as she finished, Minah Darlington quietly entered the room. Without her usual charismatic energy, she asked the nurse if Daniel was bleeding anywhere, and receiving a satisfactory answer, she took a seat by his side.

"I may have overestimated Avo's ability to deal with the unexpected. Do you remember anything that happened?"

"Parker's a sorcerer. He shot me, and—" He paused, remembering what had transpired. "Where's Blau?"

"I was hoping we wouldn't get to that right away."

Daniel raised up in the bed and winced, lying quickly back down.

"Baron Blau is dead," said Minah in a voice that grew quieter as she spoke. "Orson's gone."

"Are you sure?" Daniel asked.

She nodded. "Yes. When you and Avo didn't return, Ms. Booke went back to get you. She witnessed a fire outside the hotel. A truck ran off the road and crashed into pumps at a gasoline station. Eyewitnesses said a body fell from the top floor of the hotel through the top of the truck as it went by. There's not much left of the bodies to identify, but I believe we must acknowledge that the worst has happened."

"What about Avo? Where are Leleen and Mom?"

"They weren't there when Ms. Booke arrived," Minah said. "I can only assume they were taken by Parker and the Twilight Parliament."

"What about Johanna and Lukka and Prinse Rigel?"

"They're here. We aren't leaving the palace until we have a guarantee of safe passage. Which brings up a matter we will need to discuss." Ms. Darlington paused. "The king, and therefore the kingdom, believes you to be Baron Blau's heir. That means you are now in charge of his lands and estate."

"I'm not even a citizen," Daniel said.

"I know that!" Minah almost shouted. "I know this is a big responsibility, but it's what we have to work with under the circumstances." Her voice dropped back down to a whisper. "I know you probably expected this charade to end when you found your brother, but it would seem that this false life of yours has become your new normal. I will see that the king acknowledges Blau's wishes that you be his heir. As for the people of Tarrbly, I'll do whatever I have to in order to make sure anyone who knows you as Duun Howl—Knot Kovenant or otherwise—will acknowledge you as the new baron, Daniel Hardy. Since it turns out the closest thing to your castellan is a terrorist, that further complicates the matter."

"What about Natalie? She is as aware of Baron Blau's dealings as anyone in the manor."

"I'm having her investigated to make sure she had no ties to Parker. If it turns out she's in the clear, then she can be considered. Until then, she is not an option."

Duun swallowed. "It doesn't seem like there's a lot of options." He looked at his restraints. "In the meantime, can I get my hands untied and may I speak to my friends?"

"I'll see what I can do about both those things."

When Minah left, Duun sat in solitude unable to move. He stared at the ceiling as his stomach churned and his mind raced. He had searched for Avo and the Twilight Parliament, and now faced with both, they had both managed to elude his grasp yet again. Worse, his family had been captured by the elusive army like a crocodile leaping up from under the pond scum of a still lake.

Duun tried to turn his body toward the window, but then the fierce fire of pain shot across his chest and under his arms. He knew climbing and flying would be out of the question for a long time. He remembered Dr. Violite's kytinfiend flopping about without its wings after he and Lukka had sheared away its feathers and tail with machine-gun fire. The monstrosity could bounce and flop about with awkward motions, but even that felt impossible.

Why did a bunch of vines and leaves come popping out to guard him from a bullet if it only meant he was going to suffer afterward? He assumed this was in some way a scheme of Avo's, but that would mean Avo had to have given him the seeds or pod to make this thing grow over him. He was sure he would've remembered it, but Avo had a thing for misdirection. So did Leleen, but Avo was sly in ways Leleen wasn't. Duun remembered Avo's pat on the back before they left the elevator. It must've been then that he planted the pod. Unfortunately, though, Avo had never had Leleen's finesse with plants. Perhaps that's why the poisonous vines had squeezed him so tight and given him such an itchy rash.

Duun knew he had avoided a brush with death yet again just as he had when he had struck Lukka's plane. He had been lucky then—everyone had avoided death from that glancing blow. Now, his family faced an unknown fate, and the sanctuary of his home had been wrested from his grasp. How would he go forward? He descended deeper into despair.

The door flew open and in walked Rigel, Johanna, and Lukka. "Hey, Duun, we're here to cheer you up," said Rigel. He turned around and barred the girls' entrance. "Ladies, you don't want to go in there. He is shirtless."

"So?" Lukka asked.

"He's shredded."

"What?" Lukka asked.

"He's got incredible muscle definition," Rigel said. "It's kinda intimidating."

"Duun," Johanna said over Rigel's shoulder. "Rigel doesn't want us to see your muscles. Do you mind?"

"Not really," Duun said.

"See, he doesn't mind," Johanna said as she pushed past Rigel with Lukka.

"For Four's sake, there are ladies without scruples in my kingdom," he exclaimed.

Minah's voice came from behind him. "Speaking of being without scruples, what business do you have seeing my daughter's scar?"

Rigel darted to Duun's side. "Get back here!" Minah shouted.

Duun could not see them, but hearing the exchange was enough to set him into pained but mirthful laughter. "Oh, everything hurts," he said, but he couldn't stop.

The nurse followed Minah into the room. "Ladies, if you don't mind, I'm going to get Mr. Hardy a new gown and undo his restraints."

"Of course," Johanna said.

"Yep, do what you have to do," Lukka added.

The two ladies turned to one another and gave a silent but approving nod at what Rigel had tried to keep hidden. The nurse turned around. "There, he should be a bit more presentable now."

The nurse left and Duun's three friends returned to his side. Minah sat back down in the chair she had occupied before.

Duun carefully moved his arms and smiled. "Hi Johanna, Lukka, Rigel."

"How are you holding up?" Johanna asked.

"Well, apart from finding out my whole family is gone and that, with the Hero of Tarrkaven's death, I've inherited a title I've got no business owning…I suppose I'm as good as anyone could be."

"We couldn't believe the news when we heard what happened to Baron Blau," Johanna said.

"It's difficult to believe, and it's even harder to accept," Lukka said. "However, you can't dwell on that because a lot of people are counting on you now. Tarrbly may be the only safe place for the Knot Kovenant, and even that is in jeopardy the longer you are away. As long as we keep going, we can find and save your family."

"Where do we start?" Duun asked.

"Well, you're going to start by getting patched up," Johanna said.

"We're going to talk to Dr. Auberdine about where a hidden fortress for the Twilight Parliament could be," Lukka said.

Rigel raised an eyebrow. "Couldn't we send in additional security to clean up wherever the Twilight Parliament may appear? Lukka is the only one among us who can fight, and since they have guns and kytinfiends, I think that's a pretty tall order even if she is remarkably capable."

"We're not going to be able to manage that overnight," said Johanna's mother. "There's no telling how many of these jokers got into my company under my nose and there could be more even under the king's watch. If we just settled on the noble officers, then we would encourage Buldwikk to advance during our vulnerability and I hate to admit it, but several of the barons and dukes are hardly cut out for such a mission. Worst comes to worst, I could hire Visolian mercenaries, but I'd need to scout out a group fit for the job and by the time the ink dried, there's no telling what the Twilight Parliament would do. For the time being, it all comes down to just us."

"Maybe not," Duun said. "There is one group we know we can trust with the safety of my people. Themselves."

"The Knot Kovenant?" Lukka asked. "They don't fight."

"That's not true," said Duun. "They fight, but they don't kill senselessly. We are a community that protects one another first and foremost, and we will defend our own. If the Knot Kovenant know where to go to save our missing brothers and sisters, they won't hesitate."

"Forgive me for being stupid," Rigel said, "but how are a bunch of farmers and shepherds going to fight a secret army of sorcerers and soldiers?"

"Avo's not the only forestfolk in Tarrbly," Duun said. "They can do what he does with plants, and if we can come up with a wide variety of plants suitable for all sorts of environments, we could employ effective countermeasures against the Twilight Parliament. Not to mention the fact that some in our community hunt. You'll find that while we're not prone to violence, we are far from defenseless."

"Is it wrong that I'm almost excited to see this play out?" Rigel asked.

Duun and the others didn't mind, as everyone needed to feel some glee in the present circumstances.

"Leave finding plants to me," Minah said. "If nothing else, my resources are extensive."

"I'm happy to hear it," Duun said. "Probably a good chance I won't be flying any time soon, but I believe I've got my work cut out for me in the meantime. Find out what you can, and we'll put an end to the Twilight Parliament for good."

The friends knew there could be no room for failure—they would be fighting for the future of the kingdom itself. Duun's friends and Ms. Darlington stepped outside and left him to his rest and recovery.

After a few days of recuperation and the fine medical care of the palace doctors and nurses, Duun prepared to board the boat back to Tarrbly. As he took his ticket to return to the mansion, he wondered in silence if he really could convince his people to fight a war. This seemed a challenge greater than Daniel Hardy could manage.

Then again, he thought, it just might not be beyond Duun Howl.

Chapter 40

Daniel stood on the ship's deck, anxiously awaiting the journey to Tarrbly. He was returning to an empty and treacherous mansion that wasn't really his. Natalie, no doubt, was now in custody, under suspicion because of Parker.

His reluctance spread through the muscles of his legs and paralyzed him—after the episode with the dragon's glory, his breathing had barely recovered, but the nurses had reminded him to take deep breaths to avoid risking pneumonia. He was headed into the colder seasons and Bigby would not be there to keep him warm as he had been before. Damn Parker most of all for using Bigby as a weapon against him, he thought. Daniel stewed between sorrow and rage.

"Daniel, wait up!" A voice much louder than one he recognized called to him. He looked up to see the figure of Johanna towering above the crowd like a pillar of serenity. She moved with the crowd toward the boat.

As she neared the wharf, the ticket master stopped her. "Where's your ticket, Miss?"

"Right there," Johanna said, pointing to the port side of the boat. *Lucky Johanna* was emblazoned on the side of the ship.

"That's not a ticket," he said.

"No, it's a boat…and it belongs to me," Johanna said.

The uniformed man's eyes widened and he looked her up and down. "You're Johanna Darlington? You're a bit taller than I expected."

"If you don't believe me, we can take it up with Lottie Langhorn and the firing squad."

The ticket master stepped aside. "Right away, Miss Darlington."

"Thank you," Johanna said.

"Do you have any luggage? I can have our people put it on the ship."

"It'll be flown up later," she said.

"Yes ma'am," he said. "Enjoy your voyage."

Johanna walked up the wharf in proud strides and sat down next to Daniel. As soon as she was seated, her face turned bright red and she buried her face in her hands. "Did you catch any of that?"

"Bits and pieces," Daniel lied. He hurriedly looked around to see if Lukka was nearby to call him out on it. She wasn't.

"Mom told me to say that if I had any trouble. She calls the human resources office "the firing squad," because they mostly fire employees with foul attitudes. For the record, we don't execute employees."

"I didn't think you did," Daniel said, breathing a sigh of relief.

"Do you think I hurt his feelings?" Johanna asked.

"I think he'll live," said Daniel. He paused for a moment. "Where are *you* going? Do you have business to attend to?"

"Yes," she said. "I'm coming with you to be your castellan."

"Really?" The biggest smile he had managed all day appeared on Daniel's face. Then he reined it in. He didn't want Johanna to think he was as desperate as he was at the prospect of enforced solitude.

"Yes," said Johanna. "Mom didn't want me to go at first, which makes sense, seeing as the kingdom is quite dangerous right now. But then I showed her my plans for a secret project I've been working on in engineering. She looked it over and realized it would be a perfect deterrent against incoming hostilities."

It had been quite some time since Johanna had spoken about her secret project. Daniel figured it wouldn't have been much of a secret if she'd spoken about it all the time, and Johanna wasn't much of a talker anyway, but he felt certain he remembered some mention of it when they'd first met. "What *is* your secret project?"

"I probably shouldn't talk about it until we get behind closed doors," she said, fiddling with her hands. "You don't mind that I'm coming with you, do you? I don't mean to be rude by inviting myself over to your house."

"It's not really my house," Daniel said.

Johanna made a face. "It kinda is, now, though."

"I suppose you're right."

"You're not going to be bothered by me sharing a roof with you though, are you?" Johanna asked.

"It'd be more than a roof," Daniel said. "We'd be sharing libraries and dining rooms and parlors and boiler rooms and wine cellars and stables and kitchens and bed—"

Johanna giggled and shook her head. "It's just a general expression for the grounds of the house," she said. Daniel, it seemed, always found a way to sail dangerous waters when he spoke. They would need to work on that.

"Oh, well, then no, I won't be bothered a bit. I've actually been dreading going back to an empty house. It will be quiet without everyone. I don't think I could bear it."

"What was your life like?" Johanna asked. "I mean before you went looking for your brother."

"It feels like forever ago," Daniel said, conjuring up a memory of his old house and the pastures. "I got up early, let the chickens and sheep out of their pens. Kept them fed, safe, and near enough that they didn't get lost in the woods around Tarrbly. My brother and sister, Avo and Leelee—who are twins—tended to the trees in the orchard and the crops in the fields. They'd argue a lot. One said the beans didn't like being too near the wheat or the apple trees and thought the cherries were taking up too much sunlight. I never could tell if they were serious about the plants. It was fun to watch. Most families don't have two forestfolk, but our family was different."

He paused and a hint of contentment appeared on his face. "Our house had two rooms—one where we slept and one where we ate. If it got cold after we put out the fire for the night, then we'd bring the sheep into the house for warmth. What about you?"

Johanna shrugged her shoulders. "Well, I am an only child. Mom was usually away at work, but she still showed up when I had a golf tournament or back when I had recitals. Depending upon the season, we moved among different houses, and Mom keeps a fairly large staff at each estate. I guess I'm not used to quiet houses either, so I know how daunting it can be."

"Well, if you're there, then maybe it won't be so bad," Daniel said.
"We'll just have to wait and see," Johanna said.

***

By the time the ship arrived at the port in Tarrbly, the majority of passengers had already disembarked at more popular stops. Only Johanna and Daniel got off and wandered into town.

Johanna had never seen so many forestfolk in one place. Prior to meeting Avo, she could scarcely say she'd encountered a single one. However, here they were among their Knot Kovenant brethren who ranged in skin tones from the brightness of an apple to the darkness of forest moss. Some of the men had bark on their arms and leaves within their beards and, even though the temperatures had turned cooler, some of the women still had flowers growing in their hair.

Those who were not forestfolk had worked hard to raise new buildings along the lakeside, and in the view of the hills leading toward the diminishing forests, there were farms and fields overshadowed by the great cliffs. The baron's mansion overlooked the lake and the town.

Even Johanna perceived, however, what Daniel knew with certainty—that the vitality of Tarrbly had dwindled. It seemed as though something had been taken away even in the short time he had been gone. He was certain that Parker had been responsible.

Nobody was there to greet Daniel. He thought perhaps that word had already arrived that the baron was dead. If so, the only safe haven left for the Knot Kovenant had eroded with his demise. Even though Daniel hadn't agreed with all the changes Baron Blau had made, he still knew it was better than to see his people in fear and without hope.

"Can we go up to the manor?" Johanna asked.

"Let's do that," Daniel said. "I haven't eaten all day, and we're not going to inspire anybody on an empty stomach."

"Can you cook in your present condition?" she asked.

Daniel grinned. "Well, if the pain is more than I can bear, I'll just holler."

The two walked up to the manor. A plane emblazoned with the Darlington Company logo on its tail waited on the runway. Johanna and Daniel waited cautiously to see who would exit the plane and were relieved to see it was Ms. Booke. She directed movers to carry crates and boxes into the mansion. When she saw the two young friends, she approached at as brisk a pace she could muster.

"Ah, good to see you two arrived on schedule," Ms. Booke said.

Daniel was confused. "Why are you here?"

"A few matters mostly. One, Johanna and Ms. Darlington coordinated this little scheme of theirs so abruptly that Johanna left without packing anything for her stay. Two, we gathered a wide array of plants and seed samplings that Avo kept in his hideout. Three, I've brought the materials for Johanna's secret project. Miss Darlington, please let me know that everything is to your specifications. Four, Ms. Darlington has cleared with the authorities the alibi of one Natalie Wayneright."

As Ms. Booke said this, Natalie descended from the plane, looking tired but thankful to once again be on solid ground. Daniel went straight to her. She almost threw her arms around him, but saw the splint he wore.

"Oh, I nearly forgot about that. It hasn't been long, but it feels like forever. I heard on the radio about what happened to Baron Blau, and then the next thing I knew two soldiers took me into custody. This really enthusiastic woman drilled me with questions and then I got flown back here. She told me what happened to your family, Daniel. Poor dear. I'll do whatever I can to help."

"Right now, a good meal would help most of all—for myself and Johanna," Daniel said.

Natalie looked past him to see a girl younger but much taller than the woman who had swept her away from the estate for a barrage of questions.

"Is she Johanna? Huh, she doesn't seem as frantic as the other woman. Is she a friend of yours?"

"My very *first* friend," Daniel said. "And she'll be helping oversee the surrounding territory."

"Well then, I'll be happy to help her however I can," Natalie said. "What will you do?"

"Well, I need to figure out how to run a barony."

Natalie nodded. "There's a lot of boxes that came on the plane." She gestured toward Johanna. "She must own a lot of shoes. I'll go prepare dinner. You help her feel at home."

"Will do," Daniel said.

Natalie headed into the manor to prepare a meal while Daniel escorted Johanna to the house and into the library. "You mentioned a secret project," Daniel said. "I don't know if you need a workspace to work on it, but will this be suitable?"

"This will do for drafting," Johanna said. "Thank you."

"What's this secret plan of yours?" Daniel asked.

Johanna went over to one of the baron's drafting tables and rolled out a sheet of paper. She drew a series of elaborate drawings that made no sense to Daniel. Then she turned to him and pointed at her technical illustration.

"There exists a spectrum of light unseen to the human eye. All light reflects off everything it touches. That light can be projected and received by machinery without being seen by attackers. With it, we can measure the size, distance, and speed of attackers farther out and faster than the naked eye can manage."

"This can help us against the Twilight Parliament?"

"If it works, then we'll never face a surprise attack again," Johanna said. "And we may even be able to pinpoint where the Twilight Parliament is moving your family."

"What do you call it?" Daniel asked.

"The Shadow Light," Johanna said.

Chapter 41

When Lukka returned to Skyskape after the late summer break, the air bore the bite of the cold. Despite her reputation, she knew little of frost and autumn gusts beyond the piercing chills of a plane's cockpit. Her home sat midway up the side of a volcanic island, overlooking the fierce furnaces and foundries of the kingdom's shipyards.

Her earliest memories involved views from her room of skies of soot and shorelines of glossy obsidian glowing by the light of molten steel. When her parents took her to the beach on the opposite end of the island, she would dive under black glassy tides and feel one with them, her straight black hair melding with the waters.

At Skyskape, however, the world was different. The waves were blue and crested in white. The only lights were those from the airfield and from Landskape. There were expansive forests around the school and town, vaster and greener than anything she had ever seen on her island.

The official story about Daniel's absence was that it was a bereavement leave. Ms. Darlington's reason for Johanna's delay in returning to school was that she was on a medical leave, but Lukka knew she was helping Daniel. The faculty did not know how much he had truly lost, but they did not expect him to return to Skyskape for the remainder of the year.

Lukka had come to understand Daniel better than that. She knew that he was already hard at work on a plan to bring Parker and the Twilight Parliament to justice and to take back what still could be saved. It was up to her to do her part on campus while he was away. That meant working with the Klown Prinse.

"Lukka," Rigel said.

"Your Highness," Lukka said.

A tense silence sat between them that, under better circumstances, would've been occupied by Daniel or Johanna. Now, these two opposites had no buffer.

The first weekend back, the two met at the Wave's Break. Lukka had her cup of tea and shortbread cookies. Rigel had a stack of waffles dressed in syrup and whip cream. They sat across from one another like two duelists in one of the savage and romanticized epics of Visolian history.

"So," Lukka said.

"Yes?" Rigel answered.

"Auberdine."

"What of him?"

"We need to see him."

The prince ate a bite of his waffles. "I agree."

"Why are we here?" asked Lukka.

"Johanna, Daniel, and I always did this before a mission," Rigel said.

"What missions have you done up to this point?"

"Well, it was mostly Daniel who carried out the missions. We just talked things over with him beforehand."

"What has Daniel done?"

"He watched that film reel with us and then went off to beat you in that aerial exam."

"Okay, so what did Johanna do?"

"Johanna cracked the code," Rigel said.

"What do *you* do then?"

"I provide moral support."

Lukka munched on a shortbread cookie. "So you don't do anything."

Rigel recoiled. "I wouldn't say I do nothing. I helped get us started with all this in the first place. I found the film reel way back when."

Lukka leaned back in her chair. "So it sounds like this isn't the most important thing to do right now."

"Not so," Rigel said. "If we don't do this, then we won't come up with sudden insights that are useful for whatever Daniel is doing."

"Daniel's not here, so it can't be important."

"Well, look here, then," Rigel said. With his fork, he scooped a huge cloud of whipped cream and shoveled it into his mouth. Hunter, who'd been watching from behind the counter, looked at the prince and subtly shook his head.

Rigel wiped his mouth. "Daniel may not be here, but I'm a prince. Princes are capable sorts of people who can make things happen. Just look at any fairy tale."

"What about baronesses?" asked Lukka.

"Oh, baronesses lock princesses in castles and towers and stuff because they're jealous about something or other. Don't blame me. I don't write the fairy tales. Point is the baroness does something awful and then the prince steps in and saves the day. You see?"

A hint of a smile appeared on Lukka's face. "It sounds to me like the baronesses in the stories are proactive and the princes are reactive, yes?"

"Wait," Rigel said.

"Then we're agreed," Lukka said. She finished her tea and paid her check. "We're going to talk to Auberdine right now because coming all the way out here is a waste of time." She glanced toward Hunter. "No offense, sir."

Hunter just shrugged his shoulders. "Sounds to me like you two are in the thick of something I want no part in, so I'm not going to stick my nose where it doesn't belong."

"That's very thoughtful of you, Ol' Hunter," Rigel said.

Hunter frowned. "Did you just call me 'Ol' Hunter'? I'll have you know I'm only forty-nine. I'm not old."

"Okay," said Rigel, hopping to his feet and following her out of the diner. "Lukka's on to something. I'll be leaving now."

***

Dr. Auberdine's historic society met in a windowless room somewhere in the middle of the great spire in the center of the campus. The room was a museum of its own. Several upperclassmen examined documents, studied maps, catalogued historic artifacts, and translated handwritten papers. The vast majority came from Korona Red or Doubloon Gold.

Lukka and Rigel stepped inside and looked around for the doctor. He stood looking at what appeared to be a scrap of an old scroll, taken from the pelt of an animal and preserved between two pieces of glass. When he saw the Rigel and the baroness enter, he jumped up to greet them.

"Hello! Is His Highness here to join the Historik Preservation Sosiety? And the baroness of Pyrmunt too?"

"We're actually here on behalf of Baron Daniel Hardy," Lukka said.

The professor's countenance fell. "I didn't realize you were friends with Daniel. If you see him, tell him I'm sorry about what happened to Baron Blau. It's a terrible thing to lose a parent."

"Yes," Lukka said, eager to get the conversation over with. "I'll be sure to tell him myself. He wanted to ask you about something specific."

Auberdine cocked his head. "What is it?"

"If you know that the baron died, then perhaps you also heard about the attack the night of the premiere of *The Emerald Dragonfly*. It was orchestrated by a group calling themselves the Twilight Parliament. Someone with an interest in tracking down Buldwikk sorcerers has traced their operations to a hidden location along Tarrkaven's northern coast. They suspect they have a harbor and an airfield for large bombers and prisons for large numbers of people." The baroness paused. "We were told you know the geography of Tarrkaven better than anyone else. Can you tell us, given the geography, where that base might be?"

The doctor's eyes narrowed. "By any chance, was the person asking green and defensive about his identity?" Neither Lukka nor Rigel were able to hide their reactions. "Ah, I see you have spoken to Avo then. You can't trust that one," he said softly.

"Even if he was," Rigel said, "don't you think the kingdom would be better off knowing where a base of murderous sorcerers may be hidden along the coast? Take it from me. I may not be a very good prince, but the last thing I'd want is for ruin to come to the kingdom. If you're a good citizen of Tarrkaven, then perhaps you'd make that a priority over whatever you think Avo Howl did."

Rigel paused, glancing at Lukka, who gestured for him to go on. "And you can't make judgments of someone on only partial information. Armand and Avo were good students and good friends, just as you were their favorite teacher. Perhaps Avo didn't betray your trust but, instead, kept secrets for someone he cared about because he couldn't tell the world for fear of what dangers it would bring upon the people he most cared for.

"Avo's not a citizen. Being mixed up in danger spelled trouble for himself and his family, but he wouldn't turn his back on Armand because of it. It's selfish to think we deserve to know everything about the people in our lives, even if sometimes we'll feel cheated and lesser for not knowing. The fate of the kingdom and its people are at stake."

Auberdine sighed. "I suppose it would be poor form to let terrorists destroy the kingdom while I do nothing. I don't know what to tell you about hidden bases on the northern coast. It's mostly rocky crags, cliffs, and forests. If there was a hidden base with planes, ships, and large enough facilities to hold people then it would more than likely be noticed by air patrols. You can look over the maps in case there's something I've missed."

"That's all we ask," Lukka said.

As Dr. Auberdine went to gather the maps, Lukka turned to face Rigel. Her face registered a change in attitude toward him. "Wow. You're practicing what you preach. Maybe I misjudged you."

"Is that a compliment?" Rigel asked.

"Do you want a medal?" Lukka shot back.

"No, but I do have a question for you. Before, you mentioned to Daniel that he owes you an answer to one more question. What is it?"

"Maybe I spoke too soon. It's personal."

"I'm not going to hear it, am I?"

"Is your name Daniel Hardy?"

"Technically, *his* name's not Daniel Hardy either, but I'm not going to pry."

"Good."

Auberdine returned with several maps showing different points along the coast of Tarrkaven. "Here's what I could come up with." He looked at Rigel. "I take it the crown is responding to this danger."

"Yes, Pops has me playing messenger," Rigel fibbed.

The doctor handed the maps to the prince. "Then Father's light be with you," he said.

Lukka and Rigel left the room behind—Rigel carrying the maps, so Lukka could keep her hands free in case she needed to act quickly. She had lost her bat to the theater fire and, while she was glad it had helped Daniel survive the attack, it had robbed her of the security of carrying a threatening bludgeon to ward off people with ideas of picking a fight with her.

Rigel blabbered on but Lukka ignored him. Instead, she listened carefully to their surroundings and picked up on a footfall slightly out of sync with their own steps. With a subtle gesture, she caused a coin to fall from her pocket. As she bent to retrieve it, she whirled around and buried her foot in the solar plexus of a helmeted Twilight Parliament soldier.

The soldier crumpled to the ground. Lukka rushed forward and pulled away his helmet to reveal the prince's perpetual handler. Rigel was stunned. "Billiam! You're in the Twilight Parliament?"

"I'm not letting you run this nation into the ground with your antics and wanton disregard for consequence," said the man through gritted teeth. "You and your father have caused our people enough trouble."

"Oh, Billiam, what a bastard you are," Rigel said. "My antics may have caused you misery and hair-tearing by the looks of it, but I've never once killed anyone in a theater or bombed a town into submission. What good's boasting about power if your first act is to bully others?"

William sneered. "The weak will grow dissatisfied when their divine protectors can do nothing to save them."

"Rigel," Lukka said quietly. "He's seducing you to talk because he knows you like to."

"I do like to talk," Rigel said. "Talking is the simple pleasure of letting other people know how stupid and wrong they are."

"That's fantastic," she said, "but it looks like William here has friends… and they have us surrounded."

Rigel looked down at the captain. "The rest of school security, I presume?"

"Perfect way to keep tabs on our enemies. Parker knew you'd be trouble."

"Well, I hope Parker armed you to the teeth because Lukka can take your kytinfiends." Lukka tried to hide her uncertainty—the twelve probable sorcerers who had them cornered could be more than she alone could manage.

It would not be long before her concerns materialized. The sorcerers waved their hands and from the mists came the horrific shapes of twelve human figures with stripes of white in their hair and flowers and bark embedded in their skin.

"Even nature privileges some with power over its bounty," said William with an evil smile. "Buldwikk has shown us how to make that power our own."

Chapter 42

"Come on!" yelled Lukka. With no time to deliberate and knowing the odds were against her, she squeezed a hand around Rigel's stout wrist and, with the agility of a long jumper, dove through the security guards and their monsters—monsters likely created from imprisoned forestfolk.

She dragged the pendulous prince behind her with the maps in tow. Rigel did his best to keep pace with her but had none of the martial artist's grace. Running with Rigel behind her felt like moving through an obstacle course with a heavy chain to her wrist and a great weight rolling behind her. A skill to be learned by more advanced students of her order, she hadn't achieved this level of mastery. Perhaps, she thought, if we survive this, that exam would be a breeze.

"Stairs or elevator?" Rigel asked.

"Stairs," Lukka said.

"Up or down?"

"Down," she said. "They won't follow us into such a public area."

"They blew up Blau's town, attacked a crowded movie theater, and killed Blau. I don't think they're too concerned about acting in public now," said Rigel.

"If we go down, we can disappear into the garden."

"They have plant-speaking zombies with them!"

"Dr. Violite could be downstairs and she could help us," Lukka said.

"What in the Shadow's name is a chicken canary cat going to do against those odds?"

Lukka rolled her eyes. "Fine! We'll go up. Happy?"

"Not really!" When Rigel reached the bottom of the tower, he took wide strides up the stairs toward the top of the spire. "Can your older sister fight like you?"

"More or less," Lukka said following behind him with light brisk steps. She would have overtaken Rigel and left him behind, except for the pesky truth that she was sworn to protect the royal family with her life.

"Good enough for me," Rigel said. He narrowly missed a step and began to tumble backward when a pale and bony hand reached out to catch him. Lukka turned to see the shadowy shape of Dr. Violite—gliding up the steps beside them.

"Hey, you kids should run along. I suspect Buldwikk has figured out I'm here, and they're none too happy about it."

"Dr. Violite!" Lukka said. "They're terrorists of this kingdom using kytinfiends to cause chaos. Can you help us stop them?"

"Well, the thing is the charm I made for my most recent beast is currently attuning in the great bonekiln in the forest. I can get my backup, but I keep it in the headmaster's office as collateral." Violite moved with such speed that she almost seemed like a specter.

Rigel huffed and puffed up the stairs after her. "Surely you have some sort of counter for kytinfiends used by wayward sorcerers," he said.

"I mean, sure, but it isn't pretty," Dr. Violite said.

"If those things get to us, it won't be pretty, either."

"A fair point. There is something I could use, but it's up in the headmaster's office as well."

"Do you keep everything up there?" Rigel asked.

"Look, royal tenure works wonders, but even I have to abide by certain rules. I don't own the place. Four's sake, I never can appreciate how tall this tower is until I'm getting chased by some shoddy craftsmanship of third-rate sorcerers."

Lukka glanced over her shoulder. The kytinfiends were a mere ten paces behind Rigel. Their sorcerers followed a few paces behind them.

From the kytinfiends' hands sprouted sharp serrated claws. Dripping from their jaws was an acid that bleached their chins. As Lukka, Rigel, and Dr. Violite reached the top of the stairs and the waiting room before the headmaster's office, one kytinfiend threw what looked to be a pumpkin from a vine. It struck Rigel in the back and he was thrown forward. Lukka grabbed him by the arms and dragged him toward her sister's office and through the door. Dr. Violite slammed the door behind them.

The headmaster jumped to her feet. "What is the meaning of this?"

"Marley!" Lukka said to her sister. "We need your help. The school's under attack."

"I need a doctor," Rigel said.

"I *am* a doctor," Violite replied.

"Sion save me," he murmured.

The headmaster rounded her desk to face the three. "Slow down," she said, just as a large clawed hand broke through the door throwing splinters across the office.

"Shadow's Light!" Rigel shouted as he clambered along the floor.

"What the hell are those?" Marley turned and opened a cabinet, which held a wide array of weapons as well as Violite's kiln. She tossed Violite her bonekiln while she grabbed a shotgun and started feeding it shells.

"Twelve kytinfiends created from the bodies of forestfolk," Lukka said.

"Mother's mercy," said the headmaster.

"Look, Marley," Dr. Violite said. "Shells aren't going to fight off twelve of those shoddy tasteless creations. Neither are your sister's laxative kicks or the prince's crippleness. I need my archpriest's tonsil."

"You are not permitted by royal law to use that level of magic," said the headmaster.

Gesturing toward the door, Dr. Violite sneered. "*They're* not permitted to use that sort of magic at all. Live a little, Marley, because we may all be dead in a minute."

Rigel shouted into the void. "If it's a problem with the law, I'll get Dad to smooth it over," he said. "For the Mother's love, don't let us die here."

"Fine," said Marley. "Do what you have to, but next time monsters are chasing you, do NOT bring them to my office."

Dr. Violite grabbed a small burlap sack. She reached inside and pulled out what looked like an orange stalagmite about nine inches long.

"Is that a yam?" Rigel asked.

Violite looked at it and then broke into a wild smile. "Whaddya know? It *does* look like a yam!" Her smile waned. "It's not a yam, but we may all be in a serious mess. It's a good idea to think happy thoughts."

"Bit of a tall order, don't you think?" Rigel said.

"Maybe, but think happy thoughts like your life depends upon it!" The doctor dropped the "not yam" into the bone kiln. Deep white smoke billowed from the kiln just as the doors broke open and engulfed the kytinfiends and sorcerers. Everyone present collapsed into an instant and frightful sleep.

***

Few things in the world are less understood than an archpriest's tonsil. For starters, it did not come from a human man or woman of faith. Rather, it was found in the paleontological digs of Buldwikk.

Buldwikk is a land of countless graveyards of prehistoric beasts that no longer walk the earth. The most frequently identified fossils in Buldwikk are monstrosities of indefinable shape with long and twisted spindly bones. Study of the skeletons by Buldwikk paleontologists and sorcerers identified the beings as having a structure that resembles a skull. Some of the creatures had more than one. As no living person understood the role of these beings, they fell into the realm ruled by the Shadow, the patron of the Four that deals with the unknown. In every one of the skulls discovered, which paleontologists had named "archpriests," there existed large orange deposits sprouting from where human tonsils would rest.

When the tonsils are cooked in a bonekiln, all swept within the cloudy mist are entranced in a world of dreams. As Dr. Violite was so fond of saying, Buldwikk sorcery is far more an art form than a science, and it is from these dreams that all kytinfiends are born—dangerous only to the dreamer in whose dream the terrors appear.

***

Lukka found herself in the royal palace, far from the spire. She couldn't recall how she'd come to be in this place, but she wasn't concerned. As the frequent commuter knows, the specifics of a journey from point A to point B becomes muddled from their being overdone.

She walked down the hallway to the king's court. There, seated on the throne and surrounded by suitors, advisors, and malcontents was Rigel. He was swarmed by attention, and in the cacophony of voices, his own could not be heard.

While ladies fawned over Rigel, a red-faced citizen screamed about the taxes being too low to maintain the military and an old silver-haired man furiously shouted gibberish. The new "king" appeared deeply overwhelmed.

Lukka waded into the mob. As she looked to the suitors, she saw herself among them. She shook her head, seeking to clear it. It wasn't exactly herself, but a more shapely and provocative creature resembling her, kissing at Rigel's hand.

Lukka clenched her teeth. Just as the old man began another round of gibberish she drove her fist deep into the elder's jawbone, lifting him from his feet. He disappeared and the mob fell silent. "What's the meaning of all of this?" shouted Lukka. "Rigel is not your king. He's a second-born. King Azekiel rules this land, and, if you have something you need done, you should talk to him. If he's busy, then talk to Prinse Marzin." She paused as the crowd stared at her. "Rigel's the last person you'd want to go to because he has no authority of his own. Act like you've got some sense, people!"

With that, the crowd huffed and sneered and dispersed. As the shapely apparition of herself departed, Lukka shouted to her. "And you can do way better, lady!"

Rigel sat in stunned silence on the throne. Lukka dragged him down from it and he tried to swat her hand away. Recoiling, struck him hard on the temple with her open palm. "Are you really Rigel, or are you another one of those fakes?"

Rigel shook his head. "You're really Lukka?"

"Why? Did you think the other one was me?"

"I knew it had to be too good to be true."

"I've got plenty more smacks if you keep saying stupid things."

"Okay. So, real Lukka, real me...anything else here real?" Rigel asked. "Where are we anyhow?"

"I'm guessing some elaborate dream world."

Rigel appeared puzzled.

"Buldwikk sorcerers can be killed by their dreams," said Lukka. "Weren't you listening in Dr. Violite's class? So, naturally, to beat a bunch of 'third rate sorcerers,' as she called them, she lured them into a dream world."

"How are you so cognizant if this is a dream?"

"I'm a trained warrior. That's a matter of mental discipline as well as physical discipline."

"Well, if you're so disciplined, how do we get out of here?"

"Dr. Violite said something just before we came here."

"To think a happy thought," Rigel said.

"Oh, perfect," Lukka said, with a tone of disdain.

"Well, c'mon then," Rigel said. "How hard is that? Oh wait, forgot who I was talking to."

"You don't have to rub it in," Lukka said.

"Well, if this is a dream where your fears can destroy you, can't you just as easily imagine something that would make you happy?"

"Like what?"

Rigel considered suggesting that she think of her parents being alive, but he felt certain that would have the opposite effect. If Lukka had the mental discipline to be aware this was all a dream, then she would have the discipline to know any sudden appearance of her parents was also false. Under normal circumstances, teasing Lukka would fill him with enough joy for the dream's negatives to release him, but he knew he'd feel terrible leaving her behind. He considered, with no shortage of effort, how to make his arch-nemesis happy.

If it weren't for Daniel, he thought, he would not be associating with Lukka. Daniel isn't here right now, but I am. By Lukka's logic, they weren't the only two trapped in the dream. There was exactly one other person in a similar bind to Lukka who, without a doubt, wanted the same things that Lukka wanted.

"So, your sister's name is Marley," he said. "That's a cute name." The prince cantered down the steps from the throne. When he nearly fell on his face, he decided to walk like a normal person the rest of the way.

Lukka frowned. "Could you not talk about my sister that way? She's way out of your league."

"I'm a prince, Lukka. I'm a league of my own."

"She's also twelve years older than you."

"That *does* make it strange, I concede. Anyway, what's the deal with you two? I've been called to her office once or twice. She doesn't talk about you, and you don't talk about her. Something up with that?"

"That's none of your business," Lukka said.

"No, it's yours…and it's hers, but it seems like neither of you is willing to sort it out and maybe it's because you don't know how to," Rigel said. He looked at a painting of his family as they continued down the hall of the court. He had a great overabundance of siblings. One older brother who seemed to eat, sleep, and bathe in a military uniform. Five darling little sisters swarming the painting, two of which hung on Rigel's arms.

"Family drama's no fun. Each of us has our own unique challenges to deal with."

"Right, so how about you let me worry about my sister, all right?" Lukka said

Rigel ignored her. "My brother and I don't get along at all," he said. "He acts like you all the time, and he dislikes Pops because Pops acts like me. It's like my brother feels threatened that I will take the throne from him. But you saw that fiasco in there. Why would I want that? It's dreadful. I don't know how Pops deals with it."

"I don't think your brother feels threatened," Lukka said. "If he's like me, then he probably wants you to take the role a bit more seriously. I want you to take being a prince more seriously. Not because you're going to rule this kingdom someday, Shadow forbid that ever happened, but because the people want somebody who cares about them in power and you can be that person even if you're not the one calling the shots."

"No, thank you," Rigel said. "I'm so used to people fawning over me all day. I figure if I pull enough pranks on them, they'll learn to leave me alone."

"Some of them will, but they'll do it out of contempt. If you want people to respect your boundaries, don't do it by driving them away. Show an interest in them, and then they'll be more open to your needs."

"My brother has no interest in me," Rigel said.

"Well, then you have to seem interested in him. Otherwise, what reason does he have to take you seriously?" Lukka said. Suddenly, she saw where the conversation was leading.

"Oh, you devious bastard."

"What?" Rigel said.

"You're a dangerous one, Klown Prinse. I underestimated you."

Rigel grinned. "I love it when I outsmart myself. So where do you think she is?"

"I have an idea," Lukka said. She opened a door, but just as she did, Rigel faded from view. She told herself not to panic—that he had simply awakened. Panicking would be detrimental to having a happy thought, so she pushed that "what if" to the back of her mind.

She walked through the door and found herself at a wall of her family's manor overlooking the foundry at the foot of the volcano. Farther out to sea, she saw the incoming titanic form of a kytinfiend. She wasn't sure if a kytinfiend in the dream could hurt her, but she felt, either way, it would be best to settle this quickly. She was on the clock now.

Lukka stepped into the office. *Her* office. The place Marley left her to govern when she ran off to teach at Skyskape. She'd grown quite fond of it, enough to know it hadn't been kept the way she kept it but rather the way her father had kept it, with the telltale photograph of her parents on their honeymoon on some bright Visolian beach of white sands. They'd been so young and happy, unaware of the ending that awaited them. She and Marley didn't have that luxury. Such was the burden of the Last Light, and the price of their martial magic.

"Marley," said Lukka. "It's me."

"Yes, I know," Marley said in a calm but tense voice.

"So that's the one that will do it. The kytinfiend that will kill you one day? Your Last Light?"

"Yes, Lukka," Marley said.

"If we wake up, then that day won't be today," Lukka said.

"Well, I can't seem to wake up, and it would seem you haven't either."

Lukka paused. "I guess neither of us has been happy for a long time."

"You haven't come to visit," Marley said.

"Neither have you," Lukka said.

Marley nodded. "I guess this place has too many memories. Both those that were sweet and are gone…and those that are bitter and yet to come."

"There's a way out, Marley," said Lukka. "Let's not make any more memories here. Let's be sisters again. Let's go to Visolia and see the mountains. Let's go where there aren't rumors of war and giant monsters and cold air. Let's set aside sooty skies for a while and make some good memories before we have to face the bad ones. That way, we'll have something good to hold onto when rough days do come. That doesn't sound so bad, does it?"

"No, I don't suppose it does," Marley said, smiling. "How about you? The one who will be there when you die is that boy I tried to expel, isn't it? What's he like?"

"Kind, gentle, a little clueless, but he's so determined to help everyone that he ends up hurting himself. I was myself around him, and I still couldn't drive him off. There really is no cheating the Last Light. Still, I'm happy it's somebody like him. It makes me think there will be a lot of good days ahead too."

"Well, I'm not going to let him have *all* your good days," Marley said.

"I'll hold you to that," Lukka answered.

Then the two sisters blinked—away from the dream and back to the waking world.

Chapter 43

As the hills of the Tarrbly canyon shifted from green to rolling gold to horizons of orange, Duun welcomed the cool autumn air. His recovery had progressed so he could now function reasonably, within a few limits. He and Johanna began spending more time in town, discussing with both the Knot Kovenant and the citizens of Tarrbly what the community needed and how those needs could best be met.

Johanna joined him in the mornings to tend to the sheep. Her profound height at first seemed imposing to the small woolly animals. Duun laughed until he wheezed when Johanna tried and failed to get one of the itchy "clouds" to go over a hip-high stone wall.

For Johanna, changes to life in Tarrbly had not resembled the shifting of gears so much as putting a car in park and up on blocks. In her mother's household, every hour of every day was documented and made useful. In Tarrbly, time moved more slowly than usual. Life was somehow more refreshing. Even so, the duo kept busy. They had not forgotten that their main objective was rescuing Duun's family and the forestfolk that had been held captive.

Lukka and Rigel contacted Johanna to tell her about the attack thwarted by Marley and Dr. Violite. Lukka spared them the details of what became of the assailants that had fallen asleep by Dr. Violite's intervention, but she assured them that the sorcerers on campus would no longer be a problem. The most pressing information Lukka imparted, however, was what exactly the Twilight Parliament sorcerers were doing with forestfolk. That horror proved to be a dreadful wakeup call to Duun.

He paced the main hall with quick steps and, despite his power, wore the face of a boy torn asunder by the limits of human frailty. He needed to heal faster, but no amount of wishing for his bones to heal sped their recovery. He didn't have gifts like those of Avo or Leleen. He wasn't smart like Johanna or sly like Rigel or cunning like Lukka. When he had tried to save Leleen and his mother, he had come up short.

The doctor Ms. Darlington had brought him told him he was in no state to fly, but he wanted to go to Skyskape and fight alongside Lukka and Rigel. There were times he wanted to vent his frustrations to Johanna, but then he told himself he would be a burden if he distracted her from her work on the Shadow Light. It wasn't her place to bear his burden, and he didn't want to make her hard work more difficult for his sake.

He gingerly donned his coat and went down into the town. He hadn't given a grand speech to the Knot Kovenant since he'd been back, but even as the village entered into autumn, the Kovenant seemed to be revitalized in their devotion to rebuilding the town. He considered that his perception that they had given up was mistaken, that on the day he returned, he'd caught them on an off day. In any case, everyone seemed diligent like a hive of bees. Nobody seemed rushed, but everyone kept working toward the goal of having Tarrbly made new. He found a bench to sit upon and stopped to take in the sight of the town on the shore of the lake and to gaze up at the rushing falls down upon the river.

"Young Baron Blau," a voice said.

Duun hadn't prepared for all the possible combinations of his name at this point. Adding the title of baron to the pile made his brain go through mental gymnastics. Still, he turned to see who had spoken. A milkman making the rounds from the creamery that Baron Blau had built was standing behind him. Judging by his hair, Duun knew he was an Ulkirn refugee like him.

"Duun's fine," he said.

"Ok, then, Duun," the milkman said. "Several of we Knots haven't had the opportunity to thank you for your efforts away from Tarrbly. You've inspired us all and, for one so young, have done much to give our people hope."

"I'm happy to hear it."

To his own ears, his voice sounded hollow. What good was inspiring others if he couldn't even help himself?

"We're looking at a new chapter of our community's history, and you're leading the charge. Baron Blau picked you well. May his life spin new knots."

"*He* did all of this," Duun said. "I just inherited it. I can barely read."

"Oh, that's no big deal," the milkman said with a bright wide smile framed by the stripes in his hair. "Few of us can read either. I didn't know literacy was necessary to lead. Our families have gotten by without it, but maybe we can do that too if you've done it."

"Can you make my bones heal faster?" Duun blurted. In truth, his mouth had acted faster than his mind. He had rarely been one to lose his composure, so it surprised him more even than the milkman.

The milkman thought for a moment and then went over to his cart and fetched a pint bottle. He returned and handled it to the young baron.

"Nothin' wrong with being frustrated," he said. "Tight knots are strong knots. Nobody here was happy about bombers wiping out the folk that lived here before, but we've rebuilt their town to spin them new knots. Strong knots take time to weave."

Duun thought of something his mother had said long ago. About how Avo had the parts of his life that only he was aware of that were messy—but they had made him Avo. Now Duun knew more about Avo. Those messy knots had been his friendship with Armand. Armand no doubt had messy knots of his own, but Avo accepted them all the same.

Avo's "wrong" side had turned him into the Emerald Dragonfly, a symbol of hope for all of Tarrkaven. Duun's wrong side had made him a baron, with the responsibility to carry on Blau's mission for a united Tarrkaven where Knots and the Four could live together for a stronger future.

Duun looked at his present predicament and thought about all the knitwork he had made under his mother's tutelage. There wasn't a single project that didn't look horribly wrong somewhere midway through the knitting. More often than not, the start of a project looked like a disaster, but persistence made the needles spin and all turned out well.

That's where I am, he thought. In the middle of the needlework, looking abysmal. He could quit now, or he could see it through, and if he did, then perhaps he would be baron not only for the Knot Kovenant but also for Tarrkaven.

Johanna had begun to count on him just as he counted on her. He knew her work on the Shadow Light would help him find his family. Lukka had told him what had happened—not to scare him, but to give him the assurance that they were fine. Rigel needed a brave baron to protect this kingdom for a more just future. And most of all, Duun's family needed him to rescue them and—even if the worst had occurred—save the Knots and other forestfolk from a similar fate.

This was the tapestry of his journey. Slow healing bones were but one thread of it. He wouldn't be undone by this one obstacle, because all the previous bands still counted. He would continue for all of their sake.

Duun finished drinking the milk and returned the bottle to the milkman's cart. He stood and headed up to the manor where Johanna sat outside with a large array of metal rotating by the power of an electrical generator. She wore her Doubloon Gold scarf about her neck amid the cold wind.

She stared down upon a glass surface she called a monitor. The expression on her face appeared puzzled.

"Can I help you there?" Duun said, knowing full well he could not.

"I wanted to examine the area of the canyon from this spot and use it as a control. It looks about right, but I have no idea what *this* is." Johanna pointed to a strange and jagged patch along a long straight line. It faded from view and then appeared again as the array spun about on its axis.

"Looks like a bunch of lines to me," Duun said.

"Well, you're not wrong," Johanna said. "These long lines are the walls of the canyon. These distorted lights are the trees. We can even make out some of the buildings down by the lakeside. I'm not sure what's sticking into the canyon here, though."

"Does this spinning thing have anything to do with what shows up where?" Duun asked when he angled his head to the array.

"Yes, the direction it faces is what produces this readout."

Duun turned and stared in the direction of the canyon wall from where he stood. He remembered the patch of trees he saw from the day the fog hung low on the canyon walls and the bombers arrived to destroy the town.

From this observation, he made note of those lines. "You're saying those lines are inside the canyon wall?"

"Right, but I shouldn't be picking up that level of detail. The array isn't high enough to observe what's on top of the cliff side. This is lower."

Duun knew instantly what it was. "It's a cave," he said. "It's the cave I tried to hide my mother and sister in when the bombers came. It runs deeper, but those jagged rocks are likely from when the ceiling collapsed."

"A cave?" Johanna rushed to a stack of papers Natalie had brought her. Unspooling one set and placing it over the monitor, the paper revealed itself as a map of the surrounding canyon. Turning dials on the machine, she adjusted the screen so that it matched the images on the map. The cropping of the cave indented the canyon wall just as Duun described.

"I have an idea," Johanna said.

"I'm listening," Duun replied. He prepared to be amazed at another of Johanna's breakthroughs.

"Oh wait, but that wouldn't make any sense. Never mind," Johanna said.

Duun let a dense silence sit between them as Johanna returned to pondering. He waited expectantly for the revelation like an audience watching a stage magician who announces there is nothing in his hat only to remember he had to pick his coat up from the cleaners.

"I'm going to assume you decided whatever you were going to say makes no sense," Duun said. "May I hear it so that I can offer my opinion?"

"Okay. Lukka and Rigel were saying that they couldn't figure out where an airfield would be hidden along the coast near the school without being spotted. For a moment, I thought there might be a hidden cove or grotto dug between the cliffs, but then I realized that couldn't be."

"You don't think they could fly planes out of a cave?" Duun asked. "What if it's a very large cave?"

"Oh, I don't doubt they could fly planes *out* of a cave," she said. "It's landing the plane that's an entirely different matter."

Something about the idea sounded familiar to Duun. He had heard the exact sentiment shared by someone before. Who it was dawned on him all at once.

"Jensen's in the Twilight Parliament!" he declared.

It was Johanna's turn to be surprised. "What? How does that relate to what we're talking about?"

"Give me a second and you'll understand."

He plopped down beside her. "On the night Rigel discovered I was Knot Kovenant, I heard Jensen talking with someone on the phone about wanting to be part of some scheme or plot. Whoever he was talking to said something related to how or where they would pick him up, and he told them he didn't think a plane could go there. What if there *is* a cave, and within the cave is some mechanical means to catch a speeding plane before it strikes the cave wall?"

Johanna thought for a moment. "I suppose it's not out of the question. Mom uses a hook to catch landing planes on her carriers. Perhaps the Twilight Parliament has a similar contraption."

"Could we move this machine to Skyskape?" Duun asked.

"We have no choice but to do it," Johanna said. "Do you think you can rally the Knot Kovenant?"

"I have to. This is all of our fight now," Duun said.

"Do you know where they'll all be meeting? I don't think you want to spend your day running all around town spreading the word."

"I've got a hunch," Duun said.

***

Some things hadn't changed even after the passage of the year. The town had been rebuilt and the people in the town's center were different, but the post office still remained the gathering point for those seeking the day's news. Duun arrived dressed in his shepherd's attire. Johanna followed by his side. Sure enough, there at the post office, the heads of households for the Knot Kovenant were gathered reading newspapers and checking for updates on weather conditions so they would know when to start planting their crops. He looked around and felt lucky to have caught a few forestfolk before they all scattered to their work in the fields and forests.

Even after everything he'd been through, he still felt like a child among all these people. Johanna acted and looked more like an adult than he did.

The thought occurred to him that the same feelings were behind why Lukka acted the way she did. In any case, the success of this mission depended upon his having the support of the community, so he'd have to do his best.

"Good morning, Knots of the Kovenant. There is a matter I must tell you about. I'm sure you've heard it in part already. We the Knot Kovenant—and to a greater extent the Kingdom of Tarrkaven—are under attack by a grass-root movement of sorcerers calling themselves the Twilight Parliament. They wage war against the kingdom because they believe the kingdom has failed them, but they wage war on *us* because they feel we do not deserve the responsibility we have been given by our ancestors and the world.

"I have received news that these terrorists have been capturing our brothers and sisters to wrest control of our sacred gifts and responsibility and to abuse it to their aims. They have taken both my brother and sister, Avo and Leleen Howl—and my mother—to strike a blow against our community. They will not stop until they have made this kingdom part of the very land that destroyed many of our homes. They struck once before, seeking to wipe away Tarrbly when we were defenseless."

The crowd present stirred with uncertainty and fear at the declaration of this enemy's name. The reaction wasn't exactly what Duun wanted, but he knew it was necessary to call his peaceful people to action.

"They are a hidden enemy," he continued, "but Johanna Darlington and I have found, using newly developed technology, where they have hidden their base. I have made an alliance with the free people of Tarrkaven to strike these sorcerers at their base before they have a chance to establish a foothold within the kingdom. If we strike now, they will be taken completely off guard."

He stood up, his spine straight, and spoke as eloquently as he ever had.

"However, I cannot do it alone. I need people who are willing to fight for the preservation of our way of life and the natural world. If we do not fight, then they will do to Tarrkaven what Buldwikk did to Ulkirn." He paused. "I know it is not our way to seek violence. It is not our way to kill without cause, but if we stand idly by, we will be the first victims in their war against life itself. We are the knots that fasten humanity to the natural world. Without us, the tapestry of life would unravel. Let us fight for life itself, to free our brothers and sisters in captivity, and to make a new future for the Knot Kovenant in Tarrkaven."

Someone called from the back of the crowd. "How can we fight? We are not soldiers." Duun had anticipated the question and was prepared with the answer.

"Avo Howl, my brother and a pillar of our community, never stopped fighting for life when he was accused of being a criminal. He was just as much a gardener and a keeper of the trees as the rest of us. He didn't choose to fly to be a soldier. He flew for the freedom to travel on the wind as a symbol of our people.

"When he was alone and unable to return home, he made an identity for himself as the Emerald Dragonfly. Now, the Emerald Dragonfly is a hero to the people of Tarrkaven. Were it not for betrayal by Mr. Parker, he would be leading this fight himself. There is only one of him, but there are hundreds of us, and if one of us can threaten our enemies, then *all* of us can stop them forever. We do not fight alone. We have the kingdom and the whole of nature at our back. What can be more powerful than that?"

The crowd discussed his proposal with middling enthusiasm. Duun couldn't help but wonder what to expect. He hadn't learned to make speeches from Baron Blau or the professors at Skyskape. Avo would've been better suited, he thought.

"Let's go, Johanna," Duun said.

"Wait," Johanna said. She stepped up beside him. "Duun is one of your own. Avo and Leleen are your own. What good is it to call them brothers and sisters if you won't stand to fight for your own? Knot or Tarrkavian, it doesn't matter. We all share the land the same, we live the same, and we die the same. We're going to Skyskape to fight the Twilight Parliament. You can come with us and save your brethren, or you can stay and watch us save your brethren. But I don't want to be the one explaining why strangers showed up to save them when their own could've."

The two friends turned and started back up the hill. A voice called out from behind them It was the milkman. "Wait!" he said. "We're with you. We'll get as many as we can. Wait for us. Meet us this evening—we'll be there."

Duun smiled up to his castellan. "Not bad, Johanna!"

"Come now," she said. "You did the heavy lifting. I just gave them a push." The two continued up the hill in silence. *By the gods,* thought Johanna. *I'm beginning to sound like my mother.*

Chapter 44

When evening arrived at the airfield, Minah Darlington flew in with two additional passenger planes. She stepped down from the cockpit to greet Duun and Johanna. "Are you ready for school?" she said, with chipper enthusiasm.

Johanna and Duun groaned in response. Minah held up her hands defensively. "All right, all right, I thought that would sound better than 'Let's all go to war,' but then I said it out loud and realized school is way worse. Not to be too picky, but I hope it's not just the two of you."

"We were told others were coming, but we haven't seen them yet," Duun said.

"Okay. For sake of seating, does 'others' have a number to it? I'm being pushy, I know. I just like to know what sorts of ingredients I'm working with before I bake an ambush."

"How about us, then?" said a voice from the front of an approaching crowd. There stood a veritable company of townsfolk. The bright glowing forestfolk stood along the edges and the rest of the Knot Kovenant approached with hunting rifles, scythes, and pitchforks. They numbered around two hundred fifty, and they marched with vitality and zeal.

"Oh," Minah said. "You kiddos did well. I can make a stash of whoop-ass with this. I suppose it does feel like we're leading an angry mob right now, but I can work with that. Come on, I've got something you'll like."

Minah and Ms. Booke went into the plane and brought down several crates. When she opened them up, there were uniforms identical to Avo's. She tossed helmets to Duun and Johanna.

"This will protect you from glancing bullets, sharp objects, and fire. Don't charge a machine gun nest, but these will even our odds. Duun, yours doubles as a brace for your ribs so you can fly your plane."

She turned to the crowd. "Forestfolk among us, will you step forward? I've got seed pouches built into yours. I've also got a wide array of seeds and shoots to choose from. Stuff that binds people, stuff that paralyzes, stuff that blocks paths, and breaks kilns. All sorts of fun. Glowing moss for walls. Algae to mask our entry. Seed pods to give us smokescreens. This is from Avo's secret armory, so you know it's good stuff."

"What about you, Ms. Darlington? I know about the whole blood thing, so where will you be?" Duun asked.

"I'll be coordinating from ship to Marley Strauss in the Skyskape spire. I figure the radio signal won't reach the cave from the tower, but I may be able to relay it from one of my ships. I made headsets for the suits. They were a bit of a rush order, but they should still be good."

The planes were loaded and everyone donned their gear. Duun stepped into the manor one more time to see Natalie. She waited in the foyer where she'd swept over the same square foot of floor for some time.

"Oh, is it finally time for you to head out?"

"It would seem so. Thank you for everything you've done for me and my family, Natalie. You and the baron have both done much for the Knot Kovenant."

"Oh, I just served where I could. The kingdom would be a far better place if more people knew your family. I enjoyed your mother's conversations. Bring them home, and please stay safe," she said as she fought to hold back tears. "I'll bake those potato things your mother told me about. I don't know if there'll be enough for everyone, but I'll try."

"Thank you, Natalie," Duun said. "We'll all be home soon."

"Will that nice girl be coming back? I like her," Natalie said.

"Well, I think that's something for Johanna to talk about with her mother, but I'll let you know if they reach a decision."

"All right. It's not often the house is full anymore."

"If all goes well, then you may think the house is *too* crowded."

Natalie wrapped her arms around Duun, careful not to squeeze too tight. "It's not a home if it's not crowded." Duun noticed that Natalie's hug had not hurt him. Either the uniform Minah had brought him worked wonders, or he had sufficiently healed. He returned the hug and then went to his plane.

***

Duun flew with Johanna and Minah. The other planes were flown by Ms. Booke and Professor Thompson from Skyskape. Duun was surprised how well Minah could keep the plane steady. He had expected her to move at a breakneck pace as she had when she arrived at Skyskape all those months ago. "It's something else to see you fly, Ms. Darlington. I always knew you could, but I never really put it together in my mind that you did."

"Well, of course," Minah said. "You can't build the best airplanes in the sky if you can't fly one. When I got started, my parents repaired cars, but as soon as people started building machines for the air, I had to get into that business. The War of Kalamity was the catalyst to put Darlington on the map, and then when the baron fought for this hard-earned pause in the conflict, I went into any business that interested me. I try to keep my hands close to all my industries as possible. It's not good sport to just throw money at your problems. You can't really appreciate the people who use your work if you've never worked on it yourself."

She glanced around. "Could you be a dear and check on Johanna. She doesn't really handle flying all that well."

"Will do," Duun said. He got up from the co-pilot's chair and walked back to the fuselage where Johanna sat between two windows, looking out neither. A touch pale, she gripped the armrests as tightly as a serpent might squeeze a rabbit. She looked up to Duun and gave a nervous smile.

"You look good in the flight suit," she said keeping her eyes on him to avoid catching a view of the sky.

"Oh, yeah, it's a little tight. I'm going to assume that's the brace." He looked down at her. "I take it you're not much of one for flying."

"Not really, I will design the planes, but on the whole, I'm not crazy about being in the air."

Before Duun could offer any consolation, the low roar of thunder growled over the hum of the engines. Ms. Darlington spoke through the speakers. "We're going to have some turbulence. Forgot to mention that. Buckle your seat belts."

Duun suspected Ms. Darlington had not actually forgotten to mention the fact, but he took a seat by Johanna's side regardless. Johanna buckled her seatbelt and assisted him—his brace prevented him from turning his body too far in one direction. She took the buckle from his hand and fastened the belt. She looked to the floor to again avoid looking out the windows.

"Planes don't usually go down in storms," Johanna said. "Also, passengers tend to be safe from lightning strikes." Her foot tapped away on the floor as she rattled off other statistics about the unlikelihood of planes going down due to weather, her mother's track record as a pilot, and the steps to successfully deploy a parachute.

Duun suspected none of her strategies were actually helping, so he took her long dark fingers into his own warm, calloused hand. He felt her pulse surging through the hand, and then he realized his own pulse adjusted, syncing to the same pace. Then he spoke in a soft tone.

"Imagine yourself as a bundle of knots tightly wound and confused. Start from the top of your head and work your way down, taking time to think about unwinding each one." Duun then went down from the top of the head to the neck to the shoulders, substituting the chest with the back, and then by the time he finished, he felt the length of Johanna's arm pressing into his own. Her eyes were closed, and even against the distant rumble of thunder, she breathed in soft and restful repose.

***

When the planes landed at the Skyskape airfield, they were greeted by canvased vehicles carrying Dr. Auberdine, Dr. Violite, Rigel, and Lukka. Johanna and Duun got off the plane followed by the group he had assembled from Tarrbly. Each wore the armored flight suits that Ms. Darlington had procured for them. Lukka wore an identical suit and welcomed her two friends into the canvas truck. A caravan of trucks awaited the rest.

"Those other trucks aren't carrying students, are they?" Duun asked.

Lukka's expression was resolute. "Most students are safely tucked away in the tunnels below the school," she said, "but Krossbone Brown refused to do so. They said they came to this school to get citizenship and they didn't want the kingdom to fall before they could manage it." She looked over the pair. "You two look great in the suits. Have you healed up, Duun?"

"Well enough," Duun said, his smile hidden by his helmet. Lukka seemed to get the idea.

"Good to hear, though I don't suspect you're much of a fighter."

"My job will be to free my family," Duun said.

"Well, I believe you'll do it," Lukka said. She paused. "I'm going to take care of the sabotage. If there's a hidden base in the cliff side, then there are planes and munitions that need to be destroyed. Not to mention a potentially large bonekiln. Between the two of us, I think you may have the easier job."

"We'll see," Duun said.

The trucks turned out of the airfield and down the muddy street toward the Landskape harbor where Minah's heavily-armed ship waited. In a separate truck, Johanna's Shadow Light followed the convoy. Once they had all boarded the ship, it left the harbor behind and traveled along the coast east of the town. Johanna turned on the spinning dish, and Dr. Auberdine set out the map of the coastline.

As they sailed, the first indications of an enclosed cave appeared on the Shadow Light. By the time they had drawn near enough, it became clear how hidden away the cave had been. A gate of large imposing stones blocked both view and access by large vessels. Safe passage relied on small rafts carrying a few people at a time.

Lukka had gone on a ship with a group of the Knot Kovenant accompanying her. They had been armed by Ms. Darlington with military hardware, but many of them still favored the hatchets, knives, and tools they'd brought from home. Behind her came Duun's raft carrying several more of the Knot Kovenant. Few on the raft were comfortable—the waves grew more turbulent as they neared the entrance. By the time the raft entered the cave proper, the group was shrouded in darkness.

"Do you need a light, Duun?" a forestfolk asked.

"Not yet," he whispered. "We need to stay hidden a while longer." As he said these words, the growling hum of a plane came rising from within the cave and flew out of the cave's mouth into the sea. Shortly thereafter, the sound of flak cannons from Ms. Darlington's cruiser could be heard canvasing the sky with shells.

The intent of this strategy was to make sure any enemy fighters leaving the cave spotted the ship so as to alert the others and start moving planes from the fortress. If the enemy went to fight the ship, then they would deplete their planes and thin their numbers for the ground assault to move in.

The deafening sounds of airplane engines inside a closed cave blotted out the sounds of the ground force. As soon as the first plane was fired upon, five other planes screeched into action from the cave entrance. They left to do battle just as Duun saw the first lights of the Twilight Parliament base.

Within the cave stood a massive chamber with buildings carved in the stone walls, cages along the perimeter, runways for planes, watchtowers with machine gun nests, and, at the center, a massive bonekiln beneath an altar carved from the cold black trees of Buldwikk. Here within waited an organized military force with the resources to crush a force of trained Tarrkavian marines.

Unfortunately, all Duun and Lukka had were students, farmers, shepherds, and hunters.

Chapter 45

Leleen stood at the barred window, watching as she had for days as plane after plane arrived, unloading forestfolk who had been captured from Tarrkaven and elsewhere. It hadn't taken long for Leleen and the others to learn what was happening to them. Standing outside the cell where she and her mother had been kept out of respect for their connection to the Emerald Dragonfly were two kytinfiends made from two lovers taken some time before. From between their red beetle-like plating grew daffodils that peeked out over the red orbs upon their heads like a slug's eyestalks. Those closest to the door went first to the kiln.

At first, the radical changes to Tarrbly, made with the cooperation of the Knot Kovenant, had been repugnant to Leleen. She had worried about what the changes brought about by the baron after the attack would do to the values of the community over time.

Now, she agreed that those differences paled when compared to the abuses of the Twilight Parliament. Was there ever a more dreadful place than this for a being who thrived in nature? No plants, not even moss, could grow here. Some fungi grew in the cave, but it was too far out of reach to speak to. At one point, Leleen had tried to talk to mold on the bread, but it had had a nasty attitude. All the forestfolk in the packed cells found new disdain for mold when it mocked them.

But something was different. There was more than mold near the cave. There near the water was growing a large swath of ferns. Leleen knew there had been no ferns before because the cave was hostile to life itself. She scanned the ferns and soon saw long vines of kudzu crawling across the ground. This plant, quick to grow on normal days, was moving even faster. She watched as one of the Twilight terrorists was swallowed in the growing thicket. Then, beneath the swarm of kudzu, she saw a light, and then another, and before long, she recognized the bright blue hue of luminous algae.

She caught her breath. Forestfolk were rising from the kudzu.

Leleen turned to the others in the cell. "Everyone," she said with a raised whisper. "Our brethren have come to rescue us. We must illuminate ourselves so they can find us."

As she spoke, her skin lit up, revealing a bright color of blue. Under better circumstances, she would've been even brighter, but without communication with her beloved flora and fauna, it was all she could do to muster her algae's light. Others in the cell followed suit and before long they produced enough light to shine through the window to the shore.

"Stop that glowing or we'll shoot!" said a guard. The kytinfiends hissed and caused the daffodils to grow long venomous barbs as their handlers aimed guns within.

"We won't be your prisoners any longer!" someone shouted.

"Nature wins in the end!" said another.

The guard raised his rifle. "I've had enough of this!"

But he was too late. The blade of a hatchet came down on his shoulder. His knees collapsed beneath him and his arms twisted inward. He struggled but found he could no longer move his limbs.

Pitchforks impaled the kytinfiends, and they crashed through the stone walls of the cell. A small soldier who had disabled the guard drew two pistols and shot both beasts in the orbs, after which they dissipated like smoke. Taking a key from the belt of the guard, the soldier opened the doorway.

"Follow the plant growths," she said. "Duun will get you to the boats. Hurry!"

The huddled masses came out one by one, but more sorcerers arrived with guns and beasts in tow. Two horrifying bats clambered along the ground screeching a terrible song. The young woman cried, "Barricades!" and some of the taller soldiers dropped pine cones to the ground. In their place sprouted massive trees. Scattered pumpkin seeds burst into a blockade of squash that blocked the passage of the Twilight sorcerers.

At last, the prisoners realized that the soldiers were forestfolk and increased their pace down among the foliage. As soon as Leleen reached the door, she spoke to a small soldier who shot from behind a tree that had not been there before.

"Miss, my mother's here, and she cannot walk," Leleen said.

"Don't worry, these two will carry her down." She motioned to two of the soldiers to rescue the old woman.

"My brother is also being held somewhere else. He's the Emerald Dragonfly."

"Oh," said the soldier, pulling away her mask. "I thought you looked familiar. You're Duun's and Avo's sister, right?"

"You know Duun?" Leleen said.

"I do. Now, I'd love to stay and chat, but time is of the essence and we are being shot at. Would you kindly go down to the boats?"

"Not without Avo," Leleen said. "He's being held in a cage over the big pit."

"Of course, he is," said Lukka. She thought for a second. "I was told that despite the speed with which they grew, these trees won't last long. Go down the path, find Duun, and I'll set up the fireworks and distract the sorcerers. Go!"

Leleen went with the two forestfolk soldiers who'd returned with her mother down the path of fast swarming kudzu and ferns. Duun stood among a small squad of soldiers firing on the Twilight Parliament from under cover of mounting brush. An occasional kytinfiend drew close only to be pinned to the ground by farm equipment and shot in the orb.

"Duun!" Leleen said.

"Leelee!" Duun said. "Where's Avo?"

"In a cage over the altar. I think Parker's there too."

"Is Mom safe?"

"Two of your guys have her," Leleen said.

Duun looked to the two soldiers carrying his mother down the slope. "Get her to the boats, and then get to the ship."

"Yes, Baron," they replied.

"I'm going with you to get Avo," Leleen said. "If we don't hurry, they'll feed him to the kiln."

Duun nodded and hurried with her up the path. When they reached the trees and pumpkins, he caught sight of Lukka hurriedly planting red sticks beneath large fuel silos. She spooled out wires behind her. He turned to Leleen. "Looks like we haven't got long."

"I'm waiting on you," Leleen said, as she turned and called a series of branches forth toward the altar. Duun ascended them and made his way to the cage. The top opened like a basket and he saw Avo within—he was unconscious. His body was bruised and beaten and his skin was a sickly yellow.

"Avo, it's Duun!" he called. "I'm here to get you out!"

Avo didn't move.

"Avo! Leelee and Mom are safe. I need you to wake up."

Avo remained still.

Duun turned and called back to his sister. "Leelee! I need help!"

"Right!" she said. "I'm here." Using ivy cuttings acquired from one of the other forestfolk, she bound Avo and with Duun's help hoisted him up and out of the cage.

Once in the light, Leleen scanned Avo's body. "He doesn't look good," she said.

"What's wrong?" Duun asked.

"The algae under his skin has been taxed too hard to repair itself. But if I can get him quickly back into nature, I can transfer the vitality from the surrounding plants into him."

"We have plants here!"

Leleen shook her head. "These move too hastily. And they're far too weak to save Avo. We need to use the time we have to get him out of here."

A figure appeared outside the cage.

"It's a shame you have no time," said Parker. He pointed a gun at the three siblings. "I shot you once, Duun, but you're as resilient as your mother. If she had just died from the poison I was giving her —"

Just then, the ground shook and the fuel depots exploded. The ceiling shattered and Parker fell into the kiln.

The opening in the ceiling revealed vines from the forest above growing downward to meet them. Lukka crawled up and with the help of the forestfolk above lifted Avo out of the darkness to the morning sun and the fresh clear air above.

"Lukka! Where are the others?" Duun asked.

"They're already in the boats. You were taking too long, so I figured I'd start things on my end."

Leleen smiled at Duun. "I like her."

Lukka looked at Leleen and then Avo. "So you are the twins?"

"Can't you see the resemblance?" Leleen said, smiling. Avo groaned through swollen lips.

Then the radio receivers crackled through for the first time. The voice of the headmaster boomed through. "Baron, Baroness, do you read me? The fighters are attacking the lifeboats. The Krossbone kids are doing their best to fend them off, but they're outnumbered. We can't return fire until the lifeboats are safe."

Duun turned toward Lukka. "Get my brother up to the forest. I'll go and help the planes."

Leleen shook her head. "How about you two get to the planes, and I drag Avo up to the forest? I've been carrying Mom up and down the stairs since you two were gone. I've got loads of experience," she said.

"Are you sure you don't need help?" Lukka asked.

"Please," said Leleen. "In the woods, I am invincible." Branches reached down from the forest above, and once she had fastened them around herself and Avo, the two siblings swung upward into the forest clearing above.

"Why can't you say amazing things like that?" Lukka grinned as she sprinted down to the cavern's runway with Duun. She glanced around. "Do you see two planes that are undamaged?"

Duun scanned the empty clearing of the fortress. "Just one, but it looks like it has a rear gunner position."

"Are you sure there aren't two?" Lukka asked.

"I'm sure," Duun said.

"Ah," Lukka said. She closed her eyes. The universe had conspired against her to reach this very moment. If she could have taken a separate boat, freed the prisoners faster, even detonated the fuel beforehand, she could've stalled fate a while longer. Death looked down upon Lukka, and it had come in the form of Duun Howl.

How could she tell her friend that he was the omen of her death? Was this her Last Light, the end that had been revealed to her back at the monastery where she conducted her trials? A voice spoke in her head. "If the two of you fly together, one or both of you will die."

She slid the hatch over her head and headed to the rear, sure she had closed the casket on them both. Duun slammed the throttle forward. They would dance with death together.

Chapter 46

When Lukka and Duun took to the air over the sea, the ceiling of the cavern's entrance had not collapsed. They flew to join with the Krossbone Brown pilots whose lone bomber was fending against five enemy fighters. The bomber was cumbersome, which made firing on the enemy fighters difficult. Flak cannons from the cruiser below served to provide a defensive blanket around the students' plane in the air, but the battle quickly stalled into a dangerous stalemate.

Duun pulled the stick back to join the others. He was eager to get into the skirmish, but he had to complete another task first. He located the radio and switched it on. "Darlington, this is Sidewinder and Baroness. We're joining the fight in an enemy craft. Please make sure the Krossbone Brown gunners check fire before engaging. Over."

"Roger, Sidewinder," Ms. Darlington said. "Looks like you really did a number on the hornet's nest. Priority one is to get the rafts back on board. We'll do what we can to cover the hostages. Over."

Duun brought the plane into position over the life rafts that cruised toward the gunboat. As he strafed overhead, deep purple airplanes circled the barons. He focused his eyes on the planes and adjusted his hand, preparing to fire.

Lukka, who had been silent, yelled from the back. "Just a reminder, Duun, but this plane doesn't have rockets. If you drop a bomb by accident, you may kill the people we're trying to save."

"Oh," said Duun.

"Just worry about flying. I'll shoot."

The first planes flew overhead in a quick pass. Lukka tore into their underbellies with a hail of gunfire. The single gun in the back cut with far less power than the front cannons, but Lukka persisted, holding a tight grip of the trigger.

When the purple planes moved out of her sight, she groaned. "Whoever made these planes made them tougher than the pirates I'm used to. My gun isn't getting through."

Duun watched a plane turn back toward them, and he glanced at the bottom of it. "There are bombs underneath," he yelled.

"Yes, Duun, they're dive bombers!"

"Can you set off the bombs with your gun?"

"I'll try!"

Duun pulled back on the throttle and spun the plane on the axis of its wings. Then holding for a moment in a short pause, he thrust the throttle wide again and flew toward their enemies. Leaning back on the stick, he lined up his sights and, with a few swift taps of his guns, ruptured a fuel tank below the bomber to his left. It turned away as the wind dispersed the fuel and leaned back toward the cruiser. Duun stormed on its tailfin. Just as he drew near, he swung downward and dove toward the sea. A plane in pursuit flew into the fuel streaming from the other plane. With a long pull of the trigger, Lukka shredded the bomb that was nearest the two crossing planes.

In a fierce explosion, a wing snapped free of the bleeding bomber, and the fuel now on the wings of the pursuing bomber ignited. The canopy flew open and the pilot leaped from the cockpit. His head cracked against the tailfin and Duun watched as he dropped into the ocean following his plane. The rear gunner rolled out of the cockpit and pulled his parachute before hitting the waves.

"Not bad, Lukka."

"Thanks, but we're not done yet. There's a new guy behind us—and he's persistent."

The plane she described that had hounded them like an all-too-eager dance partner trying to "cut in" made a fast approach. With cannons blazing, it banked toward Lukka, filling the air with burning bullets.

"I can't get an opening!" she yelled. Duun knew if he tarried, she'd be pulled apart by machine gun fire. In a snap decision, he dove toward the sea.

"This guy doesn't seem to care where he shoots. He may accidentally hit our lifeboats," Lukka said.

"Don't worry, he's a bit slow on the stick. Judging by that endless barrage, I'm betting it's our classmate, Jensen. Hang on."

Duun flipped the plane level with the sea just feet above the waves and could see that he was right—Jensen was in the cockpit of the plane. The fierce force of the slipstream pushed off the waves below, kicking water up behind their plane. The sea spray struck up to obscure Jensen's view.

Bullets continued to fly from the plane but caught the waves, throwing more water over his windshield. Before Jensen's shots could connect with the plane in front of him, Duun pulled up and dropped a bomb. It slammed through the water's surface and exploded. Jensen's plane flipped twice before breaking its wings on two jutting stones. Its stripped fuselage rapidly took on water and the plane sank into the sea.

Amid the demonstration of nautical acrobatics, yet another plane prepared to strike the barons from a safer distance. However, in its narrow focus, the pilot failed to notice that Krossbone Brown's students were waiting for it to close in. Their gunners stormed the plane with bullets and decimated its hull. A shower of scrap crashed into the stone surface of the cliff side.

Ms. Darlington's voice crackled through the radio. "Excellent work, everyone! That should be the last of them. The rafts are cleared and everyone's safe aboard. Head back to the school airfield—"

A rush of thunder from the hollow of the cavern interrupted her transmission. The sky grew as dark as the devil and from the depths of where the large kiln had stood emerged the gargantuan form of a human-shaped kytinfiend with eight arms. Trees grew on its plating.

As soon as it appeared, the rain fell heavy over the cape and the fog grew thick. As the massive body rose out of the cliff side, the earth broke apart and stones and debris flew in all directions. Waves exploded toward the cruiser, vastly increasing its risk of capsizing. The kytinfiend rose astride the stone remains of the cliff, and its head and shoulders disappeared above the clouds. When it left the water, large cascades of ocean crashed down. Seawater rushed in to fill the hole where the kiln had been, sucking the cruiser closer to the sharp stones now jutting from the side of the cliff. As its feet pounded through the forest, trees were flattened in its wake.

Duun stared at the creature's shape and his heart fossilized in his chest. "Avo, Leelee," he whispered.

"Duun," Lukka said. "You have to stay with me, Duun. We're the only plane present that can achieve an operational altitude to strike its orb. The cruiser can't strike that high and neither can Krossbone Brown. A kytinfiend that large will devastate the kingdom before our armed forces can ever make it back from the front. You don't know that Avo and Leleen were in the landslide—your family may still be down there." She had always been quick to pick up on other people's lies, and she fumbled on the last sentence. Even she found it hard to believe. "After everything," Duun murmured, "they're gone."

"Johanna and her mom are still alive. Your mom is still alive. Your people are still alive. Hunter and Jaki and the teachers and so many others are still alive, and we're still alive. We can stop anyone else from dying, but we have to act now. Pull up. Let me face the beast head on."

Duun pulled back on the stick and steadily flew upward toward the heavy bank of clouds. Lukka took a breath of some relief—one of the few she would be afforded in the battle ahead. When Duun appeared marginally responsive, she spoke once more.

"This may sound strange, but if you don't mind, I'd like to ask my second question now." She didn't add that it might be her last chance.

"All right," Duun said.

"When we first met, I was outright hostile to you. I called your investigations childish. I thought you were wasteful and a fraud riding Blau's coattails. Why, in the midst of that, were you so insistent upon having me help you?"

Duun hadn't expected that question. "You just want to know *why?*"

"Yes," said Lukka. "Why? Rigel suspects you have a crush on me, but clearly he isn't paying attention. Johanna probably thinks it has something to do with my martial training, but you didn't know about that at the time. What was so critical that you needed *me* to assist in your mission?"

Duun spoke without hesitation. "That's easy, Lukka. You had something that no one else had—open, honest, and shameless truth. Blau cheated. Johanna hid. Rigel built walls around himself. Even Avo had shadows I didn't know about. But you never hid anything, and you accepted the consequences of everything you did."

She thought for a flash, knowing they had little time. "I'm flattered," she said. "However, I've learned that's not entirely true. Truth is fundamentally *un*true. The Sion and the Shadow are the same being. Where there is light there are always shadows." She took a deep breath and turned back to her gun. "Now, we've got a beast to slay, so if you still believe in me, believe this. You and I are the only ones who can protect our loved ones, so let's do that here and now. As soon as the orb comes into view, lay into it with every shell you have. Do not drop the bomb, because we will not escape the blast. It is our only chance of breaking this beast. Understood?"

"Understood," Duun said.

"On my mark," Lukka said.

The plane rose up the beast's back like a mortar shell ready to burst into a fiery hailstorm. The air thinned, and the propellers fought to find purchase. The giant red orb atop the kytinfiend's skull pulsed against the light of the sun above the clouds. Then Lukka said it.

"Mark."

The cannons pelted the creature's skull with a torrent of shells, each pointed and armed to break what stood before them. The percussion of the guns popped ceaseless in the clear air as the great shots shattered against the orb in a sparkling spray of lights.

The closer they got, however, the weaker the sound became—and the less the effects of the impacts. Even with the full power of the cannons that could shed trees, the vessel came up short. The giant continued its cumbersome steps toward Landskape unopposed.

Then, in the thin air of the sky, the cannons expended their last shells, the plane listed backward, and the barons fell into a spiral toward the distant earth.

Chapter 47

Moments after the emergence of the titanic kytinfiend, Minah Darlington picked herself back up from the floor of the cruiser's command deck. Johanna followed suit and together they looked through the glass of the bridge at the monster before them.

"That thing will destroy Landskape and the school if we don't do anything," Ms. Darlington said. "Looks like Duun and Lukka are off to try and destroy the beast. I fear they won't have the firepower to do it. Assuming this kytinfiend is proportioned like the average human male, it's taller than the maximum altitude of anything I've built. I doubt whatever these klowns were using for planes can top that."

"Does that mean we can't beat it?" Johanna asked.

Minah looked at her daughter. "That's right, love. We can't beat it. They can't beat it. No one can beat it. No one can beat it *alone*," she said. She raced to the radio. "Skyskape, do you read me?"

Headmaster Strauss's voice came through the radio. "This is Skyskape. Care to explain what I'm looking at?"

"It's a very large kytinfiend taller than any weapon we can throw at it."

"Are you saying it can't be beaten?"

"Hold your horses, schoolgirl," Minah said. "That's not what I said."

"What are you suggesting?" Strauss replied.

"It's shaped like a human. If nothing else, humans know a thousand ways to bring down a human. Is Dr. Violite there? I need confirmation."

"Rightarooney, Miss Minnie Moneybags, on both counts," Dr. Violite said. "Everyone at one point or another wants to make their monster look like a man, but they just aren't as guiley or wily enough to face a true sorceress. I'll head to the exam bonekiln and summon up what I had saved for the upperclassmen's final exams. It won't kill that monster, but it may do us a few favors."

"Good," said Minah, "if we coordinate an assault, we may be able to lay that thing low enough for Krossbone Brown to bomb its head to the Shadow's Rest. Let me know when you get to the kiln, Violite."

"I don't get a nickname?" Violite asked.

"No, because your nickname was mean," Ms. Darlington said.

"Eheheh," Violite answered.

"There's not much we can do on my end," Marley said. "I'll keep you posted on the direction of the kytinfiend. Any word on who's controlling the beast?"

"I'm guessing it's Parker, Baron Blau's traitorous attache. Judging by the size of it, I can't say where he is in the beast. Doesn't matter, really, since we can't hit it with accuracy. If we can topple it, then that should be enough. My daughter Johanna is currently drafting a firing solution as we speak. Violite, can you hold it still long enough?"

"Sure thing, dearie," Violite said over her radio. "At the bonekiln now."

A pillar of fire blasted upward from the earth from the kiln and a great bull mastiff wreathed with a mane of jellyfish tendrils and squid tentacles emerged. As it rose from the ground, the dog dug its paws into the earth and howled a hurricane up toward the clouds. In the midst of the mastiff's fervent cry to battle, those who saw the beast also saw Duun and Lukka's plane break through the clouds in a downward spiral.

"They're stalling!" shouted Rigel, who'd appeared beside Ms. Darlington.

She screamed into the radio. "Sidewinder! put the plane into a nosedive and shut off the throttle."

They watched, stomachs roiling, as the plane, in a terrible dance with gravity, turned itself toward the forest below. The distance between the barons and the earth evaporated with each second.

"Now bring the plane level with the ground and push the throttle forward," she said in the calmest voice she could muster.

Duun fought hard to push the throttle with the flat of his hand as he turned back the stick. As the mastiff's howl cleared the fog, he felt the relation of the plane to the earth from the pressure of gravity shifting from the back of his seat to the belts that fastened him to the cockpit. His muscles strained against the g-forces as he forced blood to flow through him. Finally, the propeller began to turn again and the plane leveled off. With the throttle pushed to full, the plane shot across the treeline and began to rise again.

"How are you feeling, Sidewinder?" Ms. Darlington asked.

"Shaken, but Lukka and I are still all right."

"That was bold of you. We think we've found a way to bring this thing down. We're going to shoot out one of its knees with a barrage from our vessel. When it falls, Dr. Violite will use her kytinfiend to trap as many of its arms as possible. The Krossbone bomber will hit it in the head, but you're going to keep it distracted."

"What's going to hold the free arms down?" Duun asked.

Minah paused. "Prayers. So be ready to evade when you can."

"Can't we do better than that?" asked Rigel.

"We're already doing the best we can," Minah said. "Jojo, do you have the firing solution?"

Johanna set down her chalk and turned her board to her mother. "If we fire on this bearing at this trajectory, we should be able to take out both its knees."

"Will the shots endanger Landskape?"

"The legs will be hit with a delayed impact. This should cause the kytinfiend to turn toward the sea. The cape should guard the town, but we should expect some large waves. We may capsize…unless we can angle the vessel against the tsunami."

"All right, you heard the lady," Ms. Darlington said. "Let's make it happen. Rigel, let everyone know to brace for impact."

The cannons on both ends of the vessel turned to face the kytinfiend, still moving toward Landskape. Minah took a deep breath and gave the order to fire. The flash of shells pushed the boat hard as the first and then the second broke away at the backs of the construct's knees. The monster tilted, then staggered and, as Johanna had predicted, slipped back toward the sea. As the middle of its body impacted the ocean's surface, waves rose in a torrent that seemed sure to overtake the cruiser. Johanna grabbed a bar on the console with one hand and then wrapped her other arm around her mother. Rigel, who had returned from his mission, ducked for cover.

When the wave struck, Johanna's chalkboard flew into the wall and shattered on impact. Chalkdust filled the air. The ship went up on its side and they all prepared for the worst…but then, it reversed course and began to right itself again.

Ms. Darlington steeled her composure and picked up the radio.

"Violite, can your beast get to those arms?"

"Please," said the doctor, "my creature's built for the sea. That's why I'm the best Buldwikk sorceress."

Marley Strauss watched from the spire as the bounding hound leapt into the ocean to ensnare its prey. "Dr. Violite, just how many dogs did you use in the kiln?"

"Oh, lah-ti-dah, everybody loves sausage but nobody wants to know how it's made," the sorceress said. "But don't worry. I sneak off to the pet cemetery when my husband takes me on picnics. I don't kill them myself."

"That's horrible!" Rigel exclaimed.

"Sue me for recycling!" Violite snapped back.

The hound swam hard with its legs as its webbed array of limbs held tight and planted its feet in the sand. Over the sound of the winds that had begun to rise, Dr. Violite cackled through the radio. Ms. Darlington looked at Johanna and rolled her eyes and then raised the radio to her mouth.

"Krossbone bomber, prepare to engage."

The bomber droned into view, ready to drop its payload on the monster's face. As the students opened the hatch and armed the bombs, Lukka and Duun turned back to assist with distracting the beast. However, a single hand of the kytinfiend reeled upward and swatted the bomber's tailfin. Parachutes opened all over the ocean.

The headmaster watched from the spire in horror as her last hope in defeating the behemoth vanished. Then her sister spoke through the radio.

"Marley," said Lukka, "I have an idea. Duun and I have one remaining bomb on board the plane. The impact with the sea may have cracked the orb just enough that any substantial outside force will rupture it."

"One bomb won't be enough," Marley said.

"What if it speeds at the head moving several hundred miles per hour?" Lukka suggested.

"It won't work. It's a bomb, not a rocket."

Duun piped up. "Then what if we bail from the plane and send it on a collision course with the orb?"

"Of course you'd suggest that," Marley said, fighting despair. "It's possible, but it wouldn't afford you much time to deploy parachutes."

"Let *us* worry about that," Lukka said. "Focus on rescuing the Krossbone Brown crew from the sea."

"For the record, I think this is foolish," Marley said.

"Well, if it doesn't work, just know that I regret that we didn't get to go to Visolia together," Lukka said.

She switched off her radio and turned to Duun. "Punch it, my friend."

Duun pushed the throttle to its limit and with a blast of adrenaline pried open the glass canopy above them. They rolled out of the cockpit and out into the open air. Duun watched as the plane maintained its altitude and prayed that their timing had been right.

Then he began the countdown to pull his cord.

Chapter 48

10 Free fall.

9 Free fall.

8 Free fall.

7 The beast begins to rise.

6 The beast's free hands strike Violite's mastiff through its orb.

5 The beast lifts its head.

4 The kytinfiend is drawn toward the incoming plane, which explodes on contact.

3 Tall trees wrap around the creature's legs and pull it into the blast.

2 The orb of the beast explodes and its head shatters.

1 Duun pulls his parachute cord and is horrified to feel it come free in his hand.

0 Lukka's arms wrap around him and she pulls her cord.
As one, they jerk upward.

Chapter 49

When Duun and Lukka emerged from the water, a fishing boat from the harbor awaited them. Once aboard, they stood in the cabin, scanning the sea. The plated remains of the grotesque beast had melted into small pieces and then faded like a foul slime into the ocean. The sea itself was a mess of floating debris. An air of uncertainty swept over the two barons. Was the battle truly over?

"Duun," said Lukka.

"Yes?"

"Smack me."

"No!"

"I need to know that I'm alive."

"Then smack yourself."

"Fine," she said, and then struck herself full force across the face.

Duun looked at her incredulously. "Why on earth did you do that?"

"To make sure I'm not dead."

"How does that prove if you're dead or not?"

"Isn't that what people do?" She gripped her jaw and winced at the pain.

"I don't know!" said Duun. "How would that prove that you're not dead? Also, why would you think you're dead? It was *my* parachute that broke!"

Lukka wiped water from her face with her sleeve. "It's sort of a taboo subject."

"Does it relate to me?"

"Maybe."

"Then shouldn't I know what it is?"

"You haven't asked about Johanna's scar."

"Johanna's scar doesn't have anything to do with me," Duun shot back. "This apparently does."

Lukka sighed. She waited for the sailorman to tend to the dock lines. Once he was gone, she spoke in a pensive tone.

"To learn the martial arts I have, there is a price. It's a form of magic. To move my hands through another person and block and channel energy requires me to see a vision of the day I die. It's not a clear vision—at least the one I see isn't—but you will be there when it happens."

Duun considered what she had said, but chose not to respond.

"It's written," she said. "It's fated, and I thought it was going to be today. Turns out it wasn't."

"Oh," Duun said pensively. "I'm not sorry about that. But I'm sorry to hear that you have to deal with the vision."

"Sorry?" Lukka shrugged. There's nothing to be sorry about. Do you know anyone who will never die? I don't. If anything, I'm happy a friend will be nearby when it happens. We lived today. Let's enjoy that."

They stood quietly together looking toward the shore. "You saw that thing the trees did, didn't you?" said Lukka. "I'm going to assume a forestfolk or two did that. I don't know about any trees that grow like that naturally, do you?"

He glanced at her and then back toward the town. "Do you think it was Leleen and Avo?"

"Well, how many other forestfolk climbed up through the top of the cave?"

"Do you think the people in the ship are okay?" Duun asked.

"Well, the ship was hit by a pretty big wave, but we aren't that far from shore, so doctors will no doubt be on the scene. I know your mom's situation is precarious, but there were good people with her."

Duun looked down. "It's a shame we didn't get that surgery done so she could walk, but I understand where she was coming from and respect her wishes."

"What surgery? I wasn't there for that conversation."

"She was supposed to have the tendons in her legs reconstructed, but they were going to use a baby calf's tendon to do it. She declined."

"Have you been living under a rock?" Lukka asked.

"Pardon?" Duun asked.

"In Visolia, there are doctors who can regrow tendons using one's own cells. It costs quite a bit, but since you just helped the richest woman in Tarrkaven save the kingdom, she owes you one."

"Huh," said Duun. "I'll have to look into that."

He stepped out and leaned on the rail. Although the state of the ocean around them made him feel sad, the breeze felt good on his face. Lukka joined him.

"I'm glad you flew with me today," he said.

She placed her hand on his arm and smiled. "You know, you're not a half-bad pilot."

***

When the boat finally docked, Lukka and Duun disembarked and searched through the crowd. Spying a medical tent, they headed toward it, hoping to find their friends and family present. Sure enough, Duun's mother sat comfortably in a wheelchair and both Avo and Leleen were with her. Avo looked his usual verdant self—far improved from the yellowing husk he had been when they'd last seen him. Leleen simply appeared happy to be alive.

Duun approached his family and, for the first time in longer than any of them could remember, they were united. "Avo, you look well," Duun said.

Avo looked at his younger brother. "It was a bit touch and go there for a moment. Can't say I expected a kytinfiend to come bursting out of the earth."

"It's going to take a while for the area to fully recover," Leleen said. "Not to mention that debris field isn't looking good for the ocean. The forest tells me it's a real mess, but all the plants and sea creatures are happy not to have been annihilated by a giant eight-armed human monster."

"It was Parker, I assume. Do we know how he managed to do all of that?" Duun asked.

"We do, actually," said Leleen, "though he's not really in a position to explain his motivation." She pointed in the direction of a shard of the kytinfiend's orb. Within it, Parker was preserved like a mosquito in amber.

"He can stay in there forever as far as I care since he poisoned our mother. Not to mention what he did to Baron Blau and poor Bigby."

Dr. Violite pulled up on her motorcycle and went straight for the shard. She tapped it a few times and shook it and then walked away with a patented "eh-heh-heh."

"I'm sure Violite and Parker will get along famously," Avo said.

Everyone laughed.

"How did Mom get to shore?" Duun asked.

"Me, right over here," Rigel said. "I saw her and thought I should help that lady, and I did, and it was your mother, so hooray!" He looked down at himself. "My clothes are ruined. I should've worn a suit like you and Lukka, but I didn't, because I wanted to look good. I look ridiculous now, so that's on me."

He glanced around the group and his eyes fell on Avo and Leleen. "Hey! You two, you're twins right? Love that thing you did with the trees, really couldn't have done it without the trees. Big fan of the trees, and the tree people, and I'm a prince, so I can run it past Pops to get all the tree people citizenship." He paused.

"Congratulations, thanks a bundle. Oops, Lukka's got a new bat, so I'm gonna shut up." He moved safely behind Duun.

Leleen gaped. "You're who's running the kingdom?"

Duun laughed. "He's second-born, so it probably won't happen."

A new voice was heard from the midst of an ever growing gathering.

"You! Avo Howl!" Headmaster Marley Strauss stepped into the middle of the group.

"Huh, suddenly our family is the most popular family in the kingdom," Avo said.

"I'd like to talk to the nice young lady," said their mother.

"Mom…" Avo said. "I might be getting arrested."

"Not on my watch," she said. She stared at the headmaster. "Are you in charge of the school?"

"That is my role, yes," Marley said.

"Well, my boys here are fine examples of your students. They're a real credit to the institution you're running here."

"Your boys?" Marley said, looking at Duun and Avo.

Duun stepped forward. "Yes, Headmaster. The name Daniel Hardy was a ruse concocted by Baron Blau to get me into Diamond Blue. I am actually Duun Howl, the brother of the Emerald Dragonfly—and a proud son of the Knot Kovenant."

Marley crossed her arms and frowned. "It's times like this I wish I was the human lie detector my sister is. You did something very brave although altogether reckless—just like last time. But, once again, you saved my sister."

"Oh, no," he said, turning to Lukka. "She saved *me* this time. My parachute broke."

The headmaster looked at her younger sister. "Huh, did she now? She sure knows how to play with fire." She shook her head. "Oh, well."

Then she looked at Duun and smiled. "Tarrbly needs a baron. While this news of your relationship will likely ruffle a few feathers, I'm not going to let it bother me. Your secret is safe with me."

She turned to Avo. "As for you…" He stepped up beside Duun. "I won't allow you to re-enroll at Skyskape, but, to be honest, what good would that do? But I *will* strike the crimes from your record here and, in honor of your service, henceforth, Krossbone Brown will be known as Dragonfly Green."

Avo demurred. "Thank you. Well, suffice it to say that I think you're doing a fine job as headmaster."

Marley turned back to Duun. "I'd feel better if a secret army hadn't infiltrated the school, but it looks like that's been taken care of. Right?"

Duun nodded. "I don't have a ledger of all the members, Headmaster, but I think we're good."

"Right then. One day at a time," Marley said. She joined Dr. Violite on the edge of the crowd.

"What's *your* move now, Avo?" Duun asked.

"Well, I'm going to go home, take care of Mom, help the Knot Kovenant rebuild Tarrbly, conspire with the corn crops against Leelee—and when I'm sure all that is squared away and in good shape, I'll make it my mission to find answers about what happened to Dad and Armand. As for you, it looks like you have a real job now," Avo said.

"This kingdom needs Baron Hardy, especially if the Emerald Dragonfly isn't needed now. There will be all sorts of peril because there always is, but it appears you have a good group at your back. And if it gets really serious, I'll be right back here ready to fly again."

He gestured over Duun's shoulder to someone behind him. "Now, if I'm not mistaken, it looks like a really tall girl wants to talk to you."

Johanna came forward, her mother not far behind.

"Who's that?" said Mrs. Howl, craning her neck for a better view.

"Yes," asked Leleen, "who is that?"

Duun did not speak, but the answer he gave did not require words. In his heart, pride and admiration spread through every ounce of his countenance and could be felt by all those who were near. Johanna was the brilliant mind who had sought answers in the relentless pursuit of peace for her first friend, the gentle soul who had cared for Lukka when she had faced mortal peril.

Johanna's face reflected the same. Before her stood the hero who conquered fear, loss, and the skies to bring his family back together. Each stood before the other with a unity of spirit transcending the mere distance between them, a unity that could never be destroyed.

Chapter 50

Frozen in amber, Parker was entranced by the frothing glow of a bonekiln before him. Wrapped tight in the embrace of a pulsing octopus-shaped kytinfiend, the stone that had preserved him from the fall now served as only a prison. A solitary bulb hanging from the ceiling, flickered with its last ounce of endurance to cast light across the room. Moths danced with it, ignoring the light of the kiln. It was far more dangerous.

The pale, worn porcelain face of Dr. Violite reflected her twisted delight. "Heh-heh-heh, my friend, you've done well to last this long. Few can keep their nerve in a place like this. In Buldwikk, at least five of my apprentices died after visiting my lab. My work has a way of bringing nightmares to even the most stubborn souls."

Violite crossed the floor to a wall of photo albums, removing one from the shelf. She opened and looked at it, leering at what it showed, and then back at Parker. "Sometimes reporters give me their finds from the battlefield. Well, they don't *give* them to me—I pay them. This one had me looking away for weeks." She waved a photo in front of the traitor. When after a minute had passed, she looked down at the octopus attached to the stone and saw it had not changed from its even pulsing, she turned away to hide her disappointment. "You're tough for a third-rate sorcerer, but don't worry. There's a lot more where that came from. I'll break you soon enough."

Violite flipped through more pages of the album and then paused and sniffed the air. A heavy odor of sulfur crept through the room.

"Sugar bear," Violite called through the door. "Did you check the expiration date on the eggs?"

A voice answered from the other room. "I picked them up this morning, Dolly."

"Did you get them from that no-good scoundrel Boone?"

"Now, Dolly, Boone is a respected member of our parish," the voice answered.

"I don't know. Somebody with that many windchimes on the front of their house has to be hiding something. What does he not want us to hear?"

"Maybe he *likes* windchimes, my dear. I like songbirds and kitties. It's not that strange."

"Hmmm." Violite turned her ponderous troubles inward. There was something suspicious about that farmer. She was sure of it.

"Speaking of strange," said the vicar, who now stood in the doorway with a picnic basket. "You're not still telling kids that you cooked Miss Fluffypaws, are you?"

"Not in front of the specimen, James," she said, an unusual primness enveloping her.

"Oh, Dolly," said James, "I flew under Parker back in the war. He knows you're a softy deep down. I didn't think he would do half the things you say he did but I guess I really don't know him very well. However, Blau always did have a sense for people who could keep secrets. I guess he had one more secret that even the baron didn't know."

Dr. Violite's stout husband sniffed the air. "Huh, maybe it's you who has rotten eggs. It's been a while since you've cleaned this place."

"Don't disrespect my she-shed, James."

"No disrespect, Dolly. By the way, I cleaned up your motorbike and the sidecar is attached. Anywhere in particular you want to go this afternoon?"

"How about that hill overlooking the airfield?"

The couple left Parker alone, immobilized, in the dimness of the doctor's laboratory. Bubbles churned in the kiln. The beast latched to the stone continued to thrum in the even glow of the prisoner's frustrated boredom.

Then, suddenly, the door creaked and joining its frame, closed itself tight. As the telltale scent of sulfur spread through the inside of the amber, the bulb hanging from the ceiling flickered a final time.

The rumble of a motorcycle could be heard in the distance, but no one was there to hear Parker's screams as the shadow of a man moved across the room and the flashing kytinfiend at his chest disappeared in the dark.

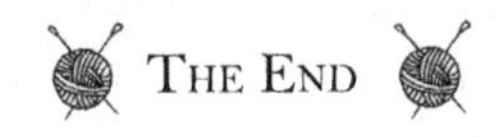

About the Author

David Mruz attended Presbyterian College where he earned degrees in history as well as English with emphasis in creative writing. While he attended Presbyterian College, he went abroad to Edge Hill University just outside of Liverpool, UK. He also studied across Central Europe how people remember war. After PC, he earned his Masters degree at Converse College.

David lives in the upstate of South Carolina. When he's not writing, he explores bookstores, builds with his hands, and experiments in the kitchen. His most requested dish is his mac and cheese. In his downtime, he's dreaming up new worlds and the people who live in them.

Made in the USA
Columbia, SC
06 November 2021